IN *DANGER* OF *JUDGMENT*

DAVID RABIN

Black Rose Writing | Texas

ISBN: 978-1-68513-000-8 (Paperback); 978-1-68513-059-6 (Hardcover)
PUBLISHED BY BLACK ROSE WRITING
www.blackrosewriting.com

Printed in the United States of America
Suggested Retail Price (SRP) $22.95 (Paperback); $27.95 (Hardcover)

In Danger of Judgment is printed in Baskerville

*As a planet-friendly publisher, Black Rose Writing does its best to
eliminate unnecessary waste to reduce paper usage and energy costs,
while never compromising the reading experience. As a result, the final
word count vs. page count may not meet common expectations.

Credits:
"Legs"
Written by Polly Jean Harvey
Published by Hot Head Music Limited

For Colonel Lowell Gene Sidwell, USAF
1918-2012

Recipient of the Distinguished Flying Cross, the Croix de Guerre,
and others too numerous to mention

IN DANGER OF JUDGMENT

Ye have heard that it was said by them of old time,
Thou shalt not kill; and whosoever shall kill shall be in danger of the
judgment.
–**Matthew 5:21**

Prologue

1968 - 1972
South Vietnam

The eight men filing into the Tactical Operations Center had six days' beard growth, they reeked of sweat and jungle, and their clothes were smeared with soil and grime and still-wet enemy blood.

Major Henry Sampson waited for them at a table at the rear of the TOC, as far away as they could get from the beeping, static, and chatter of the radios. The men settled themselves around the table and didn't wait for Sampson to ask a question. They'd just completed their fourth mission, and by now they knew the debriefing procedure.

"Eleven," said the first man.

In due course, Sampson would steer them to other aspects of the mission, but they always started with what was most important: the number of enemy killed in action.

Sampson had had a rude awakening a few years earlier, during his first tour in South Vietnam. He was a West Point man, a professional soldier to the core, but Vietnam was a war unlike any he'd prepared for. In every war America had ever fought, the objective was to capture and hold territory, but in Vietnam, that was never the goal. The only metric that mattered was the body count.

"Tell me about the first one," Sampson said.

"Sentry in the southwest sector. Older than usual, thirties, maybe, leaning against a tree with a Chicom AK slung over his shoulder. He wasn't even scanning, just gazing into the distance, probably thinking about his old lady back in Hanoi. I snake-crawled from the rear, put my hand over his mouth, and pulled back. Three stabs and a slash through the neck. No sound."

The man described the rest of his kills and then they went around the table. By the time they finished, the count reached 102. It was a good night's work.

Sometimes the body count was so high that Sampson wondered whether they were exaggerating, but he questioned them carefully and they convinced him the count was true. When the two guys from the Department of Defense had given him the assignment, he didn't dream the men would kill so many.

* * *

The DOD men had arrived by helicopter on a soggy December morning in 1968, late in the rainy season at Phu Bai, South Vietnam, where Sampson was stationed with the 101st Airborne Division. They weren't in uniform, but from the way they exited the Huey—quickly and gracefully—Sampson could tell they'd spent some time in the bush.

There was no fanfare on their arrival. That was by design. Sampson had been told the men would meet with him and then leave, and the fewer the people that knew about the meeting, the better.

The DOD men introduced themselves as Robinson and Reese, and it occurred to Sampson that whoever gave them their code names must have been a Dodgers fan. They wore identical navy-blue suits, white shirts, muted ties, and blank expressions.

Robinson was black and Reese was white, but otherwise they could have been twins.

Sampson took them to his hooch, a rudimentary structure of plywood elevated a foot off the ground and divided into four living quarters. Inside, the décor was olive drab, drab being the operative word. Sampson's corner had a cot, a small desk, makeshift shelves, a locker, and a table fan.

He pulled over a couple of folding chairs for the two men to sit on. Sampson wished he had a conference room befitting their importance, but the hooch was the only venue at the base where they could be assured of privacy. He'd made sure that the other three officers who lived there would be absent for the meeting's duration.

Reese got it started as Robinson shook a Marlboro out of a hard pack and lit it with a Zippo. "We're going to tell you some stuff you may already know, but bear with us. We'll get to the good part shortly."

Sampson sat up straight and did his best to look attentive. "I'm at your disposal, sir."

"When you got here," Reese said, "you were fighting the Viet Cong and the North Vietnamese Army. The VC are still around, but we hit them so hard during Tet that they're no longer a major threat to the South. That's why you're now focused on the NVA."

Robinson took the baton. "The NVA's constantly moving men and supplies down the Ho Chi Minh Trail, infiltrating into the South, probing for weaknesses. Occasionally, they attack us and the South Vietnamese, and then they hightail it back to the North. Now, we both know that in a war you're supposed to pursue the enemy, take the fight to them instead of the other way around. That's how it's always been done, but this is Vietnam, where nothing gets done the way it's supposed to."

"We're not allowed to send ground troops into the North," Sampson said.

Reese nodded. "That's right, and it's not because our civilian leadership is spineless, contrary to what you guys in-country may believe. North Vietnam has a great, big patron on its northern border called Communist China. In '64, the Chinese told us that if we sent boots north of the 17th parallel, they'd intervene on behalf of their North Vietnamese comrades. Meaning, they'd send a few million Red Chinese soldiers down south, just like they did in Korea when we drove too far north, and we all know how that turned out for us."

"Not real well."

"Yeah. Not real well. We want to help the South Vietnamese, but we don't want to start World War Three. Frustrating for us, frustrating for you."

"I don't make policy, sir. My duty is to follow orders and execute the mission."

"I'm glad you mentioned that," Robinson said, "because we came here to give you a mission."

"Sir?"

Robinson stubbed out his cigarette and leaned forward. "You are very quietly going to insert ground troops into North Vietnam."

They proceeded to tell him about the operation they wanted him to supervise: how the men would be selected, how they'd be trained, and the nature of the missions. They spoke for nearly an hour. Sampson listened intently, saying nothing. When they finished, they asked if he had any questions.

He did indeed have a question, though he hesitated to ask it, fearing they might think him insolent. But it was such an obvious issue, he just had to ask. "Why go to all this effort? All this planning, the massive selection process, the special training? Why don't you use the men you already have?"

The DOD men looked at each other without a trace of reaction, communicated telepathically, and turned back to Sampson. "That's above your pay grade," Reese said, "but if you're not comfortable with this op, we can find someone else."

Now Sampson wished he hadn't asked, but he recovered quickly. "I can do it," he said.

"There's one more thing. The body count is important—the higher the better, of course—and it needs to be accurate. You'll have to drill it into the men to keep an accurate count. Can you do that, Major?"

"I can do it."

Sampson thought the whole thing was a crock, just another foolhardy operation in a senseless war. But they got through the selection process and trained the men, and when they were finally let loose on their missions, they surpassed everyone's expectations. The body counts were staggering.

* * *

It was now late 1972, and Team One was nearing the end of its sixth mission. The Huey had inserted them six nights ago. They'd spent three nights approaching the target camp, followed by three nights of recon. Seven of them would attack the camp, and the eighth would remain just outside the camp's perimeter to cover them as they withdrew.

They wore no insignia and bore no identification, all to give the government plausible deniability if things went south. For the same reason, they never called each other by name during their missions. They were Ares Numbers One through Eight, a bit of theater they deemed absurd but acquiesced to nonetheless.

They killed time with the usual idle chatter: their favorite bands, best road trips, girlfriends good and bad. In their three years together, they'd told the same stories so many times that the telling was no longer the point. It was how they reinforced the bonds among them.

"Okay, guys," Ares One said, "fifteen minutes till go time."

They synched their watches, and as they went through one last gear check, Four addressed the elephant in the room. "The war's almost over, so this is probably our last mission."

Silence. No one wanted to talk about it.

"You know I'm right," Four continued. "The Paris peace talks are barreling down the tracks. Kissinger went on TV and said peace is at hand." He absent-mindedly checked his M16 again. "When we started out, I thought you guys were a bunch of losers, and now I don't want it to end."

"Jesus, you're a downer," Five said. "Look, when we get back, we'll do it up right. Get us a case of that black-market champagne, put on some CCR and turn it all the way up."

"Temptations," said Seven.

Everyone laughed. Seven *loved* Motown.

"Enough of this shit," Three said. "If this is our last mission, I don't want the perimeter again. I want some action. Lemme be on the assault team."

Two shook his head. "If Sampson and Thornton find out you violated the orders—"

"Fuck 'em," Three said. "What're they gonna do, fire me?"

No one had a response to that unassailable logic, and Three turned to Six. "Let me take your place," Three said. "Take the easy duty tonight."

Six looked at the others. They all nodded.

Three and Six exchanged weapons and ammo, Six getting the sniper kit. They all gave each other thumbs-up, and the seven men on the assault team moved silently into their assigned sectors.

Six checked his watch. The men would breach in twenty minutes and return one hour after that. He had nothing to do now but wait.

He stared into the darkness, listening to the sounds of the jungle and imagining the men—

Gunfire.

There should not have been gunfire.

It was not the treble staccato of American M16s. It was the bass thuds of Chinese AKs.

The gunfire ended abruptly, and then all was silent.

A flood of thoughts coursed through his brain.

His friends were dead.

The enemy had known they were coming, and so the enemy knew he was here.

And now, the enemy would come for him.

* * *

Sampson sat in his hooch, drinking his fourth Scotch of the night. The operation had gone along like clockwork until that bastard Thornton went rogue, the chief instructor selling out his own men.

The higher-ups had immediately terminated the entire operation, and Sampson could just imagine the hysteria now playing out at DOD. First, there would be recriminations. Who picked Thornton? Who vetted him? How in the hell did no one foresee this? Then they'd have to invent stories to tell the families, explaining why the bodies of their sons and brothers weren't coming home. They'd prime people to describe how heroically the men had died, so the families would buy it and not inquire further. And once the cover-up started, they'd have to cover up the cover-up. It would feed on itself and grow exponentially until the cover-up itself was more important than the events that birthed it.

As distasteful as it was, Sampson knew there was nothing else they could do. If the public ever learned the whole story, there'd be more heads rolling at DOD than bowling balls at the local alley on dollar night.

* * *

Three weeks after the operation ended, the DOD men visited Sampson again.

In the four years since he'd last seen them, Sampson's world had changed dramatically. The war was winding down and would end soon—and for Sampson, that was a problem. The way to get ahead in the military was to serve in a war zone. He'd done multiple tours in Vietnam, but once this war ended, who knew when there would be another one? He would have to find a way to make himself invaluable.

When the DOD men arrived, they looked just the same as before, all the way down to their navy-blue suits and inscrutable faces. They assured Sampson that no one blamed him for the unfortunate way the operation had ended. They complimented him on how well he'd run it, and on the results the men had obtained. A promotion to lieutenant colonel was already in the works.

When he heard the word "promotion," Sampson knew they were about to get to the real point of the meeting. Guys like them always dangled a prize before asking for something.

"There are two other things," Robinson said. "DOD wants to keep the operation and its outcome confidential."

No kidding, Sampson thought. "What else?"

"The upper echelon at DOD considers the remaining men to be somewhat unstable."

"What you mean is, you think they're crazy."

"However one puts it, given their, uh, mental disposition, we consider it prudent to monitor them until the last of them has passed away."

Sampson saw the logic of it. "Where do I fit in?"

"The perpetuation of secrecy and the observation of the men are related tasks, and we need someone to oversee both. We'd be pleased if you could do that, at least until your retirement, which we hope will be many years from now. Can you do that, Major?"

At that moment, Sampson saw his future.

These assignments were delicate. They were critical. They would last the rest of his career.

They were giving him a way to make himself invaluable.

He took his time and pretended to think about it, not wanting to look too eager, then slowly nodded.

"I can do it," Sampson said, though it would be another fifteen years before he'd discover just how complicated it could get.

Chapter 1

Sunday, May 10, 1987
8:02 p.m.
Chicago

Marcelle leaned against the railing of an apartment building at the south end of the 3700 block of Wilton Avenue, waiting for someone, though not for anyone in particular. She'd been there for five minutes and decided to wait another two before moving on.

The street was deserted, the residents having battened down the hatches in anticipation of twilight. An empty Old Style can rolled down the street in a grating, metallic rhythm, pushed by the wind coming off Lake Michigan a mile to the east. The only sign of life was the rumbling of an L train on the tracks a half-block from where she stood. The neighborhood seemed peaceful, though she knew its tranquility could be deceiving.

She was about to give up on this spot when two men in their late teens rounded the corner at the other end of the block and began walking toward her. They wore the gray and black colors of the area's predominant street gang, the Latin Eagles, and they walked with a slow swagger as if they owned the place, which they pretty much did. One was taller and one was shorter, and thus became, in her lexicon, Mr. Tall and Mr. Short.

The instant they saw her, they broke into big smiles and started conversing energetically. She'd gotten their attention. It didn't surprise her, because she was accustomed to getting attention. She was about five-eight and in her late twenties, with dark brown hair that barely touched her shoulders and a face that belonged on a magazine cover. Tonight she wore a light coat that was open at the front. Marcelle always dressed for success.

The men were five steps away now.

She put her right hand in her coat pocket.

"Que pasa, mami chula," said Mr. Tall.

They walked back and forth around her from opposite sides, examining her from head to toe and leering at her, no doubt expecting she'd panic and try to extricate herself.

Except she didn't.

Instead, she smiled at them.

It was a beautiful, radiant, magazine-cover smile, and because it was the last thing they'd expected, they froze in their tracks.

Her hand came out of her coat pocket.

It held a badge case.

"Detective Marcelle DeSantis," she said, "and I want you to know I do appreciate the compliment."

"Mierda," said Mr. Short.

"We don't talk to police," said Mr. Tall.

Her smile turned into a pout. "A minute ago, you thought I was sexy, and now you don't even want to talk to me? My feelings are hurt."

The men looked dumbfounded. Marcelle figured no police had ever spoken to them that way, and she took the opening. "I'm not here to hassle you guys. You're just two fine-looking dudes strolling down the street. Fact is, I need your help."

Now they looked intrigued. "Help with what?" asked Short.

"I want to find the guy who killed your friends. Hector, Ramon, Angel, and Luis."

"We take care of our own business," said Tall.

"That's good to know. Have you found the guy yet?"

Again, they were speechless.

"I know you want to find the guy who did it," Marcelle said. "You want revenge, and you want people to know they shouldn't screw with the Latin Eagles. The problem is, you won't find him on your own."

"Why not?" asked Tall.

"Because he's a pro and you guys aren't exactly Sherlock Holmes. If he gets found, it's going to be the Chicago Police Department that does it."

Tall shrugged. "We don't know anything."

"Okay," she said, "but maybe you'll remember something or hear something."

"What do we get if we help you?" Short asked.

Now she knew she was getting somewhere. When they asked for something, it meant they were interested.

"I'll tell you what you'll get. If we convict the guy, he'll get a life sentence or death row. Either way, he'll go to a prison. Probably Pontiac, Stateville, or Joliet, and you've got members in all three. I'm sure your buddies will give him a warm welcome when he arrives."

It was the men's turn to smile.

"I'm gonna go now," Marcelle said, "but I want you to remember something. I didn't give you any shit. I didn't ask for ID or search you. I treated you like men because that's what you are."

They nodded their agreement.

"Here's how I work," she continued. "You play straight with me and I play straight with you. As long as you're law-abiding, I'll treat you like you live on Lake Shore Drive." She handed each man a card. "If you learn anything that might help us, call me. I don't know your names and you won't have to give them."

The men pocketed the cards. Short looked ready to leave, but Tall stood still, his face gripped in concentration, as if trying to recall something from long ago.

Now, he looked like he remembered.

He stood up straight and looked her squarely in the eyes. "It was good to meet you, Detective. Have a nice night."

Chapter 2

Sunday, May 10, 1987
8:11 p.m.
Chicago

Bernie walked slowly and deliberately down the stairs of the building in the 3500 block of Fremont Street. With 260 pounds haphazardly distributed on a six-four frame, slowly and deliberately was the way to go.

When he reached the sidewalk, he stopped and surveyed the street. It held two- and three-story apartment buildings and an occasional single-family home, with barely any space between them. There were few yards to speak of, mostly just miniscule plots of weed-covered soil. Many of the buildings were decorated with graffiti—LATIN EAGLES; its derivative, L/E; and the *noms de guerre* of gang members—spray-painted in elaborate street calligraphy.

Bernie let himself rest for one minute. He'd walked building to building, apartment to apartment, speaking with every resident he could find, since ten o'clock this morning.

Eight murders.

All drug-related.

All professional hits.

No witnesses.

No evidence.

Cold trail.

For Detective Bernie Bernardelli, it was just another day at the office.

The next building was a three-story six-flat. He walked through the front door into a small vestibule that housed the residents' mailboxes. A door stood between the vestibule and the interior stairwell. Half the time, these doors weren't locked.

He turned the knob and pulled, but it didn't give. Time to play buzzer roulette. All he needed was one person to let him in.

He looked at the mailboxes of the two first-floor units, Murphy and Popovich. *Eeny, meeny, miny, moe.* Murphy was the lucky winner.

He pressed the buzzer and waited. Finally, the speaker crackled and a woman's voice said, "Who is it?"

"Detective William Bernardelli, Chicago Police. I'd like to ask you some questions about a crime that occurred near here."

"I don't know anything."

"Do you know which crime I'm talking about?"

"Don't know that either."

"Lady, do you mind telling me that face to face?"

"You got ID?"

Bernie's shoulders heaved, and he glared at the speaker over the mailbox. "Yeah, I got ID. Now open up, okay?"

The door's buzzer trumpeted. He opened it and walked up the single flight to the first floor, where he saw a door opened just a crack and secured by a chain. Through the opening he saw an elderly, white-haired woman, who looked annoyed and apprehensive in equal measures.

Bernie opened his badge case and held his credentials up to her eyes. She looked at his star, then his photo, then his face, and then his information. Most people never went past the star.

"Do I have to let you in?" she asked.

"Not if you don't want to."

"I'm gonna keep it chained. This neighborhood's not safe, you know."

"So I've heard," Bernie said.

The woman inspected him. The dark circles under his eyes, wrinkled forehead, and sagging jowls gave him the look of a tired bloodhound. He wore a brown plaid sport coat, a white shirt, a green tie, and gray slacks that had never met an iron. The only pieces of apparel that matched were his black shoes.

She clicked her tongue and frowned. "I thought detectives dressed better."

"If I dressed better, would it help me catch offenders?"

"Probably not."

"Then there's no reason to dress better."

He wanted to talk about the murder, but the woman still seemed fixated on his clothes. She said, "Can I give you some advice?"

"Sure."

"Ask your wife to pick out your clothes."

"If I had a wife, I would."

"If you dressed better, maybe you'd have one."

Bernie smiled for the first time that day. *Score one for the old lady.*

"Are we done with the clothes now?" he said.

"I suppose."

"Could I get your name, ma'am?"

"Mrs. Ethel Murphy."

"Does anyone else live here?"

"Just me. My husband died five years ago."

"I'm sorry to hear that."

"It happens," she said.

"Do you mind if we talk about the crime now?" Bernie asked.

"Talk about any crime you want."

"Last October, there was a murder over on Wilton, a couple blocks from here. Do you remember hearing about it?"

"There've been lots of murders around here and there'll probably be more."

"The only one I'm interested in right now is the one on Wilton last October."

She looked at him blankly.

"Let's try it this way," he said. "Mid-October, last year. The leaves were falling, it was getting colder, you'd probably just started wearing your winter coat. The Cubs season had just ended two weeks earlier."

The word "Cubs" elicited a visible response. Wrigley Field was only two blocks away, and everyone in the neighborhood followed the Cubs.

"Yeah, I remember now," she said. "Lots of hubbub. Police cars, big crowd. The dead guy was a drug dealer, right?"

"That's right."

"So why do you care?"

He got that question a lot. "Society runs smoother if people know we catch murderers."

"I never thought of it that way."

Most people don't, he thought. "They found the body right after dawn. That night, did you hear anything or see anything that might be related to the incident?"

"Like what?"

"People arguing. Loud noises. One person buying something from the other. Someone running away. Anything else that might be unusual."

"None of those things are unusual around here, but no, I don't remember any of that."

"Okay. I know it was months ago, but is it possible you were out and about that night?"

She shook her head. "I'm never out there past sunset. I make sure I'm home, I lock the doors, I draw the curtains. Don't want anyone looking in."

"Maybe you drove somewhere and got back late?"

"I don't drive. Never learned how. My husband did all the driving. If I want to go somewhere, I walk or take the CTA."

"Was anyone else living here at the time? Maybe one of your children?"

Another head shake. "I've got one daughter. She lives with her no-good husband in Naperville." She stopped and looked like she'd thought of something clever. "Now you're gonna ask me if maybe they were here that night."

"You get a gold star."

"They weren't. They only come here on Mother's Day."

There were thousands of people in Chicago like Ethel Murphy. She'd probably lived in this apartment for decades, and she'd stay here until she just couldn't stay any longer. This neighborhood was her entire universe, but now, in her golden years, her life was ruled by the movement of the sun, her imperative being to barricade herself after dark. She was on her own, her only child over an hour away and living the good life in the suburbs, uninterested in driving back to this crummy area.

Bernie pulled out one of his cards and, under his name, wrote, "DRESSES POORLY" so she'd remember him. He gave it to her, and she took it in both hands.

"If you remember anything about that night that might help us, please call me."

"Okay."

"And one other thing. Any time you don't feel safe, if you ever need help moving something that's too heavy for you, if it's bad weather and you can't go out to get groceries, you can call me. If I'm not in my office, they'll know how to find me, and if I can't help you, I'll be sure to find someone who can."

Her hands trembled and her eyes filled up. She unhooked the chain, opened the door, and hugged him.

"Have a good night, Mrs. Murphy, and be sure to lock the door."

She closed the door, and Bernie heard the lock engage. He leaned against the wall, pulled a narrow notebook out of his coat pocket, and opened it to the first blank page.

He wrote the day and time, the address and apartment number, the occupant's name, and a brief physical description of her. Beneath it all, he wrote, "DKA."

Doesn't Know Anything.

He wondered how rich he'd be if he had a dollar for every time he'd written "DKA" over the last twenty-six years.

He walked two steps over to the other first-floor apartment and knocked on the door to start the process all over again.

Chapter 3

Monday, May 11, 1987
7:21 a.m.

Bernie entered the headquarters of Area Six of the Chicago Police Department the same way he always did, head down and looking as if he bore the weight of the world. He nodded at Weems, the shoeshine man, and pushed his way through the metal gate that separated officers from the public. He walked slowly and deliberately up the stairs to the second floor where the detectives were housed, and was greeted by the familiar tap . . . tap . . . tap of the manual typewriters, always at a slow rhythm because detectives did all their typing with their index fingers.

Before him lay forty metal desks, four columns of ten desks each, with an invisible line separating Violent Crimes from Property Crimes. His desk was on the Violent Crimes side, the last one on the left at the end of the floor. A couple of detectives were typing reports, swearing occasionally and applying liberal amounts of correction fluid. Three others cradled phones to their shoulders, taking notes with one hand and holding a cigarette in the other. Clouds of cigarette smoke drifted hither and yon, congealing at the ceiling tile that had once been white but now was stained a yellowish-brown. The floor tiles used to be white, too, but now were a dull gray from thousands of scuffs from soles and heels.

The whole room looked tired and worn down, as did most of the people who worked in it.

Marcelle had the desk next to Bernie's, and she was already there, just as she always was. Bernie dropped himself into his chair, the springs loudly registering their objections, and no sooner had he settled in than Marcelle rolled her chair over and handed him a slip of paper. It bore the handwriting of their superior officer, Commander Michael Kozinski. *You and Bernie, my office.*

"It was on my desk when I got here at 6:45," she said. "You think he knows about Andretti?"

"It was three days ago. By now, the whole department knows about it. You really ought to stop beating up your colleagues."

"This time was different."

"I don't think that matters to Andretti."

Marcelle looked at him optimistically. "Maybe Mike wants to talk about the Arroyos."

"Maybe he wants to talk about both."

"Okay," she said. "If it's Andretti, I'll handle it. If it's the Arroyos, you handle it."

"Not much to say. Should I make something up, or just tell him the truth?"

"The truth is easier."

"The truth is boring."

"Go for it," she said. "You're good at being boring."

They walked up to the third floor and on to Mike's office. Bernie knocked on the open door.

"Have a seat and shut the door," Mike said. He leaned back in his chair and looked over his reading glasses at Marcelle. "Tell me you had a good reason to break Andretti's nose."

"I'm the only woman detective in Violent Crimes, and I can't let people think I'm a doormat."

Mike took off his glasses and wearily rubbed the bridge of his nose. "Give me the whole thing from beginning to end."

"Friday night at Angie's," she said. "Me, Bernie, Andretti, and a bunch of the other guys from the two-three. Andretti starts needling me like he always does." She looked over at Bernie to give him a chance to provide confirmation.

"It's true," he said.

She turned back to Mike. "Andretti tells me I need a man to make me a complete woman. I tell him that martial arts classes make me a complete woman. To which he replies, 'Martial arts are Hollywood bullshit, and you wouldn't last ten seconds in a street fight.'"

Mike waited for more, but there wasn't any. "That's it? That's what set you off?"

"Well ... yeah."

"And you couldn't just ignore it?"

Marcelle sat forward in her chair and locked eyes with Mike. "I did what you and Bernie and every other male cop would've done. I invited him to show me how I can't last ten seconds in a street fight."

"Jesus, Marcelle, he outweighs you by a hundred pounds."

"Yeah, I know that's not much. Maybe if he were bigger, it would've been a fairer fight. Anyway, we went to the alley behind Angie's where these things get settled, and everyone followed us out."

"How long from beginning to end?"

"Right around ten seconds."

"And then you put an elbow in his nose and decked him."

"Yes, sir."

Mike threw his head back and laughed.

Marcelle said, "You're not mad?"

"Hell, no. Andretti's an asshole. But you really ought to stop beating up your colleagues."

"Does that mean we can go now?" Bernie asked.

"Not so fast. While you're here, I thought you could update me on the Arroyos. I bet you're typing arrest warrants already."

"Not exactly."

"How much not exactly?"

Bernie shifted around in his chair. "Here's where we are. Last week we started canvassing the areas where the Garza boys and the Latin Eagles were found. Seems the original interviews weren't too comprehensive."

"You're doing door-to-doors?"

"Some street stops, too. Nothing fancy, no other way to do it. And so far, no one knows a thing, not that I expected anything different."

"Anything else?"

Marcelle said, "You know Victor Ramos from Narcotics?"

Mike nodded.

"Victor and I have been going to a club on North Avenue where Arroyo and his buddies hang out. We haven't decided yet whether we're boyfriend and girlfriend or pimp and hooker. The plan is to get Victor a job with Arroyo, and we figure having me as eye candy can't hurt."

"They think you're a neighborhood girl?"

"Yeah, I've got the right look and my Chicago Spanish is as good as theirs. I'm Maricela DeSoto, and I grew up near Halsted and Addison."

"That's it?"

"That's it."

Mike looked at them for a few seconds, digesting what they'd told him. "You guys have bupkis."

"It's gonna be a long process," Bernie said.

"I know. And I'm sorry to have to crap on your Monday morning, but it's about to get more complicated. Ever heard of a Southeast Asian heroin group called the Quan organization?"

"I have," Marcelle said. "DEA was monitoring them when I worked there. They're active in Europe and Australia, but never sold here."

"Well, that's about to change," Mike said. "Last month, Quan sent his head of security here with twelve men. The security guy is an American named Thornton. The feds think Thornton and his guys want to make Chicago the US beachhead for Quan, and once they start selling here, they're going to square off with the Arroyos real quick. And that's why it makes sense to work their case and yours together."

"Ohhhhh, shit," Bernie said.

"Yeah, that's right. You'll be working with the feds on this one."

"Look on the bright side," Marcelle said. "After all, I used to be with the DEA."

Bernie shot her a side-eye. "That's exactly what I'm afraid of."

"We have a show-and-tell tomorrow, here, eight a.m.," Mike said. "We tell what we have, and their guy tells what they have."

"Guy, as in one man?" Bernie asked.

"For now. He arrived from DC yesterday. You guys are his liaison."

"You want us to babysit a fed."

"Who said anything about babysitting? The guy's a pro, Bernie. He's got a list of major busts longer than your arm."

"I can't wait to meet him."

"Well, I'm glad you feel that way. I thought it would be a real nice gesture if you two could go over to his apartment this morning—he doesn't have an office yet—and introduce yourselves."

Marcelle said, "I have to meet with an assistant state's attorney at 26th and California at nine o'clock."

"Then you're off the hook." Mike handed Bernie a slip with an address. "His name is John Shepard, and he's expecting you in an hour."

Chapter 4

Monday, May 11, 1987
8:56 a.m.

The address Mike gave him brought Bernie north to a residential street in Rogers Park. He eased himself out of the car and checked the address again. It was a two-story, four-flat apartment building. If the man was renting an apartment, he was planning on staying awhile.

He walked through the front door into the vestibule. The door leading to the stairwell was locked, so he found the right mailbox and pressed the buzzer. Thirty seconds later, the intercom came to life.

"Yes?"

"Mr. Shepard, I'm Detective William Bernardelli, Chicago Police Department. They said you'd be expecting me."

"Yes, of course, I'm not sure where . . . oh, here it is."

The buzzer blared forth, and Bernie pulled the door open. He made his way up the three flights of stairs, expecting to find Shepard waiting to greet him, but the apartment door was still closed.

Bernie knocked and waited again.

"Yes?" came a voice from behind the door.

"It's me, Mr. Shepard."

"I'm sorry. I never open the door without knowing who it is. Could you hold your credentials up to the peephole, please?"

Bernie did as he was asked. A few seconds later, he heard three locks being turned. He was looking straight ahead, but when the door opened, he realized he'd been aiming too high.

The man standing in front of him was about five feet seven and looked like he might weigh 120 pounds in winter clothing. His age was hard to place because of his boyish face, maybe mid-thirties. He had neatly combed light brown hair and a pale complexion indicating a life spent indoors. His eyes were as wide as saucers, no doubt because the blinds in the apartment were drawn shut and not a single light was on.

"Johnshepardpleasedtomeetyou," he said as they shook hands. He looked away as he spoke. "I'm looking forward to working with you."

"Likewise." Bernie scanned the apartment. "Nice place."

"Do you really think so? The rent is quite reasonable."

"It should be, for a place that doesn't have electricity."

"Excuse me?"

"Don't you have any lamps here?"

"I'm sorry." John switched on an overhead bulb and began squinting.

"Something wrong with your eyes?" Bernie asked.

"No, not at all, it's just that the light is a little bright for me."

John was distracting to watch. His eyes kept opening and narrowing, and his eyebrows were moving up and down according to some silent rhythm only he could hear. Occasionally, his mouth and head would twitch. If body language could be measured, his would be clocked at 100 miles per hour.

They entered the dark living room. John sat down on a couch, and Bernie sat to his side in an armchair. There was no offer of a glass of water or coffee. John just sat there, twitching away, saying nothing.

"So, did you just fly in from DC?" Bernie said.

"I drove."

"From DC?"

"Yes."

"You have something against airplanes?"

"I do."

"What?"

"They leave the ground."

"Well, you're right," Bernie said. "I never thought of it that way."

John looked away, waiting for Bernie to say something.

"Well, I understand you'll be over at Area Six tomorrow," Bernie said.

"Yes, I'm looking forward to it."

"If you don't have any plans today, I could take you to our range. You could get in some practice with your sidearm, blow off a little steam."

"I don't think that's necessary," John said. "I rarely carry a gun."

"Why not?"

"Why should I?"

"Most DEA agents I know carry guns. I guess that sometimes bad guys shoot at them."

"Yes, of course, but I'm not DEA."

"What are you?"

"I'm an accountant."

Bernie blinked twice, trying to process what he had just heard. "You're a fucking *accountant*?"

"No, I'm just a regular accountant."

"I'm sorry. I—I just—I'm surprised. I didn't mean to be rude."

John's face remained blank. If he was offended, he sure didn't show it.

"I don't understand rude," he said.

"Look, maybe there's been a mistake," Bernie said. "I thought you were here to work a drug case."

"I am."

"If you're not with the DEA, then who are with you with?"

"I'm a Special Agent of the Department of the Treasury, Internal Revenue Service."

"You're an accountant," Bernie said in wonderment.

"Detective Bernardelli—"

"Bernie."

"Bernie. Al Capone was one of the most prolific and violent criminals the country has ever known. Do you know what he was finally convicted of?"

"Tax evasion."

"That's right. And do you know who made the case against him?"

"The Untouchables?"

"No. Special Agents of the Internal Revenue Service, just like me."

"Mr. Shepard—"

"Please call me John."

"John, I didn't mean to get off on the wrong foot."

"Which foot is bothering you?"

"It's just an expression."

"I'm not good with expressions."

"Let me say it this way. I wanted to make a good impression."

"You have. Your reputation precedes you. I understand that Ms. DeSantis is also quite competent."

"That she is."

"Well, then, now that we've introduced ourselves, we don't need to waste time on it in the morning. Eight o'clock tomorrow?"

"Eight o'clock," Bernie said.

* * *

Bernie parked his car at Area Six and walked up to the second floor. Marcelle wasn't back yet, so he proceeded to the third floor. Mike's door was open, and when he saw Bernie approaching, Mike's face turned sheepish. Bernie walked in and sat down.

"You knew, didn't you?" Bernie said.

"I knew some. I spoke with his boss a few days ago."

"And you didn't want to tell me?"

"I didn't want to prejudice your opinion. How weird is he?"

"Weird isn't a strong enough word. He's a little, bitty guy, and he's got a bunch of tics. Real disconcerting to watch. Kind of socially inept. Want me to go on?"

"No, sounds like what his boss said."

"Care to fill me in?"

"His boss, guy by the name of Street, said John's the best agent he's ever had and the strangest person he's ever met."

"The second part, I can see. The first part's hard to swallow."

"It's true," Mike said. "You remember when the feds took down the Volkov brothers in New Jersey last year?"

"Sure."

"That was John's gig. And there's a whole lot more." Mike pushed a manila folder toward Bernie. "That's his jacket. Read it at your leisure."

"What else did Street tell you that's not in his jacket?"

"Nothing that'll surprise you, now that you've met him. John's not too social and he's not on the floor with the other agents. At his request, they gave him an office in the building's basement next to the custodian's office. No windows. Nice and dark, real quiet. No family or friends that Street knows of, never talks about himself. But the no friends or family seems to work out, because they have him going all over the country and he stays in one place for months at a time. Never complains, never argues, just says, yes, sir, and goes on about his business."

"Sounds like your kind of guy," Bernie said. "You'll have a ball with him tomorrow."

Bernie returned to the second floor, and a few minutes later, Marcelle arrived.

"How'd it go with the ASA?" Bernie asked.

"I think he likes me. His eyes were all over me."

"That's not exactly what I was asking, but it'll do."

"Did you meet John?"

"Oh, boy, did I meet him." Bernie ran through the meeting with John and what Mike had told him.

"Is that his jacket?"

"Yeah." Bernie flipped it open and began skimming. "Let's see. Born 1947, Greencastle, Indiana. Goes to Indiana University, does four years of ROTC, gets a BS in accounting with honors. Joins the Army as a second lieutenant. Goes through the Army Finance School at Fort Benjamin Harrison, Lawrence Township, Indiana, then reassigned to Fort A. P. Hill, Bowling Green, Virginia."

"What was his job?"

"Finance Corps, finance and payroll accounting. Completed his active-duty service commitment, discharged in '73 as a captain. No disciplinary actions."

"Any Purple Hearts for paper cuts?"

"Not that it says here. Joined Internal Revenue Service later that year, assigned to the Intelligence Unit, now known as Criminal Investigation."

He flipped to the next section of the file. "Here's his case list." He read her the list—it was every bit as impressive as Mike had said—and closed the file.

"What do you think?" Bernie asked.

"I think tomorrow is going to be mighty interesting," Marcelle said.

Chapter 5

Eighteen Days Earlier
Thursday, April 23, 1987
10:15 a.m.
Washington, DC

General Henry Sampson was having a good day. He had no meetings until the afternoon. His secretary had successfully diverted all of his calls. The fax machine, the bane of his existence, hadn't spit out a single emergency. On this beautiful, peaceful spring day, he allowed himself to reflect upon his good fortune.

The promotion to lieutenant colonel had come through two months after his meeting with the DOD men, followed by colonel, brigadier general, and major general. He was less than two years away from his thirtieth anniversary with the Army, and it had all worked out beautifully. He'd gotten two stars, and with them, the perks: a spacious, wood-paneled office with a good view on the outer wall of the Pentagon, his own secretary right outside his door, and a brigadier general to do his grunt work.

He swiveled his chair around and looked out his window at Arlington—the lush green trees, the perfectly manicured grass—

And row after row of gravestones. Hundreds of thousands of them, each one marking a soldier just as indispensable as he was.

Sampson turned back around, put his feet up on his desk, and opened the sports section of the *Post*, but he'd barely started reading when one of the bulbs on his phone lit up. It was an outside line, probably something his secretary could refer to the brigadier, but that hope evaporated when he heard his intercom buzz.

"Yes?"

"A gentleman who wishes to speak with you, sir. I asked whether General Willingham could help him, but he said you'd want to take the call."

"Who is it?"

"A Professor Thornton."

Sampson's feet came flying off his desk as he bolted upright in his chair.

"General?"

Sampson picked up the handset. "Thank you, put him on." The line clicked once. Sampson didn't wait for a salutation. "I'd hoped you were dead," he said.

The response from the other end was laughter. "Now, Henry, after all these years, I thought I'd get a more cordial greeting. Or should I address you as 'General'? Congratulations, by the way—I always knew you'd go far."

"Where are you?" Sampson asked.

"Chicago."

"How'd you get into this country?"

"Why, I'm an American citizen, a veteran at that. The passport was easy."

"Why'd you come back?"

"I was homesick, Henry. I longed for things American. I want to go to baseball games on Sunday afternoons and eat hot dogs. There is, however, just one slight problem."

Sampson's chest tightened, and he gulped down a breath. The past was about to rear its ugly head and bite him right in the ass.

"Do you still keep tabs on my former students?" Thornton asked.

"Of course, we do," Sampson said. "We never know when one of your killing machines might get his wires crossed."

"Don't be so harsh. They served you and your superiors quite well. Unfortunately, now that I've returned, I need protection from them. One in particular."

"Good luck. When he finds out you're here, you won't be able to stop him."

"Perhaps not. After all, he did have an excellent teacher. Nevertheless, I think we ought to try."

"What do you mean, 'we?'" Sampson said. "I hope he slits your throat from ear to ear."

"That's a very unfortunate attitude, Henry. How close are you to retirement, a year or two?"

Fifteen months and twenty-two days, you bastard, Sampson thought.

"What a shame it would be," Thornton continued, "so late in your career, for the public to learn of the rather unusual operation you supervised in Vietnam."

Sampson was momentarily dumbstruck, but then found his voice. "After what you did, now you're going to blackmail me?"

"That's such an ugly word. I simply propose an exchange of favors. My vow of silence in return for a small service from you."

"What do you want?"

"I'm an old man, but I wish to live a while longer. He will indeed discover I'm here. All I ask is that you arrange to protect me from him. Can you do that for me?"

Sampson's jaw clenched, and he resisted the urge to scream obscenities at the man. He had no good choices.

"I can do it," he said.

"I knew I could count on you. I'll be in touch to discuss the details."

The line clicked again, and Sampson heard a dial tone. He stared at the phone for a moment, then finally hung it up. His good mood having vanished, he pushed himself out of his chair, turned to his window, and looked out at Arlington and its endless gravestones.

Chapter 6

Thursday, May 7, 1987
6:44 a.m.
Northeastern United States

Ed Stepanek was working, but didn't want anyone to know it.

He sat on a park bench reading a newspaper, casually glancing at the occasional cyclist or jogger. He was slim, balding, and of medium height, and because he was utterly nondescript, no one paid attention to him.

Ed liked it that way.

He lived alone in a quiet neighborhood in a town a four-hour drive from here. At first, his neighbors were curious about him because he told them he didn't work. People would believe whatever made them comfortable, so Ed told them he lived off an inheritance. By the same token, people were less apt to be suspicious of someone they liked, so he always made sure he was a good neighbor. He eagerly participated in all the neighborhood functions. Every Halloween, he patrolled the street to keep the children safe as they made their way through the dark. And every few months when he went on one of his extended vacations, he hired a service to care for his yard.

Ed's neighbors didn't know he worked while he was out of town. And he was working right now, waiting for a particular man to jog by. Watching and waiting were very important parts of Ed's job. After all, killing a person was easy. The hard part was getting away with it.

Seven benches were within visual range of the path that the subject took through this part of the park. Ed had come here each morning for two weeks, each time wearing different clothes and hats. One of the benches was next to the path, though he never sat there. The others were between seventy-five and 200 yards away. He rotated among those six.

Ed could tell the subject never noticed him. The man lived in the lowest state of alertness, noticing nothing beyond what he needed to see to perform whatever function he needed to perform. It never crossed his mind that he was anything but safe.

At that moment, the subject jogged down the path about one hundred yards from where Ed sat. 6:48 a.m. It never varied by over seven minutes in either direction. *The subject is an idiot.*

This subject would not require the use of a gun, a circumstance that brightened Ed's mood. A gun dispensed a bullet over which one had no control after it was fired. A gun could also be traced. And most importantly, it was not artful.

Whenever he thought about the inelegance of guns, Ed thought about the man who taught him that. It didn't take much to make Ed think about the man. He thought about Robert Thornton every single day.

When they'd met eighteen years ago, this man had seen something in Ed that he himself had never seen. Thornton had recognized Ed's talent and had helped him develop and hone his skills. Sometimes guns were necessary, he said, but killing by hand was always preferable. It was quieter, more reliable, and exhibited more craftsmanship.

Ed had admired Thornton more than anyone else he'd ever met. Thornton was the father he'd never had, the only male in his life he'd ever looked up to. Ed wanted nothing more than to please him, to show him what a good pupil he was, and to earn the man's respect.

But Thornton never gave Ed the recognition he deserved. There were fifteen others and Thornton treated them all equally, never acknowledging that Ed was the best of them, as Ed knew he was. It grated on Ed, became his obsession. Ed decided that the ultimate proof of his ability would be to kill Thornton, to show that his skills exceeded his master's.

But Thornton abruptly left Vietnam before Ed could carry out his plan, and that was the man's worst sin—abandoning Ed just as Ed's father had abandoned him. It was no longer just a matter of proving his superiority. It was a matter of retribution.

Ed's hatred for Thornton burned relentlessly. Eventually he learned Thornton was in Southeast Asia. Ed could have gone there, but the circumstances would have made the mission difficult and time-consuming. He would have been in unfamiliar territory where he didn't know the language, and the man undoubtedly would be well-protected.

Ed thus put his plans on hold. It was always possible, though, that Thornton would return to the United States. So as not to miss the opportunity, Ed had passed the word around the underground society through which his work came: if the man were ever sighted, the information would be well-rewarded. And every single day, Ed passionately hoped that time would come.

Chapter 7

The Present
Monday, May 11, 1987
11:47 a.m.

Preparing for the next day's meeting at Area Six, John reread the DeSantis and Bernardelli personnel files. He had no doubt about it: they were going to be a problem.

John often worked with the local police, and they usually gave him their least productive officers to serve as liaisons, not wanting to waste good people on federal projects. CPD, though, had done exactly the opposite—it had assigned him its best two investigators. Their records showed they would stop at nothing to close a case.

And that was why they were going to be a problem. He couldn't let them get close to the truth.

Most of his presentation tomorrow would be routine, but there would be two gaps in the chronology. The first would be Thornton's first seven years after World War Two. John could finesse that one by telling them the information was classified, which was both truthful and plausible, and thus unlikely to arouse suspicion.

The second gap, from 1968 to 1973, was a bigger problem. If he told them that information was classified, they'd know Thornton had worked for the government during those years, a fact too sensitive to disclose. If he fabricated a story, he risked being caught in a lie if they followed up on it. The safest course was to tell them he knew nothing.

John finished reviewing his notes and thought through the sequence of tasks he needed to accomplish. The first order of business was to arrange protection for Thornton, but with two motivated detectives involved, he'd also need to slow them down. The key to both would be the meeting tomorrow.

John practiced his presentation, hoping he could pull it off.

Chapter 8

Tuesday, May 12, 1987
7:42 a.m.

Bernie walked downstairs to the first floor to retrieve John. He sat on one of the benches with the rest of the public, but he wasn't hard to spot—he was the one whose head was jerking. It would go to his left, vibrate for a few seconds, and then it would center up and repeat the cycle.

"Good morning, John."

"Yes, it is," John said.

"Ready for the big day?"

"I don't think it'll be big. My presentation shouldn't take long."

John stood up, hefting a large briefcase, and followed Bernie up to the second floor. Mike and Marcelle were already in the conference room, and Bernie watched John make his introductions. With each one, John looked off to the left side of their head, thrust his hand out, and said, "Johnshepardpleasedtomeetyou." His head jerking settled down to a twitch, but he was blinking more and his eyebrows were going up and down. Mike offered coffee but John declined it, saying it made him nervous.

They took their seats, and Mike kicked it off. "Marcelle and Bernie are the lead officers in our Arroyo investigation. Both are detectives assigned to Area Six, which I command, and they're both in Violent Crimes."

"You've classified this matter as homicide, and not narcotics?" John asked.

"That's right. And just to complete the loop, why don't you tell us a little about yourself and what you do?"

"I'm a Special Agent of the Department of the Treasury, Internal Revenue Service, Criminal Investigation, what used to be called the Intelligence Unit. I'm in Narcotics-Related Financial Crimes, which pursues narcotics investigations from the financial angle. We document the movement of money during the course of a crime—where the money comes from, who gets it, when it's received, and where they put it—because drug dealers typically do not pay taxes on their income."

Mike thanked him and asked Bernie to start.

"What do you want to know?" Bernie asked John.

"How the heroin trade operates in Chicago."

"Okay. Right now, all the heroin in the Chicagoland area is supplied by a Mexican drug trafficking organization called the Arroyo family. Up until a few months ago we had another Mexican DTO, the Garzas, and we'll get to them in a minute."

"All right."

"The Arroyos are based in the Mexican state of Durango," Bernie said, "and they've been in the heroin business since the mid-fifties. They run a farm-to-the-arm operation—they grow the poppies, process the opium into heroin, and move it to Chicago, mostly Mexican brown powder but also some black tar. Family members control the whole process from start to finish."

"How do they smuggle it?" John asked.

"Mostly in vehicles. Sometimes they mix it in with legal freight, but usually they stash it in hidden compartments. They also use something we call the Durango drive shaft—a sleeve that wraps around the drive shaft that can hold several kilos. The head of the family in Chicago, Javier Arroyo, owns a garage called Lakeview Auto Repair, and we suspect that's where they extract it."

"How do they distribute it?"

"Street gangs control retail sales, mostly black gangs on the West Side and South Side, and Latino gangs on the North Side. The Arroyos wholesale the dope to some of the bigger gangs. Those gangs retail some themselves, and also wholesale some to smaller gangs that do their own street sales. Altogether, you're looking at a three-tier system."

"How do they launder the money?"

"The usual," Bernie said. "Cash-based businesses, used car lots, beauty salons, car washes—anywhere they can commingle drug money with legit money."

"Have there been any recent changes in the retail price of heroin?"

"No, it's been ten bucks for a tenth of a gram for years. They adjust for cost and profit by changing the purity. What we've seen the last few years is a range of three to seven percent purity at the retail level, and it's gone down some since the Garzas left the market."

"Is that the other DTO you mentioned earlier?" John asked.

"Right. The Garza family is out of the state of Nayarit, next to Durango where the Arroyos are based, and they compete with the Arroyos."

"What happened to the Garzas?"

"Last year, dead drug dealers started turning up. Not that dead dealers are exactly a novelty, but it's usually some minor turf war or one guy pissing off another."

"How were these murders different?"

"It all happened in the space of four months," Marcelle said, "and there were some aspects that made the deaths unusual. The first thing was the way these guys died. Typically, these gang guys kill each other in a public place—though there never seem to be any eyewitnesses—and they shoot each other or use baseball bats."

"And in these cases?"

"No gunshots or blunt force," Marcelle said. "There were eight bodies, six with cut throats and two strangulations. And these weren't done by ordinary street guys—they looked like professional hits, something we haven't seen before with street gangs."

"The other odd thing was where they were found," Bernie said. "The first guy was sitting in the driver's seat of his car. One guy was in the gutter of an exit ramp off the Chicago Skyway. They were just random places, no attempt made to make it public. We saw it as another indication it was someone professional."

"And due to those factors, you consider them related?"

"Those and one other thing," Marcelle said. "Four were members of the Garza family, and the other four were Latin Eagles that bought wholesale from the Garzas. None were ordinary citizens, and none were associated with the Arroyos. They were all Garzas or doing business with Garzas."

John looked back at Bernie. "You were going to tell me what happened to the Garza family."

"Not long after we found the eighth body, the Garzas exited the heroin business here. We understand they're still distributing in the southwest, but not in Chicago."

"And you think the killings were meant to drive them out?"

"Exactly."

"Are any members of the Garza family still here?"

"Quite a few," Marcelle said, "including the head of the Chicago family, Manuel. Their extended families live here and they own businesses here."

"Were all the bodies found in Area Six?"

"I'll address that," Mike said. "Some of the bodies were found here and some in other areas, but none were originally assigned to

Bernie or Marcelle. The assigned detectives worked the cases for a while, didn't find any evidence, and moved on."

"It sounds like they moved on quickly," John said.

Mike's face went taut. He leaned across the table. "Chicago had 744 murders last year. When a citizen dies, we'll work it till it's solved or until the next one comes in. Plus, all these guys were known members of either the Garza family or the Latin Eagles, and six of them had felony sheets."

"But later you resumed the investigations?"

Mike nodded. "Because one of the dead Garzas had an aunt who works for an alderman."

"Alderman?"

"What they call city council members in Chicago. Anyway, the aunt complained to the alderman, the alderman complained to the mayor, and the mayor asked us to reopen the cases and to assign all eight to Marcelle and Bernie. That's also the reason I'm supervising the cases directly, which someone at my rank usually wouldn't be doing."

John asked, "What's the status of the investigation?"

"We've been on it three weeks since it reopened," Bernie said. "Our working theory is that the Arroyos did it. We're doing interviews, plus Marcelle and one of our undercover officers, Victor Ramos, are frequenting a bar where the Arroyos hang out. Victor's next move is to try to infiltrate by getting a job with them. That's pretty much it."

Mike looked at the clock. "We've been going awhile. Let's take a break, and then John can tell us all about the Quans and Mr. Thornton."

Chapter 9

Tuesday, May 12, 1987
9:07 a.m.

Manny Garza always got disoriented when he drove outside the city. He was accustomed to the grime of Chicago, with its pavement and congestion and old buildings, but as he drove northwest and passed O'Hare Airport, he entered a different universe, leafy suburbs with beautiful houses unmarked by gang graffiti. An hour into the trip, the houses became less frequent, and when he exited the expressway and started driving north on Route 31, he found himself in a rural area, prairie grasses alternating with tilled land, and only an occasional house or grain silo. Finally, he saw the McHenry County Forest Preserve, which meant he was nearing his destination.

Everything on his left was dense forest, and before long Manny noticed a black metal fence running alongside the edge of the woods, parallel to the road. He slowed down, but the gate to the Lowell Mansion was wedged so inconspicuously among the trees that he almost missed it. The gate was black wrought iron, a good fifteen feet high, with a quaint old guardhouse on the left. He pulled up to the gate, and a man came out of the guardhouse holding a photograph. The guard looked at the photograph, and then he looked at Manny.

"Good morning, sir. May I see your driver's license, please?"

Manny handed it to him, and the guard took a long look at it before returning it. "Please wait for the gate to open fully, then follow the driveway until you see the house."

The guard flipped a switch, and the gate's doors slowly opened. When Manny saw them stop moving, he drove forward, surrounded on both sides by trees. The driveway curved around and eventually the trees ended, and he saw the mansion and the building connected to it.

They were beautiful structures. The mansion itself was three stories, with a light, weathered, brick facade and several gabled roofs that made it look like multiple buildings in one. Porches and bay windows adorned the first and second floors. The roofs and the bay windows had wide, overhanging eaves with elaborately carved brackets underneath. Even to Manny's untrained eye, he could tell that whoever built this place had spared no expense.

To the right of the mansion was a long, three-story building with a similar, though not identical, brick exterior. Closely spaced windows ran the length of the building's top two stories, a design that reminded Manny of a hotel.

Manny pulled up to the front door of the mansion, where a man waited for him. The man wasn't big—slim and a shade under six feet—but he looked very fit. His hair was short, gray, and cut in a military style.

The man's most distinctive features were his eyes, a silver-blue that made them look like mirrors. When he looked at Manny, they seemed to bore right through him. The man did not seem pleased with what he saw.

"Good morning, Mr. Garza. My name is Arthur, and I'll be accompanying you today. Please follow me."

They walked into the mansion. The floor just inside the door was marble, with a large, inlaid "L," and beyond it the floor was wood parquet, obviously old but polished to a high gloss. They walked down a hallway and stopped at a carved wood door.

Arthur knocked on the door. Manny heard someone inside say, "Enter."

Arthur opened the door, and Manny looked into the most impressive room he'd ever seen—black walnut bookshelves lining the walls floor to ceiling and filled with books, a white marble fireplace, sculptures on pedestals, a large desk, and several leather-bound chairs.

In the center of the room was a man who walked toward them. He had a full head of perfectly coiffed, wavy white hair. He wore a gray suit and a starched white shirt, with a deep red tie in a Windsor knot. His face looked old, but he moved with the ease and fluidity of a young man.

He gave Manny a broad smile.

"Welcome, Mr. Garza," said Robert Thornton. "Would you care for something to drink?"

Chapter 10

Tuesday, May 12, 1987
9:18 a.m.

John opened his briefcase, pulled out three binders, and handed them to Mike, Bernie, and Marcelle. "I took the liberty of preparing some written materials. I'll describe the contents as I proceed, and you can read them at your convenience."

Mike gave Bernie a *why didn't you do this?* look. Bernie just rolled his eyes.

"I'll start out with Robert Thornton," John said, "who prefers to be called 'Professor.' He actually was a professor briefly, and we suppose he got attached to the title. We know quite a bit about his early life because he described it in an appendix to his doctoral dissertation."

John pulled out some notes, laid them next to his notebook, and read. "Thornton was born in Michigan in 1914. When he was two, his parents joined the Methodist Missionary Society and moved to China, taking young Robert along. If you look under tab one, you'll see a series of photographs of Thornton during his youth in China.

"Thornton's parents believed in immersing themselves in the local culture as a way of earning the citizens' trust, so they encouraged Robert to learn the language, and by the time he was six, he was fluent in Mandarin. At age seven he began studying the Chinese martial art of Taijiquan."

"Taiji-what?" Mike asked.

"What we call tai chi," Marcelle said.

John nodded. "In 1927, the civil war broke out between the Chinese Communists and the Chinese Nationalists, and three years later, when Thornton was sixteen, he and his parents moved back to Michigan. He finished high school and then enrolled at Columbia University. He spent the next eight years at Columbia, ultimately earning a PhD from its Department of Chinese and Japanese."

John reached back into his briefcase, pulled out three volumes, and passed them out. "These are copies of Thornton's dissertation, 'Ancient Chinese Martial Arts.' His biography is the last section. We've been told that his dissertation was one of the first scholarly Western treatments of the subject."

"What year are we in now?" Bernie asked.

"1940. After Thornton received his PhD, he became an assistant professor at Columbia. Late in the following year, the Japanese bombed Pearl Harbor, throwing the US into World War Two. For us, it was the start of the war, but by then the Chinese had been fighting the Japanese in China for ten years. The US decided to help the Chinese against their common enemy, which brings us back to Thornton.

"Someone in the government learned of Thornton's dissertation and background and realized he'd make an ideal operative, so early in 1942, the government recruited him to join the Office of Strategic Services. Nominally, he was commissioned a second lieutenant in the Army, but they detached him to the OSS for the duration of the war."

John turned to the third section in his notebook and held it up. "This is Thornton in 1942, wearing his military fatigues, while training at an OSS camp in the Catoctin Mountains in Maryland. He also trained at a school called Camp X in Ontario, Canada, operated by the British Special Operations Executive."

"What were they training him to do?" Bernie asked.

"A whole host of things—close combat, guerrilla warfare, demolitions, sabotage, intelligence collection, and escape-and-evasion techniques. They then deployed him to China and Burma, where his and other OSS teams trained and led hundreds of indigenous guerrillas, attacking Japanese transportation and communications, and gathering intelligence whenever they could. Thornton compiled a spectacular record, and by the time the war ended he was a major and had a Silver Star. Shortly after that, the OSS was dissolved, but its constituent parts were merged into other bodies, and most of them ended up in the CIA. Thornton stayed in until 1952."

"Doing what?"

"The CIA is still classifying those parts of the files, and we haven't yet been able to get access to them."

Marcelle said, "Did you check to see whether he's got a deepfile?"

"What's a deepfile?" Bernie asked her.

"Everyone employed by the federal government, civilian or military, has a personnel file," she said, "but there's a parallel file system—the deepfile system—that houses highly classified information, like the activities of CIA operatives and undercover personnel. There's probably one on me because of my work at DEA. Getting access to a deepfile—even just to find out if there is one—is an extensive process because each request has to go through multiple approvals."

"We checked," John said, "and there wasn't one. If there was ever one on Thornton, it's been purged, which wouldn't be unusual given how long it's been since he was active. And just to follow up on what Marcelle said—it took three months to process our request."

"What happened after he left the CIA?" Marcelle asked.

"At this point, his government records end. We understand that in 1952 or '53 he moved to Malaya and ran mercenaries defending landowners against the Communist insurgency. The next place he surfaced was the Congo in 1960, again running mercenary units, and that's when he became famous for his mercenary work."

John held up his notebook again. "Under tab four, you'll see an article about Thornton published in 1965 in a men's pulp magazine called *Warfighter*. The author supposedly traveled to the Congo and interviewed Thornton about his exploits there, but it reads like a puff piece so we don't give it much credibility. It is, though, the only published piece about Thornton that we could find, so we included it for the sake of completeness. As best as we can determine, he stayed in the Congo until 1968."

John paused and looked at his notes. "We lose track of him for a few years after that, but in the mid-seventies we got reports he was involved in the opium trade in Southeast Asia."

"Whoa," Bernie said, leaning across the table. "Slow down there, hoss. You've got the first fifty-some years of his life figured out, this famous mercenary guy, and you're telling me he disappears for six or seven years?"

"No. I'm saying we lose track of him."

"Seems strange, doesn't it? With all the resources the feds have? Did you try—"

Mike swiveled his chair around. "Lighten the hell up, Bernie. He's not some punk you picked up for shoplifting. He told you they don't know."

Bernie looked at John for a moment, then gave a half-apologetic shrug. "Sorry. I didn't mean any offense."

"None taken," John said. He ran his finger down his notes, trying to find where he'd left off. "As I was saying, in the mid-seventies we got reports he was involved in the opium trade in Southeast Asia, and that's where we get to the Quan organization."

He turned to the next section in his notebook and held it up. "This is a 1968 photograph—the most recent one we have—of General Trinh Van Quan, formerly of the North Vietnamese Army. We know little about him beyond what I'm about to tell you."

John put the notebook down and flipped to the next page in his notes. "Quan was born in the province of Thanh Hóa in the area we used to call North Vietnam, and he's around the same age as Thornton. He fought the French during the French Indochina War, and then joined what became the North Vietnamese Army and fought the United States."

John stopped and looked up from his notes. "Before I go any further, let me ask you something. How familiar are you with the opium trade in Southeast Asia?"

"I know a little," Marcelle said, "but I'm not sure about these guys."

Mike and Bernie shook their heads.

"All right. The area I'll be referring to is commonly called the Golden Triangle." John held up the notebook and showed them a map. "Northeastern Burma, northern Thailand, and northern Laos, an area of around 150,000 square miles."

He put the book down. "Most of the opium is grown in northeastern Burma—hill country that includes an area called the Shan states. Opium has been grown in the region since the 1800s, and many of the hill tribes in Burma, Thailand, and Laos grew it as a cash crop. But the pivotal event causing the area to become a major source of opium occurred in the late forties, when the Chinese Communists drove the Chinese Nationalist forces out of China."

"I thought they went to Taiwan," Mike said.

"Most of them did, but there were portions of the Nationalist Army—also called the Kuomintang, or KMT—that retreated through southern China into northern Burma. Over the next three years they tried to invade China a few times, but the Communists beat them back."

"What's that got to do with opium?" Bernie asked.

"The KMT needed a source of income to finance itself, so it terrorized the local population and forced the farmers to grow more opium. The KMT expanded production exponentially, and ultimately controlled ninety percent of the Golden Triangle's opium smuggling—that is, until Quan and Thornton entered the picture."

Mike asked, "How did an American mercenary hook up with a North Vietnamese general?"

"We don't know, but we believe they began their takeover of the region's opium trade in 1973."

"How'd they do it?" Marcelle asked.

"They allied themselves with a local Shan warlord named Lo Chi-Fu. Lo had a small private army and controlled a minor part of the region's opium smuggling. Quan expanded Lo's army, and over a period of years they eliminated their competitors and established their own refineries to process the opium into heroin. They finished pushing out the KMT three years ago, and now they're the world's predominant opium and heroin organization. We don't know all the particulars, but our intelligence suggests they now manage the activities of the middlemen and distributors either directly or indirectly."

Mike asked, "What do you know about their organization?"

"We understand Quan provided the capital. We have little visibility into their structure, but we know Quan is at the top of the chart and Thornton oversees security and enforcement."

"How good is their stuff?" Marcelle asked.

"It's the purest heroin in the world—number four heroin, also known as China White, made by chemists Quan brought in from Hong Kong. You said earlier you've seen the street purity of the Mexican heroin in Chicago at between three and seven percent?"

"That's right."

"What Quan is going to bring here will retail at sixty to eighty percent purity at the same price."

"Jesus," Marcelle said, "at that level, users can insufflate."

Bernie looked at her, baffled. "Not all of us know what that means."

"They'll be able to snort it," she said. "That means a lot more buyers—people who don't want to mess with needles, but are willing to inhale. It'll also mean a lot more overdoses."

The room got quiet.

John folded his notes and placed them into a file folder. "Does anyone have any more questions?"

"I'll ask the most important question," Mike said. "How do you propose to stop this guy?"

"I was about to get to that," John said.

Chapter 11

Tuesday, May 12, 1987
9:28 a.m.

What Manny really wanted was a cold beer, but he didn't want Thornton to think he was some yokel. "What are you drinking?"

"Tea," Thornton said.

"Tea would be great."

"Arthur, I think the Earl Grey would do nicely."

While Arthur made the tea, Manny noticed an unusual-looking instrument on Thornton's desk. It had an iridescent, teardrop-shaped handle, and a blade that looked sharp enough to shave with.

Thornton picked it up and displayed it to Manny. "I see you've noticed my letter opener, a gift from a former employer. The handle is mother-of-pearl, the band is sterling silver, and the blade is high-carbon steel. A tremendous amount of craftsmanship went into this simple implement, and it's one of my most prized possessions." Thornton carefully returned it to the desk. "But you didn't come all this way to discuss my stationery tools. Shall we sit?"

Arthur handed Manny a cup of tea on a saucer, and Manny and Thornton sat down in two of the leather-bound chairs.

"Mr. Garza, I'm delighted we're finally able to meet. I apologize for having to communicate through intermediaries, but I'm sure you understand our need for secrecy."

"Always pays to be careful," Manny said.

"I was sorry to hear of your misfortunes at the hands of the Arroyo family, but consider it a stroke of profoundly good luck for General Quan and myself that your organization is now available to joint venture with us. Rest assured, we shall square your account with the Arroyos in short order. I trust the financial arrangements are suitable?"

"Yeah, they're fine."

"How does your family in Mexico feel about you distributing for us?" Thornton asked.

"When our people got killed, my family washed their hands of Chicago. The southwest was always a better market, anyway. As long as I send them their share of the profits, they'll be happy. Do you need any help bringing the stuff in?"

"Thank you, but no. We've already made those arrangements, and I hope you won't be offended if I can't share those details with you."

"No problem. Is it true we don't have to cut it when it gets here?"

"That's correct. When you receive the product, it will already be packaged in glassine envelopes, one-tenth gram apiece, and the envelopes will bear a trademark that we've selected for the Chicago market: '100% Super Tiger,' stamped in red ink. And since our trademarks carry with them an assurance of quality, we go to great lengths to maintain the goodwill associated with them. Diluting the product further will neither be necessary nor tolerated, and anyone who cuts it before retail sale will be dealt with swiftly and permanently. I hope that won't be an issue for your distributors."

"I'll make sure they understand," Manny said.

"Speaking of which, have you notified your distribution channel that you'll be supplying them?"

"I talked to the head guys at the Vice Lords, the Gangster Disciples, and the Latin Kings, and told them to keep it quiet until we're ready to go."

"Do they have any qualms about leaving the Arroyos?"

"They said if I can sell them seventy percent pure dope, already packaged, at the same price they're paying for Arroyo's shit, they'll be all over it. They'll have lines a mile long for this stuff."

"Perfect."

"One thing worries me," Manny said. "Arroyo's gonna come back hard on us and he's got a lot of soldiers, way more than I do. We need to figure out a game plan."

"You needn't be concerned. As is our custom, my men and I will handle whatever conflicts arise. Your organization is strictly distribution. My organization provides security and enforcement."

"How many men do you have?"

"Twelve, plus myself."

"How many more are you getting?"

"I think what we have now will suffice."

Manny shook his head. "We're gonna need a lot more than twelve men."

"Trust me, Mr. Garza, we've done this before."

"How fast do you plan to move?"

"I expect the process to be complete within two weeks."

Manny couldn't hide his disbelief.

"Chin up, Mr. Garza," Thornton said. "A month from now, you'll be awash in money and all your doubts resolved. I would, though, like to ask you for a favor. Are you able to get a message to Mr. Arroyo?"

"Yeah, I can do that."

"General Quan believes in trying to resolve conflicts peacefully, if possible. Please tell Mr. Arroyo I'd like to meet with him, preferably by week's end, to discuss the possibility of his voluntarily withdrawing from Chicago, in exchange for joint venturing with us elsewhere."

"No way he's gonna do that."

"Well, there's nothing to lose by trying. Can you ask?"

"Sure. I can ask."

"Very good. One more request, if you don't mind. Given your former involvement in the heroin business here, the authorities may view you as a potential source of information about my activities—you know, the word on the street sort of thing. If they contact you, I trust you'll report it to us promptly?"

"Absolutely."

"Thank you. It's been a pleasure meeting you, Mr. Garza, and I look forward to a long and prosperous relationship with you. Unfortunately, this meeting is the last time we'll speak face to face, as I expect the authorities will soon have me under surveillance. That's not an altogether bad thing, but it will preclude personal contact."

Arthur walked Manny to his car and returned a few minutes later. "He's a moron."

"I agree, but he'll be quite useful."

"What are the odds that Arroyo agrees to meet?"

"Almost nil. Tell Johnson and Lattimore to continue their surveillance on the house, and to be ready to move when the shipment comes in."

Chapter 12

Tuesday, May 12, 1987
10:51 a.m.

"The way we work isn't glamorous," John said, "and requires time-consuming, painstaking attention to detail. We look at how the target lives, how he acquires his wealth and spends his money, and how he reports his income when he files his tax return."

Marcelle asked, "Where's Thornton living now?"

"He bought a property called the Lowell Mansion near Diamond Lake in McHenry County, northwest of Chicago."

"That's outside our jurisdiction."

"It's taken care of," Mike said. "The McHenry County Sheriff's Office agreed to a joint project with CPD, and the Illinois AG's office blessed it. We can put people over there, and McHenry County SO will notify us if there's unusual activity."

Mike turned to John. "What's your plan?"

"I expect evidence-gathering to last several months. For the next few weeks, I'll be working alone, acquiring high-level information, working out of my apartment. At the appropriate time, we'll bring in a team and set up an office in one of the federal buildings."

"How can we help?"

"The first thing I want to do is learn the area, as I'm not acquainted with Chicago. I especially want to get familiar with the areas where heroin sales take place, but I need to understand the entire city's dynamics, how its transportation flows. Specifically, I'd like someone to drive me through the city's neighborhoods and educate me as we go along."

Bernie and Marcelle looked at each other and then looked at Mike, who finally spoke.

"No disrespect, John, but is that a good use of our time? We have eight homicides we have to clear and a new dealer in town, and you want us to drive you around?"

"In my judgment, it's the way to do it. I'd suggest two to four hours per day, so your people can attend to other matters each day, and we should be able to finish by the end of next week."

Mike looked unhappy, but didn't push it. "Bernie, can you handle it?"

"Do I have a choice?"

"The second thing," John said, "is that we need twenty-four-hour surveillance on Thornton. Two-man teams who follow Thornton whenever he leaves his mansion. They don't need to be surreptitious. If he stops, they stop. If he walks into a building, they do, too. And I suggest they be well-armed."

"You think Thornton's going to shoot at our cops?"

"No. I think his enemies may shoot at him."

"In our business, we call that a favor," Bernie said.

"I understand your point, but it's imperative we keep Thornton alive. Our plan is to get enough evidence against Thornton to turn him against Quan, but that can't happen if he's dead."

"From what you've told us," Mike said, "he doesn't sound like a guy who turns. Unless—"

"Unless what?"

Sometimes Mike's mouth got ahead of his brain, but he decided he may as well spit it out. "Do you guys already have a deal with him?"

"We do not."

Mike scowled at him. "We are not in the bodyguard business, and we've never given someone protection without a deal and sworn testimony beforehand. Two men, eight-hour shifts, that's six man-days per day, and you don't even know if he'll cooperate."

John nodded politely. "I understood you spoke with Supervisory Special Agent Street about cooperating with us."

"Well, I did, but I didn't know we'd be giving a drug dealer free security."

"I also understood that Mr. Street agreed to lend certain investigative resources to your department, as a token of our gratitude for your cooperation."

Marcelle and Bernie looked at Mike again.

"I'll tell you what, John. We'll do it for a while and see how it goes, but if things get hot, I reserve the right to pull them."

"Thank you."

Bernie asked, "When do you want to start your driving tours?"

"I'll be occupied tomorrow and Thursday. I'll come by at ten o'clock Friday morning."

"I can't wait," Bernie said.

Chapter 13

Tuesday, May 12, 1987
11:38 a.m.

Marcelle had taken the detective's exam at the first opportunity, three years after joining CPD, and she'd passed it with the highest score anyone could remember seeing. That was how she came to the attention of the Deputy Superintendent, Bureau of Investigative Services.

When he read her file, he realized she was an exceptional candidate. She spoke French and Spanish and was a second dan in aikido. She'd graduated first in her class at Marquette with a degree in Criminology and had joined the Drug Enforcement Administration, where she worked undercover in the southeastern US for four years and received glowing reviews from her superiors. And then she resigned and came to Chicago, where she joined CPD and became a patrol officer.

The Deputy Superintendent couldn't understand it. This woman had solid-gold credentials. She'd been on a straight upward trajectory at a prominent federal agency. Why would she resign and become a Chicago copper?

So when he interviewed her, he asked her.

"I had a disagreement with my supervisor," she said.

"About what?"

"Correct use of hands."

"Excuse me?"

"He put his hand on my ass, so I broke two of his teeth."

"I see. Were there any witnesses?"

"Yeah, about a dozen people."

"Was there any doubt he was the aggressor?"

"None at all."

"Then why didn't you report him?"

"I did," she said, "mostly to keep him from doing it again to someone else. He got demoted and transferred, and then I resigned."

"But why?"

"Because at that point I knew I was damaged goods. Whether I stayed at DEA or transferred to another federal agency, I'd forever be known as the chick agent who beat up her male boss. They protect each other, you know. I'm sure everyone would've been nice to my face, but they'd have made sure that every assignment I got after that was a shit sandwich, so I came back home and joined CPD."

"Well, for our sake, I'm glad you did. Welcome to the Detective Division."

"Thank you, sir."

"You'll be assigned to Youth Investigations. I trust you'll find it challenging and rewarding."

"I want to work with Bernardelli," she said.

He knew that wouldn't happen, but he needed to let her down diplomatically. "In Detective Division, we don't assign partners."

"That's okay. Just give me the desk next to his, which I happen to know is vacant right now."

"Look, Bernardelli's a good detective, but difficult to work with. Why are you so keen on working with him?"

"I've been here three years, so I've had a chance to ask around—you know, who are the good detectives? The first name everyone gives me is Bernardelli."

"Miss DeSantis—"

"*Ms.* DeSantis," she said. "Or Officer DeSantis, if you prefer."

He took a deep breath before continuing. "*Ms.* DeSantis. Bernardelli works Violent Crimes. Women do not go into that section. It's only been since 1974 that CPD even let female officers go on patrol. We slot female detectives into Youth Investigations— child abandonment, child abuse cases, and so forth. The hours are much more regular, more conducive to raising a family."

"Is that a rule, or just the way you do it?"

"Well, um, just the way we do it."

"How many times have you seen a résumé like mine?"

"Probably never."

"I want to work with Bernardelli," she said.

They asked Mike to break the news to Bernie, who was not having it.

"There's about a million reasons why it won't work," he said. "First off, I resent being the butt of some silly, female upward mobility project."

"She asked for you," Mike said.

"I don't care. You know my style. I am not going to stop every fifteen minutes so she can touch up her makeup."

"Fine. Don't stop. Run her around. Do like you always do. In a few days she'll realize it's not for her and request a transfer to Youth. Everyone'll be happy."

Bernie decided he was not going to wait a few days.

He knew what was going to happen. She'd walk into the second floor all dressed up in some professional-looking business suit she'd bought at Marshall Field's. She'd stride up, introduce herself, and make a wonderful speech about what a pleasure it would be to work with him, the pinnacle of her ambitions ever since she was a child, and blah, blah, blah. He'd wait patiently until she was done and then knock her down a few pegs.

She walked through the door the next morning while Bernie sat at his desk. He glanced at her, then looked down again. She wore a blue dress that hugged her body and ended two inches above her knees, and the highest high heels he'd ever seen. She sure didn't get that outfit at Field's.

There were six other men in the room, and they stared at her all the way along her walk down the aisle. She walked around to the back of her desk, set her purse down, and then turned and looked down at Bernie, who was still pretending he was reading something.

"This is my new desk," she said.

Bernie turned in her direction, but without looking her in the eyes. Instead, he looked down at her shoes, then shifted his gaze up to her legs and her thighs, where he lingered for a moment. He continued upward until he got to her chest, on which he spent the most time. Finally, he looked at her face and made eye contact with her for the first time.

Marcelle looked at him indifferently. "You think you're going to scare me off by staring at my boobs? I like it when men stare at my boobs."

"How come?"

"Because it makes them stupid."

"So now you think I'm stupid?"

"You tell me. So far, you haven't done anything smart."

He forgot about knocking her down a few pegs. He was starting to like her.

She turned her chair in his direction and sat down directly in front of him. "I worked undercover at DEA for four years. I had guns pointed at me five times and a knife to my throat twice. Then I came here and worked patrol for three years in the 27th District. You can just imagine what a joyride that was. And compared to all that, you're not so scary. You are not going to run me off, so man up and get used to it."

The only thing he could think to say was, "Why me?"

She looked like she was reconsidering whether she'd made the right decision. "Everyone says you're the best detective in the city, so you're the one I want to learn from. Now tell me where the coffee is, and go back to pretending you're reading."

It wasn't an auspicious beginning, but Marcelle was glad she'd stuck with him. Most cases couldn't bear the freight of two detectives, but she and Bernie worked together every chance they got. Even when they weren't officially on the same case, they worked their cases jointly, helping each other however they could, even if it meant off hours without overtime. She could tell it pleased Bernie at some elemental level that someone wanted to learn from him. She also knew he would have eaten glass before he'd ever use the word "mentor," but that's what he became. And every now and then, they'd be discussing a case and Bernie would pause and say, "It's time for an educational moment."

Which was why, as they walked back to their desks after the meeting with John, she knew what Bernie was going to say and decided to beat him to the punch.

"I'll bet it's time for an educational moment," she said.

"You got it. Tell me your impression of John."

"At the beginning, he was just as you described. Real fidgety, so much so I felt sorry for him. Can you imagine the life he has?"

"No, I sure can't."

"And the way he introduced himself, he sounded almost robotic, like someone had written out what he's supposed to say when he meets people and he was just reciting it from rote memory."

She stopped and thought through her images of him. "But then, when he started his presentation, his whole demeanor changed. The fidgeting diminished, and he did a great job."

"I've met people like him before," Bernie said. "Very nervous most of the time, but when they have to perform a task, it's like they zero in so much they forget to be nervous. Other than that, though, did anything strike you as unusual?"

"I thought the weirdest part was this bit about protecting Thornton. I understand John wanting to preserve the guy as a witness, but I think it's a dumb idea and a waste of resources to do it without an agreement."

"When you were at DEA, did they ever protect someone before they agreed to cooperate?"

"No, and I never heard of any other federal agency doing it, either."

"It might make more sense if we knew something about John's strategy, but Mike asked him twice what his plan was and he was pretty vague both times."

"Yeah, and there's no excuse for it. He gave us more detail about guarding Thornton than he did about investigating him."

"Anything else strike you?" Bernie asked.

"The fact you're asking suggests there's something else, but I can't think of anything."

Bernie drew the moment out. It wasn't often he got ahead of Marcelle, and he wanted to savor it.

"John lied to us," he said.

"When?"

"When he said they don't know what Thornton did between '68 and '73."

"*That?* Just because he didn't know something?" She shook her head, looking askance at him. "In all the time we've worked together, this is the first time I've heard you say you had a hunch."

"And I'm not saying it now. I don't believe in hunches; I believe in facts. But somewhere along the spectrum between the two is judgment, and that's something we exercise every day."

"Fair point. Tell me what you based your judgment on."

"Okay. Thornton's seventy-three years old. For sixty-eight of those years, the government knows where he was or what he was doing or who he worked for—they at least know *something*. But right in the middle, in the prime of his life, this famous guy just falls off the face of the earth, and they don't know squat?" He paused to see if she'd respond, and when she didn't, he continued. "The federal government has massive intelligence resources—you know that from your DEA days."

"True enough, but how can you be so sure he's lying?"

"I'm not sure. But we don't deal in certainties, Marcelle, we deal in probabilities. What's the likelihood the government knows zero about what Thornton did during those five years?"

"Probably not too high, but what difference does it make?"

"Because it just happens to be the five years right before he got into the drug business. And because ninety-nine percent of the time when people lie, they lie for a reason. If John's lying about it, he's got a reason he doesn't want us to know, and that makes me damned queasy about this whole thing."

Marcelle had worked with Bernie for two years, and two years in cop time was like ten years in civilian time. She knew him as well as she knew anyone, and one thing she knew was that when he latched onto something, he would not let it go.

"I guess that means we're going to try to find out what Thornton was up to."

"At least make a run at it," Bernie said. "You still have friends at DEA?"

"Yeah, but the folks I know are on the Latin American cocaine cartels. They wouldn't have any details on Thornton. And now that the file's at IRS, if they ask around, we run the risk that John finds out we're going behind his back. I'll call them if you want, but can you think of another way to do it?"

Bernie rocked back and forth in his chair, pondering the question.

"I think," he said, "we should pay a visit to my Uncle Mario."

Chapter 14

Tuesday, May 12, 1987
1:44 p.m.

"Is Mario really your uncle?" Marcelle asked.

They were in Bernie's car, turning onto Lake Shore Drive. They proceeded north, with the Outer Drive on their right and the beach and the lake just beyond it.

"No, but he may as well be," Bernie said. "They lived down the block from us and I've known him since I was six. Bobby and I were inseparable all the way through high school and until I joined the Army."

"When did you realize Mario was a mob boss?"

"He wasn't a boss. He was, like, their bookkeeper. And to answer your question, I was nine or ten. Everyone in the neighborhood deferred to him, and sometimes he'd get a lot of visitors, large men in very nice suits. Bobby would come over and spend the night at our house because they didn't want kids around."

"So now we're going to ask an Outfit guy to help us catch a drug dealer."

"He's not an Outfit guy anymore. He retired and turned over the family business to Bobby."

Marcelle snickered, but said nothing.

"I owe him a lot, Marcelle. When I got out of the Army, I had no job prospects. My only skills were being a military policeman and fixing shoes. I'd fixed enough shoes to know I didn't want to do it anymore, so I asked Uncle Mario to introduce me to CPD. He greased the wheels for me."

Marcelle cocked her head in disbelief. "You never told me that before."

"Well, the subject never came up before."

"You're saying a mob boss got you your job as a policeman."

"Sometimes you still think like a fed. This is Chicago, Marcelle. I happened to know a very successful businessman who, along with his partners, owns the biggest liquor distributor in the state. He's also been voted Chicago's Italian-American Man of the Year three times, he's donated so much money to Daughters of Mercy Hospital that they named a wing after him and his wife, and he gives generously to the Democratic Party."

"Even though he's retired and all, do you suppose it might put him in a weird position to talk to us?"

"I don't think so. Mario's folks stayed away from heroin, and these days it's all street gangs, anyway. And the worst that can happen is they'll play dumb and say they never heard of the guy."

"Is there some reason we couldn't just call him?"

"Uncle Mario doesn't like to talk business on the telephone."

They passed the Lincoln Park totem pole and turned left into the driveway of Mario's condominium building. The security guard, who'd already been notified they'd be visiting, waved them into the parking garage and told Bernie where to park. They took the elevator to the twenty-eighth floor and saw a large man in a very nice suit standing outside Mario's door.

"We're carrying," Bernie said.

"I know. Mr. Torelli said it was okay." He spoke into a radio, and a few seconds later Bobby Torelli opened the door.

The first thing Bobby did was hug Marcelle. "You look more beautiful every time I see you."

"I love the way you talk."

Bernie said, "I'm here, too, Bobby."

"So you are. Pop's waiting for us in the living room."

The living room was bigger than Bernie's entire apartment. The outer wall was lined with windows, giving a magnificent view of the lake. Mario rose to greet them, looking dapper in a sport coat and tie. Bernie had never seen him without a tie on.

"William, it's so good to see you." Mario and Bernie's mother were the only two people who still called him William. "And you must be the famous Marcelle. I've heard so much about you."

"It's a pleasure to meet you, sir."

They declined his offer of drinks and spent the next several minutes on small talk. Mario inquired about Bernie's mother, "one of the most wonderful women who ever walked the earth," and confirmed that Bernie visited her once a week. Then he decided it was time to get down to business.

"You know, I have many good friends in the Chicago Police Department, and I'm happy to assist however I can."

Bernie took the cue. "We've been working some murder cases, drug dealers who turned up dead."

"Yes, Alderman Perez told me about it. Very tragic, bad for the neighborhoods. Do you think they're related?"

"Could be. It's something we're trying to figure out. But now we have a new wrinkle, a Southeast Asian heroin group trying to move into Chicago, the Quan organization. Their advance man just got here, a guy named Robert Thornton."

Mario's face remained impassive. Bobby's did not. He didn't look startled, but his eyes flickered just enough that Bernie realized Bobby had heard the name before.

"I'm not familiar with him," Mario said. "How can I help?"

"We're trying to learn as much as we can about him. We were hoping you could steer us in the right direction."

Mario gave a modest shrug. "I'm just a retired liquor salesman, but we can ask our acquaintances and see if anyone knows of this man. Bobby, perhaps you can make some inquiries and get back to William and Marcelle tonight."

"Be glad to."

They thanked him and said their goodbyes, and Bobby walked them to the door. "Meet me at Angie's at eight," he said.

"You can do it that fast?"

"Anything for the Chicago Police Department."

Chapter 15

Tuesday, May 12, 1987
8:04 p.m.

Angie's wasn't busy on this Tuesday night. The White Sox game was on the television above the bar, a few men sitting and casually watching it. Bernie leaned across the bar and shook hands with Angelo Ricci, the bar's nominal owner, who took excellent care of it for its money owner, Mario Torelli.

"What's the score?" Bernie asked.

"Yankees three, Sox one. Looks like it's gonna be another lousy season." Angie tilted his head toward the back. "Bobby's in his booth, drinks waiting for you."

Bobby rose when Bernie and Marcelle walked up, and he hugged Marcelle again. "I have to say, I am enjoying working for you guys."

"No more hugs till you deliver," she said.

"Yes, ma'am." They sat down, and Bobby looked over at Bernie. "I guess you saw my reaction when you mentioned Thornton. My poker face still isn't as good as Pop's."

"Give it time," Bernie said. "I hope we didn't put you guys in an awkward position."

"No, not at all. You know we never got mixed up with heroin. But if you're wondering how we knew—" He stopped and turned his palms up. "We're businessmen, right? And when a powerful businessman moves into our area, we pay attention, even if he's not in our line of business. Who knows, maybe he wants to branch out, so it's only natural we keep up with these things."

"When did you find out he was here?"

"Hell, Bernie, we knew he was coming three months before he left Thailand."

"It figures. Now I know how you could get back to us so fast."

Bobby pretended to stretch, just an excuse to take a quick look around and make sure no one had sat down near them. "It took us the better part of the last three months to gather the information I'm about to give you, some of it very expensive, and my father wants you to know it's with the compliments of the Torelli family."

"Tell him we appreciate it, and no one will know where we got it."

"I'll do that. Most of this comes from some acquaintances of ours, Corsican gentlemen in the adult entertainment business in Bangkok."

"Good euphemism, Bobby."

"Thanks, Marcelle. I thought of it myself."

"And how would they happen to know about Thornton?"

"Because they used to be in the heroin business in Vientiane, Laos. That is, until Quan and Thornton pushed them out."

"Now I understand," she said. "They spy on him, hoping they'll have a chance to get back in."

"I didn't ask about their intentions. Anything in particular you want to know about?"

Bernie and Marcelle looked at each other and Bernie gave her a go-ahead nod. "We've got some gaps in our information," she said. "The first one starts right after World War Two, until the early fifties when he goes to Malaya."

"Sorry, can't help with that. What's the next one?"

"He leaves the Congo in 1968 and by the mid-seventies, he's in the drug business with Quan. What was he doing in between?"

"I've got a little there," Bobby said. "The first place we see him after the Congo is South Vietnam."

Marcelle and Bernie perked up.

"When we learned Thornton was coming here, we put the word out—anyone who knows anything about the guy, no detail too minor, tell us what you know. Turns out one of our acquaintances in Philadelphia has a bodyguard, an ex-Green Beret, who saw Thornton at Nha Trang Air Base in South Vietnam. He didn't remember the exact date, but said it had to have been '68 or '69, because that's when he was there. He said Thornton was recruiting mercenaries."

"Mercenaries for what?" Marcelle asked.

"He didn't know."

"Did he talk to Thornton?"

"No, never even got close to the guy."

"Did it sound like a secret thing?"

"Not at all. He said the whole base was buzzing over it because Thornton was this big, famous guy, like some kind of mercenary rock star."

"You think we could talk to this bodyguard?"

"Not a chance, but he wasn't holding out on us. The more he could tell us, the more we'd owe his boss, and the more his boss would owe him. He was already motivated. You wouldn't get anything else."

"Where'd Thornton go next?" Bernie asked.

"Okay. From there, our trail goes cold until 1973, but then things get really interesting. You know anything about opium smuggling in the Golden Triangle?"

"We got a crash course today, but tell us what you know."

"You're gonna love this," Bobby said. "Let's go back to the sixties for a second. There was a bunch of groups—gangs, really—that smuggled opium out of the hills in Burma and brought it south to Thailand and Laos. The 800-pound gorilla was these Chinese soldiers that controlled the biggest piece."

"The KMT?" Marcelle asked.

"The very ones. After the KMT, there were warlords that picked up the scraps, but they were always at each other's throats so none of them got big, except for this one guy named Lo. Enterprising guy, he built up a pretty good-sized army, not as big as the KMT, but still pretty good for a warlord. Now tell me this: when a smaller gang starts feeling its oats and sees a bigger gang in the way, what's the smaller gang do?"

"It goes to war with the bigger gang."

"Right—and that's exactly what Lo did. He got into a huge firefight with the KMT in Laos, just over the Mekong River from Burma. The papers called it the 1967 Opium War, but it was really just a battle that went on for a few days."

"How'd it turn out?" Bernie asked.

"Both sides got clobbered, but Lo took the worst of it. He and what was left of his men slunk back to the hills in Burma. A couple years later, the Burmese army arrested him and threw him in jail, so now you're thinking, that's the end of Lo."

"I sense he's going to make a comeback."

"You bet. Fast forward to April 1973. Lo's been in jail for four years. Two Russian doctors get kidnapped from a hospital in Burma, smack in the middle of opium country. Lo's men parade the doctors in front of a film crew and say they'll return the doctors if Burma releases Lo."

"The stones on those guys."

"I know, right? You can't make this stuff up. The Burmese spent a year trying to find the doctors, but finally gave up and exchanged Lo for the doctors."

"Good story," Bernie said, "but what's it got to do with Quan and Thornton?"

"Lo's men claimed they were the ones that kidnapped the doctors, but the Corsicans tell me it was actually Thornton and his guys that did it, after Thornton had partnered up with Quan.

Thornton's supposedly a guru at penetrating military bases, so grabbing a couple doctors from a hospital was probably a breeze."

Bobby leaned forward, wanting to end with a dramatic flourish. "And that, my friends, was how Mr. Lo was introduced to his new best buddies, General Quan and Professor Thornton."

"Hell of a way to make an introduction," Marcelle said. "What happened after Thornton sprung Lo?"

"Now Lo's out of jail, but he needs to rebuild his army. In comes General Quan with a big war chest."

"Where'd Quan get his money?"

"Don't know. Could have been Chinese syndicates, could have been a government, could have been all of the above. But with Quan's money they built a big damn army with plenty of armament, plus Quan and Thornton know a thing or two about mountain and jungle fighting."

"What's their structure?" Marcelle asked.

"They've got two armies, a big one and a small one. The big one is up in Burma, maybe ten thousand men. Lo's the figurehead leader, but everyone knows Quan's the power behind him."

"And the smaller army?"

"That's Thornton's group, based in some mountains seventy kilometers from Bangkok called Khao Khiao."

"How many men?"

"Judging from the traffic in and out, the Corsicans figure around a hundred."

"Who does what?" Bernie said.

"Quan's is the regular army and Thornton's is the special ops guys. The two groups together took on the other warlords and the KMT and polished them off. Nowadays, Quan's army fends off anybody that tries to get in on the smuggling action in Burma, and they guard the mule caravans that bring the opium out of the hills to Quan's heroin refineries in Thailand and Laos."

"And Thornton's army?"

"They do two things. First is, they take over after the opium's been refined into heroin. They get it to Bangkok, and from there it goes to distributors. Basically, a security detail."

"And the second thing?"

"Thornton's the enforcer for the whole organization, and I am here to tell you, he is a bad man. If anybody steps on Quan's toes, if Quan needs to take someone out of the distribution chain, whatever, Thornton gets the call. Our Corsican friends have some very unfortunate, first-hand experience with his work. And the really creepy part is how he kills people." Bobby paused for effect. "But I guess you guys already know about that."

"Pretend we don't," Marcelle said.

"Ooh, something else you don't know. I get *two* hugs for this."

Bobby took a sip of his drink and continued. "Here's the deal. You know how drug gangsters like to kill people—real flashy, machine guns blazing, a hundred bullets when one would do. They blow stuff up, they like to do it big and loud because they think it makes their organ bigger, excuse my language, Marcelle."

"Don't worry, I've heard worse."

"But Thornton—he doesn't use guns unless he needs to. Sometimes, yeah, they get into shootouts, but he tries to avoid it. He prefers surgical strikes—lots of cut throats, garrotes, strangulations, all nice and quiet. And sometimes they can't even figure out how he did it."

"Now it's sounding like urban legend," Bernie said.

"Yeah? Well, try this for urban legend. A few years ago, Quan was having some problems with a Chinese syndicate in Hong Kong that was helping him move his dope. Next thing you know, five Chinese gangsters were found on the same night in different parts of the city, stone dead, not a mark on them, no poison in their system. The coroner wrote them down as heart attacks, but the strange thing is, they were young, healthy guys, and they all just happened to drop dead the very same night. And before you ask—

yes, we checked it out, even got copies of the death certificates, because we were just as skeptical as you."

Bobby shook his head. "The way Thornton takes care of business, it's pretty effective. People know if they cross Quan they're going to die up close and personal, and there's something about it that scares the hell out of people."

"Let me ask you something," Marcelle said. "This stuff you just told us about how Thornton kills people—how well known is it?"

Bobby looked surprised at the question. "How well known? Marcelle, everybody in Asia and Europe knows about it."

Chapter 16

Tuesday, May 12, 1987
9:52 p.m.

"The way Bobby described Thornton's methods," Marcelle said, "sounded an awful lot like the way our bodies got killed."

She and Bernie were sitting in a diner near her apartment, drinking decaf and comparing notes. They'd both thought the same thing, but Marcelle said it first.

"It sure did," Bernie said. "It's either a coincidence or Thornton started working here way before now. And taking out one of the cartels before getting here would be a smart move."

"I'll tell you what really bugs me," Marcelle said. "If it's so well known how Thornton does his business, I have to believe the government knows about it, but John sat there stone-faced when we described how our bodies got killed. Why didn't he want to tell us?"

"Maybe the government didn't tell him. Either way, I don't like it. And what are the chances that Thornton was at a US military base in Vietnam, recruiting mercenaries, and the government didn't know about it?"

"Okay, you told me so. But what do we do now? Have you exhausted your supply of Mafiosi?"

"I'm afraid so, but maybe there's another way to do this."

He opened the notebook John gave him that morning and turned to the magazine article about Thornton.

"*Warfighter*," Bernie said. "*True-Life Stories of Real Fighting Men*. Catchy masthead, huh?"

"Oh, yeah. Makes me want to subscribe."

"Summer 1965 issue," Bernie continued. "'Robert Thornton, the Professor of Congo Mercenaries,' by Gene Richards." He pointed at the author's name. "Maybe this guy knows something."

"I read it," she said. "Vignettes about Thornton's adventures in the Congo. Search and destroy missions in the dead of night. How can he help us?"

"The author claims he spent a week with Thornton at his compound in the Congo, but this article doesn't have a week's worth of material. Maybe he learned some things he didn't put in the magazine."

"That article's over twenty years old," Marcelle said. "Is the guy still around?"

"I bought the latest issue at the newsstand today. Richards was the editor-in-chief when the article was published, and still is."

"Where's he located?"

"The publication office is in New York City. I'll call him first thing tomorrow and see if there's more to be had, and if there is, I'll be on the next plane out."

"Can't you do it over the phone?"

"People talk a lot more when you're sitting in front of them, looking them in the eye."

She sensed they'd just had an educational moment, but decided not to rib him about it. "How can I help?"

"I want to know more about John. What sort of guy is he? Can we trust him? Do we need to be looking over our shoulder?"

"Good luck with that. Mike said he's got no friends or family, and we sure can't talk to the people he works with."

"He was in the Army," Bernie said, "and no matter how anti-social you are, the people you serve with get to know you. You can't avoid it—you work with them, eat with them, live with them. And the kind of person John is, I doubt he's still in touch with any of them, so we don't have to worry about them blabbing to him."

"Then we need to find out who he served with. Something like unit rosters?"

"Exactly like that. His first posting was the Army Finance School at Fort Benjamin Harrison. That's near Indianapolis, three to four hours from here. You mind taking a road trip?"

"I'll try, but we don't have jurisdiction there. Do you think they'll talk to me?"

Bernie tilted his chair back, the corner of his mouth raised just enough to signal his amusement. "Marcelle, those Army boys are going to love you."

Chapter 17

Wednesday, May 13, 1987
6:17 a.m.

The ground was still covered with dew and a light fog hovered inches above it. The air smelled crisp, with a slight chill but starting to warm. The birds flew their figure eights, chirping their excitement. It was thirty-nine minutes past sunrise and a beautiful day was beginning.

Ed Stepanek was happy.

He was going home today.

He entered the park at the east entrance. He walked at a medium pace and carried a newspaper in his left hand. It would take fifteen minutes to walk to his destination. The subject never arrived at the bench before 6:41. Ed had plenty of time.

The path curved, and Ed saw a baseball field. He had never played baseball. His father had left him and his mother before he was born. His mother had told him his father was evil, just as all men were evil. She forbade him from playing with other boys so they would not influence him to do evil things. Ed never resented it. His mother had smothered him with love. Every evening when she returned home from work, they would cook together. His mother had been a wonderful cook, and Ed prided himself on his own cooking skills.

He looked at the baseball field again. Teams of boys would play there later that day. Only once in his life, when he was in Vietnam, had Ed ever been on a team.

There had been two teams, Ed's and another one. The men on the teams were gross and hideous, just as his mother had warned him. He'd worked well with them when they were working because he wanted to please his teacher. When they were not working, Ed kept away from them. They competed with him for Thornton's attention, and they were the reason Thornton never acknowledged that he was the best one. He hated them as much as he did Thornton. Every time he thought about them, he wanted to kill them.

Ed finally arrived at his destination: the seventh bench, the one next to the path the subject took through this part of the park, the one Ed had never sat on. In front of the bench was a field. Behind the bench were dense woods. There were only three sides where someone might see him.

Each morning for over two weeks, except Sundays, Ed watched the subject stop jogging when he arrived at this bench. The subject would walk in circles and huff and puff and then sit down on the bench and catch his breath. He never saw Ed watching him. The subject was an idiot.

Ed did not know who wanted the subject dead, or why. Those items were irrelevant to his job. What he knew was that the subject ran a real estate development company. He lived in a large house in an upscale neighborhood. He came home each weekday at seven o'clock to his wife and three children. He visited his mistress every Wednesday afternoon at the apartment he paid for, never earlier than four o'clock or later than five o'clock.

And every morning except Sunday, the subject jogged through the park, stopped, and sat down on this bench while he caught his breath.

The bench was long enough to seat three people. There was never anyone else on the bench when the subject arrived. What would he do when he saw Ed sitting there? Would he feel comfortable sitting down next to someone else? It was the only contingency in Ed's plan. Ed assessed it and concluded it was a low risk. The man was a creature of habit.

Ed sat down just to the left of the center of the bench, leaving enough room on the right so the subject would feel comfortable sitting there, but close enough for what Ed needed to do.

Ed unfolded his newspaper and found the crossword puzzle. It was the Wednesday puzzle, so it would not be difficult. He pulled a mechanical pencil out of his shirt pocket and clicked it open. He liked his mechanical pencil because the lead never got dull, and he could print his letters precisely with it.

He worked the puzzle for seven minutes and got most of the way through it. The next clue was "Old Thailand." Four letters.

In his peripheral vision, he saw the subject approaching from the left. Ed clicked his pencil closed and put it in his pocket. He turned the page to the home and garden section and started reading it.

The subject slowed down and stopped.

He walked in circles.

He huffed and puffed.

He looked at Ed.

"Mind if I sit down?" he said between breaths.

Ed gestured at the bench with a seemingly absentminded wave.

The subject sat down.

Ed looked forward and to each side. He saw no one. The dense woods were behind him. No one would be there. He reached over with his right hand and pressed his thumb into a space between the subject's fifth and sixth left ribs.

The subject's head shot backward as if lightning had struck him. Ed started counting to himself.

One, one thousand, two, one thousand . . .

The man felt pain—excruciating, searing, unimaginable—

. . . four, one thousand, five, one thousand . . .

—pain that was unlike anything he'd ever experienced. His brain was so focused—

... *seven, one thousand, eight, one thousand ...*

—on the new, unusual stimulus, and was so distracted that it could not attend to anything else—

... *nine, one thousand, ten, one thousand ...*

—and abandoned its usual role of directing his systems. One by one, each of his organs stopped functioning, and then his heart stopped and he slumped forward—

... *thirteen, one thousand.*

Ed caught him and laid him back against the bench, his head facing up, his eyes shut. He looked like he was sleeping.

They never make it to fifteen, one thousand, Ed thought.

He looked around again and still saw no one, but just in case someone saw the man slump down, Ed decided to wait a few minutes. It wouldn't look good to leave immediately.

A four-letter word meaning "Old Thailand."

He opened the newspaper to the crossword puzzle and printed S-I-A-M in Forty-Five Down. He spent the next two minutes completing the puzzle, then folded the newspaper, put his pencil in his pocket, and walked away.

* * *

A woman walking her dog discovered the man's body two hours later. The medical examiner listed the immediate cause of death as acute myocardial infarction, the underlying cause of death as physical exertion, and the manner of death as natural. He noticed a small contusion over the fifth left intercostal space at the anterior axillary line, between the fifth and sixth ribs, but deeming it insignificant, did not mention it in his report.

Chapter 18

Wednesday, May 13, 1987
10:34 a.m.

Fort Benjamin Harrison didn't match Marcelle's image of a fort. It had no wood stockade and not a single blue-coated soldier riding a horse. There was a modest entrance framed by two stone columns, and a sign telling her that the Fort Benjamin Harrison Military Reservation was established in 1906.

She drove right in and flagged down the first person she saw, a young soldier on his morning run. She put down her window, and when he looked at her, he became enthusiastic about wanting to help her.

"You are so nice to offer and I wish I could, but I won't have time for a tour," she said. "I'm just looking for the personnel department."

"Civilian or military?"

"Military."

"That'd be the PAC. Weston Hall, a half-mile down on your left. I'll be jogging around here for a while, so let me know if you change your mind about the tour."

"I sure will. Thank you so much, and have a wonderful day."

She parked in an empty parking lot, opened her visor mirror, and freshened her makeup. Not because she wanted to, but because she expected to be dealing with men today. The same consideration drove her wardrobe—a white, low-cut, sleeveless top; a black, form-fitting pencil skirt with a hem just below her knees; and black three-inch heels, an outfit guaranteed to render most of the male population instantly pliable. As she always did, she'd brought a spare set of clothes in case she ended up in front of a different audience.

She got back on the road and soon arrived at Weston Hall, an old but well-maintained brick building. She walked inside, found an office entitled "Personnel Administration Center," and peeked through the window. All men. It was a good start.

She walked in and stepped up to the counter. Two men, an older one and a younger one, sat at their desks, and when they saw her, they almost collided in their haste to get to her. The older guy won.

"Can I help you, Miss?"

"Gosh, I sure hope so." She pretended to fumble around in her purse and finally brought out her badge case and opened it.

"A lady detective, huh? I think you're the first one I've ever met."

"Well, there aren't many of us, and my boss—he's *such* a jerk— he doesn't think women ought to do this kind of work, and he always gives me the worst assignments, hoping I'll fail."

"Miss, I will do everything in my power to help you prove him wrong." He sounded like he meant it.

"You are so nice! The thing is, we're doing a background check on this guy who attended the Finance School here in the late sixties, and I'm looking for the names of the people who were there with him, so we can do interviews. Unit rosters or whatever you call them."

He looked worried. "Late sixties? I'm afraid we wouldn't have anything that far back."

"Maybe on a computer?"

"I can't remember if we even put that stuff on computers back then. If we did, it would have been several systems ago and there's no way I could retrieve it from here."

"Where do you suppose I might find it?"

"Your best bet would be the National Personnel Records Center in St. Louis. There's a written form you send in."

"Any idea how long it might take?"

"Maybe five to six months."

"Oh, no, my boss is gonna *kill* me." She rested her forearms on the counter and leaned in close. "Isn't there *anything* you can do to help me?"

It took him a few seconds to restart his brain, but when he did, he looked like he was thinking harder than he'd ever thought in his life. "You just need the names of the people in his class?"

"Uh-huh."

"Back during the Vietnam War there was this older lady who lived near here, Mrs. Worthington, and she used to put on these dances for the Finance School classes. The people in the class would get all dressed up, and they'd have someone taking pictures, and then she'd put together these little books with their photos and their names and hometowns. If you could find the book for his class, then you could see who was there with him."

"That'd be perfect. Does she still live here?"

"Well, she passed some years ago, but one of her daughters still lives in her house. I'm trying to think of her married name." He shut his eyes and looked like he was concentrating for all he was worth. "McIver . . . McIntosh . . . *McIntire*. That's it—Annie McIntire."

"I don't suppose you have an address for her?"

He pulled a phone book out from under the counter, looked it up and read her the address and phone number. "Is there anything else I can help you with?"

"I think that'll do it, but you've been so great. I can't tell you how much I appreciate it."

"You're welcome, Miss, and if you need anything else, let me give you my name and phone number." He wrote them down on a slip of paper and handed it to her.

"You're wonderful. Thanks again for all your help."

She walked into the hallway, found a payphone, and called Annie McIntire. Annie didn't sound hopeful, but did sound friendly. She invited Marcelle to "come on by" and gave her directions.

After driving out of the base, Marcelle stopped at the first restaurant she saw, grabbed her bag of spare clothes, and went to the ladies' room to change. She kicked off her heels, replaced them with flats, and put a blouse over her top. It had long sleeves and a collar, and she buttoned it almost all the way to her neck. She now looked like the daughter every woman wanted to have.

Annie's home was only three miles away. It was a classic Midwestern two-story brick house with a spacious front porch, complete with a swing. Annie answered the doorbell quickly and greeted Marcelle warmly. She looked to be in her mid-fifties, her hair swept back in a ponytail, and she wore blue jeans with a T-shirt bearing the name of a local charity.

Annie offered coffee, and while she went to get it, Marcelle looked around the living room. The furniture looked old, almost like antiques, but it was in flawless condition and there wasn't a speck of dust in the room. The walls were covered with paintings, mostly watercolors of landscapes and farm buildings, but none had an artist's signature.

"These are beautiful," Marcelle said as she accepted the coffee. "Are they all by the same artist?"

"I confess they're all by me," Annie said.

"Don't be so modest. I love these." Marcelle walked up to one of the paintings and asked about it, starting a twenty-minute conversation as Annie walked her through the collection.

"I'm sorry," Annie said, "you're trying to do your job and I'm just prattling on about my pictures. You mentioned something about the yearbooks my mother used to make?"

Marcelle nodded. "We're doing a background check on someone who went through the Finance School in the late sixties. I'm trying to get the names of his classmates, but the fort doesn't have the records, and I'd rather not wait six months for the Army to find them. I understand your mother made books with the names of the students?"

Annie beamed at Marcelle. "Mom's labor of love. She was part of a very patriotic generation, you know, and considered it her duty to do what she could for her country."

"That's really admirable. How'd the books come about?"

Annie's eyes got a distant look. "Back in the mid-sixties, a lot of people started going through Fort Ben. Mom wanted to do her bit, as she put it, so she put on dances for the folks going through the Finance School. The school had four classes a year, eight weeks each, and at the fourth week of each class she'd put on a dance at the base, kind of like a high school prom."

"What a great idea! I'll bet they appreciated it."

"They did. Mom wanted to make sure there were plenty of people for the students to dance with, so she'd post flyers at the local churches and colleges inviting people to the dance—men and women ages eighteen to thirty, to mirror the makeup of the class."

"She thought of everything."

"Let me tell you, no detail escaped her. A photographer would take a picture of each student as they entered the hall, along with pictures of the activities at the dance."

"And then she'd make the books?"

Annie nodded. "She called them 'yearbooks,' one book for each class. Each book had the year on it, and a letter designation showing which class it was, A, B, C, and D. There'd be a photo of each person in the class, with their name, service branch, and hometown, and the Army would distribute them to the students."

"Did the dances get a good turnout?"

"Oh, yes," she said with a laugh, "because the base commander ordered them to attend. We might have lacked a few who were on emergency leave or in the hospital, but Mom included them on a separate list so they wouldn't feel left out."

"I can tell you're proud of her. She sounds like she was a marvelous woman."

"She was, and I miss her dearly." Annie got the distant look again, but recovered quickly. "I guess you're curious about whether I have the books for the year your person was here."

"You didn't sound optimistic on the phone."

"I'm afraid I'm not. When Mom passed in 1981, she was seventy-nine and she'd accumulated quite a few belongings. My sister Jessica came down from Minneapolis and we spent a week figuring out what to do with it all. We kept some things for ourselves, gave some to family members, and donated some to charities. And as for the rest . . ."

She sighed and looked away for a second. "I hate to say this, but we just disposed of whatever we couldn't find a home for. After you called, I tried to remember what we did with her copies of the yearbooks, but I can't even remember seeing them. I was in such a haze the whole time I barely remember it at all."

"I don't blame you. I'll be a mess when my mom dies."

"I appreciate your saying that. If you don't mind getting some dust on your clothes, we can go up and look now if you like."

"As long as it's no trouble."

"None at all."

They walked up to the second floor. Annie tugged on a rope hanging from the hallway ceiling and pulled down the attic stairs. "Watch your step, dear, these stairs are a little wobbly."

The attic had some old furniture and lamps and even a dress form mannequin. A couple of dozen cardboard boxes sat on the floor, and Marcelle and Annie spent the next hour going through them to no avail.

"I'm so sorry," Annie said. "You came all this way and I hate to see you go back empty-handed."

"Annie, you've been wonderful. I'm so grateful for the time you've given me."

"I'll tell you what—maybe Jess took the books. She's out of town till next week, but I'll call her when she gets back. What's the name of the gentleman you're checking on?"

"John Shepard, S-H-E-P-A-R-D."

"And when was he here?"

"I'm not sure. Probably 1969 or '70."

Annie wrote it down. "You have such a long drive ahead of you. Can I fix you a sandwich before you go?"

Chapter 19

Wednesday, May 13, 1987
10:52 a.m.

The badge is designed to evoke respect and fear—a shield of bright gold with contrasting navy-blue lettering, announcing its bearer as:

CRIMINAL INVESTIGATION
DEPARTMENT OF THE TREASURY
US
SPECIAL AGENT

The badge is a harbinger of unknown peril, and even law-abiding citizens tremble at its sight. Today, John was counting on that.

His meeting the day before had gone well. He'd obtained police protection for Thornton and arranged some busy work to split the detectives and stall one of them. Now he had to attend to the next task on his list.

The Lowell Mansion, where Thornton and his men lived, had been purchased early last year by a company called LPI, Inc. The IRS had determined that, through a maze of intervening companies, LPI ultimately was owned by a Swiss corporation, which, according to Interpol, was a front for the Quan heroin organization.

Last week, John had spoken with the head of the McHenry County Building Division, who informed him that the county had required LPI to complete an extensive series of renovations to the property. John knew those activities must have generated reams of documentation—among which would be floor plans, invaluable to anyone who wanted to invade the structure.

He'd ended the conversation quickly, preferring instead to continue it in person and without warning. People were more amenable when the gold badge and its owner unexpectedly faced them.

John left the expressway and drove north until he reached the county seat of Woodstock. He parked next to the county's administration building and re-read his script for how he was going to justify his request. Telling them the real reason was out of the question.

He walked into the office, where a woman sat at a desk. She saw a man whose mouth, eyebrows, and head were twitching. She reacted, as people often did upon seeing John, with a mixture of revulsion and fear of catching something.

He thrust his badge toward her. "Special Agent John Shepard, Internal Revenue Service, Criminal Investigation."

She stared at the badge and swallowed. "I swear to you, my husband does the taxes and I just sign what he gives me."

"I'm sure you do. However, you're not the reason I'm here. Is Mr. Easley in?"

She looked as if she'd just gotten a reprieve from the gallows. "Yes, sir, he's here. Is he in some kind of trouble?"

"Should he be?"

"No. I mean, I don't think so. He's a very nice man and—"

"Please tell him I'd like to speak with him."

She placed the call, and thirty seconds later Easley appeared. He was a large man whose triple chin drooped over the tie he wore on his short-sleeved shirt. His face was flushed and he was sweating profusely.

John held up his badge again. "Special Agent John Shepard, Internal Revenue Service, Criminal Investigation."

Easley swallowed even harder than did the woman, but then he got his bearings. "Yes, of course, we spoke on the phone about the Lowell property."

"Correct. Would now be a good time to continue our conversation?"

Easley's perspiration accelerated. "All our permits and expenditures are in order. We dot every i and cross every t."

"I'm sure you do. May we speak in private?"

They went to Easley's office. "I'm at your service, Mr. Shepard. Anything you want to know, anything at all, McHenry County is pleased to help."

"Thank you. I understood from our conversation that the county required a great deal of work on the property before it would issue a certificate of occupancy. I was hoping you could elaborate on that."

Easley looked relieved at the question. "Sure thing, I'd be happy to. The property had been vacant for some time, and the previous owners had done little to keep it up, so it was in a sorry state of disrepair. It was truly a shame, because it's a landmark in our county. The two structures are pretty large, you know, and we made them bring the whole place up to code. That right there was a lengthy, expensive process, and then we had the historical issues."

"I don't understand."

"We've classified it as a place of historical significance, so there are limits on the kinds of changes a new owner can make. We went back and forth for quite some time before we finally got it all straightened out."

"I see. I presume there is documentation backing up everything that was done?"

"Absolutely. Like I said, every i dotted and every t crossed. In McHenry County, we do everything by the book."

"Can you give me some examples?"

Easley leaned back in his chair and thought about it. "Let's see. Lists of all the items that required repair or replacement. Work orders with contractors and receipts proving payment. Detailed architectural plans, both before and after, with all fixtures and HVAC included. The records of our negotiations over the changes and what we agreed to. And then, of course, inspection records and permits. I guess that pretty much covers it."

"Mr. Easley, if I disclose something confidential, would I have your word you won't repeat it?"

"Of course."

"We have reason to believe the property's owner may have under-reported its income. We investigate that by comparing its expenditures with the income it did report. If expenditures vastly exceed reported income, then that suggests under-reporting."

Easley nodded, and John continued. "Your records would lay out the expenditures on the property, which would be quite useful to our investigation. I trust you wouldn't mind if I borrowed them for a while?"

Easley squirmed in his chair. "Well, normally, people have to file a public records request, and then we process it, and—"

"Mr. Easley. If I made a formal request, then the form I filed would itself be subject to disclosure. I would prefer that the target of our investigation remain unaware of our interest."

"Yes, I understand, but—"

"I had hoped that McHenry County would demonstrate its good faith by cooperating, but if it doesn't, we can pursue other means."

"No, no, that won't be necessary. We pride ourselves on our good relationship with the law enforcement community."

They walked down to the basement and Easley loaded three cartons onto a hand truck. He wheeled it to John's car and helped John put them in his trunk.

"Mr. Easley, I appreciate your cooperation and assure you I'll return these in good order."

"Glad to help. And if you don't mind, perhaps you could tell your superiors how I facilitated your investigation?"

"I shall. Thank you again."

John decided to stop for lunch before making the long drive back to the city. He drove through downtown Woodstock and stopped at a small restaurant, taking a seat next to the window where he had a view of the street.

Before long, he saw a gaggle of teenagers walk past. They wore sweatshirts with the logo of the local high school and appeared to be on a trip somewhere. They had all separated into small groups and were chattering and laughing, the boys trying to impress the girls and the girls egging them on.

All, that is, except for one boy. He had difficulty balancing and moved with a waddling gait, probably, John thought, from a degenerative muscle disease. The boy was all alone, several yards behind the pack, and falling further behind. No one spoke to him or noticed how far he'd gotten separated. He was different from them, and, therefore, an outcast.

John knew that boy.

That boy was him, twenty-five years ago.

Chapter 20

Wednesday, May 13, 1987
2:05 p.m.

LaGuardia was just as Bernie remembered it: cramped, dingy, and wall-to-wall people moving at the speed of light. It even made O'Hare look good.

The cab dropped Bernie at a five-story building in SoHo that looked past its prime, and he took the elevator to the third floor. "Warfighter Publishing Suite 320" was stenciled on the door's frosted glass window. Bernie knocked, and Gene Richards promptly appeared.

Gene appeared to be in his fifties. He was tall and lithe, with unkempt hair and a kindly visage that reminded Bernie of his high school English teacher. As for the headquarters of Warfighter Publishing, there wasn't much to the place—a small reception area with a desk and one adjacent office.

"Yes, I know," Gene said, smiling. "Time-Life it's not. There's a woman who comes in once a week to handle advertising and subscriptions, but alas, I'm the only other employee." He offered, and Bernie declined, a cup of coffee.

Gene's office was well-kept, and the walls were covered with photographs. Photos of Gene in uniform; photos of him in civilian clothes, posing with people in uniform; and photos of him wearing a leather shooting coat and holding a rifle.

"Looks like you've done some shooting," Bernie said, pointing at the photos.

"Now and then."

"There's got to be more to the story than that."

Gene gave a *no big deal* shrug. "I started shooting smallbore rifle when I was young, and did well enough on my high school rifle team to earn a ticket to West Point. I shot on the Academy's team for four years and had a glorious time, but eventually they made me graduate and join the real Army."

"Do you miss shooting?"

"I haven't had a chance to miss it. I still compete in smallbore and highpower, and make the annual pilgrimage to the national matches at Camp Perry."

"How'd you get from West Point to *Warfighter*?"

Gene responded with a self-deprecating laugh. "Believe me, I've asked myself that same thing many a time. In its infinite wisdom, the Army decided that my history degree qualified me to be an infantry officer. I did eight years and got out as a captain. I'd always been interested in literature and history and I enjoyed the company of fighting men, so I combined my interests and started the magazine. Fortunately, I had an extensive network of contacts in the military, men who were chock-full of war stories and would give them up for the price of a few beers, so I didn't want for material. As time went on, I started getting submissions, and these days I mostly just edit."

"You said on the phone you had a lot on Thornton that you didn't put in the article. I was curious about why you'd leave it out."

"Well, you have to understand the nature of my audience. My readers aren't academics or historians who want to plow through a thirty-page piece. They're mostly men with dull lives who want to live vicariously through the adventures of others, and I try to keep each article at coffee-break length. The Congo was a hot topic at the time, and Thornton's escapades there were more than enough to fill my quota."

"I'm impressed you could lay your hands on a file that's over twenty years old," Bernie said. "I can't find my files from last year."

"It's not as impressive as it sounds. The Thornton piece was the apex of my otherwise undistinguished literary career, and I made sure I always kept the file someplace where I wouldn't lose it."

"Why was it so special?"

"Because Thornton was a celebrity. One of the notable aspects of the Congo Crisis was the quite influential role played by mercenaries, many of whom were government-sponsored. The Congo was all over the news, as I'm sure you recall, and some of those mercenaries became internationally famous."

"I remember reading about it," Bernie said. "Was there a guy named Hoare?"

"Oh, yes, 'Mad Mike' they called him, and a fellow named Denard, they were the most prominent. But along around 1964, word started filtering out about a privately employed mercenary—Professor Thornton, as he called himself—who was wreaking havoc on his enemies. The mainstream news outlets all took a crack at him but he rebuffed them all, as he had a fairly low regard for the news media."

"How'd you swing it?"

"Let's just say that he owed a big favor to someone who owed me a big favor, and leave it at that."

"I understand how that works," Bernie said.

"In any event, I scooped the big boys. The whole experience was quite an adventure, let me tell you."

"Was Thornton cooperative?"

"At first, he seemed to regard me as a nuisance, but when he learned of my background, he warmed up to me. He favors well-educated people, a scarce commodity in his immediate environs at the time, and we had some wide-ranging conversations."

"I'm glad to hear you say that."

"No offense, but it's really a shame that I'm now talking to the police about him. In retrospect, though, it's interesting that his life has come full circle."

That last bit puzzled Bernie. "I'm not following you."

"You know, that whole affair with the Chinese Nationalists after World War Two."

"Sorry, still not following."

"I beg your pardon," Gene said. "You're with the police. I thought you'd know."

"We know Thornton was in the CIA from the end of the war until 1952, but we can't get any information about what he was doing because the Agency is still classifying the files and won't release them."

Gene's mouth curled to a half-smile. "I guess it shouldn't surprise me. It's a horribly embarrassing chapter for the CIA."

"I am all ears," Bernie said.

"You do know that Thornton was in the OSS during World War Two?"

"That much I know."

"After the war ended, the OSS was dissolved, but Thornton stayed in its successor units and eventually landed in the CIA. From the end of the war until 1949, Thornton stayed in China, trying to help the Nationalists—the KMT—in their civil war against the Communists. When the Communists won in '49, most of the KMT went to Taiwan, but parts of the KMT fled to Burma, and Thornton went with them."

"Doing what?"

"The idea was that the KMT would re-arm and reorganize, and then they'd invade China. Pretty quixotic when we look back at it, but that was the plan. And the CIA, through Thornton and his fellow operatives, was helping finance and re-arm the KMT."

"How'd it turn out?" Bernie asked.

"In a word—badly. The KMT invaded China several times and got their butts handed to them. Their last try was in 1952, and by then Thornton had had enough and he quit. But to help finance itself, the KMT turned to opium and forced the locals to grow more of it. Before long, the KMT's mission was less about re-taking China than it was about opium smuggling. And even though the CIA didn't actively help them with the opium trade, it certainly turned a blind eye to what they were doing, and helped enable the KMT to become the region's opium lord."

"How do you know all this?" Bernie said. "My government source didn't even know about it."

"If your government source didn't know about it, then he didn't try very hard. The CIA's role in this sordid affair has been public knowledge for years. The only thing I just told you that's not public record is the fact that Thornton was one of the operatives involved in it."

"He told you he was?"

"He did. In fact, he told me gleefully that he *knew* he wasn't supposed to tell me, but he did it anyway because he no longer gave a damn about the CIA and the US government."

"You said a couple minutes ago that he came full circle?"

"Look at it this way," Gene said. "In the early fifties, Thornton worked for the government, indirectly helping the KMT take over and expand the opium trade in Burma. Years later, he went back to Burma, and helped someone else take over the opium trade *from* the KMT."

"I see your point."

"It's also why I'm not surprised the CIA is still classifying the files. Imagine its embarrassment if the word got out that its former operative was involved at both ends of this debacle."

"Would it be embarrassing enough that Thornton could blackmail the government with it?"

Gene looked intrigued by the question. "The journalist in me wants to know why you're asking that question."

"Would it surprise you if I said I can't answer?"

"I suppose not, though it was worth a try. But to answer your question—yes, conceivably Thornton could use it for blackmail."

That tidbit alone made the price of the trip worth it, but Bernie decided to go for broke. "Why was he so mad at the government?"

"I wouldn't call it anger. It was really that he no longer felt any allegiance to the US. He'd spent only a small part of his life in this country and had never gotten attached to it. And even when he joined the OSS, it was less about serving the US than it was about helping the Chinese, whom he loved deeply. But when the Chinese civil war revved back up in 1945, well—" Gene's voice trailed off. "There were no good guys in that war, and I think he felt disillusioned. I got the impression that when he quit in '52, he was determined from then on to look out for number one, if you get my drift."

"I understand," Bernie said. "I know he went to Malaya after that, but not much about what he did there. Did he talk to you about it?"

"He did indeed. Are you familiar with the Malayan Emergency?"

"Not at all."

"Back then, Malaya was still a British colony, and in 1948 a Communist insurgency broke out. Thornton saw it as an opportunity, so after he quit the CIA, he went to Malaya and got the lay of the land."

"Which was what?"

"The Communists were waging a guerrilla war, and some of their primary targets were the rubber plantations and tin mines. The British forces couldn't be everywhere at once, so the landowners hired contractors to help guard the properties and their workers. Bear in mind, at this point Thornton knew as much as anyone in the world about how to fight a guerrilla war, and he saw instantly that the landowners were doing it all wrong."

"What was wrong with it?"

"They assumed a completely defensive posture, which played right into the guerrillas' hands. Thornton knew that to beat a guerrilla, one must be a guerrilla. He impressed the owners of several contiguous plantations with his OSS experience and Silver Star, and made them an offer: give him eight men and three months to train them, and if they weren't happy with the results, his services would be free."

"Pretty good offer," Bernie said.

"Which, unsurprisingly, they accepted, and once he got his men trained, they took the offensive. They went on deep penetration patrols into the jungle, and when they found a guerrilla camp, they'd formulate a plan and attack at night."

"With only eight guys?"

"The object wasn't to defeat the enemy; it was to terrorize the enemy. As he explained it, they'd kill as many insurgents as possible, as quickly as possible, and as quietly as possible, focusing mainly on men who were sleeping. And that strategy achieved its intended result. It's one thing to be awake and to see the enemy in front of you—that's horrifying, to be sure—but the prospect that someone might stand over you while you're sleeping and cut your throat is absolutely terrifying."

"When you said it achieved its intended result—"

"The insurgents decided they wanted no part of Professor Thornton. They agreed to stop harassing the plantations he worked for, in exchange for him standing down and not bringing other plantations under his flag."

"I'll bet his employers were happy."

"Oh, absolutely. He became something of a local hero, and that's when his reputation as a mercenary began to rise."

"How long did he stay there?" Bernie asked.

"The conflict was pretty much over by the end of 1959. That year, he moved to Singapore and lived there while awaiting his next opportunity. That came in the form of the Congo Crisis in 1960, when the colony achieved its independence from Belgium. The country quickly descended into chaos, and as you saw in the article, what he did there mirrored what he did in Malaya, except now he was working for palm oil plantations."

Bernie thumbed through his notes of last night's conversation with Bobby. "One of our sources said Thornton is an expert at penetrating military bases. Would you agree with that?"

Gene pursed his lips and considered it. "I would, but I'd say it differently. He's an expert in small-unit tactics, and using small units to penetrate and terrorize larger ones."

"Anything else about his time in the Congo that you thought was interesting?"

"There is one other thing, though I don't think he really meant to tell me about it."

"What, he just blurted it out?"

"No," Gene said, laughing. "I assure you, Robert Thornton does not blurt. On the last night I was there, I broke out a bottle of some very nice Scotch and we consumed a goodly portion of it."

"That'll do it," Bernie said.

"Yes, and it did it for him. Do you remember from the article that there was a lull in the Congo fighting from the beginning of '63 to the beginning of '64?"

"Yeah, but you didn't say much about was he was doing."

"That's what I was getting to. Thornton had mentioned during my stay that it was difficult for him to find qualified men. He advertised in the newspapers in Johannesburg and Salisbury, but few of those that responded had military experience, and even those men weren't necessarily the cream of the crop. Adding to the headache was the fact that the men had six-month contracts, so there was periodic turnover and he had to keep replacing them. That left him with frequently having to separate wheat from chaff, and the type of fighting he did required fairly specialized skills, which made it even more difficult."

"What did he do, put 'em through boot camp?"

"In a manner of speaking. During our Scotch episode that last night, he told me he spent that year devising a system for quickly and positively identifying men who could excel at the type of warfare he conducted, and the way he said it, he made it sound like a trade secret."

"Did he explain it?"

"I remember nothing beyond what I scribbled in my notes the next morning." Gene stopped and paged through his file. "Here it is. Two types of tests, physiological and psychological."

"That's it?"

"That's all I have on the method. The only other thing I wrote down, because I found it impressive, was that he'd hired a doctor to help him with the psychological tests. He called the man 'Rupert,' and I don't even know whether that was a first name or a last name. I didn't follow up because I guessed I wasn't supposed to know about it to begin with."

"Did you have any more contact with him after that?" Bernie asked.

"No, sorry to say. I heard about him falling in with General Quan, but that was pretty common knowledge, at least in the circles I run in."

Bernie thought through his checklist. Gene had filled the CIA gap, but the gap from 1968 to 1973 was still unresolved. "Other than hearing that Thornton aligned himself with Quan, do you have any idea what he did after the Congo?"

"None at all."

"You said earlier you had a lot of contacts in the military. We know of a Green Beret who saw Thornton at Nha Trang Air Base in South Vietnam in the late sixties. Do you know any Green Berets who served there?"

"Nha Trang, specifically? I have no idea, though I do know some Green Berets who served in Vietnam. Mind you, that was over fourteen years ago, so my contact information may be dated." He turned to his credenza and leafed through his Rolodexes. "Your most likely bet is Ezra Simons, Hollywood, Florida." He read the phone number and Bernie wrote it down.

"Gene, you've been tremendously helpful. I can't tell you how much I appreciate it. One last question before I go?"

"Sure."

"Thornton sounds like a very smart, very capable guy, but everyone has a weakness. What's his?"

"The same one that afflicts many great men," Gene said. "He's a slave to his own massive ego."

* * *

Bernie still had two hours before his flight, so he went to one of the airport payphones and called Simons.

"Sorry," Simons said, "I was never at Nha Trang. I was in the Seventh Special Forces Group, mostly in Laos, a little in Vietnam, but never had a reason to go to Nha Trang."

"How would I find a Green Beret who was there?"

"Look for someone who was with the Fifth Special Forces Group. That was the biggest SF group in Vietnam, and they were based at Nha Trang."

"Know anyone who was with them?"

"The only one I've kept up with is a guy named Sam Harrison, but contacting him might be difficult. Sam doesn't have much use for people, so he doesn't have a phone."

Bernie heard pages ruffling. "Here's what I've got. P.O. Box 8, Blinkem, Georgia. I don't have a street address for him and don't know if he's even got one."

"Will this guy even talk to me?"

"There's no telling. Within the first minute, you'll either be his best friend or his worst enemy, so make a good impression quickly. Feel free to invoke my name and tell him he still owes me five bucks from the bar in Fayetteville."

Bernie thanked him, then went to the ticket counter. The ticket agents pored over a map and told him Blinkem didn't appear to be a city, just an area name, but it was in the northern part of Georgia. His best bet would be to fly into Atlanta. Ninety minutes later, he was on a plane headed south.

Chapter 21

Thursday, May 14, 1987
8:45 a.m.

Bernie thought Chicago traffic was bad, but Atlanta's was even worse.

After arriving in Atlanta the previous night, he checked in at an airport motel and called Marcelle. They debriefed each other, and Bernie commiserated with her about striking out in Indiana.

"Do you want me to try the records place in Missouri?" she asked.

"May as well," Bernie said. "John's going to be with us awhile. And they usually expedite it for law enforcement, so it may only take a couple weeks."

He rented a car at the airport. The rental car people knew nothing more about Blinkem than did the airline people, but they advised him to drive to Dillard, the closest city of consequence, and ask for directions.

He was now crawling northbound on I-85 through Atlanta's morning rush hour. The scenery gradually became suburban, then rural, and the traffic finally eased up. At 11:30 he saw a sign: "Lions Club Welcomes You to Dillard, Georgia, Gateway to the Mountains." He stopped at the first restaurant he saw, ate a delicious meal, and handed the waitress a nice tip, his entrée to ask for directions.

"Blinkem's a real small place," she said, "just a stretch of road and no more than ten houses. Who're you going to see?"

"A guy named Sam Harrison."

"Ohboy."

"That didn't sound good."

She bit her lip and her eyes darted around. "He's not so bad once you get to know him."

"How long will that take?"

"Probably more time than he'll give you. Does he know you're coming?"

"No, and I couldn't call him—"

"Because he doesn't have a phone. Yeah, I know. When he wants to call someone, which isn't real often, he comes here and uses our payphone."

"Well, I still need directions," Bernie said.

She described the route and ended with, "Go real slow there, because it's easy to miss."

"Got it. One last thing—why do they call it Blinkem?"

"Like I said, it's a real small place, so if you blink your eyes while you're going by—"

"I'll miss it."

"Uh-huh."

"Perfect. Thanks for your help."

In half a mile Bernie was in the mountains, and for the next twenty minutes he was either on his brakes, trying not to veer off the mountainside, or in second gear trying to ascend, negotiating one hairpin turn after another. The road finally leveled out, and remembering the waitress's admonition, he slowed down. He passed three houses, each with a mailbox with the owner's name. The fourth house didn't have a mailbox, but it did have signs on both sides of the driveway: "POSTED NO TRESPASSING." He guessed this was the place.

He drove up and heard the dog before he'd even exited his car, barking loud enough to wake the dead and throwing itself against the door of the house. The door was a massive wood affair with no windows or openings except a peephole. Before he could knock, he heard a voice inside.

"Chester, hush." The dog went silent and then he heard the voice again. "Who's there?"

Bernie held his star in front of the peephole. "Bernardelli, Chicago Police."

"Lemme see your warrant."

"I don't have a warrant."

"Then come back when you do."

"I'm not here about you."

"Then I doubly don't want to talk to you."

It was time for Bernie to play his hole card. "Ezra Simons sent me. He says you owe him five bucks from the bar in Fayetteville."

Bernie heard a lock being turned, and the door opened.

"I do not owe that sumbitch five dollars or any other amount. I sunk that eight-ball just like I called it."

Sam Harrison had a perfectly round, perfectly bald head that sat atop a muscular body, and he looked Bernie up and down. "Sit yourself down at the kitchen table."

They sat down across from each other, but the dog walked around and parked himself facing Bernie, sitting at attention and eyeing him the way Bernie had eyed his lunch an hour earlier.

"Don't worry about the dog," Sam said, "but I do recommend you refrain from sudden movements."

"Unusual name for a dog. The only Chester I ever knew was Marshal Dillon's sidekick on 'Gunsmoke.'"

Sam's face went from suspicious to impressed. "You, sir, are a man of the arts—that is in fact the origin of my sidekick's name. Kind of an inside joke, though I'd guess it's lost on the dog."

Sam now looked more interested in Bernie. "Did you ever serve your country?"

"Four years as an MP."

"Well, you're big enough for it. Stateside or overseas?"

"Two years stateside and two in West Germany."

"I thank you for your service," Sam said. He looked around, as though unsure of what to do next. "I don't get many visitors. You want a beer or something?"

"No, thanks, I'm on the clock."

"Good man. Duty before pleasure. Now, did you come here to collect five dollars or for something else?"

"I'm after a man named Robert Thornton. Hope you might know him."

Sam let out a long, low whistle. "Thornton," he said. "That was a long time ago. Last I knew, he'd thrown in with a dadgum NVA general to sell drugs."

"And they're still together, except now Thornton's opening up shop in Chicago."

"Ahh, now it's all clear, but you came a long way to hear me say I never met the man."

Bernie's head dropped and his shoulders slumped forward.

"Though I did see him once," Sam said.

"Remember where?"

"Hell, yes. Nha Trang, the HQ for the Fifth Special Forces Group." He leaned back in his chair and cocked his head toward the ceiling, squinting his eyes and trying to dredge up an image. "I'd guess it was 1969."

"What was he doing there?" Bernie asked.

"That, sir, is a damned good question. I'll tell you what I know, and you can draw your own conclusions."

"Fair enough."

"At the time," Sam said, "Thornton was a merc with a big reputation. Now, as you know, most soldiers don't have any idea what they're going to do after the service. They've got the first day planned, but not much after that. All that most of them know is soldiering, and a lot of them have this pie in the sky ambition to be a big, bad merc and make lots of money. When Thornton arrived, there was a rumor he was looking for recruits, and naturally that caused quite a stir."

"Why'd they let him on the base?"

"At first, I thought they did it for the men's morale, you know, give the men something to look forward to after the service, though later on I wasn't so sure about that."

"So, you just saw him, no contact?"

"Right. I never spoke to the man myself. Didn't have a high regard for mercs, if you want to know the truth. But the word comes back he is indeed interviewing people. He's there a couple days and then leaves. Good riddance, right?"

"Right."

"Next morning I'm looking for one of my noncoms, a big ol' farm boy named Johannsen. 'Johannsen's gone,' they say. What do you mean, gone? 'Just gone.' So I go to my CO, he says the same thing, and now I'm getting pissed. I ask him, is he AWOL? Did he get new orders? 'Damn it, Sam, he's gone, that's all you need to know and don't ask about him anymore.' That's when I knew he wasn't AWOL. The response would've been different, plus Johannsen never would have gone AWOL, anyway."

"And you connected his leaving to Thornton?"

"It was either a correlation or a coincidence, and I am always skeptical of the latter."

"Did you ever hear from Johannsen again?"

"Not a word. And I'll tell you something else: Johannsen was raised right, he had manners. We had a good relationship, and he never would've left without saying goodbye unless he was under orders to do it that way."

Bernie nodded, taking it all in. "What can you tell me about Johannsen?"

"Good soldier. Good leader. Had the respect of those around him. Never hesitated to take point, and he killed a pile of VC. I'm not surprised he caught Thornton's eye. He was the best NCO I had."

"I don't guess you know where he is now, do you?"

"No, but I bet I know how you can find him. Back in Vietnam, when soldiers were sitting around the hooch with their buddies, you know what the number one topic of conversation was?"

"Tell me."

"The first thing they were gonna do when they were discharged and got back to the world. Yes, sir, *the* number one topic."

"I hear you," Bernie said.

"Now, most guys would say, when they got back to Shitkicker, Texas, or wherever, they were gonna go drinking with their old buds, get absolutely hammered, and then get themselves some good, old-fashioned American muff. You follow me?"

"Uh-huh."

"But not Johannsen. No, sir. Johannsen was gonna go back home to Shitkicker, Iowa, marry little Susie, his high school sweetheart, and spend the rest of his life on the family farm. Man, he loved that farm, talked about it every chance he got. If I were a betting man, I'd bet he's on that farm right now, with little Susie and a tubful of kids."

"Iowa, you say?"

"Yes, sir."

"Any idea where in Iowa?"

"No, but Iowa's not a big place, and it probably doesn't have many Steven Johannsens." He spelled both names and Bernie wrote them down.

Sam could tell the conversation was drawing to a close. "You sure you don't want that beer?"

"I wish I could, but I've got a three-hour drive to Atlanta to catch a plane to Chicago."

"Understood. If you ever find yourself back here, you look me up, we'll tie one on."

Bernie rose slowly, watching the dog, and the three of them walked to the door.

"If you find Johannsen," Sam said, "tell him I understand the circumstances and I've got no hard feelings about how he left."

"I will."

"And tell Simons I ain't never paying him that five dollars."

"You got it, Sam. Thanks for your help."

Chapter 22

Thursday, May 14, 1987
9:10 a.m.

"We just heard from Garza," Arthur said. "Arroyo declined to meet with us."

Thornton appeared neither surprised nor unhappy. "Was that the way Mr. Arroyo phrased it, or was he more colorful?"

"The latter, sir."

"It's all right, Arthur, I can handle it."

"He said he'd rather drink his own piss than meet with you, and if we try to sell in Chicago, he'll cut your balls off and feed them to his dog."

"I see," Thornton said, looking mildly amused. "What kind of dog, I wonder?"

"He didn't mention it, sir."

"No matter. But now that we've expressed our intentions and the die is cast, it's possible Mr. Arroyo may elect to strike first."

"You think he'll start a war?"

"I doubt it. We taught Mr. Arroyo the value of professional assassins, and he may decide to hire one. Please notify the men we've elevated to condition orange."

"I'll do it, sir."

"Any word on the shipment?"

"Based on the last one, Frank thinks it'll be no later than tomorrow."

"That will work out well. Tell Johnson and Lattimore they have a green light, and to let us know when they're going to move."

"Anything else, sir?"

Thornton looked out the window for a long time, then finally turned back to Arthur. "Please ask Frank to come in. I want to send him to Boston."

Chapter 23

Thursday, May 14, 1987
9:42 a.m.

The fifty empty brass cartridge cases stood tall and parallel and proud in their loading block, like obedient soldiers awaiting their orders, and it made Ed Stepanek happy just to look at them. Yesterday evening Ed had run them through a vibratory tumbler filled with crushed corn cob and brass polish until they gleamed. Now they were so clean and shiny he could practically see his reflection in them. He knew that polishing them did not make them work better. He did it because otherwise they would not be perfect.

The world was a dirty, disorganized place, and it had taken Ed many years to accept the fact that he could not make it clean and well-ordered. He had finally made his peace with the imperfect world by striving to achieve perfection in those things within his control.

The process of reloading—making his own ammunition from its constituent components—was one of Ed's favorite pastimes. He could control every step in the process, and he loved all the minute details required to make it perfect. It was just like his other favorite activities, cooking and baking. He first gathered and prepared the necessary ingredients and then assembled them according to a recipe, working in a particular sequence, and if he did everything properly, he was rewarded with something wonderful.

Ed neither liked nor disliked guns, at least not as a general proposition. He regarded them simply as tools. One did not like or dislike a hammer; it either drove the nail or it did not.

Because Ed had no particular affinity for guns and rarely used them in his work, he owned only two. One was a .45 ACP Series 70 Colt Government Model semi-automatic pistol, lightly modified to assure reliable functioning with hollow-point bullets. The other was the one for which he was now making ammunition: a pre-'64 Winchester Model 70 target rifle in .30-06, identical to the sniper rifle he had used in Vietnam, except that his military rifle wore a Unertl eight-power scope and his present one had a ten-power Zeiss Diatal-C. With this rifle and his own handmade ammunition, he could shoot five bullets into a circle smaller than a quarter at a distance the length of a football field.

Ed turned his attention to the fifty empty cases. He had already fired them once, which caused the necks and bodies of the cases to expand. Now he needed to squeeze them down so they could hold a bullet and fit properly in his rifle's chamber. He screwed a resizing die into a reloading press and resized the cases by raising them into the die. He cleaned the residue out of the primer pockets and pressed a fresh primer into each, using a hand-held priming tool. Next, he charged each case with precisely 53.5 grains of smokeless gunpowder, meticulously dropping in the kernels of powder until his balance beam scale was absolutely level.

Now it was time for the last step: inserting the bullets into the cases. Ed replaced the sizing die in his press with a bullet-seating die. He placed a charged case into his press, plucked a 190-grain Sierra MatchKing bullet out of its green box, and set it in the mouth of the case. He held it in place as he pulled down on the press handle and raised the case and bullet into the die. He felt the bullet pressing into the case as it reached the limit of its upward travel, then lowered it back down and removed the now-completed cartridge from the press.

Ed used a caliper, with graduations of one-thousandth of an inch, to measure the distance from the base of the case to the leading edge of the bearing surface of the seated bullet. He wanted to make sure the length was correct, a dimension he had arrived at through shooting tests. It was perfect, and he proceeded to seat bullets in the remaining forty-nine cases.

Ed placed the completed cartridges in a plastic cartridge box and took one last look at them before closing it. Fifty rounds of ammunition, and each of them as perfect as man could make them. It made Ed feel proud.

It was time for his second chore of the day: mowing his lawn. It was spring, and the grass grew quickly. Ed's neighbors mowed their lawns once a week, and by the end of the week their lawns were unkempt, with the blades of grass at non-uniform heights. How could they stand to look at their lawns in such a condition? He could not make them mow more often, but he could mow his own lawn as often as he wished, and at this time of year, he did so every other day.

He had gotten home from his job yesterday afternoon. His lawn service had mowed the lawn two days ago, and it was time for him to mow it again. He worked the mower intently, making sure all the paths were parallel, and then shut the mower off.

Ed walked to the corner of his lawn, knelt down, and craned his neck so that his eye was level with the top of the grass. He looked across the entire expanse to make sure every blade was at the same height and noticed he'd missed one spot. He restarted the mower, mowed that spot, and checked again. Now it was perfect. His lawn looked like a carpet. Ed was proud of it.

He cleaned up and made two grilled cheese sandwiches. His mother had made him grilled cheese sandwiches, and his were almost as good as hers had been. Eating grilled cheese sandwiches reminded him of his mother. It made Ed happy to think of his mother.

He had one chore remaining: buying a copy of his local newspaper and checking the personal ads, the first of a two-step process that led to his jobs.

Ed received his jobs through the mail. He had a box under an alias at a post office twenty miles away. He had three brokers through whom he received his work. When they had a job for him, they would mail an envelope to the post office box. There was never a return address, and the postmark was always from a different place.

It was always possible, though, that the authorities would try to ensnare him by mailing him a fake job, and that was where the personal ads came into play. If one of his brokers had a job for him, the broker would place an ad in the personals with an identifying code. One of them would name three animals in the ad; another would name four flowers; and the third would name five geographical locations. If he saw a coded ad in the personals, he knew an envelope would be waiting for him and he would go to his post office box.

Ed did not think there would be an ad today. He received only two or three jobs a year, and had just completed one. All the same, he checked the personals every day.

He went to the nearest convenience store and bought the newspaper. He opened it to the personals. He saw an ad referring to roses, carnations, lilies, and orchids. Another job, so soon after his last one! It made Ed happy.

He drove the twenty miles to his post office box. Sure enough, there was an envelope for him. He resisted the temptation to open it then and there. Someone might be watching.

He drove home and finally opened the envelope. As usual, it contained two smaller envelopes, one letter-sized and the other larger. The smaller one would contain a receipt for a deposit to his bank account in the Cayman Islands, which he had opened under an alias. If he rejected the job, he would reverse the deposit. The deposit would be for one-half the total price of the job, with the other half due upon completion. His usual charge for a job was a total of $40,000, $20,000 in advance.

He opened the smaller envelope first. It had a receipt showing a deposit of $30,000, fifty percent higher than normal. That meant it would be a difficult job.

The larger envelope would have photographs of the subject and pertinent information, such as the subject's name and location. It would also have a deadline.

Ed opened the larger envelope and spilled the contents face down onto his table. He turned them over and beheld the face of a man he had last seen fifteen years ago.

Ed's heart skipped a beat. He blinked several times, afraid he might be hallucinating, but the photograph did not change. It was the most incredibly good luck he had ever experienced. For fifteen years, he had dreamed of killing this man, *and now someone was going to pay him to do it.*

He read through the rest of the materials. Of all places, the subject was in Illinois. Ed had a two-day drive ahead of him and a short deadline, so there was no time to waste.

He thought about what he would need to do before he could leave tomorrow. He had to pack and prepare some meals for the trip, but before he did either, he had one priority: he called his lawn service and asked them to mow on Saturday and every other day after that until he returned.

Chapter 24

Thursday, May 14, 1987
9:28 p.m.

Marcelle checked herself in the mirror and pronounced herself satisfied. She was wearing one of the ensembles she'd bought when working undercover at DEA, and it was one of her favorites—a bright red strapless minidress with matching stiletto heels. It was practically painted onto her, which made it hard to move in, but it never failed to achieve the desired effect.

She walked out of the locker room and into the detectives' room on the second floor. The men greeted her with the usual applause and cheers, and she curtsied to acknowledge them.

"How much for an hour, baby?"

She turned in the heckler's direction. "George, that's fifty-nine minutes more than you'll use."

More applause and cheers.

Undercover officer Victor Ramos bowed his head in admiration as she walked over to him. "You pulled out all the stops tonight."

"Got to dress well for your job interview. Baby needs a new pair of shoes."

They got into Victor's car and headed to Zona Norte. The uninitiated thought the club's name was a play on its North Avenue location, but those in the know recognized it as Tijuana's red-light district.

"I think it may work better if you're my girlfriend," Victor said. "If Javier Arroyo thinks I'm pimping you, he may wonder why I need a job."

"Suits me. Have you figured out your elevator pitch?"

"Everyone in Chicago thinks I've been doing cocaine transport, contract work, and I'm sure Javier has heard it by now. I'm gonna tell him I need a more regular paycheck because I've got an expensive girlfriend."

"That'll work."

"By the way, I found out something new yesterday. You know that guy Alejandro, who always sits next to Javier?"

"The guy with the big hair, the dopey one who thinks he's smart?"

"That guy. I knew he ran Javier's garage, but now I'm told he's Javier's second-in-command."

"Couldn't Javier have found someone a little sharper?"

Victor shrugged. "Alejandro's a nephew. They like to keep it in the family."

Marcelle said, "I'll try to park myself between them. You sit on Javier's other side, and while you're schmoozing him, I'll be extra special nice to Alejandro."

Victor pulled up in front of the club and handed the keys to a valet. The weekend started on Thursday night, and a long queue waited outside the club. The doormen scrutinized people as they walked up, admitted those who met their criteria, and told the rest to get in line. They took one look at Marcelle and waved her and Victor through.

Marcelle could feel the thumping bass in her bones as soon as they walked in. The room was dark, lit mostly by rotating, multi-colored lights, and it took a moment for her eyes to adjust. They made their way to a relatively quiet corner, where Javier held court in a large, semicircular booth. Both Javier and Alejandro were there, and Marcelle was glad to see plenty of space available. Javier waved them over.

"Maricela! Victor! *Cómo te va?*"

"*Todo bien,*" she said.

Javier gestured at the bouncer, who unhooked the red velour stanchion rope to let them through. Javier and Alejandro stood up and shook hands with Victor, and gave Marcelle polite hugs.

"I want to sit between you handsome men," she said. Alejandro made a dramatic sweep of his arm and she got the catbird seat, with Victor on the other side of Javier. So far, so good.

A waitress took their drink orders quickly. They spent the first twenty minutes making small talk, and then Marcelle deftly turned her attention to Alejandro. She needed to get him out of the loop so Victor could have Javier to himself, and it worked to perfection.

Unfortunately, it also meant she had to endure Alejandro one-on-one. For the next half-hour, she pretended to be profoundly interested in his jabber about his condominium and how expensive and well-furnished it was; his two cars, a Corvette and a Porsche; and his gold, diamond-encrusted Rolex, which he spent a good three minutes showing her. He was, well and truly, a supreme dumb-ass, and she wondered with some horror whether there were women who actually fell for this shit. All the while, she made sure her leg was rubbing against his.

Now she saw Victor and Javier huddled together, heads bowed, and she knew it was time to clinch the deal. She put her hand on Alejandro's thigh and stroked it, which he most definitely did not mind at all. He was breathing heavily now and most of his breath was landing on her neck, and she silently prayed that Victor and Javier would wrap it the hell up.

A moment later, her prayer was answered. Javier stood up and motioned for Alejandro to exit the booth with him. They walked a few feet away and conversed briefly. At the end, she saw Alejandro say something. Javier gave a conclusory nod, as though agreeing with whatever Alejandro had said.

Javier gestured for Victor to come over. The three of them spoke, then Victor shook hands with the other two men. Victor gave Marcelle a *let's go* head shake, and they said their goodbyes and walked out.

They were in a crowd, so they said nothing of consequence while waiting for the valet to retrieve the car. As soon as it arrived, they got in and she asked him how it went.

"It looks like I have a job, but not immediately."

"Why not immediately?"

"That's the interesting part. Javier said they've got something going on right now, occupying his attention. He said it should all be settled next week, and wants me to see him after that to discuss the details."

"I don't suppose he mentioned Thornton, did he?"

"No, but that's got to be it." Victor's face turned grim. "It looks like there's a war brewing."

Chapter 25

Friday, May 15, 1987
8:25 a.m.

"Let's do a timeline," Marcelle said.

She pulled out a blank pad of General Progress Reports that detectives used to record their notes during investigations. She turned her chair toward Bernie and wrote while she spoke. "Thornton's in the CIA till 1952, helping set up the KMT in Burma. He leaves Burma, goes to Malaya, and stays until '59. Hangs out in Singapore for a year, then goes to the Congo in 1960. Okay so far?"

"Okay," Bernie said.

"He leaves the Congo in 1968 and shows up at a US military base in '69. We think he was recruiting people, but we don't know for what."

"Check."

"Then we have a four-year gap until April of '73, when he grabs the Russian doctors to get in Lo's good graces." She stopped and tapped her pencil on her desk. "I think we've narrowed it down to those four years. Am I missing anything?"

"I'd add one thing," Bernie said. "January of 1973, the Paris Peace Accords get signed, ending the Vietnam War."

"How's that fit in?"

"I don't know if it does, but here's how I see it. We think Thornton recruited an active-duty Green Beret with the Army's permission, and for the next four years Thornton went completely dark. Three months after the war ended, he showed up in Burma to start his drug career. Maybe a coincidence, maybe not."

"I see what you mean," Marcelle said.

"And something else sticks out. Thornton's a prominent guy. His movements are well known. In a few conversations, we got his whole life figured out except for four years. If no one knows what he was doing then, it has to be because he deliberately stayed under the radar. I'm thinking he was doing something with the military in Vietnam, and when the war ended, he needed a new job."

Marcelle said, "Maybe this guy Johannsen can help us. Have you started looking for him?"

"I called all three Directory Assistance numbers in Iowa and got one Steven Johannsen. Turned out he was an auto mechanic in Council Bluffs who's never even been in the service."

"Damn. What do we do now?"

"I asked Wanda to find him."

"Oh, geez, do you think she'll live long enough to do it?"

"Don't worry, Wanda's immortal. The real problem is that I have to start driving around with John this morning."

"Didn't Gene Richards say Thornton might be blackmailing the government? If we go to Mike with what we have, maybe he'll pull you from John."

"Gene said it was conceivable, which is another way of saying maybe yes and maybe no. IRS has its hooks in Mike, and he's not going to piss them off with an unsubstantiated story accusing them of colluding with Thornton. If you and Victor are right, I expect things to heat up real soon, and then I can ditch John. In the meantime, I've got to play nice."

Chapter 26

Friday, May 15, 1987
9:58 a.m.

Bernie found John in the waiting area, his head doing the left-center jerk.

"Good morning, John."

John turned and looked out the window, considered it momentarily, and said yes.

Bernie knew it was going to be a long day.

John stood up and pointed to the man working at the shoeshine stand. "That gentleman doesn't look well."

"His name is Weems," Bernie said, "and he doesn't look well because he's a heroin addict."

"You allow a heroin addict to work here?"

"Sometimes we have to adapt."

"I don't understand."

"Weems is a real nice guy, but no one would give him a job because he's a junkie, so he did what a lot of them do—he broke into houses and stole stuff to support his habit. We'd bust him, he'd go to jail and dry out, and then he'd get back on the street and the whole process would repeat itself. We finally decided it'd be a lot easier for everyone involved if he could earn a living, so we all pitched in and bought him the shoeshine stand and enough supplies to get him started. Now he gets here at six a.m. sharp every day, 365 days a year, and works till he's made enough to pay for his living expenses and two dime bags."

Bernie waited for a reaction, but got none. "Do you know where you want to go first?" he asked.

"I thought you might have some ideas."

"I'd like to see where Thornton and his men live. You interested?"

"Okay."

They got in Bernie's Crown Vic and headed to the expressway. By now, John's head had stopped jerking, but in its place were two other tics—a grimace that looked like a half-smile on the right side of his face, coupled with his eyebrows going up and down. His mouth and eyebrows seemed to move in a rhythm with each other, and he would keep it up for the rest of the day.

Neither said a word for the first twenty minutes, with John just staring out the window. He didn't seem to need human interaction, but Bernie was a talker and it was driving him nuts.

Bernie said, "You know anything about this place?"

John turned slightly in Bernie's direction, though not enough to make eye contact. "Some."

"Well, would you mind sharing it?"

"No, I wouldn't mind."

He resumed staring out the window and said nothing.

"Then please share it, okay?"

John finally started speaking more than one sentence at a time, looking straight out the front window while he spoke. "Charles Lowell was a Chicago grain merchant who built the estate on a thousand acres near Diamond Lake in the 1860s. The mansion was considered an architectural masterpiece at the time. Three stories, gabled roofs, wood and marble interior. The property eventually was sold, and by the early 1900s it was owned by ice companies, which harvested ice from Diamond Lake and shipped it to Chicago. Later on, they sold off portions of the land and donated most of the rest to the county for a forest preserve, and now it consists of thirty-three acres."

John went silent again.

"Good start, John. Only eighty more years to go."

John's head jerked to the left, vibrated a few times, and then re-settled. "In the early 1920s, the property was sold again and the new owners turned it into a country club. They built a large annex with a ballroom and reception areas and forty-four bedrooms. The country club went defunct after the 1929 stock market crash, and later a Catholic order bought the property and made it a boys' prep school. The school closed a few years ago, and the place was vacant until one of Quan's front companies bought it last year."

They pulled off the expressway and drove north on Route 31. Bernie would have passed the property's entrance, nestled as it was in the trees, but for the fact that he saw a CPD cruiser parked in a field across the road from the gate. Two bored-looking patrolmen, Larson and Herrera from the 27th District, were lounging next to their car. Bernie pulled alongside and asked how it was going.

"It's the best gig we've ever had," Herrera said.

"Tell me."

Larson pulled out his log. "Yesterday was day one. We got here right at six a.m. At seven a guy came out and brought us breakfast—coffee, eggs, bacon, the works. An hour later he came back with a Thermos of coffee and took the plates away. At eleven twenty-five the gate opened, and Thornton and his driver drove out in a brand-new Lincoln and we followed."

"Where'd they go?"

"West side. Mostly K-Town and a little into the L streets. They drove around slowly for about an hour."

"He's learning the city and how it flows," John said. "Same as I'm doing."

Bernie asked, "Did they ever try to lose you?"

"Just the opposite. The driver made sure we were always right behind, left just enough space so no one could get between us. If a light was turning yellow, he slowed down so we didn't get separated."

"He just drove around? No stops?"

"They stopped for lunch at a Mexican restaurant. We sat a few tables away and his driver came over and said for us to get anything on the menu, they'd pick up the tab."

"Next shift had it even better," Herrera said. "Thornton's guy brought out a three-course dinner."

"Is there much traffic in and out?" Bernie asked.

"They've got a few cars. Guys go in and out on errands."

"Anything happen today?"

"They brought breakfast at seven o'clock and gave us a heads-up that Thornton's going out again at one this afternoon. I guess they want to make sure we're ready to go."

"I'm happy for you guys," Bernie said. "Try not to work too hard." He and John got back in the car and drove across the road to the mansion's gate. The guard came out, and Bernie lowered his window and held up his star and ID.

"Good morning, Detective. Bernardelli, is it?"

"In the flesh." The guard tried to see who was in the passenger seat, but Bernie was blocking his view. "Who's that with you, sir?"

"Ernie Banks. You need Cubs tickets?"

"Thank you, but no. May I ask the purpose of your visit?"

"We'd like to take the tour. When's the next one start?"

"Do you have a search warrant?"

"Damn, I flat forgot it."

"Then I'm afraid we can't let you in. There's an area just past the guardhouse where you can turn around. Have a good day, Detective."

They turned back onto Route 31. "That wasn't very productive," John said.

"You have a gift for stating the obvious. Now, I don't know about you, but I'm hungry."

They drove to the nearby City of Diamond Lake, a small, quaint, tidy town, and went to a family-owned diner, Bernie's favorite type of restaurant. They placed their orders and another ten minutes of silence passed.

"Tell me, John," Bernie said, "what do you do for fun?"

"I work."

"Yeah, I know the feeling. I get on a case, it's all I can think about." He paused and waited for John to reciprocate with a similar question, but it never came. "Ever been married?"

"I have not."

"I was married once," Bernie said. "Got married a couple years out of the academy, got divorced three years later. I worked too much overtime; I don't blame her for leaving me. Do your parents live near DC?"

"My parents were killed in a car accident when I was in college."

"Oh, no. I'm so sorry."

"You don't need to be sorry. It wasn't your fault."

"John, I was—never mind."

Their food arrived, and a minute later, John surprised Bernie by speaking without being spoken to first. "I read your file. Why have you never taken the sergeant's exam?"

Every time Bernie started working with someone new, he got the same question.

"Because I don't want to be a sergeant. If I make sergeant, I have to go back to patrol. I like being a detective."

"It's a promotion in rank and more money."

"I've got enough money. If I watch my spending, I can go bowling once a week and take in a ballgame now and then. And I don't care a bit about rank."

"What do you care about?"

"I care about being a good detective, okay? That's it—I just want to be good at what I do."

They ate in silence for several minutes, and then Bernie picked up the conversation again. "The other day you said you don't usually carry a gun. Does IRS teach you guys how to shoot?"

"It does. All special agents in Criminal Investigation have to complete firearms training, and we have to qualify twice a year with our issued handgun."

"Have you ever had to fire your gun?"

"No."

"Me neither," Bernie said, rapping his knuckles on the wood table.

"You just knocked on wood."

"Yes, John, I knocked on wood. What about it?"

"It's a superstition. It doesn't prevent an event from occurring."

Bernie stared at him in mock surprise. "I had no idea. Thanks for letting me know."

"You're welcome. I should think someone would have told you by now."

They paid their check and returned to the car. "Want to go rattle someone's cage?" Bernie asked.

"Who's in a cage?"

"John, it's just—"

"An expression?"

"Right."

"I told you I'm not good with expressions."

"Sorry. Remember the other day when we told you about Manny Garza?"

"The head of the heroin cartel that the Arroyos forced out?"

"Yeah. He and I have some history."

"You didn't mention it at our meeting."

"Because it's a sore spot with me and Mike. Anyway, it might be interesting to pay Manny a visit and see what kind of reaction we get."

Bernie made a U-turn across three lanes of traffic and headed back to the expressway. "Here's the story," he said. "A few years ago, before Marcelle, I got sent out on this hit-and-run that looked like it would end up being a homicide. The victim was a nice girl, by herself at a local bar, when some coked-up numbnuts tried to pick her up. She wasn't interested, but numbnuts was too wired and wouldn't stop. It got bad enough that the girl just decided to leave. She walked less than a block before numbnuts drove his car right at her and hit her."

Bernie took a deep breath, then continued. "She didn't go under the wheels. She was flung into the air and landed behind his Camaro. Then numbnuts put it in reverse and tried to run her over again, but he missed her and hit a lamppost, and then he sped off.

"When I got to the scene, there were witnesses who'd been outside the bar, and one of them had most of the plate number. We ran what we had and got a match to a yellow Camaro. Ten minutes later I was at the front door of numbnuts' home with a couple patrol cars, and guess what? He streetparked it. *Streetparked*. With bloody bits of skin and Levi's still stuck to his grille.

"Mama answered the door in her robe and slippers, and while she was still half asleep, one of the Spanish-speaking officers convinced her she should bring numbnuts to the door. Probably told her we just needed him to move his car or something. Anyway, mama brought him to the door and as soon as he was in the threshold, we grabbed him.

"We cuffed him face down in the front yard while mama was standing there, wailing and getting ignored. And guess who chose this very moment to come home?"

"Who?"

"Manny Garza. Numbnuts, it turned out, was one of Manny's more worthless sons, and mama was Manny's wife. I guess it's a blow to one's image as a *jefe* to have the whole neighborhood see your impotent rage as the cops drag away your son, and your wife is rending her clothes in anguish. Afterward, Manny tried to go after me, you know, make it a political thing. Fortunately, I did everything by the book so it didn't go anywhere, but Mike told me to give him a heads-up the next time I plan to raid the home of a cartel boss."

"What happened to the perpetrator?" John asked.

"In Chicago we call them offenders, and this one jumped bond back to Mexico."

"And the victim?"

"She got a happy ending. She had broken bones, but no brain damage. The whole thing inspired her to go back to school to get her nursing certificate, and now she works at Children's. And to this day, there's an empty seat at the table at the Chicago Garza home, thanks to me."

They exited the Kennedy at Division Street and drove the half-mile to Manny's Place, a typical Chicago corner tavern with an "Old Style on Tap" sign hanging above the door. Inside, it was like every corner tavern in Chicago—dark, smoky, and saturated with the damp odor of stale beer and unlicensed plumbing.

There were five souls inside: a young man playing a pinball game in the corner; two older guys nursing beers and watching a game show on the television over the bar; a bartender watching along with them; and Manny Garza, sitting at a table and reading a newspaper. He looked up and made a face when he saw Bernie.

"If it's not the big, brave cop," Manny said. "When are you gonna find the people who killed my family?"

"All in good time, Manny. So many people hated their guts we've got hundreds of suspects."

Bernie and John sat down across from Manny. "Who's he?" Manny asked, lifting his chin at John.

"My bodyguard." Bernie looked around the room. "Pretty slow here, Manny. At least the Arroyos let you keep this place."

"I got no idea what you're talking about."

"Of course, you don't. But actually, I came here to give you some news. Did you hear the Quans are moving in?"

Manny had no reaction. "The who?"

"You mean you haven't heard? I guess no one tells you anything anymore. They're Asian and they're real men, not like the little babies you have. Maybe they'll be able to give the Arroyos a run for their money."

"All I do is run a bar."

"Yeah, I know, and I'm the mayor of Chicago. Now let me give you some advice: stay as far away from the Quans as you can. If you work with them, we'll take you down with them. And if you go up against them, they'll beat your asses worse than Arroyo did."

Bernie and John got up and walked out. Thankfully, John refrained from pointing out that this trip had been as big a dud as the one to Thornton's mansion.

They drove back to Area Six and Bernie dropped John off at his car. "Do you ever work on Sundays?" he asked John.

"I can."

"I'm sorry I wasted your time today. Come by here on Sunday afternoon and we'll go back out. You can pick where you want to go."

"All right."

"And John, I'd appreciate it if you wouldn't mention our Manny visit to Mike."

"I won't," John said. "You can trust me."

Chapter 27

Friday, May 15, 1987
2:26 p.m.

Bernie walked back inside Area Six, and the desk sergeant told him Wanda was looking for him.

Wanda Pawlowski was the longest-serving employee of the Chicago Police Department. Bernie didn't know how old she was, but he guessed she was around 150, and that was both good and bad. The bad part was that she was hard of hearing. The good part was that after being on the job for 130 years, she'd gotten pretty good at it. When you wanted to find someone, you went to Wanda.

He walked to the other side of the floor and headed in her direction. Wanda had lost a foot of height over the years, but she was easy to find because she had the brightest snow-white hair he'd ever seen. She wore it in a bun, and it looked like it had been polyurethaned into place. He found her in her smoke-filled cubbyhole—she'd been a chain-smoker since age six—and bent down next to her ear and shouted so she could hear him. "You look lovely today, Wanda."

"Oh, hi, Bernie."

"Is that a new hairdo?"

"No, I've had it around thirty years." She reached up and patted her hair with her fingers. "Do you like it?"

"It's perfect for you."

"Thanks, sweetie."

"Did you find my guy?"

"Yeah, and I won't even tell you what I had to go through. Directory Assistance didn't have him." Bernie had already told her that, but she'd forgotten.

Wanda proceeded to tell him everything she'd gone through, concluding with, "And the reason this dipshit was so hard to find is because he lives in a cornfield in East Jesus, Iowa." She tore a sheet off her steno pad and handed it to him. "He doesn't have a physical address, just a rural route, but I got his phone number."

"Thanks, Wanda. You're a doll."

"Anything for you, sweetie. And anytime you want to have a drink, I'm available."

"I'll keep it in mind."

Bernie walked to his desk and called the number. It was answered by a young female voice that was replaced thirty seconds later by an authoritative male voice.

"Johannsen."

"Mr. Johannsen, this is Detective William Bernardelli, Chicago Police Department. I'm investigating someone you may have known a while back."

"How can I help you?"

Bernie decided it was time to take a leap of faith. Sometimes, people were more forthcoming when they thought you knew more than you really did.

"Could you tell me about your relationship with Robert Thornton in Vietnam?"

There was a long silence.

Much too long of a silence.

"Mr. Johannsen?"

"I can't help you. Please don't call again. Goodbye."

Bernie looked back at the sheet Wanda had given him. Johannsen didn't live in East Jesus; he actually lived in a place called Halsey. Bernie turned to the Iowa page in his road atlas and found the town, a tiny dot in central Iowa, just six hours from Chicago.

Chapter 28

Saturday, May 16, 1987
3:23 a.m.

"I hate these jobs," Lattimore said. "It's a lot easier just to kill them."

Johnson felt the same way, but didn't want to say so. As good an operator as Lattimore was, he tended to be whiny, and Johnson didn't want to encourage him. "Don't sweat it. If we do our jobs right, we'll be in and out in under three minutes."

They sat in their car in the 300 block of South Keeler Avenue in K-Town, watching a house they'd been surveilling for two weeks. Two weeks of living in a motel, away from the rest of the group, alternating in eight-hour shifts. It wasn't difficult work, but it was mind-numbingly monotonous. At least it was about to end—that is, if Frank's intelligence was correct, as it had been so far.

The building was one of Arroyo's stash houses, a two-story brick structure painted green with white trim. For two weeks they'd seen only the same three people go in and out of the house, but ninety minutes ago, during Johnson's shift, a black van had pulled up and a half-dozen people got out. They scanned the street and, concluding incorrectly that no one was watching, all but two—the front and rear lookouts—walked into the house.

If Frank was right, that expedition was the shipment of heroin from Mexico. Later today, Arroyo's people would start cutting it, and from here it would go to distributors.

Or at least that was their plan.

* * *

The lights on the second floor finally went off. It was go time.

"Let's sync up," Johnson said. "I have three-three-seven. Set to three-three-eight when your second hand hits twelve."

Each waited until the second hand on his watch reached 12:00, pulled out the crown to stop it, and reset the minute hand. "On my mark: three, two, one, *mark*." They pushed the crowns in.

Each of them had a Heckler & Koch MP5SD3, a 9mm submachine gun with a retractable buttstock and an integral suppressor. In this op, the guns' primary function was intimidation, and they were to be used only as a last resort; if they had to fire them, it would mean they'd done their job wrong. They had thirty-round magazines already inserted and rounds chambered, and now each of them tugged on his mag to make sure it was fully seated.

"Frank says it'll be in the dining room, middle of the first floor," Johnson said. "You've got the front, I've got the rear. Breach at three-five-five."

"Three-five-five, copy." Lattimore got out of the car and started walking.

* * *

The front lookout sat at the bottom of the stoop. He had just lit a cigarette when he saw a skinny white dude in a ratty-looking overcoat shuffling toward him.

Junkie. He was probably going to ask for a free bag.

The junkie walked up to him, his head lolling around. "Brother, could I get a smoke?"

Okay, not so bad. He turned to reach into his right coat pocket, and the butt of Lattimore's subgun smacked him squarely in the cranium.

Lattimore dragged him to the side of the house. He pulled out three pairs of plastic cuffs, used two to cuff the man's wrists and ankles, and used the third to attach his hands to a gas pipe. He finished by cutting off a short piece of duct tape and sticking it over the man's mouth.

He pulled the man's keys out of his pocket and walked up the front steps in a crouch. Only one key had a logo matching the lock. That had to be it.

He looked at his watch. Seven minutes, twenty-two seconds to breach.

* * *

Johnson saw Lattimore take his position at the door. He looked up and down the street, saw nothing, and exited the car. He wore a jacket that easily concealed the subgun with its stock retracted. A satchel hung over his shoulder.

He walked past Lattimore without acknowledging him and turned toward the side of the house. He passed the still-unconscious front lookout and stopped when he reached the rear.

He set the satchel down, made sure the subgun's safety was off, and took it in both hands. This was where it got tricky. He didn't give a shit about having to kill the rear lookout, but Thornton had a strict rule against unnecessary killing, and Johnson didn't want to have to explain himself. He'd have to at least try to avoid killing the guy.

He went belly down, holding the gun in front of him, ready to bring it up to fire if necessary. He turned in a quarter-circle until he was facing toward the rear lookout and looked up.

The lookout was sitting on the back steps, holding a shotgun and looking toward the alley behind the house.

Johnson calculated the odds. It was four yards to the stairs. If he stayed down and avoided sudden movements, the guy might not notice him in his peripheral vision, and if he did, Johnson could give him a burst and be done with it.

He was getting ready to move when the lookout leaned his shotgun against the railing and opened an ice chest to pull out a beer.

Johnson leaped up and quickly closed the gap, and just as the lookout saw him and reached for his shotgun, Johnson rammed his gun's butt into the man's face. The man rolled down and lay still, blood spewing out of his nose and mouth.

Johnson checked his pulse. Still alive.

He cuffed the man's wrists and ankles, cuffed his hands to the railing, and duct-taped his mouth. He searched the man's body, but found no keys. This guy was smarter than the other one.

He retrieved his satchel from the side of the house and returned to the back stairs. The stairs led to the kitchen. The room was dark, though he could see light coming from the interior of the house. He walked up the stairs in a crouch, keeping his head below the door's window, and listened. A television was on, and he silently thanked them for giving him some cover.

The door had a deadbolt lock. Johnson pulled out the pouch with his lock pick set and laboriously worked the lock. It took him close to a minute, but finally the bolt retracted.

He looked at his watch. One minute, fourteen seconds to breach.

* * *

Five, four, three, two, one—

They breached within a half-second of each other. They were on opposite ends of a hallway and they inched toward each other, backs to the wall, until Lattimore was on one side of the dining room entrance and Johnson was on the other.

Johnson held up three fingers, then lowered them one by one. *Three, two, one—*

They turned into the room, pointing the subguns forward. Four men watching TV. Pistols on the table in front of them and a shotgun propped against it.

"Hands in the air *now*," Johnson said.

The only things the four men saw were submachine guns pointed at them, and they saved their lives by sticking their arms straight up.

Johnson spoke in a low voice. "If we wanted you dead, you'd be dead already. Do as we say and you live, otherwise, you die. Nod if you understand."

They all nodded.

"If you make a sound, you die. If anyone comes downstairs, they and you all die. Nod if you understand."

They nodded again.

"Clasp your hands behind your head, stand up real slowly, and back away from the table until your back hits the wall."

He waited for them to comply, then glanced at Lattimore. "I can take it from here. You've got the doorway."

Lattimore put his back to the wall next to the room's entrance, ready for anyone who might venture downstairs.

Now Johnson could turn his attention to the table. It was filled with the tools of the trade—scales, face masks, vinyl gloves, razor blades, aluminum foil for making dime bags, and powdered milk for cutting the product.

And in the center of the table, eight packages of Mexican brown powder. Eight kilograms, nearly eighteen pounds of uncut heroin.

Jackpot.

He kept the gun slung over his right shoulder, but held it with only his right hand to free up his left. He set the satchel on the table and tossed in the eight kilos. Before he closed it, he pulled out an envelope and tossed it on the table.

"Everything Arroyo needs to know is in there, but I'll give you a preview. Professor Thornton thinks businessmen should always be willing to sit down and talk, and he was very disappointed that Arroyo declined his invitation. He regrets having to resort to such an extreme measure, but deemed it necessary to get Arroyo's attention. If Arroyo wants his dope back, he'll agree to meet. Him and his assistant, Thornton and his. No one else besides those four. No guns, no knives, no weapons of any kind. We'll have measures in place to make sure everyone's clean. Professor Thornton gives you his word that if everyone plays by the rules, Arroyo and his assistant will walk out of the room with every gram of this stuff."

Johnson waited for it to sink in.

"Who's in charge here?" he said.

A short, stocky man on the left responded.

"What's your name?"

"Bosco."

"Okay, Bosco, you're our insurance policy. I'm gonna cuff you and you're gonna walk with us back to our car. If your guys stay put and don't sound the alarm, we'll let you go when we get there. Otherwise, you die. Everyone nod if you understand."

They all nodded.

"Cover me," Johnson told Lattimore. Lattimore turned and held his gun on the men while Johnson cuffed Bosco's hands behind him. "Now, just relax, son. I'm gonna grab your collar, but I won't hurt you. I just want to make sure you don't cut and run, okay?"

"Okay."

Johnson grabbed the back of Bosco's shirt collar and pulled up on it. The three of them walked out of the house and down the block to the car.

Lattimore opened both doors and kept his gun on Bosco. "I'm gonna let go now," Johnson said. "You gonna be good?"

"I'll be good," Bosco said.

Johnson let go and Bosco stood still. "Have a nice night," Johnson said, "and make sure Arroyo gets that envelope pronto."

Chapter 29

Saturday, May 16, 1987
9:20 a.m.

For once, John had nothing he needed to do.

Although he'd been to Chicago before, he'd never had a chance to sightsee. With the forecast calling for mostly sunny skies and a high of seventy-five, today would be perfect for it.

He got on the Outer Drive and drove south. On his left were a park, a beach, and Lake Michigan. Chicago had a fantastic park system, and people had come out in force to enjoy the good weather. The bicycle paths were filled with riders, and people were walking and jogging and throwing plastic discs to each other and playing games of fetch with their dogs.

His destination was the Lincoln Park Zoo. He exited the Outer Drive at Fullerton and began the arduous process of finding a place to park. He drove through a parking area embedded in Lincoln Park near a lagoon, and after what seemed an eternity, he saw someone pull out of a parking space just ahead of him and filled it quickly.

The zoo was just a short walk away. On this beautiful Saturday, the zoo was crowded—parents with young children, groups of teenagers carrying on as teenagers always did, and couples holding hands. He wondered what it would be like to walk through a zoo as part of a couple.

John spent the next two hours touring the exhibits. It was a wonderful place, one of the best zoos he'd ever seen, and he so enjoyed being in the warm spring air that he decided to venture forth and explore the surrounding area. He walked toward the lake and soon arrived at the lakefront beach, a wide expanse of sand with the lake on one side and a sidewalk on the other.

He walked north along the sidewalk, and within minutes, the sandy beach ended. In its place was a vast area filled with stone blocks, each several feet square, which appeared to be a buffer to prevent erosion from the lake's waves. They were arranged in rows that descended to the water like long, rocky stair steps, and they were level enough that one could walk on them. Here and there, people sat on them while reading or sunning themselves. Nearby was a refreshment stand that sold hot dogs and ice cream and soft drinks.

John walked to the stand and asked for ice cream. The vendor handed him an ice cream cup and a small, flat, wood spoon. The cup was made of paperboard and had a cover with a tab at one end.

John stepped away, sat down on a bench, and examined the cup and spoon. He carefully pulled the cover away, exposing the vanilla ice cream inside. The ice cream was frozen, and the small, flat wood spoon appeared to be no match for it. He guessed the spoon would break as soon as he tried to use it, and he spent a good thirty seconds looking at the ice cream and the spoon, trying to figure out his next move.

"It'll be easier to scoop out once it warms up," said a voice to his left.

He looked up and saw a woman who must have been behind him in the line, holding an unopened cup and a wood spoon. She had short blonde hair and an attractive, round face, pleasant and friendly looking, but not intimidatingly beautiful. She said, "Want me to show you how?"

"Please."

After peeling the cover off her cup, she stabbed the end of her wood spoon into the top of the ice cream and broke off a small piece, and when she got it balanced on top of the spoon, she tilted her head down and brought the spoon up to her mouth. "Now you try."

John applied himself diligently and got a sliver of ice cream into his mouth. He was surprised at how good it was.

The woman looked delighted. "You did it on the first try! I'm going to eat mine on the Rocks. Want to come with?"

"Um, sure."

They walked to the stone blocks. The woman sat on the edge of one block and scooted down to the next row. John followed her lead, and they sat down next to each other, their backs against the block from which they'd just descended.

The woman crossed her legs beneath herself and stuck her hand out. "Mary Ellen Rodocker."

"Johnshepardpleasedtomeetyou."

"I'm pleased to meet you, too." She began rocking lightly back and forth. "I love the Rocks, don't you? I come here every weekend when it's warm and even when it's not so warm, because I'm from North Platte, Nebraska, and it gets cold there just like it does here, and I'm used to it. Do you come here every weekend?"

"It's my first time."

"Oh my God! Why'd you wait so long?"

"I don't live here, so it's the first chance I've had."

"Oh." She looked unhappy. "Where do you live?"

"Washington, DC. I'm here on business."

"I guess that means you're going home soon."

"Actually, I'll be here awhile."

"Are you staying with family?"

"I've got an apartment."

"An *apartment*." She looked pleased with what she'd just heard.

She resumed talking while rocking back and forth the whole time. "When I come here, I pretend I'm at the ocean because Lake

Michigan kind of looks like an ocean, don't you think? And even though I've never been to a real ocean, I imagine it must look like this, and I shut my eyes—"

John was always uncomfortable and nervous with women in social settings. How were you supposed to know what to say to them? Work was different—you discussed what was necessary and moved on—but social discourse was filled with mysterious rules, and he struggled to come up with something to say. It made his ticcing even worse, and no matter what he said, women came up with an excuse to exit the conversation. He was surprised when he realized he was twitching only a little, and Mary Ellen didn't seem to mind it.

"—and I have two older sisters and an older brother so I'm the baby in the family, and you know how that goes, and when I was nine my parents gave me a beagle and I named her Betty, and she was my best friend and followed me everywhere, and then she ran away and we couldn't find her, and it was the *worst* thing that ever happened to me—"

Mary Ellen didn't seem to expect him to talk, which meant he didn't have to risk saying something foolish. There was no pressure on him. He could just relax and let her carry the conversation.

"—and after high school I went to junior college and got an associate's degree as an administrative professional, and then I moved here, and I work at an apartment management company in the Loop as an administrative assistant, which is like being a secretary. What do you do?"

"I'm an accountant."

"Oh, wow, I bet you're good with numbers."

"Pretty good, I guess."

"Then we have something in common, because people say I'm good with numbers, too, and I don't think they're saying it just to be nice. Do you think it's weird that I rock this way?"

"Not in the least," John said, his mouth twitching.

"It makes me feel better," she said. "I don't know why, it just does. Sometimes people make fun of me for it, but I'm not hurting them, so why should they care? Do you like the ice cream?"

"It's delicious."

They consumed the rest of their cups while Mary Ellen talked. "—and I didn't like the men in North Platte so I came here, and now I'm thirty-five but people tell me I look younger, and I joined a church but all the men are married, and I tried a singles club but all the men had only one thing on their mind." She stopped and looked at him. "You don't say much, do you?"

"I enjoy listening to you."

Her eyes went wide. "Oh my God! I've never heard a man say that before! Men don't like to listen. They just want to do-do-do all the time. Do you know how rare you are?"

"I never thought of it that way."

"Well, you are, believe me. You're not wearing a wedding ring. Are you married?"

"No."

"Ever been?"

"No."

"Do you have a girlfriend?"

"No."

"Why not?"

"Well, um, I guess I've been busy."

"I know exactly what you mean! You work all day and then you're tired out, and how do you even meet people in a big city? Do you like to eat?"

"As much as the next person, I suppose."

"Me too! I like to eat and I like to cook and those things go together, don't you think? Do you like meat loaf?"

"It's my favorite food."

"I make the *best* meat loaf." Her face was serious for a moment. "You probably think I'm exaggerating, but it really is the best. Want me to make some for you?"

"I'd enjoy that."

"Do you have a kitchen with an oven and all?"

"I do."

"Then I could go to your apartment and make you meat loaf." She paused and seemed to be thinking hard. "I get off work at 4:30. How about next Friday at 5:30?"

"That'd be fine. But if you're going to make meat loaf, I should get the rest of the food."

"That's fair. Let me make you a list."

She rifled through her purse and pulled out a pen and a crumpled piece of junk mail. She straightened it out and wrote a list.

"I put a bottle of wine on there. Do you drink wine? You don't have to get it if you don't."

"I drink it sometimes. I can get it."

"I'll need your address."

He gave it to her, and she wrote it down.

"This is exciting," she said. "You like to listen and you like meat loaf." She stood up and threw her purse over her shoulder. "I have to go now. I'm glad I met you, John Shepard."

"I'm glad I met you, too," John said.

Chapter 30

Saturday, May 16, 1987
2:17 p.m.

There wasn't much going on in Halsey, Iowa. From what Bernie could see, it had three things: a service station, a restaurant that also housed the post office, and a grain elevator with railroad tracks alongside. The service station, where he now stood, wasn't one of those places that just sold gas and were staffed by clerks that had never looked under a hood. Halsey's was a real service station, the kind where you could get your car fixed, with jacks and grease and tools lying all over. Bernie filled his gas tank, and the friendly proprietor gave him directions to what he called "the Johannsen place."

Four miles later, Bernie turned into the driveway. Two enormous oaks cradled the house, and behind it were vast fields as far as the eye could see, gently rolling land with small clumps of trees intermittently punctuating the landscape. The doorbell was answered by a woman who he guessed was little Susie from Sam Harrison's narrative.

"Good afternoon, ma'am. I'm looking for Mr. Johannsen."

"What do you want with him?"

"I'm a salesman for Thedford Life Insurance Company."

"He doesn't need any, and he doesn't like salesmen."

"Ma'am, he's on my route and I'm gonna get fired if I don't at least talk to him."

She eyed him suspiciously. "He's in the shed out back. If he asks you to leave, you best leave the first time he asks."

"Yes, ma'am, thank you."

Bernie walked around to the shed and saw a tall, heavily muscled man trying to break loose a bolt on an ancient John Deere tractor. His face fell as soon as he saw Bernie.

"Mr. Johannsen?"

"You're the cop I talked to yesterday."

"Yes, sir." Bernie held open his badge case. "Detective William Bernardelli, Chicago Police."

"Did my wife send you back here?"

"She did. For what it's worth, I told her I was a life insurance salesman."

Johannsen nodded as though Bernie had done something right. "Thank you. I appreciate that."

"And just so you know, she tried to get rid of me."

"She's a good woman," Johannsen said. He wiped his hands on a rag and tossed it on the floor. "I figured you'd show up, though I didn't think it'd be this fast. Have a seat if you can find one."

Johannsen sat on the back of the tractor, and Bernie sat down on a trailer. "Sam Harrison wanted me to tell you something," Bernie said. "He understood the circumstances and hasn't got any hard feelings about how you left Nha Trang."

Johannsen looked pleased. "Sam was a damn good officer. I felt bad about how I left, but I was under orders."

"He figured as much."

"How's he doing?"

"He lives with his dog in the north Georgia mountains. Looked to be in good health when I saw him a few days ago. Kind of cranky, and a lot sharper than he wants you to think."

"Yeah, that's Sam." Johannsen sighed and his face turned grave. "When you called yesterday, I was so surprised I didn't know what to say. Now you know why I don't play poker."

"You know why I'm here, sir."

"You want to know all about Thornton."

"That's right."

"Well, I already told you—I can't help you."

"Can't or won't?"

"I don't see how it makes any difference either way." Johannsen bowed his head and looked down at the floor. "What's Thornton done now?"

"He's in Chicago, trying to take over the heroin trade."

Johannsen looked up, startled. "He's back in the States?"

"Yes, sir, got here a short time ago. Does that surprise you?"

"Yeah, it surprises me. I didn't think he'd have the guts to come back."

"Why not?"

"Because there's a lot of people here who want to kill him."

"Including you?"

"Including me."

"Then why won't you help me?"

"Why?" Johannsen jerked his head toward the house. "I've got a wife and five kids back there that need me, and if I talk to you, they won't have me around much longer."

"I'd never name you as my source," Bernie said.

"I don't doubt that, but you don't understand. There's just a handful of us that know the whole story, and if the government finds out you know they'll probably kill all of us just to make sure they got the right one."

Johannsen was a man who'd faced down worse things than an out-of-state detective. Bernie knew he wouldn't make headway trying to intimidate him. He'd have to take a different tack.

"You said there's just a few people that know the entire story."

"That's right."

"But there must be lots of people who know little bits and pieces—I mean, that's how I found you. They can't possibly identify all those people."

"So?"

"So tell me some bits and pieces."

Johannsen was silent for a beat.

"Ask me a question," he said.

"What were you doing with Thornton in Vietnam?"

"I was his assistant."

"At what? What was he doing there?"

"I guess you could say he was a teacher. The Army gave him the sixteen craziest men it could find, and he taught them how to kill."

"Sounds like basic training."

"There wasn't anything basic about it."

"What was so special about it?"

Johannsen shook his head. "I've already said too much. It's time for me to get back to this tractor and it's time for you to go."

They walked out to Bernie's car, and Johannsen turned to him with a plaintive, almost desperate expression. "If I didn't have a family, I'd go after that bastard myself. I hope you nail him, Detective. I hope you nail his ass right to the wall."

"I will, Mr. Johannsen. Thanks for your help."

Chapter 31

Saturday, May 16, 1987
3:28 p.m.
Boston, Massachusetts

I Love Lucy was wrapping up, which meant that in half an hour Frank could drive by the house.

When they gave him the assignment, Thornton and Arthur had cast it as a vacation, a reward for a job well done. He didn't doubt their sincerity, but he'd rather have been back at the mansion with the guys. It would have been easier to swallow if they'd given him some idea of why he was doing it, but as usual they didn't tell him jack. That was the thing about working for Thornton—he told you what you needed to know and nothing more.

Not that he was complaining. No, sir, because working for Professor Thornton was the best job a fighting man could have. He just never expected he'd have a soft assignment like this one when it all began two years ago.

* * *

On the night two years ago when his life changed, Frank sat in a roadhouse bar five miles outside Fayetteville, North Carolina, the home of Fort Bragg. There was a joint just like it near every military base he'd ever been stationed at—a place where the liquor was cheap, the hookers were passable, and people left you alone if you wanted to be left alone. And on this particular night Frank did want to be left alone, because he was pondering a topic he'd considered only once before: what he was going to do with his life.

The only other time Frank had thought about his future was when he was a high school senior, and he'd been just as clueless then as he was now. He'd been a good student but not a scholar, a decent second baseman on his high school baseball team, but not good enough to attract attention from scouts. College held no attraction for him, and there wasn't anything in particular he wanted to do. He'd been perfect fodder for the Army recruiter who promised him three hots and a cot and told him the Army would teach him a skill. And over the next eight years, the Army did indeed teach him some skills, though they were skills without much demand in the outside world.

Frank enjoyed military life and had figured on being a lifer, but then the Army notified him it wasn't renewing his enlistment contract. There was some form language blaming force structure reductions and noting he'd get an honorable discharge and all of his veteran's benefits, but to Frank it meant only one thing: in four months he'd be a civilian.

Now, as Frank sat at the bar nursing a bourbon, he was forced to contemplate his future again. Who would pay him to do what he was good at? He had a vague notion of being a cop or a security guard, but that was far as he'd gotten.

There was, of course, the plum job: being a contractor. Anyone who'd spent time in special operations had heard the stories. Mercenaries got good pay, good women, and good action, which, after all, were the only three things a man needed. And the pinnacle of all mercenary jobs was working for the legendary Professor Thornton, supposedly a drug baron who gave you the best pay, the best women, and the best action.

He never really knew if such stories were true. Lots of bullshit was exchanged among military men, and Frank had been around long enough to develop a healthy skepticism of such tales. He'd assigned it to a mental file that had grown thick over the years—a story that probably wasn't true, but was so attractive he held out some hope it was.

He was halfway through his second drink when the door opened and a man walked in. The man had buzz-cut steel-gray hair and looked like he'd been born to be a soldier. He was dressed plainly, in jeans and a T-shirt, but he wore his character like a uniform. Frank had known many such men, and he pegged the guy instantly: an ex-NCO who had seen and done everything there was to see and do, and had not been particularly impressed by any of it.

The man had silver-blue eyes that even in the dim light shone like mirrors, and he paused just long enough to scan the entire bar. It didn't look deliberate; it looked natural, as though he did it every time he entered a room. He didn't look happy or sad or bored or excited or curious. He just looked ready.

He looked like he had never been afraid of anything in his life.

He sat down next to Frank.

"What are you drinking?" the man asked.

"I don't drink with people I don't know."

"My name is Arthur, and I work for Robert Thornton."

Three thoughts raced through Frank's mind.

Holy shit.

Don't fuck this up.

Stay cool.

For a moment he stared nonchalantly at the remaining well whiskey in his glass, then downed it and rapped the glass back on the bar. "Double Jack Daniels and water," he said.

Arthur ordered tonic water. Their drinks came, and they sat down at a table in the farthest corner of the room.

"Francisco Velez," Arthur said, "Sergeant First Class, United States Army, Seventh Special Forces Group. You were born in Los

Angeles and joined the Army right out of high school. You've been in for eight years and you're going to be discharged in four months. You're the assistant operations and intelligence sergeant on your A-team, and you're fluent in Spanish."

"So you've read my file. So what?"

"Your file doesn't mention what you did in '84, in Chalatenango province in El Salvador."

"That's classified information."

"You bet it is," Arthur said with a laugh. "If it wasn't, you'd be staring at a wall in Leavenworth right now, instead of sitting here, sipping on a Jack black."

"What's your point?"

"My point is, we know a lot that's not in your file. Have you thought about what you're going to do after your discharge?"

"I've got some irons in the fire."

"Do any of those irons pay eighty thousand dollars a year and come with room and board and all the women you care to have?"

"Okay," Frank said, "you've got my attention. What could I possibly do to deserve all that?"

"You have certain skills, Frank. They're skills that don't translate well to the civilian world, but in our business they're very valuable."

"And what business is that?"

"Heroin," Arthur said. "The biggest, most integrated heroin enterprise in the world. We are the almighty General Motors of heroin. Does that bother you?"

"I can't say that it does."

"Can you still kill on command?"

"I've done it before. I s'pose I could do it again."

Arthur smiled approvingly. "Here's how it works. You'll get an unmarked envelope in the mail. It'll have three thousand dollars in cash and an airline ticket from DC to Bangkok, departing two weeks after your discharge. Use the time to get the Army out of your system, but keep yourself in shape."

"What's next?"

"We pick you up at the airport and take you to our compound. You get three days to get over your jet lag, and then we put you through three days of tests."

"What kinds of tests?"

"I can't be specific, because we don't want you to be prepared. All I can say is that some will be physical and some will be psychological."

"Then what?"

"We give you another three thousand dollars and drop you off in Bangkok for a few days while we evaluate your scores. You can have a very good time in Bangkok, Thailand, with three thousand dollars in American cash money. All we ask is that you don't draw attention to yourself. Then we come get you and tell you how you did."

"That's it?" Frank asked.

"That's it," Arthur said. "Any questions?"

"Yeah, I've got a question. What's to stop me from going to the cops with what you just told me?"

"The certain knowledge that no matter what you do and no matter where you go, we will hunt you down and kill you."

"Fair enough," Frank said.

The envelope arrived a few days later, and four months after that, Frank was discharged. He spent some of the money on hookers, but saved the rest. He laid off the booze, limited himself to smoking weed just once a day, and did his PT religiously. Frank knew he'd never again get a shot at something this good.

* * *

Two weeks after his discharge, Frank stepped off the plane at Don Mueang Airport in Bangkok. The terminal looked a lot like those in the States, though it was cleaner than most of them.

Within a minute, a man walked up. "Welcome to Thailand, Frank. My name is Johnson and I'll be your camp counselor for the next week."

They got into a Land Cruiser and headed to the mountains. Before long, they were on dirt roads without a person in sight.

"I don't want you to spill any secrets," Frank said, "but can you give me a hint about what I'm in for?"

Johnson was silent for a few beats. "We don't care about brute strength."

"What do you care about?"

"Speed, timing, agility, and balance, and that's all I can say."

"Understood. How much farther to your place?"

"We've been in it for the last ten minutes."

"I didn't see any sentries."

"We've already been scoped by four snipers," Johnson said.

The fun began bright and early on the fourth day with the most comprehensive physical Frank had ever gotten. They poked him and prodded him, took a blood sample, did an EKG and an EEG, took x-rays, and tested his vision and hearing. When he finished dressing, Johnson took him to a gym.

"Ever done gymnastics?" Johnson said.

"I sure haven't."

"Don't worry, most of us hadn't before we got here. You don't need to qualify for the Olympics. We just want to test your agility and balance and see how fast you can learn."

They started with a pommel horse, and a guy named Chuck ran him through some basic routines: holding onto the pommels and swinging his legs from side to side; holding onto one pommel and swinging his body in a circle; and laying his hands on the surface of the horse and circling some more. It was harder than hell, and Frank's arms felt like spaghetti. All the while, Johnson took notes on a clipboard. After twenty cycles, Frank was exhausted but improving.

"Okay, Frank," Johnson said, "that's the toughest men's routine. Now let's try the toughest women's routine."

They walked over to an apparatus that was four feet high, sixteen feet long, and four inches wide.

"Ever seen a balance beam?" Johnson asked.

"Only on TV."

"It's a women's event, but you're going to do it, anyway. Let's see if you can stay on."

"How do I mount it?"

"You can use that springboard to get yourself aloft. After that it's for you to figure out."

Frank removed his shoes and socks. He jumped on the springboard and propelled himself upward, but when his feet hit the beam, he promptly fell. The beam's surface was a rough suede, and it burned his feet a little as he slid off. On the fifth try, he managed to stay on, gripping the surface with his toes to stabilize himself.

"Nice job," Johnson said. "Now walk back and forth."

The beam was so narrow he couldn't walk normally with his feet side by side. Instead, he had to walk one foot in front of the other, carefully placing his toes down first and then rolling his foot down to the heel until his whole foot made contact. He fell twice more until he realized he could balance himself by holding his arms out to the side. He panicked a little the first time he got to the end, but turned himself around by rising on the balls of his feet and pivoting. After five successful mounts and back-and-forths on the beam, Johnson called it quits.

"This next part is fun," Johnson said. They walked out of the gym and into a room with a wood floor. A Thai woman who looked to be in her sixties was already there, and she walked up to Frank. She pressed her hands together and held them straight up and centered in front of her chest, as if about to pray, then bowed her head until her forehead touched her fingertips and the tip of her nose touched her thumbs. She held the pose for a moment before raising her head. Frank imitated her as best he could.

"I am honored to meet you, Mr. Frank. I am Khun Suda. My compliments on how well you performed the *wai*. Have you done it before?"

"No, ma'am."

"Then you've already shown an ability to emulate a series of movements, very important to mastering the art of dance. Have you ever done ballroom dancing?"

"I have not, ma'am."

"It requires footwork, rhythm, agility, balance, and timing. We'll start with a box step."

She took his hands and taught him the sequence of steps. Frank caught on quickly, and soon he was doing it well enough that Khun Suda put on some music and showed him how to do a waltz. Johnson was right—it really was fun. After an hour they said goodbye and this time Frank initiated the *wai*, which seemed to please Khun Suda immensely.

"Last exercise of the day," Johnson said. They returned to the gym and Johnson pulled a tarp off a pitching machine.

"I haven't seen one of these since high school," Frank said, "but there's not much room in here to hit balls."

"You're not going to hit, just dodge." Johnson handed him a catcher's mask and chest protector, and Frank put them on.

"The object of the game," Johnson said, "is to see how well you anticipate contact from a moving object, how much you move to avoid it, and how well you time your reaction. You'll be sixty feet, six inches from the machine. We'll aim some balls to hit you and some we won't. I want to see you stand still when they won't hit you and to dodge them when they will, and you get more points by minimizing your movement. Speeds from seventy to ninety-five miles an hour. Today you get straight stuff, tomorrow we'll mix in breaking balls."

Johnson showed Frank where to stand and they started, with Chuck operating the machine and Johnson taking notes. The machine spit the balls out. At first Frank erred on the side of avoidance, but in a few minutes, he reacquired his batting eye. He got hit a few times, but by the end he was avoiding contact pitches with only slight movements. After an hour, they shut off the machine.

"When do I get to fight?" Frank asked Johnson.

"You won't be doing any fighting this week."

"Don't you want to see if I can?"

"We presume you know how to fight. The US Army gave you the best training it has to offer, and your record says you can do it."

"Then what are we doing here?"

"Figuring out whether you'll be able to fight our way."

They walked to a cafeteria. "Eat up," Johnson said. "You'll need to use your brain cells this afternoon."

When they finished eating, Johnson led Frank to an office and introduced him to a slim man with wavy gray hair, rimless glasses, and a warm smile that immediately put Frank at ease. His name was Dr. Rupert.

"Just out of curiosity," Frank said, "are you really a doctor?"

Rupert didn't seem to mind the question. "I have a PhD in clinical psychology from George Washington University."

"Okay then," Frank said.

For the next hour, Dr. Rupert interviewed him, not in an interrogation sort of way, but in a friendly, conversational manner. He asked open-ended questions: "Tell me about yourself." "Tell me about your family." "Which classes in school did you like or dislike?"

Frank understood the drill. The Army had trained him in how to question people. Rupert wasn't just interested in the substance of Frank's answers, but also in the way he responded. Did he give short answers or long answers? Was Frank being straightforward or playing games? Was he making eye contact? What was his body language saying? Frank knew he couldn't fool an experienced examiner, and he played it straight the whole way.

The interview took an hour, and when Rupert finished, he asked Frank to sit at a desk. "Now we're going to do some testing," Rupert said. "Three tests today and five tomorrow."

The first was what Frank guessed was an IQ test. He had to define words and solve arithmetic problems; figure out what certain things had in common; look at several strings of symbols and determine which string didn't fit; and repeat strings of numbers that Dr. Rupert read aloud, either in the same order or in reverse. It went on for an hour and a half.

They took a break and then Rupert gave Frank a pencil and a stack of blank sheets of paper. "I'm going to hand you some cards with pictures on them and ask you to copy each one as best you can."

He handed Frank a three-by-five card with a circle and a diamond-shaped figure next to it. Copying it was pretty easy. He copied eight more cards and finished in ten minutes.

"One more, Frank, and then you're done for the day."

The last test was a true-false test with 175 items. Frank finished it in twenty-five minutes.

The second morning followed the same pattern as the first: the pommel horse and balance beam, ballroom dance with Khun Suda, and the pitching machine. Johnson asked Frank to perform different moves on the beam, and Khun Suda taught him the foxtrot. He got breaking balls from the machine, just as Johnson had promised. Following lunch, he saw Dr. Rupert again.

"We'll start with another true-false test," Rupert said. This one was much longer than the one he'd taken yesterday, 550 true-false questions.

They took a quick break and then Rupert handed Frank a sheet with twenty-one questions. "Difficulty breathing?" "Racing thoughts?" Each question had the same four multiple choice answers, ranging from "not at all" to "severely." The questionnaire was easy, and Frank filled it out in a few minutes.

Rupert followed it with another questionnaire with twenty-one sets of four related statements. For each set, Frank had to choose the one he felt was most applicable to him. "I don't feel particularly guilty." "I feel guilty a good part of the time." This test was harder and took him fifteen minutes.

They took a twenty-minute break and then returned to the desk. "I'm going to show you some pictures and ask you about them," Rupert said. "There's no right or wrong answer. Just be yourself."

Rupert handed Frank a card with a picture that looked like it had been drawn in charcoal or pencil. It was some sort of farm scene with three people in it: a young woman in an old-fashioned dress, holding some books; a muscular, bare-chested man standing behind a horse, apparently plowing a field; and an older-looking woman leaning against a tree with her arms resting on her stomach, who looked like she might be pregnant.

"I want you to tell me a story about this picture," Rupert said. "What's happening at the moment shown here?" Frank made up an answer as best he could, and Rupert followed it up with more questions: "What led to the event shown in the picture?" "What are the characters thinking and feeling?" "Tell me the outcome of the event in this picture." Over the next hour, Rupert handed him nine more pictures and asked the same questions about each.

"Last test, Frank. It's similar to what we just did. I'll show you some pictures and ask you some questions about them. Just like before, there's no right or wrong answer."

Rupert put a card in front of Frank. It was seven inches by nine inches and showed a black inkblot on a white background. "What might this be?" Rupert asked.

It didn't look like anything in particular, which Frank guessed was the whole point.

"Could be a lot of things," Frank said. "Do you want one answer or more than one?"

"As many as you want to give me."

"How much detail do you want?"

"However you want to do it," Rupert said.

Rupert showed him ten cards altogether. The first five were black and white, the next two were black, red, and white, and last three were in multiple pastel colors on a white background.

When Frank finished the last card, Rupert took him through the cards again. This time around, he asked Frank to hold each one and questioned him on what he'd said about the card during the first cycle. "Where did you see that?" "What makes it look like that?"

"Can I turn it?" Frank asked.

"You can do whatever you wish."

They kept at it for nearly an hour, and Frank was relieved when they got through the last one and there were no more questions.

Rupert patted him on the shoulder. "You're done with the hard part, Frank. Tomorrow will be easy."

On the third day, they switched it up a little. They skipped the pommel horse and worked Frank on the beam for an hour. Frank and Khun Suda danced both the foxtrot and a waltz, and when they said goodbye, Frank did a perfect *wai* and thanked her profusely. The pitching machine threw mostly breaking balls, and Frank felt like he had his timing down. He was feeling good about his chances.

After lunch, Johnson led Frank to a room in a different part of the building. The room had a tile floor with a drain in the center, as if it might once have been a shower room, and it had a weird odor, disinfectant masking something else.

At one end of the room was a movie projector, and at the other end was a movie screen. In the center of the room was a table with a machine on it. One side of the machine had graph paper covered by a clear plastic screen.

"Do you recognize it?" Rupert asked.

"It's a polygraph."

"Most people would call it a lie detector."

"It doesn't detect lies," Frank said. "It measures physiological reactions. I learned to use it as part of my intelligence training."

"Well, we're not going to use it the same way you did."

"What are we going to do?"

"We're going to watch movies," Rupert said.

Frank sat down next to the table, facing the movie screen. Rupert attached a blood pressure cuff to Frank's upper arm, then wrapped two rubber tubes around his chest and abdomen, and finally put electrodes on two of his fingers.

"We'll begin momentarily," Rupert said. He turned the lights off and the projector started to whir.

The movie showed a park with people doing park things. Joggers running by. People riding bikes. A woman lying on a blanket reading a book. It was just dull, everyday activity.

Why is he showing me this?

Frank thought back to his polygraph training. He'd start out by asking control questions to establish a baseline for the subject's reactions, a standard he could use later to evaluate the subject's responses to the relevant questions. If this movie of dull, everyday stuff was the control, it meant there'd be another movie that wasn't dull, everyday stuff.

The lights came on again. "There will be a brief intermission while we change reels," Rupert said.

A minute later, the lights went off, and the projector came on.

Dios mío!

A bunch of Asian soldiers were bayoneting people tied to wood stakes. An officer would give a command and the soldiers would step forward, thrust their bayonets into the people and step back again, to be replaced by another line of soldiers. The people tied to the stakes were men, women, and children of all ages, also Asian, but different-looking from the soldiers. There was no sound, but there didn't need to be—Frank could practically hear their screams just looking at them. Before long, they were covered in blood, some with their limbs severed.

It was pretty gruesome, but not a whole lot worse than what he'd seen in El Salvador. Hell, it wasn't a whole lot worse than what he'd *done* in El Salvador.

The film went on for a couple of minutes. Rupert turned it off, switched on the lights, and removed the attachments from Frank's body.

"How'd I do?" Frank asked.

"You kept your lunch in your stomach, which puts you ahead of most people."

"I'll bet no one's ever had flat lines during that movie."

"Only one."

"Damn. When do I get to meet him?"

"Hopefully, you won't," Rupert said, "because if you do, you'll be dead within seconds."

"He's not in your group?"

"No, not anymore."

An hour later, Johnson gave Frank three thousand US dollars and drove him into Bangkok. Just as Arthur had predicted, Frank had a very good time. Three days later, Johnson retrieved him.

"Don't keep me in suspense," Frank said.

"You got good scores and checked all the boxes."

"So I'm in?"

"Not yet. You still need to meet the Man and answer one question."

They drove back to the mountains and Johnson escorted Frank to a part of the compound he hadn't seen before. Johnson opened the door and there was Professor Thornton himself, dressed to the nines, who greeted Frank cordially. They sat down on comfortable couches across from each other.

Thornton said, "I trust you've had an enjoyable experience here?"

"Yes, sir, I have."

"Everyone was quite impressed with you. Did Johnson tell you I have a question for you?"

"He did."

"Then without further ado, I shall ask it: do you enjoy killing people?"

There it was, the eighty-thousand-dollar question. He had a fifty-fifty chance of getting it right, but had no idea which answer the man wanted.

When in doubt, tell the truth.

"Not really," Frank said. "I just do my job."

Thornton's expression told Frank it was the right answer. "Thank you, Mr. Velez. I'd like to offer you a position, and hope you'll accept."

"Absolutely, sir. It'd be my honor."

"I'm delighted to hear that. Do you have any questions?"

"Right now, just one, sir. How did you come to choose me?"

"A perfectly reasonable question," Thornton said. "Over the years, we found that men with special operations experience were more likely to possess the traits and abilities we were looking for than those in the general population, no doubt because of the extreme winnowing process such services use. You were in Special Forces and your history there showed you were likely to meet our profile. And besides all that, you are fluent in Spanish."

"Begging your pardon, sir, but there aren't many Spanish-speakers in Thailand."

"You are quite correct. In Thailand, there are not, but in Chicago, there are many."

* * *

They trained Frank for the next five months, and at the end of the fifth month, they finally explained his first mission. He was to go to Chicago and gain employment with the Arroyo family, the larger of the two heroin operations in the city. Once he was entrenched, he'd learn everything he could about the organization and how it conducted its business. He would convince the Arroyos to eliminate their competitor, the Garza family. And in the last phase, Frank would do the eliminating.

A month later, Frank flew to Chicago. After a couple of weeks, he gathered that the head of the family, Javier Arroyo, had a favorite nephew, Alejandro, who ran Arroyo's garage. Frank ingratiated himself with Alejandro, a nice but not very bright guy, and one night over drinks, he asked Alejandro for a job.

"You know how to fix cars?" Alejandro asked.

"Not at all."

"Then what can you do for us?"

"I'm good at killing people," Frank said.

Alejandro burst out laughing, but stopped when he realized Frank was serious.

Frank seized the initiative. "I figure you guys have ways of checking federal service records. Check mine, and I guarantee you'll be interested."

"I have no idea what you're talking about."

"I know," Frank said, "but check it anyway."

The following week, Alejandro took Frank to Javier's office and introduced him. They searched him, satisfied themselves he was free of electronics, and then Javier opened the conversation.

"I'm meeting you because Alejandro thinks highly of you, but he says you know nothing about cars."

Frank said, "Just listen for a minute. I'm guessing you'll say you don't know what I'm talking about, and that's okay. Don't feel you even need to say it. I'll just assume it."

"I'm listening," Javier said.

"The Garzas are a thorn in your side. You could have a monopoly on dope in Chicago, cut your stuff more and make lots more money, if Garza wasn't competing with you. Problem is, you don't know how to get rid of him. Wars are expensive and bad for business. Civilians get hurt, the newspapers get the politicians fired up, and then the cops make life difficult. It's easier just to share the city with Garza."

"As you said, I don't know what you're talking about."

"I know you don't, so I'll just finish my speech and leave. There's another way to do it that maybe you haven't considered— take them out quietly. No guns, no noise, no flashy stuff, no cops breathing down your neck. We both know the Garzas don't have the manpower to fight back. You keep going until they decide Chicago's not worth it anymore. And I, Mr. Arroyo, am the man who can do it for you."

"It was nice meeting you, Señor Velez. Enjoy your stay in Chicago."

A few days later, Alejandro approached Frank.

"How do we know you're not a cop?" Alejandro asked.

"Do you think a cop would commit murder?"

Alejandro just gawked at him.

"Pick a target," Frank said. "The first one's free, but after that I expect the job."

The target turned out to be a low-ranking Garza named Eduardo. Alejandro gave Frank a photograph and an address. Frank asked one question.

"Which drugs does he like to do?"

"Cocaine," Alejandro said.

Frank spent the next five days doing his recon and growing his beard out. He hated the beard, but knew he could shave it when he finished the job.

Late in the evening of the fifth day, Frank followed Eduardo to a strip club on the northwest side, just past the city limits. He waited until Eduardo had been there for fifteen minutes, then put on a White Sox hat, walked inside, and sat down at the table next to him.

For the next two hours, Frank was Eduardo's best friend. Frank bought the drinks and lap dances, and when Eduardo looked sufficiently buzzed, Frank leaned over and whispered.

"I just got the best coke I've ever had."

"I'd like to try it," Eduardo said.

"I don't have it on me. Meet me in an hour and you can do a couple fat lines."

They arranged a meeting place, and Frank left the club. He already had the coke with him; he just didn't want people to see them leave together, and he figured an hour would be enough delay to avoid suspicion.

They met outside an abandoned warehouse near the club. Frank sat down in the passenger seat of Eduardo's car and opened a leather pouch.

"You first," Frank said. He handed Eduardo a small mirror, a bag of cocaine, a razor blade, and a dollar bill.

Eduardo expertly chopped a rock with the razor blade, arranged the powder into two lines, rolled up the bill and snorted one. As he tilted his head back for the last inhale, Frank picked up the blade and slit his throat with surgical precision.

Two days later, Frank had a job.

It didn't take long for Frank to work his way up the Arroyo ladder. Javier himself was a smart guy, but he surrounded himself with imbeciles, and Javier confided in Frank more and more as time went on. Javier chose the targets, mixing in Garza family members and Latin Eagles who distributed for the Garzas. Frank made sure he left the bodies in random places to avoid an appearance of a pattern.

Over the course of four months, Frank assassinated eight people, and the plan worked to perfection: the Garzas were reeling and their distributors were abandoning them. And when Frank felt he'd learned as much about Arroyo's operation as there was to know, he walked out of his apartment with a single small bag, took a cab to O'Hare, and flew back to Thailand.

* * *

After Frank and the rest of the group got to Chicago, he had to lie low in the mansion, lest anyone recognize him before they moved on Arroyo. But on Thursday morning, Thornton and Arthur finally gave him something to do. Thornton had reason to believe that a man named Stepanek might leave his home near Boston and come to Chicago, and they wanted to know when Stepanek left so they'd be ready.

They didn't tell Frank who the guy was or why they thought he was coming or why they even cared. He didn't need to know any of that, because it was a simple damn mission: drive by the guy's house once a day, and if he's left town, call it in and come home.

"How will I know if he's left?"

"This man is fastidious about his yard," Thornton said. "When he goes out of town, he hires a service to take care of it, and they put a sign on his lawn."

"Simple enough," Frank said.

"One more thing. Mr. Stepanek is an extraordinarily skillful man. If he is outside when you go by, do not look at him or give any indication whatever that you're interested in him. He will notice it, I assure you."

Frank flew into Logan late Thursday afternoon. On Friday morning, he rented a car and made his first pass by the house, but saw no sign.

He returned the car, went to another agency, and rented a different car. He'd make Saturday's pass in the afternoon to avoid a pattern.

Frank now sat in a perfectly clean and perfectly dull room in a chain motel, watching Saturday afternoon reruns and waiting for the clock to reach four. *I Love Lucy*'s closing credits were rolling, which meant that in thirty minutes he could make his daily drive by the house.

Next up was *Gilligan's Island*, one of Frank's favorites. He smiled at the age-old question: Ginger or Mary Ann? Frank was a Mary Ann guy.

Finally, the clock struck four, and Frank turned off the TV. He put on a blonde wig, which made him feel ridiculous, but it was necessary just in case Stepanek saw him drive by. Sunglasses and a baseball cap completed the outfit.

He drove to Stepanek's neighborhood and turned onto the street. The house was halfway down on the right. Frank made sure to keep his head facing forward.

Hot damn. There it was, right next to the driveway: "PETERSON BROS. LANDSCAPING."

Frank kept driving until he reached a gas station. He dropped four quarters in the payphone, pressed the number, and it was answered on the first ring.

"Hello?"

"Yunnan," Frank said.

"Report."

"The sign is in the yard."

"Copy. Come on home."

Chapter 32

Saturday, May 16, 1987
11:43 p.m.

Ed's stomach was hungry.

Before leaving for Chicago, he had prepared enough food to see him through the two-day trip: chicken sandwiches, peanut butter sandwiches, hard-boiled eggs, sliced peppers, and sliced apples. Ed never ate in restaurants because they were filthy places, and one never knew what they did with their food. But it was four hours since he'd last eaten, and his stomach was telling him it was hungry.

Ed did not want his stomach to be hungry. He made his living with his body, and he wanted his body to be happy so it would work properly. His body was happiest when he ate small portions several times a day, but the trip required him to drive all day and now he was out of food. He told his stomach to be patient because he'd soon arrive at his destination, and then he could make dinner.

It was slow going through Chicago's expressways, but he finally turned off the Outer Drive and headed toward an area on the North Side the locals called New Town. He'd had a job in Chicago previously and found this neighborhood to be ideal—it was so diverse and crowded that no one stood out. Ed did not want to stand out.

He drove down Broadway Street and found the type of place he was looking for:

HOTEL LEMOYNE

DAILY, WEEKLY & MONTHLY RATES

KITCHENETTES & PRIVATE BATHS

TRANSIENTS WELCOME

Ed parked his car in the garage behind the hotel and walked in with two pieces of luggage: a suitcase and a salesman sample case that was a tad over four feet high and rolled on four wheels. The clerk showed him a room and Ed inspected the kitchen area. The stove was small but adequate, and had enough pots, pans, and utensils to get him through the week. He paid cash in advance for six days.

Ed opened the suitcase and laid his clothes on the bed. He hung his shirts on one side of the closet and his trousers on the other. He stacked his underwear in a drawer. He washed his face and combed his hair. Ed felt refreshed.

Now it was time to buy groceries. He walked downstairs to the front desk and asked the clerk if there were any all-night supermarkets nearby. Luckily, one was a half-mile away. Ed had been sitting for most of the last two days and decided to walk instead of drive. He could buy just enough for one meal and carry it back to the hotel.

Ed walked out of the hotel and into the night air. The temperature had dropped, and his body felt chilled. Ed's body was unhappy when it was cold. Ed zipped his jacket all the way up and began walking. At this hour, only an occasional car drove by, and the street was deserted of pedestrians.

Ed decided to make chicken and rice. While he walked, he silently recited the ingredients and their proportions—four boneless chicken breasts, a half a clove of garlic, one cup of basmati rice—

Someone was walking a few yards behind him, matching Ed's cadence step for step.

Ed didn't see anyone else on the street, but he knew someone could appear at any moment, and people in the adjacent apartment buildings might be watching. He needed to get off this street so no one would see what was about to happen.

Halfway down the block was an alley, and Ed turned into it. The buildings on both sides were businesses, closed at this time of night, and none of their lights were on. A single dim streetlamp in the middle of the alley was the only illumination. He walked halfway to the streetlamp where the alley was darkest, and the footsteps followed him in.

Ed stopped and turned around. The man following him stopped as well, ten feet in front of Ed.

Ed examined the man. He was young, unkempt, and wore a faded green Army fatigue jacket. His right hand was inside his coat pocket.

The man looked mystified, and Ed knew why. Victims never just stopped like he had. They ran or they pleaded or they offered to give the mugger whatever he wanted. No one ever just stopped and stood mute.

The man said, "Give me your wallet."

"No," Ed said.

Now the man looked even more perplexed.

He took two tentative steps forward. Ed still did not move.

"Last chance," the man said.

Ed said nothing.

The man pulled a knife out of his coat pocket and thrust it straight at Ed's chest. Ed rose on the balls of both feet and pivoted sharply right, and as the knife passed harmlessly by, he chopped the man's knife wrist with the edge of his hand. The man yelped and dropped the knife. Ed pivoted left, jammed his fingers into the man's eyes, and kicked his leg out from under him. The man fell face down, and the instant he hit the concrete, Ed lifted his leg to waist level and brought it down again. His shoe heel smashed the man's head against the concrete, once, twice, three times, stopping only when he heard the skull shatter.

Ed took a moment to review the sequence. The pads of his fingers had not touched the man. There wouldn't be any fingerprints.

He dragged the body to the side of the alley and propped it up against a dumpster. The knife was still on the ground, and Ed was afraid children might find it and hurt themselves with it. He kicked it to the nearest sewer grate and waited until he heard it hit the water below.

Ed surveyed both ends of the alley and thought through his next move. It wouldn't be a good idea to walk back to the same street from which he'd entered. What if someone in one of the apartment buildings had seen him and the man walk in? They might wonder why Ed was returning alone. Ed decided instead to walk to the street at the other end of the alley and circle around.

Ed traversed the remaining length of the alley, and as he stepped onto the sidewalk, he wondered whether the supermarket had basmati rice. If it didn't, he could substitute Arborio.

Chapter 33

Sunday, May 17, 1987
11:37 a.m.

"Arroyo changed his mind," Arthur said. "We're on for tomorrow."

Thornton looked pleased. "Right on schedule. Have you notified the teams?"

"Yes, sir."

"Has Frank returned yet?"

"He got in last night."

"Would you ask him to come in? I'd like to learn more about the silos."

Frank walked into the library carrying a folder. He'd thought this question might come up, and he was ready for it.

"Welcome back, Frank."

"Thank you, sir."

"Given the fact that I'll be at the silos tomorrow, I was hoping you might give me more detail about them."

"Of course." Frank opened the file and arranged his notes. "The official name is the Santa Fe Railroad Grain Elevator, but everyone calls them the Damen Silos, after a nearby street."

"And their location?"

"On the southwest side of Chicago. As the crow flies, around three-and-a-half miles southwest of downtown, close enough that you can see the downtown buildings from there."

"It seems an odd place for grain silos. A historical artifact, perhaps?"

"Exactly. Back in the 1800s, Chicago was a major player in the grain trade, one of the largest in the country, and it had dozens of grain elevators and silos. The problem was that they're dangerous. When grain dust mixes with the oxygen in the air, it can become combustible and a spark can set it off. It used to happen frequently, and that's what happened here. Silos were first built on the site in 1906, then in 1932, there was an explosion and they were rebuilt. Ten years ago, it happened again—a huge explosion and fire—and they've been abandoned ever since."

Frank pulled out a pad and sketched as he spoke. "The property sits on twenty-four acres. The South Branch of the Chicago River is on one side and the Chicago Sanitary and Ship Canal is on the other."

"And what exactly is on the property?"

"There's three major sets of structures still standing. On one side, next to the river, there's an elevator building with fourteen silos attached. The silos are made of concrete, fifteen stories high, and the elevator building is even taller. There's a driveway in front, and across the driveway there's a group of thirty-five more silos. Then there's a large empty space and a warehouse on the other side. The Stevenson Expressway is just south of the property, and there's always a steady din from the traffic. It'll provide some cover."

"What condition are the structures in?"

"Very dilapidated. Lots of debris and garbage inside the buildings, graffiti everywhere."

Thornton studied the diagram. "I'm getting a sense for it. Where will we be meeting?"

"On the second floor of the elevator building. You walk in through the doorway on the ground floor, then there's a narrow stairway. It's in bad shape, so I'd recommend you walk carefully."

"And many places people can hide?"

"Yes, sir. In the buildings themselves, plus a maze of tunnels below."

"And the grounds? Is it open space?"

"Mostly, yes." Frank started drawing again. "Off to the side of the elevator building there's an area with tall weeds and hundreds of concrete blocks stacked a few feet high, almost like barricades."

"Are we likely to encounter people?"

"On a weekday afternoon, highly unlikely. On the weekends there may be a few people walking around, but you shouldn't see anyone tomorrow."

"Well done, Frank, as always. Are you looking forward to seeing your friends again?"

"I sure am," Frank said. "I'll bet they've been wondering where I went."

Chapter 34

Sunday, May 17, 1987
1:20 p.m.

Bernie finished describing his visit with Johannsen and leaned back in his chair. "What do you think we have right now?"

Marcelle considered it. "Thornton was in cahoots with the Army, training men for wet work the government didn't want anyone to know about."

"Agreed."

"Did you get the feeling Johannsen may have been exaggerating the whole secrecy thing?"

"No way. This guy was on Special Forces A-teams in the bush in Vietnam, and Sam Harrison described him as fearless. He's not someone who'd scare easily. I have no doubt he wanted to lay waste to Thornton, but even with that much motivation, he still didn't want to help me. He was genuinely afraid of anyone finding out he'd talked."

"Then here's what I think," Marcelle said. "Whatever Thornton did with the government, he knows things they wish he didn't know. He's probably beyond their reach, which means he can blackmail them and they have to play ball with him. That would explain why the feds are protecting him, and Johannsen's comment explains why he needs it. Am I on the right track?"

"Absolutely. And now we need to do the job that's right in front of us. As curious as we are about Thornton's background, we have to put that aside right now and focus on stopping the war he wants to start."

"Should we tell Mike?"

"I'd vote against it," Bernie said. "We can't prove anything yet; we just have deductions we're drawing. And if we tell him, he's liable to get mad about the government playing him, mad enough to do something rash like kick John out."

"And then we're made," Marcelle said. "The government knows we know, and we still haven't accomplished anything."

"Exactly."

"Do you think John knows about Thornton, or are they playing him, too?"

"I doubt he knows. He's a front-line agent, he just does what he's told. And he's not a bad guy—he's weird, but in a way that makes you feel for him. And speaking of John, he's going to be here soon."

Marcelle said, "On another subject, you know today's the third Sunday of the month."

"Yeah, yeah, I know."

"I'm going to call Mama B and ask if I can bring something."

"She always says no."

"It's polite to ask, anyway."

A half-hour later, John arrived for the day's driving tour. "I'll meet you back here at five o'clock," Bernie told Marcelle.

Bernie and John walked to Bernie's car. "Have you thought about where you want to go?" Bernie asked.

"Officer Larson said Thornton drove around a place called K-Town, which makes me curious about it."

"It's a major drug sales area. I'm not surprised he'd want to see it. You want to go there?"

"Please."

They got in the car and Bernie headed south. "Let me tell you about K-Town," Bernie said. "There's a big, north-south street on the West Side called Pulaski. For a mile west of there, the north-south streets start with K, like Karlov, Keeler, Kildare. For the next mile after that, you've got the L streets. That pattern keeps going through the P streets."

"And you say it's a drug area?"

"Biggest in the city, and it's concentrated around the Eisenhower Expressway, which goes east and west. There's an L train that runs in the median strip, so there's both an expressway and a train running through the area. That makes it easy for people to get in and out. It's basically an open-air drug bazaar."

"Aren't they afraid of police interference?"

"There's no way we can shut them all down. Now and then we make sweeps, but other guys take their place right away. As long as people want to buy drugs, there'll be people selling them."

They drove to the 400 block of South Karlov. Bernie slid into a parking space and pointed to two young men standing in the middle of the block. "See those two guys?"

"I do."

"Probably Vice Lords. That guy riding his bike up and down the street is the lookout. If you want some heroin, you go to the two guys. One of them takes your money, the other takes you to an alley or around the corner where they stashed the dope. They never keep the money and the dope together. Thing is, though, we're not going to see a transaction because they've already made us, and right now they're pissed because we're hurting their business."

Bernie pulled out, and they drove around Pulaski and the K and L streets, both north and south of the Eisenhower. Bernie noticed John seemed different today, not his usual blank self. The twitching was still there, but he had a different demeanor, like he was almost happy. Bernie just had to ask.

"How's your weekend been?"

"Good," John said.

"We had great weather yesterday. Did you do anything fun?"

"I went to the Lincoln Park Zoo and walked along the beach and sat on the Rocks and ate a vanilla ice cream cup."

"One of those paper cups with the wood spoon?"

"Uh-huh."

"They're good, aren't they?"

"Yes, very good."

This information was a revelation to Bernie. The guy actually did something normal. Maybe he was human after all, and now Bernie regretted how he'd treated him. "John, I feel like I haven't been real nice to you, and I'm sorry."

"It's all right. I have enough self-awareness to know I'm strange and it puts people off. People just don't know how to deal with me."

Now Bernie felt even worse, but he didn't know how to respond, so they drove in silence back to Area Six.

When they arrived, Marcelle was standing in front of the building, holding flowers in one hand and waving them over with the other. She looked worried. Bernie pulled up, and he and John got out.

"What's going on?" Bernie asked her.

"Don't get mad."

"That is a hell of a way to start a conversation."

She addressed John. "Every Sunday, Bernie goes to his mother's apartment for dinner, and the third Sunday of the month, I go with him. I called Mama B and asked her if I could bring something, you know, just like I always do—"

Now Bernie got worried.

"—and I told her about John being here from out of town, and working with us, and how he's living all by himself—"

"Oh, no," Bernie said, "you didn't—"

"—and she said he has to come with us."

John's head started jerking violently—left-center, left-center, left-center—and then he began stammering.

"I-I-I-I-I-I-I-I—"

Marcelle put her hand on his shoulder. "John, do you want to lie down? Do you need a doctor?"

He clenched his fists and took deep breaths, eventually calming himself, and the jerking subsided. "I can't go."

"Why not?"

"Because I have a high level of generalized anxiety, which is exacerbated by social situations because I am socially awkward and occasionally inappropriate."

"Says who?" Bernie said.

"The psychologist my parents sent me to."

"Well, he was a quack," Marcelle said. "Look, you don't need to worry about making chitchat. Mama B is an expert at carrying a conversation. Just say yes to whatever she says, and you'll be fine."

"But what if I want to say no?"

"No one," she said, "says no to Mama B."

Chapter 35

Sunday, May 17, 1987
5:35 p.m.

Bernie parked a few doors down from his mother's apartment building. When he walked back to his trunk to retrieve a bottle of Chianti, Marcelle leaned down and whispered in John's ear: "She's going to tell him he doesn't look so good."

They walked up to the second-floor apartment, and Mama B was ecstatic to see them. She hugged Marcelle, told her how pretty she looked, and gratefully accepted the flowers. Next up was John. "I'm so glad you came," she said, and she hugged him like a long-lost relative.

"Johnshepardpleasedtomeetyou."

Then she turned to Bernie.

"You don't look so good."

"I'm fine, Ma."

"You look like you got a temperature."

"I don't have a temperature, Ma."

"Everyone sit down in the front room. I'll be right back."

She returned carrying a tray with three glasses of orange juice, passed them out, and stared at Bernie until he'd drunk half of it.

"Now, you'll feel better."

"What's that noise?" Bernie asked. "Is the toilet still running?"

"Yeah, it's still running."

"Did you tell the landlord?"

"No, I didn't tell him. He's a busy man. I don't want to be a bother."

"Why won't you let me fix it for you?"

"I'm afraid if you do chores when you come here, you won't want to come back."

He stood up and headed to the bathroom with Mama B following behind, both of them bickering all the way.

John looked alarmed.

"Don't worry," Marcelle said, "they peck at each other all the time. It's how they show they love each other."

John walked to a bookcase filled with family photographs. One of them, in faded black and white, showed a man and a woman in wedding clothing in a studiously formal pose. Another showed an older version of the same man and a young Bernie, both wearing leather aprons, standing in front of a shop. Behind them was a neon sign:

BERNARDELLI SHOE REPAIR
We Fix Your Shoes With Old World Care

A minute later, the sound of the running toilet stopped. Bernie returned to the front room while Mama B walked to the kitchen.

Marcelle said, "Can I help, Mama B?"

"No, sweetie, you sit. You've been running around all day catching murderers."

Bernie walked up to the bookcase, and John handed him the photograph. "You and your father?"

"Yeah. I'd guess I was twelve or thirteen here."

"Did you work with him?"

"Every Saturday, from the age of nine until I joined the Army. I started out shining shoes, then graduated to soles and heels. Got pretty good at it, but not as good as Pop. He was the kind of guy who didn't know the meaning of 'good enough.' You either did it perfectly or you did it over. Back then, people appreciated craftsmanship, and everybody in the whole area came to his shop for shoeshines and repairs. He worked six days a week, never took a vacation."

"What happened to him?"

"He developed Parkinson's in his mid-sixties. The tremors got so bad he couldn't do the job as well as he thought he should, and he had trouble standing all day. Three years ago, he sold the shop and retired. Six months later, he had a stroke and died. Not working killed him."

"Is that why you work so hard?"

"I don't know why I work so hard."

Mama B called them into the dining room, and no sooner had they begun eating than she turned her attention to John. "I understand you're working with William and Marcelle?"

"Yes, ma'am."

"And where are you from?"

"Originally from a small town in Indiana, but now I live in Washington, DC."

"*Washington.* I've never been. I imagine it's very interesting. What do you do for a living?"

"I'm an accountant."

"An *accountant!*" She said it as though he'd just announced he was the Archbishop of Chicago. "We have a dear family friend, Mario Torelli, who's also an accountant. A wonderful man, and so successful. His son and William were practically brothers. Did you go to college to be an accountant?"

"Yes, ma'am, I did."

She stared at Bernie. "Some people go to college."

Bernie looked up at the ceiling, but said nothing.

For the next hour, Mama B ferreted out every last detail of John's life. She almost cried when he told her his parents had died.

She clapped her hands when he told her he'd graduated from college with honors. At the end, she looked at John's plate.

"You didn't eat anything."

"I just ate more than I did the last three days put together."

"Well, if you don't mind my saying so, you look like you could stand some more weight." She scanned the table, as if trying to remember something. "I almost forgot the dessert."

She disappeared into the kitchen, came back with cannoli, and distributed them two to a person. "I made these myself. I hope you like them."

John looked at his cannoli like a mountain climber facing Mount Everest.

For the second time that day, Marcelle leaned over and whispered in his ear. "You have to eat it. She won't let you leave until you do."

When they finished, Mama B surveyed the table. "No one was hungry today, there's so much left over." She looked at John again, apparently concerned he hadn't eaten enough. "Here, I'll make you a plate."

The plate turned out to be a gallon container of pasta that weighed a good five pounds. "Now you'll have something to eat if you get hungry later."

Bernie, Marcelle, and John cleared the table and helped clean up. Marcelle and Bernie said their goodbyes, and then Mama B addressed John. "I hope you liked the meal."

"Yes, ma'am, very much." He stopped, looking like he was struggling to say something. "I want to tell you something, but I don't know how to say it."

"However you say it, I'm sure I'll understand."

"It's been a long time since I had dinner with a family. I enjoyed being here. It made me happy."

"I am so glad to hear that. You'll come back sometime?"

"I would like to," John said.

Chapter 36

Monday, May 18, 1987
7:57 a.m.

Marcelle and Bernie were discussing the dinner at Mama B's when Bernie got a look on his face that Marcelle recognized. She said, "That's the look you get when you have a crazy idea."

"This one's only half-crazy."

She folded her arms and leaned back in her chair. "Go ahead."

"Like I said, John's not a bad guy. You saw that last night. He's just unusual and awkward and lonely, and he looks like he could use a friend. And I was thinking—what's the harm in being nice to him? If he knows what the government's up to and he's playing us, then we're no worse off, and if he doesn't know, then we might make him an ally."

He turned his palms upward. "Is it a crazy idea?"

"Like you said, only half-crazy. You know what else I think?"

"What?"

"You're as tough as they get, but you've got a soft spot for people in need—and right now you're looking at John as someone in need."

"Is that so bad?"

"No," she said, shaking her head. "It's not bad at all."

* * *

When John arrived, Bernie asked him where he wanted to go.

"What's another major drug area?" John asked.

"Yesterday, we saw some of the West Side. Want to go to the North Side today?"

"All right."

"The area we're going to is called Uptown. It's a depressed area—lots of poor, Southern Appalachian whites, lots of drugs, lots of alcohol abuse."

They pulled out of the parking lot, and Bernie decided it was time to broach the subject.

"John, do you mind if I talk to you about something?"

"I don't mind."

"Last night, when Marcelle said my mom wanted you to come over, your reaction—well, it concerned me. If you don't want to talk about it, that's okay, but I'd like to help if I can."

John's head-twitching accelerated, and Bernie wished he hadn't said anything. John just sat there and twitched, looking out the passenger window like he usually did, saying nothing. Bernie figured he didn't want to discuss it, but then John surprised him.

"I know I'm different," John said. "I've been painfully aware of it ever since I was a child. Do you know what my classmates called me?"

"What?"

"Shakin' Shepard."

"I'm sorry, John."

"It's not your fault. The point is, I know I'm different and I've tried to adapt the best I can. Work isn't so bad—I have a job to do, and everyone else does too, and when I focus on my job, I function acceptably. But social situations are a mystery to me, and that's why I reacted the way I did when Marcelle brought up dinner at your mother's house."

"What's so mysterious about social situations?"

"People speak in a secret language I don't understand, which makes it difficult to interact appropriately with them. Do you laugh at jokes, Bernie?"

"I do if they're funny."

"I don't," John said, "because I don't understand humor. I also don't understand metaphors or sarcasm. I'm aware such things exist, but I can't process them."

"But you're good at your job," Bernie said.

"Because it's straightforward, black and white. There are rules I can follow to determine how to characterize a transaction. But in a social context, I never know if someone means what they say. I misunderstand them and say something inappropriate, they don't know how to respond, and then my tics get worse and it's all very awkward. So I try to avoid socializing altogether, and that's why I panicked yesterday."

"Maybe I can teach you the secret language," Bernie said.

John turned and looked at him, not all the way to eye contact, but as close as John ever got to it. "No one's ever offered to do that before."

"Well, I'm offering now."

"I would like that," John said.

"Okay. Let's say we're eating lunch. I take a few bites, I throw my fork down, I push the plate aside, and I say, 'Boy, was *that* ever delicious.' Now tell me—did I like my lunch?"

"You thought it was delicious."

"No, John, I thought it stunk."

"How am I supposed to know that?"

"Because it's not just what I said, it's how I said it and what I did. I wouldn't stop eating and push my plate aside if I liked it."

"Then why did you say it was delicious?"

"Because . . . hmmm." He thought about it and drew a blank. "I don't know."

"See? You don't even know why you do it, so how am I supposed to realize you didn't mean it? Wouldn't it be easier just to say what you mean?"

"I'm sorry, John, that was a poor example. We'll work on it, okay? By the time you leave Chicago, you'll understand the secret language."

"The sooner the better," John said. "I met a woman."

The statement startled Bernie. "You met . . . a *woman*?"

"Yes."

"Well, that's good, John. Tell me about her."

"What do you want to know?"

"Start with her name."

"Her name is Mary Ellen Rodocker, and she's from North Platte, Nebraska, and she has two older sisters and an older brother, and she works in the Loop and likes to cook."

"She sounds nice, John."

"Oh, yes," he said, his head vigorously bouncing up and down. "She's *very* nice."

"How'd you meet her?"

"She walked up to me and showed me how to eat the ice cream I bought at the Rocks."

That last bit piqued Bernie's curiosity. "*She* approached *you*?"

"Yes. Is that good or bad?"

"It's good. Just a little unusual, though."

"I think she's looking for a boyfriend," John said.

"Even better. Did you get her number?"

"Her social security number?"

"No, John, her phone number."

"No. Was I supposed to?"

"Well, it's kind of customary if you want to see her again. How else will you contact her?"

"I don't need to. She's coming to my apartment on Friday evening to make meat loaf."

Bernie's opinion of John shot up several notches. "She's going to your apartment to make dinner?"

"Yes. I'm going to buy the food, though."

"How'd you work up the nerve to ask her to do that?"

"I didn't ask her. She volunteered."

"She just up and offered to go to your place and make dinner?"

"Yes. Is that good?"

"John, it's not just good, it's great. If she wants to fix you dinner, it means she wants to impress you, and that means she really likes you."

"Are you sure?"

"Positive."

John looked happy for a moment but then went to looking worried. "I don't know how to act."

Bernie nodded sagely. "Now that's something I can help you with. If you want to make a good impression on a woman, there are three rules you need to follow."

"Should I be writing this down?"

"No, I think you'll remember. The first rule is, you have to listen to her. Men usually don't listen well; they just want to take action. Even if it's the most ordinary thing in the world, listen real well and ask follow-up questions. 'Oh, your friend just changed her hair color? What was it before?'"

"Mary Ellen said I'm a good listener."

"I agree," Bernie said. "You'll be great at it. Now, the second rule is that they always like flowers. Doesn't need to be for an occasion. In fact, it's even better when it's not an occasion. Give her flowers when she comes over."

"Like what?"

"Go to a florist that afternoon. Tell them she's coming over for dinner and it's a first date. They'll fix up something nice and put it in a vase. Just set it on your table and tell her they're for her. I guarantee she'll like them."

"I can do that. What's the third rule?"

"They want you to smell good."

"Should I wear cologne?"

"No, no, she'll probably be wearing perfume and you don't want to clash. Just wash your hair and shower and put on clean clothes."

"I was already going to do that."

"See? You're a natural. You'll be fine."

John looked more relaxed now. "Can I ask you a question?"

"Sure."

"Are you my friend, Bernie?"

Bernie thought back to what John's boss had said about him: *the strangest person he's ever met.*

"Yes, John," Bernie said, "I'm your friend."

Chapter 37

Monday, May 18, 1987
2:45 p.m.

Pickett wore a gray suit, a white wig, and sunglasses when he and McNally walked into the library.

"How do I look?"

"You're the spitting image of me," Thornton said, "or at least you will be, behind tinted windows."

"Thank you, sir."

"Arthur and I will go ahead now. We'll meet you back here later."

Thornton and Arthur walked to the garage, and Arthur opened the rear door of one of the small cars. Thornton lay down on the back seat below the windows.

Arthur said, "Will you be all right there, sir?"

"I think my old bones can manage it for a few minutes."

Arthur shut the rear door, got in the driver's seat, and pulled out.

Across the road, Officers Matic and Jackson saw the gate open. It was one of the small cars, with just a driver and no passengers. That morning, Thornton's man had told Larson and Herrera that Thornton would leave the mansion around four o'clock, so there was still an hour and a half to go until Thornton's daily drive.

The car turned onto Route 31, and when it was out of sight of the police officers, Thornton sat up. He stretched, made himself comfortable, and then picked up his radio and turned it on.

"Team One check."

There was a moment of static followed by a response. "One is ready."

"How many do they have?"

"Four hiding, plus the two."

Thornton did a quick mental calculation. "You'll have forty-five minutes to deal with the four after I enter the doorway."

"Forty-five, copy."

"Base out."

Thornton put the radio down and settled in for the rest of the ride.

Chapter 38

Monday, May 18, 1987
4:37 p.m.

The silos rose from the ground like the ruins of an ancient civilization, forty-nine gigantic concrete cylinders and a concrete elevator building that towered over them, silently ruling a desolate landscape. For decades, they were majestic symbols of Chicago's regional dominance in the grain trade, but now they were weathered and decaying, defaced by spray paint, relics of a bygone age. Where once they'd been a hive of commerce, today they looked lonely and forsaken, and so foreign to their surroundings that they seemed an illusion.

Arthur stopped the car near the entrance to the elevator building, the tires crunching against broken concrete. As planned, Arroyo's car was already there.

Arthur stepped out of the car with a hand-held metal detector and a radio. Thornton took the driver's seat with the engine still running, ready to leave if anything went awry.

"Good luck, Arthur."

"Thank you, sir."

Arthur climbed the stairs to the second floor, and they were as treacherous as Frank had said. Garbage and chunks of bricks and broken concrete were strewn all over. He walked gingerly, because he deliberately avoided holding on to the handrail. When he reached the second floor, he saw Javier Arroyo and his assistant, Fernando, waiting for him. As they'd agreed, Arthur walked in with both arms raised.

"Your boss said we can check you first," Javier said.

Arthur handed the metal detector to Fernando, who waved it over a metal table to make sure it worked. "Do it fast," Arthur said. "If I don't call him in the next sixty seconds, he takes off with your dope."

Fernando passed the wand over Arthur without incident. Arthur did the same with the other two men.

Arthur switched on the radio. "All clear, sir."

Thornton shut off the engine. He put on gloves, got out of the car, and hoisted the satchel with Arroyo's heroin over his shoulder. He started for the entrance, but stopped when his eye caught some graffiti on the pavement, spray-painted in blue:

I MIGHT AS WELL BE DEAD
BUT I COULD KILL YOU INSTEAD

Thornton couldn't help but smile at it. Life was full of little ironies.

He walked inside to the stairwell and held onto the handrail with his gloved hands as he went up. When he was just below the landing, he stopped and removed the gloves, put them in his pocket, and ascended the remaining stairs without touching the rail.

Thornton entered the room with his hands raised, and Fernando passed the wand over him. Thornton's wristwatch was the only thing that registered.

"You may take the bag," he told Fernando, and then he looked at Javier. "As promised, Mr. Arroyo."

They sat down across from each other on rickety tables, Thornton and Arthur on one and the Arroyos on the other. As

Thornton sat down, he casually pulled his watch down to his wrist, past his shirt cuff. Javier opened the bag, inspected its contents, shut it, and placed it on the floor.

"I regret we have to meet under these circumstances," Thornton told Javier, "but I'm glad to have the opportunity to speak with you directly."

"I'll say this much. You guys have balls of steel, stealing our stuff."

"As I'm sure you'd agree, anything with the potential of high reward always comes with high risk. Each of us has prospered in an industry filled with risk, and I hope we can join forces to our mutual benefit."

For the next forty-five minutes, Thornton and Javier played the roles of businessmen exploring a potential alliance. They discussed heroin supply and purity, pricing, smuggling, manpower, wholesale and retail distribution, and profit sharing. Pretending he was considering a comment from Javier, Thornton looked down and inconspicuously checked his watch. They were at forty-eight minutes, and the conversation was at a good breaking point.

"I'll consider what you've said and discuss it with my superior," Thornton said, "and I trust you'll do the same with your colleagues?"

"Sure," Javier said. "Your instructions said you and your man would leave first."

"And we shall. Thank you for the meeting, and I hope it will be the first of many." Thornton lifted his hand toward Arthur and they departed.

Javier and Fernando sat still, and a minute later, they heard two gunshots. "Just like we planned," Javier said. He bent down and spit on the floor. *"Pinche pendejo."*

They laughed and congratulated each other. Fernando picked up the satchel and they stepped out the doorway.

Two men swung out from behind the wall, their knives beginning a choreographed sequence of slashes. Their arms and hands moved in graceful, balletic curves, each slash flowing seamlessly into the next, their motions in perfect unison like synchronized swimmers of death. A diagonal slash across the torso from shoulder to hip, and then another, crisscrossing the first; a lateral slash across the stomach from left to right and then reversing into a parallel cut in the opposite direction; and finally, a straight thrust deep into the top of the abdomen.

Javier and Fernando staggered, wide-eyed, their mouths vainly trying to form sounds. Lattimore and his partner stepped back and watched indifferently as the men went through their last throes.

They wiped their blades on the men's shirts. "Thornton wants us to leave the bodies and the dope here," Lattimore said.

His partner looked at him in disbelief. "This stuff's worth a fortune."

"Thornton said it's shitty dope and not to sully our hands with it. Besides, by tomorrow no one in Chicago will buy it."

They walked downstairs, where Thornton and Arthur waited for them. Four more dead Arroyos were arranged in a row, propped up with their backs against the wall.

"Well done, gentlemen," Thornton said. "Did they exit the room?"

"Yes, sir."

"Then I kept my word. They walked out of the room with every gram."

Thornton and Arthur returned to the car, and even before the wheels were rolling, Thornton picked up the radio. "Team Two check."

"Two is ready."

"You are green."

* * *

The '84 Impala with tinted windows rolled lazily into Lakeview Auto Repair and stopped. Alejandro Arroyo and his three mechanics were sitting on a couch watching television. One of the mechanics waved at the car and said, "We're closed."

The car's doors opened simultaneously. Johnson and Frank slid out, each with an H&K MP5SD3 pointed at the men, who froze instantly.

"Everyone stay real still," Johnson said. He walked to within ten feet of the men and stood before the middle of the couch.

Frank backed up to the overhead door switch, hit it, and the door came rumbling down. He walked to the back and checked the restroom, the office, and the storage area, then returned and took his position next to Johnson. "All clear."

The four men on the couch stared at Frank, stunned and furious.

"Hey, guys," Frank said. "Long time, no see."

"Which one is Alejandro?" Johnson asked.

"The guy with the jewelry and the big hair."

Johnson stepped over to Alejandro and pointed the subgun at him. "I've got good news and bad news, Alejandro. The bad news is, Javier's dead, along with his assistant and the other four guys that went with them. All dead. The good news is, you're now the head of the Arroyo family in Chicago."

"*Chupa mi verga, maricón,*" said one of the men.

"What did he say, Frank?"

"You're not gonna like it."

"Say it politely."

"He said you're homosexual, and he wants you to perform oral sex on him."

"Really?" Johnson seemed more amused than angry. He sidestepped to the man and put the muzzle of the gun against the man's forehead. "I don't think so," he said, and he pressed the trigger. The gun emitted a slight pop, and a 147-grain bullet entered the man's skull and exited the other side, spraying bone fragments, brain tissue, and blood onto the man next to him, who promptly pissed his pants.

Johnson stepped back in front of Alejandro and put the gun's muzzle an inch in front of his eyes. "Your friend died because he thought I wasn't serious. Do you think I'm serious?"

"Yeah, I think you're serious."

"Good. Now listen well, because I will not repeat myself. Starting at noon tomorrow, the Arroyos will no longer sell heroin in Chicago. That'll give you enough time to get the word out, and don't think we won't be able to tell the difference between yours and ours, because we can. Noon tomorrow, that's the end. If anyone sells Arroyo dope after that, we'll kill whoever sold it and then we'll kill you. Do not make the mistake of thinking we won't find you. We'll put a price on your head, and you won't survive twenty-four hours. Remember this, Alejandro: the Arroyos are gangsters, we're a military operation, and there is a shitload of difference between the two."

Johnson waited until he saw comprehension on Alejandro's face.

"Do you still think I'm serious?"

"Yes," Alejandro said. "I still think you're serious."

Chapter 39

Monday, May 18, 1987
5:48 p.m.

"Six bodies at the Damen Silos," said the 9-1-1 caller. His voice was muffled and pitched high to prevent identification, but his message was clear and concise.

Within minutes, a patrolman drove in and saw four bodies just inside the entrance of the elevator building. Rather than venturing inside and possibly contaminating the scene, he called in and requested a patrol supervisor, a detective, and forensic services personnel.

Detective Alan Urbaniak of Area Four arrived at 6:45. He found two additional bodies on the second-floor landing, and visually identified one of them as Javier Arroyo, reputedly the head of the Arroyo drug trafficking organization. That set in motion another chain of events that led to Bernie, Marcelle, Mike, and John being notified.

Bernie picked up Marcelle on his way there and they arrived at 8:10, before the others. Yellow barrier tape was strung around the outer perimeter of the crime scene along the side street, the buildings, and the chain link fence. A CPD patrol car with lights flashing was parked outside the yellow tape, blocking the road that led to the silos, with two patrolmen standing next to it. Red barrier tape marked off the crime scene's inner perimeter around the elevator building and its connected silos.

Going to someone else's crime scene was like going to their house. You didn't just open their door and walk right in; you rang the bell and waited to be invited in.

Bernie pulled up to the patrol car. One of the patrolmen came over to his window, and Bernie handed over his and Marcelle's credentials. "Who's the assigned detective?" he asked.

"Urbaniak."

"I know Alan. Ask him if we can go through."

The patrolman radioed in, had a brief conversation, and bent back down to Bernie's window. "You can drive in. Urbaniak will meet you at the red tape."

One of the patrolmen moved their car out of the way while the other lifted the tape. Bernie drove to the inner perimeter. He and Marcelle got out and Alan Urbaniak arrived a minute later. They spoke while standing on opposite sides of the red tape.

"Hell of a mess," Bernie said.

Alan shrugged. "Lots of bodies, but I've seen messier ones."

Marcelle and Bernie explained their interest in the Arroyos, and Alan briefed them quickly. Javier and Fernando, the two upstairs, had been slashed to death and were unarmed. The four downstairs were Arroyos as well, all armed, but their guns had not been drawn. Of those four, three had had their necks cut, as Alan put it, "by someone who knew what he was doing."

"What about the fourth guy?" Marcelle asked.

Alan shook his head. "The forensics folks are still in there, but I didn't see any signs of trauma on that guy. The ME will have to tell us."

Marcelle and Bernie looked at each other, but said nothing.

"Can we go in?" Bernie asked.

"Not yet."

"C'mon, Alan, you're not gonna pull 'assigned detective' on us, are you?"

Alan visibly bristled. "Look, I've got a building that's been abandoned for ten years. God knows how many people have walked through there over the years, leaving footprints, handprints, fingerprints. The only thing we've got going for us is that there's so much dirt and dust in there that we can try to isolate the most recent disturbances, but that means limiting how many people go in and coordinating their movements."

"When do you think you'll have enough locked down that we can go in?"

"Sun's already set, so we're on artificial light now. Let's say nine tomorrow morning."

"That'll work. Do you have an estimate of time since death?"

"The evidence techs are taking rectal temps now. We'll have a better idea after we get them to the lab, but when I got here at 6:45, I didn't even see rigor."

"Pretty fresh," Marcelle said, "no more than two hours before you got here."

"I agree. And speaking of that, have you listened to the 9-1-1 tape?"

Marcelle and Bernie shook their heads.

"Someone talking in a weird voice through a handkerchief or something. Obviously had the presence of mind to make sure it'd be hard to ID him, but that's not the strangest part. Usually when someone calls in a body—much less six bodies—they're freaking out, right?"

"Yeah."

"This guy was completely calm, sounded like he was reporting a stray cat."

"You think he was the offender?" Marcelle asked.

"I do, and for another reason, too. You may get a few people exploring this place on the weekends, but hardly anybody comes by during the week. What are the odds that some dude just happens to walk by here on a weekday and just happens to see the bodies within minutes after they died?"

"I see your point, but why in the world would he call it in?"

"I have no idea," Alan said.

Bernie told Alan that Mike and John were coming, and Alan agreed to let them through. "You mind if we hang around a little while?" Bernie asked.

"As long as you stay behind my red tape, you can hang around as long as you want."

Alan returned to the elevator building. A few minutes later, Mike and John arrived, and Marcelle brought them up to speed on the conversation with Alan Urbaniak.

"Looks like Thornton's started his war," Mike said, "so let me tell you what I learned on the way over. Thornton's tails today were Matic and Jackson. They said Thornton and his driver left the property at four, drove around the North Side for a while, and were back at the mansion at six-thirty. Pretty good alibi, I'd say."

"Now it makes sense," Bernie said.

They all waited for him.

"Thornton wanted an alibi," Bernie said, "and being under observation by two cops is a pretty damn good one, except for one thing. He needs to be able to prove the deaths occurred while he was riding around—and that's why he had his guy call it in so fast. Thornton knows that the more time that elapses before bodies are examined, the harder it is to estimate time of death. He wanted us to be able to make an accurate estimate so he could perfect his alibi."

"Or maybe it wasn't Thornton to begin with," John said.

"It was Thornton for sure."

"What makes you think so?"

"Because this is how he kills, isn't it? No guns, does everything by hand. Scares the hell out of the enemy and all that crap."

"How do you know?" John asked.

"The whole eastern hemisphere knows it, so how come the United States government doesn't?"

"You should ask the United States government."

"That's exactly what I'm doing," Bernie said.

"I'm only one man."

"Everyone settle down," Mike said, and he looked at Bernie. "John asked a good question. How *do* you know all this?"

Bernie pressed his lips together and avoided Mike's stare.

Mike said, "Is this one of those times when it's best I not know?"

"Something like that," Bernie said.

"What do you think?" Mike asked Marcelle.

"I agree with Bernie."

"Okay. I'm tired of us spinning our wheels. Let's get a search warrant for Thornton's mansion."

"You will do no such thing," John said.

Mike's face turned red as he spun around to John. "We've now got six dead Arroyos on top of the dead Garzas and Latin Eagles, City Hall's breathing down my neck, and you're blocking me? Are you here to help us or Thornton?"

"Perhaps it's you who should settle down."

"You better have a damned good reason for this position."

"I do have a good reason," John said. "First it was Garzas and Latin Eagles who were killed. Now it's Arroyos being killed. The most logical conclusion is that they're at war with each other, and you've got no probable cause to get a warrant issued for Thornton." John stopped and glanced at Marcelle and Bernie. "At least none your detectives will swear to."

"This is Chicago," Mike said. "We can get a warrant."

"Even if you got one, it wouldn't do you any good to make a search. Whoever killed these people obviously was experienced, and while we're standing here, they're burying their clothes and knives. You won't find a thing."

"Can't hurt to try," Mike said.

"No, it can hurt to try, and that's why I don't want to do it. After you find nothing, Thornton's high-priced lawyers will accuse us of harassment and sue the city."

"He'll lose."

"Even if he does, it'll still cost a lot to defend. The city's government won't appreciate the bills it has to pay. They'll be angry with you and your department, and they'll make sure the judges demand more the next time you want a warrant against Thornton."

Mike had no response, so John continued. "When we ultimately go for a warrant, we need to make sure we have a clean record. I will not jeopardize this case with a premature, foolhardy search."

Mike looked at Marcelle and Bernie. Both remained silent.

"Okay, John," Mike said, "you win this one. But we've got a war here, and we are way behind. We can't devote six men to chasing Thornton and keeping him safe. I am pulling them off as of now."

Chapter 40

Tuesday, May 19, 1987
8:32 a.m.

Rifle ranges are always in out-of-the-way places. Ed had been driving for an hour and still had an hour to go.

When Ed got the job, he knew it would be difficult, no doubt the reason his employer was paying far more than his usual fee. For the first time in his career, he'd been assigned a subject who knew him and could recognize him, which meant he could not get close enough to kill the subject by hand. It would be one of the rare jobs where he'd have to use his rifle.

Ed finally arrived at the range. There were only two cars in the parking area. Ed parked as far away as he could. He opened his salesman sample case and transferred his rifle to a cloth rifle case. He put on his backpack, picked up his rifle case and shooting mat, and walked in.

The clerk was a bored-looking young man. "It's twenty dollars, and you can shoot till sunset."

Ed paid him. He looked at the range and saw only one person on it.

"He's been here a while," the clerk said. "Probably leaving soon, and then you've got it to yourself. When you want to put up a target, get together with him and the two of you agree to call the range cold."

Ed put on his earmuff hearing protectors, walked onto the range, and surveyed it. The shooting pad was concrete, the wood target frames one hundred yards away. The field was flat and covered with grass and dirt. Trees lined the sides of the range sporadically. Behind the target frames were tall weeds that would be useful wind indicators.

Ed hoped the other man would leave soon, so he kept his rifle cased. He sat down and began watching the wind.

Most people gave little thought to wind, unless it was blowing so hard that it was dangerous or interfered with what they wanted to do, and because they took the wind for granted, they knew nothing of its mysteries. But Ed knew that a precision rifle shot at distance required patient observation of the wind's idiosyncrasies at any given time and place—how it ebbed and flowed, moved in cycles, changed direction, and was diverted by vegetation and topography.

He watched the wind for a good twenty minutes, oblivious to the muffled but still audible noise of the other man's rifle. He estimated the wind was blowing between five and ten miles per hour, moving in an arc from 6:00 to 9:00, and in the 9:00 position its velocity would remain steady long enough to take a shot.

The other man set his rifle down and walked up to Ed. "I'm done for the day. You mind if we go cold?"

"Suits me," Ed said.

While the other man retrieved his target, Ed walked forward and stapled a blank, letter-sized sheet of white paper to a target frame. There were no bullseyes or other aiming points on it. Human beings did not wear bullseyes.

The other man left, and Ed uncased his rifle and took his cartridge box out of his backpack. He unrolled his shooting mat and arranged it at a slight angle to the target. He set his stapler on the concrete pad and removed a ruler from the backpack. Now the backpack had nothing in it but old clothes.

Ed massaged the backpack until its shape was suitable as a rifle rest. He set it in front of the mat and got into a prone position with the rifle, its forearm resting on the backpack and its butt nestled in precisely the correct position in his shoulder pocket.

He put his cheek on the stock, adjusting its location so that he had a complete image through the scope. Through years of practice, his cheek had learned to recognize when it was on the stock at precisely the correct angle and with precisely the correct pressure, and once it found its memorized position, it would be welded to the stock for the duration.

Ed looked through his scope at the target. He adjusted his body's position until the intersection of the scope's crosshairs was exactly where he wanted it. His point of aim was slightly below the center of the target and a half-inch to the right. Ed wanted to shoot the 9:00 wind condition, and he knew that a right-to-left wind would move the bullet left and upward.

The object of this endeavor was to verify where the bullet would go when he shot from a cold bore. The rifle's barrel behaved differently when it was cold than it did when it was warm, and when it came time to take the money shot, the bore would be cold. The last time he had shot the rifle, he had cleaned it at the range and shot three fouling shots through the bore, because a clean bore adversely affected the bullet's path.

Satisfied with his position, Ed took a round out of his cartridge box, pressed it into the magazine, and closed the bolt, thus chambering the round. He wrapped his right hand around the grip, his index finger pointing forward and laying against the side of the stock. He looked through the scope and saw the crosshairs oscillating slightly up and down, as they always did at the beginning.

Ed breathed slowly, deeply, all the way down to his stomach. As he inhaled, the crosshairs moved down, and as he exhaled, they moved back up again.

His heart rate slowed, and the crosshairs' movement was almost imperceptible. Through his left eye, he looked at the movements of the weeds. He was waiting for the 9:00 condition, and soon it would be time to take the shot.

Ed placed the pad of his right index finger on the trigger.

He was at the most delicate point of the shot process. His brain disliked the noise of a rifle shot and the thump of recoil, and if his brain knew when the shot would break, it would make his body flinch in anticipation and thus throw the bullet askew. He had to trick his brain, and he did so by applying such gradual pressure to the trigger that his brain could not predict when the shot would occur.

The weeds were at 6:00, but he saw them start to move through the arc he'd observed earlier. He exhaled and held his breath, the crosshairs were where he wanted them, his finger applied more pressure to the trigger, he saw the weeds shift to 9:00—

The shot broke and the rifle recoiled, and in the split-second before he lost the sight picture, he saw the crosshairs' position on the target and how they moved in recoil, and he called the shot good.

Ed waited until the rifle settled down from its recoil, and looked through the scope. The bullet hole was around three inches above the center of the target, right where he wanted it. He opened the bolt to extract and eject the spent case, pulling the bolt back gently so the case would land on his mat and not hit the concrete. Ed wanted to re-use his cases, and a dented case would have to be scrapped.

Now it was time to wait. Ed wanted to confirm his scope's zero by shooting two more rounds, but he had to wait until the bore was cold again. He waited twenty minutes, his body maintaining its position throughout.

He loaded two more rounds into the magazine and closed the bolt. He repeated the process he'd followed twenty minutes earlier, and when the time was right, he took two quick shots in succession. Two of the bullet holes were touching, and the third was just above them. He estimated the group size at four-tenths of an inch. Ed was happy.

He pulled the target from the frame, took it back to his mat, and put his ruler on it. The center of the three-shot group was 2.7 inches above the target's center. With his scope zeroed this way, his bullets would never deviate more than three inches above or three inches below his point of aim, all the way out to 283 yards. Within that distance, he could hold center without having to compensate for trajectory, because a six-inch kill zone was plenty good enough for a human being.

Chapter 41

Tuesday, May 19, 1987
8:49 a.m.

Bernie picked up Marcelle and John at Area Six. On the way to the silos, they stopped to get bagels and coffee for Alan Urbaniak. It was Alan's crime scene, and they'd have to earn their way in.

They again met Alan at the red inner perimeter tape. Marcelle introduced John, who was wearing his IRS credentials. Bernie handed over the bagels and coffee.

"I know what it's like to work a scene all night," Bernie said. "Can you talk right now?"

"Sure," Alan said.

While Alan ate a bagel and drank his coffee, Marcelle and Bernie gave him a sketch of the Thornton investigation and why they thought he was behind the deaths at the silos. They didn't mention where they'd gotten the information regarding Thornton's methods, and Alan didn't ask. Bernie explained his theory about why someone had called in the bodies so quickly.

"Makes sense," Alan said while munching on the bagel, "and now I need to tell you something I forgot to say yesterday. On the second-floor landing, next to the two bodies, was a leather bag with eight bricks of Mexican brown powder."

"A buy that went bad?" Marcelle asked.

"That was my first thought, but why would the killer leave the dope?"

No one had an answer.

"We sent the bag and its contents to the lab," Alan said, "hoping we can lift prints. They're going to analyze the dope and compare it to known samples, but I've got to believe it's Arroyo stuff."

Alan took a long gulp of the coffee. "One more tidbit: the bag smelled like someone had cleaned it recently, inside and out, and the wrap on the bricks had the same smell."

"We are dealing with some very careful people," Marcelle said.

Bernie asked Alan whether he had time to give them a walk-through.

"I didn't think you were here to deliver breakfast." Alan lifted the red tape, and they followed him to the entrance of the elevator building.

Alan pointed at the floor. "The first four bodies were here."

"Were they killed here or somewhere else?" Marcelle asked.

"Probably in the tunnels. Lots of fresh footprints in the dust there. Looks like someone dragged them partway and then lifted them and brought them here."

"Any word on the clean body?"

"I checked with the ME's office an hour ago. They couldn't find anything indicating cause of death. They'll have to run a tox report."

Alan pointed at the stairwell rail. "We got partial hand and fingerprints. Some looked fresher than others, but they'll all be hard to date. Some might belong to our bodies, but we'll have to wait for the analysis."

He climbed up one step and pointed at a section of the handrail. "See that smudge? It looks recent, and it reappears at regular intervals on both rails."

"Someone wearing gloves," Bernie said.

"That's my guess. Another example of someone being careful."

They walked up to the bloodstained landing at the second floor. Small triangular evidence markers, each bearing a number, stood next to each puddle of blood. "This is where we found Javier and the other guy," Alan said. He pointed to another marker near the wall. "And that's where the bag was."

They walked into the room, and Alan pointed to the two tables. "Both tables were so dusty you can see where they were sitting. Two guys on one table and another two on the other. Javier and Fernando had the same type of dust on the back of their pants. The dust patterns on their pants pretty closely match the smudges you see here. They had to be sitting on one of these tables."

"Sitting, not standing," Marcelle said. "This encounter wasn't just a quick transaction. They were meeting about something."

They walked back downstairs. "We checked out the warehouse," Alan said. "Plenty of footprints, but hard to tell which are most recent. Lots of underage drinkers, runaways, and vagrants go tramping through there, so I doubt we'll get anything useful. Right now, we're still going through the tunnels."

"You mind if we walk around?"

"Be my guest."

For the next four hours, Bernie, Marcelle and John walked the property. They started on the second floor of the elevator building, then explored the warehouse, and finished with a walk through the tunnels. When they returned to Bernie's car, he pulled his radio out of the pouch on the back of his driver's seat and checked in. It turned out to be a longer conversation than he'd expected.

"They put me through to Victor Ramos," Bernie said. "The whole city's buzzing about new dope on the street. It's being sold by the Gangster Disciples, the Vice Lords, and the Latin Kings, plus the second-tier gangs. Pure white powder in plastic envelopes with a stamp on them."

"What's the stamp look like?" John asked.

"Says 100% Super Tiger, in red."

"It's Quan's heroin. The stamp is similar to what they use overseas. They always brand their product."

"I haven't even gotten to the best part," Bernie said. "Guess who's running the distribution?"

Marcelle and John shook their heads.

"The Garzas. My good pal Manny figured out a way to get back in business. I have to give him credit—he did a damn good job of playing dumb when we were there the other day."

Marcelle said, "So Garza got in bed with Thornton, and Thornton's getting rid of the Arroyos?"

"Looks that way."

"Where do we go from here?"

Bernie leaned against the car, his head bowed. "Have I ever told you about Slinky Skoryk?"

"Yeah, but I've never met him."

"Let's take a ride to Uptown," Bernie said.

They pulled out of the silos and headed north. Marcelle already knew the story, but Bernie retold it for John's benefit. "A few years back, I was walking down Wilson Avenue one night, headed to a bar, when this guy comes around the corner from the alley real fast and surprises me."

"Scared the shit out of you," Marcelle said, "or at least that's what you said the last time you told the story. And you were drunk and walking away from the bar."

Bernie's face screwed into a grimace. "Same difference. Anyway, the guy looked emaciated, like he hadn't eaten in days, and he was just as startled to see me as I was to see him. He must have made me for a cop because the next thing I knew, his hands were in the air and he's telling me, 'Man, these aren't even my pants!'"

Bernie laughed at the memory. "Which, of course, told me he had something in his pants. I went ahead and checked him and, sure enough, he had three dime bags of dope in his pocket. No weapons, just the bags."

John asked, "Did you arrest him?"

"No, I'm not gonna arrest a guy for three bags, not even worth the trouble."

"What did you do?"

"He looked so hungry and pathetic I took him to a fast-food place and bought him dinner. You never saw someone eat so fast."

"And now he's your CI?"

"Right. Slinky's a user and a seller, basically an independent contractor. He buys a couple of packs a day from one of the gangs and sells them to support himself. He's been on the same corner for years, and anyone who survives that long has some street smarts, which makes him a good CI."

They arrived at Slinky's residence, an old, broken-down motel. "Can't go in through the front," Bernie said. "We don't want anyone to know he's talking to cops."

They walked around to the back and on to the door of the boiler room. "They don't lock this thing," Bernie said, "they just jam it shut."

Bernie rammed his shoulder against the door. It groaned, and after a couple more pushes, it gave way. They walked inside, went up the stairs to the second floor, and proceeded to Slinky's room in the middle of the hallway.

Bernie knocked on the door. "It's Bernie, Slinky. Open up."

"I don't wanna talk."

"Why not?"

"I don't wanna talk."

"C'mon, Slinky."

"Go away."

Bernie motioned to his left, and they walked a few doors down. "He's never acted this way; there's something weird going on. If he sees us standing here when he comes out, he might run back inside."

Bernie looked down both ends of the hallway. It was long, a good fifty yards. "Marcelle, you take that stairwell and John and I'll take the other. Stay behind the wall until you hear his door open and close. Count to five to give him time to get away from his room, and then come out. We'll walk toward each other and pinch him between us."

They walked to their assigned stairwells.

"May I ask a question?" John said.

"Sure," Bernie said.

"He's going to see Marcelle at one end and us at the other. Won't he head for Marcelle?"

"That's the plan. Gives us better odds of grabbing him."

"Are you sure?"

"Just watch."

Three minutes later, they heard the door open and close. They counted to five, turned into the hallway, and started walking toward each other, with Slinky between them.

Slinky saw Bernie and John in front of him, turned around, and saw Marcelle. He ran straight at her.

She held her badge up. "Stop! Police!"

Slinky tried to shove her aside. She stepped inside him with a circular motion, grabbed his arm, and redirected his momentum into the wall. As he slid down to the floor, she grabbed his right wrist with both her hands and jerked his arm up, then bent his wrist sharply inward and pulled his pinky back.

"Eeeeowww! You're hurting me!"

"Shut up, asswipe. When a woman tells you to stop, you should stop."

Bernie and John arrived, and Bernie looked down at the writhing Slinky. "Marcelle?"

"What?"

"I think you can let go now."

Marcelle released him. Slinky rose unsteadily, flexing his fingers and glaring at her. "You got lucky."

"Try it again and I'll get even luckier."

"Now, now," Bernie said, "let's all be friends. Slinky, let's go to your room so we don't disturb your nice neighbors."

Slinky's room was small—a bed, a table, a chair, and a bathroom, but it was surprisingly clean.

"Tell me what's going on," Bernie said.

"I'm scared," Slinky said.

"What are you scared about?"

"All these years I've been buying from the Latin Kings, right? This morning, some guy I've never seen comes to my room, says he's with the Arroyos, and gives me two packs of Arroyo dope. I didn't know the Arroyos even knew about me. I said, where's my regular guy? He says he's my dealer now, he'll be back tomorrow morning to get his money for the packs."

"What's so bad about that?" Bernie said.

"Two hours ago, my regular guy from the Kings comes over, right on time, just like always. I tell him about the other guy. He says don't worry about him. New dope in town, China White, best stuff ever, and he hands me two packs."

Slinky reached under his shirt, pulled out the packs, and showed them to the group. Each had thirteen dime bags, and they looked just as Victor had described. "He says no one sells Arroyo stuff anymore. It's shit dope. The new stuff is way better, people can snort it."

Slinky looked scared now. "And then he says, anyone who sells Arroyo dope is gonna die. I tell him they just gave me two packs, I gotta sell them to make the money to pay them back. He says that's my problem, if I sell them, I die."

"Jesus," Bernie said.

"What am I gonna do? If I sell them, I die. If I don't sell them, I can't pay the guy when he comes back tomorrow, and he'll kick my ass."

"How much do you owe for the Arroyo packs?"

"Two hundred bucks."

"I'll buy them from you."

Slinky looked concerned.

"Don't worry, I'm just going to flush them down the toilet."

Bernie opened his wallet and handed Slinky ten twenties. Slinky pulled the Arroyo packs from beneath his mattress and handed them to Bernie.

Bernie said, "You've got to promise me you'll use the money to pay him and not blow it on something."

"I promise. But what happens when he comes back tomorrow and wants me to take more? He won't like it if I tell him I'm selling the other stuff now."

"We'll worry about it then." Bernie handed Slinky a card. "If he makes you take more, you call me, okay?"

"Thanks, Bernie."

"You're welcome. And if you hear anything else about what's going on, you call me as soon as you can."

Chapter 42

Tuesday, May 19, 1987
7:08 p.m.

The first body was discovered at 4:27 p.m. in an alley behind South Kildare Avenue in K-Town. Laceration of the throat.

The second body was discovered at 4:55 p.m. between two buildings on North Clark Street in Lakeview. Strangulation by garrote.

The third body was discovered at 5:14 p.m. in an alley behind North Ravenswood Avenue in Uptown. No visible signs of trauma.

Each body was in possession of bags of Mexican brown powder heroin.

Marcelle got off the phone with Victor Ramos and swiveled her chair toward Bernie.

"How bad is it?" Bernie asked.

"Crowds gathered where they found the bodies, yelling at the cops on scene. The Arroyos have gone into hiding. People on the sidelines are wondering how far the war is going to spread." Marcelle closed her eyes and rubbed her forehead. "Two more things. The drug guys on the street won't talk to Victor anymore, don't even want to be seen with him. They associate him with the Arroyos because we spent all that time palling around with Javier and Alejandro."

"I'm not surprised," Bernie said. "The Arroyos are radioactive now. People figure Victor could be next and they don't want to get tainted by him."

"Exactly. And because his cover's useless now, Narcotics just pulled him out. He's on the street trying to locate witnesses with the other cops."

"Just great. Now we've lost him as a source. What else?"

"The word's out on Alejandro—$50,000 to whoever gives his location to the Garzas."

"For that kind of money, his mother would turn him in."

"You got that right," Marcelle said. "Seems to me that Alejandro needs some friends right now."

"What are you thinking?"

"Javier put a lot of faith in Alejandro—I can't imagine why, but he did. Something led to Javier being at the silos yesterday, and I'm betting Alejandro knows something about it. He may be willing to talk if we can give him an incentive."

"If you want to do that, you'll have to involve the State's Attorney's Office."

"I know just the guy. You remember me mentioning that assistant state's attorney I was working with?"

"The one whose eyes were all over you?"

"That guy. Dan Brewer, he's in the Felony Review Unit. Very bright, went to law school at Chicago-Kent. I can call him and see what he says."

"You think he'll still be at his office?"

Marcelle looked sheepish. "If he's not, I happen to have his home number."

"Ah, jeez—"

"Give me a break."

Marcelle got Dan at his office and skipped the small talk. She spoke quickly and concisely, and the conversation was over in three minutes.

"Dan's on board," she said. "If we can bring Alejandro in, Dan'll interview him. If Alejandro has a good story to tell and gives a sworn statement, Dan will take it to the FBI because it's likely there are federal charges here. If the FBI likes his story, they can put him in witness protection."

"What if they don't?"

"Then we'll relocate Alejandro and give him a month's worth of living expenses. At least he'd have a fighting chance of staying alive, which is more than he's got now."

"What's your plan?" Bernie asked.

"If anybody's still on Alejandro's side, it'd be the guys at Zona Norte. I've always suspected the Arroyos had an interest in that place."

"You think they'll give up Alejandro to you?"

"No, but they might be willing to get a message to him."

"You'll blow your cover with them if you do that."

"My cover got blown as soon as Victor's did."

"I don't like it," Bernie said. "When they find out you're a cop, they'll be pissed, and you don't even have a backup team to extract you."

"Would you say that to me if I were a man?"

"I'd worry about any partner I had. At least let me go with you."

She shook her head. "I don't know if they'll talk to anyone about him, but at least they know me. If you're there, they won't talk for sure."

Bernie knew he couldn't talk her out of it. "What can I do?"

She took a moment to think through the sequence. "I'll ask them to have Alejandro call me. If he does, I'll tell him to stay put, and we can send in a tac team to get him out. Can you call Jimmy Hannigan and ask him to alert a team?"

"I'll do it. And call me when you've left the bar."

"Here or at home?"

"I'm not leaving until I hear from you," Bernie said.

Chapter 43

Tuesday, May 19, 1987
8:14 p.m.

Marcelle skipped the valet and parked her car herself. As she walked toward the door of Zona Norte, she realized this visit would be the first time she'd gone there in street clothes, and not all tarted up. She wondered if they'd make her wait in line.

Sure enough, the doorman stopped her. "You need to get in line."

She held her star in front of his face. He still looked unconvinced.

"Step aside or I'll take you downtown," she said.

He stepped aside.

She walked up to a bartender she knew. He did a double-take, then looked like he recognized her. "Where's your boyfriend?"

"He couldn't make it. Is Edgar managing tonight?"

"Why do you care?"

Marcelle showed him her star. "I need to talk to him."

The bartender looked around, as if inventorying everything she might have seen there. "You're police?"

"Yeah, and I'm in a bad mood, so don't make me ask you twice."

"He's here."

"Call him. Tell him I'll meet him at the dumpster in the alley where no one will see him talking to me." She handed him a twenty. "I'll have a diet pop and you can keep the change."

By the time Marcelle walked around to the back, Edgar was already there and looking extremely unhappy. "Did Javier and Alejandro know you're police?"

"No."

"What do you want?"

"I know the word's out on Alejandro," Marcelle said. "The people backing up the Garzas are very bad men, worse than anyone you've ever seen. Alejandro won't last the night unless we help him, and we're the only ones who can save him now."

"I don't know where he is," Edgar said.

Marcelle gave him her card. "My office number's on the front. Home phone on the back. I'll be home in twenty minutes. Just in case you find out where he is, tell him to call me and to stay hidden. If he shows his face, he's a dead man. We'll send in a tac team and get him out safely."

"I don't know where he is," Edgar said again, though this time he sounded less convincing.

"As soon as possible, Edgar, and remember to tell him to stay hidden until we get him."

She got home in sixteen minutes and called Bernie.

"You think Edgar knows how to contact him?" Bernie asked.

"If he doesn't, we're no worse off than we are right now. Can you call Hannigan and update him for me?"

"I'll do it. Call me if you hear from Alejandro."

"Where will you be?"

"Going home now," Bernie said.

She wolfed down a sandwich, second-guessing herself the whole time. She'd thrown a plan together on the fly, and Bernie, always wanting to show confidence in her, had gone along with it. What if Alejandro came in and Dan didn't like his story? Or the FBI didn't? Maybe Alejandro was safer where he was. Where would they move him if he couldn't get witness protection? Wisconsin? Or maybe—

Someone knocked on her door.

She ran over, looked through the peephole, and saw Alejandro. Her heart almost thumped out of her chest. "Who's with you?"

"No one."

She drew her pistol. "Stand away from the door."

She held the pistol in one hand and unlocked the door with the other, threw the door open from the side and backed up, ready to shoot.

Alejandro was alone.

"Get your ass in here," she said, and she slammed the door behind him, locked it, and holstered her pistol. "What in the hell is wrong with you? Didn't Edgar tell you to stay put?"

Alejandro gave her the same dumb, overconfident look he always had. "I don't know any police except you. How would I know if the people who came for me were real cops?"

"You could've called me and asked, dumbshit." She pointed at the couch at the back of the room. "Sit yourself down and do not move unless I tell you to."

She called Bernie and explained the situation.

"I'll call Hannigan right now." Bernie said. "They'll be there in ten minutes. Call me when you can."

Marcelle hung up and turned her fury on Alejandro. "How'd you get my address?"

"We know people at the phone company. I gave them your number; they gave me your address."

"You should've stayed where you were. Did anyone follow you?"

"Not to worry, *mamacita*, I'm a careful—"

The battering ram breached the door on the first swing. Two men in black ski masks. The rear man dropped the ram and the lead man rushed forward with a pistol at low-ready. Marcelle was between them and Alejandro.

Before she could draw her weapon, the lead man swung his pistol sideways at her head. She blocked his arm with both of hers, then swept his leg out from under him and pushed him to the floor.

She turned to face the other man, but she was too late. A triple jab to her face, jackhammer blows, harder than she'd ever been hit. She felt sick to her stomach, and the room was spinning and the floor was rushing up to meet her, and that would be the last thing she'd remember.

Chapter 44

Tuesday, May 19, 1987
10:50 p.m.

Bernie had been waiting an hour and a half to hear from Marcelle. He wanted to call either her or Hannigan, but he was afraid he might interrupt something, so he paced the floor of his apartment and stared at his phone, willing it to ring, and when it did, he grabbed it within a second.

"Marcelle?"

"Bernie, it's me."

It was Mike.

"Listen to me," Mike said. "Marcelle's been hurt. The tac team found her on the floor of her apartment, barely conscious, and Alejandro Arroyo dead. I'm at Cook County with her now."

"I'm coming over," Bernie said.

"Bernie, just stay—"

Bernie hung up. He walked to his car, put the blue light on top, and made it to County in a time that would have made Richard Petty jealous.

He parked in the lot next to the emergency room entrance, and when he got to the door, he saw two patrolmen on the other side. He held up his credentials, but they stopped him anyway.

"Sorry, you can't go up there."

"I'm her partner," Bernie said.

"Kozinski said you'd be coming and to stop you right here. She's with doctors, and you can't see her now. Make it easy on us, okay? Have a seat and wait for Kozinski to come down."

Fifteen minutes later, Mike appeared. "She's got a concussion. Her face is beat up, but they don't think there's any other damage. They're still checking her out."

"Security?"

"Hannigan's got two uniforms at every entrance. They'll be here through tomorrow morning, and there'll be a uniform outside her door until she goes home. Now, do you mind telling me what in the hell Marcelle was doing and why no one told me she was doing it?"

Bernie ran through the events and explained why Marcelle went alone. "We were afraid they'd get to Alejandro before we could, and when Marcelle decides she's going to do something—"

"I know. Wild horses won't stop her. But next time, pick up the damn phone and call me." He heaved a long sigh. "Now go home and don't come back till tomorrow."

"I want to stay," Bernie said.

"You can't do anything for her; you can't even talk to her. The best thing you can do is to go home and get some sleep so you're fresh tomorrow. Just this once, will you do what I ask?"

Bernie didn't like it, but he knew Mike was right. "Okay. Just this once."

Chapter 45

Wednesday, May 20, 1987
5:25 a.m.

Bernie tried to sleep. He'd doze off, wake up, look at his clock, and repeat the cycle. Now he looked at his clock for the twentieth time and decided he'd waited long enough. He got up, showered and dressed, and drove back to County.

Bernie walked in through the main entrance, glad to see the two patrolmen eyeing him carefully. He showed them his star, and they told him which room Marcelle was in. He rode the elevator up and saw Norm Vukovich, a good cop from the 27th District, outside Marcelle's door. Bernie gave Norm a perfunctory greeting and asked about Marcelle.

"She got a bad concussion," Norm said. "No broken bones. They don't think there's any brain damage, but they'll have a neuropsychologist check her out. Her face is bruised, but the doctor said she'll heal without scars, and in two weeks she'll be winning beauty pageants again."

Norm stopped and just looked at Bernie.

"What are you not telling me?" Bernie said.

"She had a mild seizure overnight."

"Oh, Jesus—"

"Listen, the doc said it's normal in the first twenty-four hours after a concussion. But just to be safe, they're gonna hold her here a few days, run some tests, and observe her."

"When can I see her?"

"No visitors till two o'clock," Norm said.

"Does Mike know?"

"I talked to him a little while ago. He said he and a guy named Shepard are coming over at two, and told me to tell you when you got here."

"Mind if I keep you company?"

"Suits me. You can get a chair from the waiting area."

Bernie carried over a chair and set it against the wall on the side of Marcelle's door opposite Norm. He sat down, lay his head against the wall, and was asleep in fifteen seconds.

At 12:30, a nurse shook him awake.

"Are you the Bernie she keeps asking for?"

"Probably."

"No one's supposed to go in until two o'clock, but she's getting very agitated about wanting to see you." She paused and took stock of him. "If I let you in, do you think you can calm her down?"

"Oh, yeah. I'm an expert at calming her down."

The nurse gave him an icy stare.

"Look, I'll do my best and I won't make her any worse."

He stood up and turned toward the door, but she blocked him. "Not so fast; I need to tell you something. Marcelle is a beautiful woman, but today is not her most beautiful day and she won't look the way you remember. When you go in, don't look surprised because it'll just make her feel worse."

"Okay, okay."

She knocked on the door. "Honey, do you still want to see that Bernie guy?"

"Yeah."

The nurse turned the doorknob and opened the door a crack.

Bernie walked in.

Marcelle had an IV in her right arm. Her face was red and swollen, her left eye was black, and her lower lip was split. She looked pale and tired and vulnerable.

Bernie stood still for a moment and composed himself, then pulled a chair to the side of her bed next to her good arm and sat down. He looked at her and smiled warmly. He leaned over and gently took her hand in both of his. Finally, he spoke.

"You look fabulous, kid."

She laughed, but stopped because it hurt too much. "You should see the other guy."

"I'll bet. I'm glad it wasn't me."

"No one will tell me anything. Did Alejandro make it?"

Bernie shook his head. "I'm sorry."

She slammed her head against her pillow. "All that for nothing." She digested it, accepted it, and moved on. "I need to tell you what happened."

"Not now. Mike and John are coming over at two. Save it, so you only have to tell the story once."

"All right." She relaxed her head on the pillow and looked up at him. "Will you sit with me awhile?"

"Marcelle, I will sit with you for as long as you want."

* * *

Mike and John arrived at two o'clock. Marcelle went through the whole story, dispassionately and without omitting a single detail. She was articulate as ever, but Bernie could tell the effort was tiring her. When she finished, she asked them a question.

"Why didn't they kill me?"

John responded right away. "You weren't the designated target."

They waited for him to continue.

"They were wearing masks," John said. "If they'd planned on killing whoever was there, they wouldn't have bothered with the masks. Those men were professionals, and professionals try to avoid collateral damage."

"You figured that out pretty fast," Bernie said.

"It's the logical explanation," John said.

The nurse walked in, ignored the three men, and hovered over Marcelle. She checked the IV, felt Marcelle's pulse, and looked in her eyes. "How're you feeling, honey?"

"I'm fine," Marcelle said.

"Well, I bet you'll feel finer if you get some rest." She gave the men a harsh look. "Isn't that right, guys?"

They said their goodbyes and Bernie promised to come back tomorrow.

They walked out of the room, and John proceeded to his car. Mike and Bernie walked a few steps down the hallway, away from the guard, and Mike turned to Bernie. "Are you aware of what's going on?"

Bernie shook his head.

"Other than Alejandro, there haven't been any more bodies since the three we found yesterday, because the rest of the Arroyos are all hiding. That's the only good news."

"I'm sorry I was useless today," Bernie said.

"No apology necessary. We were all worried about Marcelle. But the thing is, I need you doing something more likely to produce an arrest than driving John around. I'm pulling you from him."

Bernie didn't look as happy as Mike had expected.

"John and I have developed a good rapport," Bernie said, "and I'm afraid I'll lose it if I just dump him. Let me ride with him tomorrow, one more time, and I'll smooth it over with him. Can't hurt to keep Treasury on our good side, right? I'll go in right now, read all the reports, and I'll be ready to roll when I'm done with him tomorrow."

Mike didn't like it, but it was a reasonable request. "Okay, ride with him tomorrow, but after that I get you back full time."

Chapter 46

Wednesday, May 20, 1987
4:22 p.m.

Ed had had a productive day. He'd finished his reconnaissance—or at least as much as he could with his Friday deadline. He'd formulated a primary plan and a contingency plan, and though both presented hurdles, he felt confident.

Tomorrow he would follow the subject and wait for an opportunity to set up a shot, a location where the angles would be good and he could exit discreetly. The only contingency was that the subject might recognize him, but he would wear a hat and sunglasses to minimize that risk. If a suitable opportunity did not present itself, he would set up outside the subject's residence on Friday and take the shot as the man departed.

The hotel room felt small and cramped. Ed had nothing else he needed to do, so he decided to go for a walk.

He left the hotel and walked north on Broadway Street. At this time of day, New Town was filled with people and the sidewalk was congested.

Ed walked six blocks and turned left. Soon he saw an elementary school with a large playground. The school was a handsome structure of three stories, and he wondered how many thousands of children had passed through its doors.

Ed walked into the playground. He saw children playing on swing sets and slides and monkey bars. Another group of boys and girls played hopscotch on a diagram they had drawn on the asphalt with chalk. Nearby, two little boys played basketball.

Ed sat down on a bench. He loved to watch children play. Children were pure and innocent and good. And best of all, unlike adults, children were real.

It wasn't as if adults were imaginary. Adults were *there,* just as the bench he was sitting on was *there.* But just because adults were *there,* that didn't make them real. That was why Ed thought of his targets as subjects and not by their names. Names fostered the illusion they were real.

Unfortunately, the fact that adults weren't real created a conundrum for Ed. Children eventually became adults, so if children were real, why weren't adults real? Ed thought about it from time to time, but it always made his head hurt, so he stopped thinking about it.

Now, though, Ed was not trying to resolve the conundrum. He was enjoying watching the children. The two little boys were trying to throw the basketball through the hoop, but they were so small and the hoop was so high that they got the ball through the hoop only occasionally. They didn't get frustrated or mad. They were having fun just trying. Ed loved children.

One of the boys heaved the basketball up. It hit the rim and bounced away. He started to run after it but then froze, fear written all over his face. The other boy ran away.

Ed turned to where the first boy was looking. A young man in his early twenties had picked up the basketball. He was tall and heavy and his nose had a ring through it. His hair was greasy and combed into spikes, as though he were trying to imitate a porcupine. He wore a black T-shirt, black jeans, and military surplus boots.

Ed assessed him quickly. The young man was someone who was trying to make himself look tough.

He wasn't real.

The young man bounced the basketball on the ground as the boy nervously approached him. Ed wanted to tell the boy he was in danger, to run away, but then he realized: it was his ball, and he wouldn't leave without it.

"Gimme my ball back," the boy said.

The young man continued bouncing the ball. "It's mine now."

The boy tried to grab the ball in midair, but the young man caught it. He cradled the ball with one hand and swatted the boy hard with the other, knocking him to the ground.

A chill went through Ed and his jaw clenched.

He hurt the little boy.

Ed stood up and walked over. He was so quiet and inconspicuous that the young man didn't notice him until he spoke.

"It's not yours," Ed said. "Please give it back to the boy."

The young man sized up Ed. He was a thin, bald, old guy. He wasn't a threat.

"None of your business," the young man said. "Get the fuck outta here."

"You're brave when you face a little boy. How brave are you when you face a man?"

The young man grinned and turned to his side, the feint before the strike, and then he dropped the ball and threw a right hook at Ed's head. Ed blocked it and kneed him in the groin. The young man doubled over, and Ed knocked him out with an edge-of-hand blow at the base of his skull.

The boy walked over and looked down at the young man. "Is he okay?"

"He's just sleeping," Ed said, "but he'll wake up in a minute. You should get your ball and run home before he does."

The boy retrieved the ball, looked at Ed again, and thanked him.

"You're welcome," Ed said, "but next time you should be more careful. You never know who you might run into."

Chapter 47

Thursday, May 21, 1987
5:31 a.m.

Ed ate a big breakfast. It might be many hours before he'd have a chance to eat again. He did not drink any coffee. Ed wanted to make sure his hands would be steady.

He snugged his pistol into the holster behind his right hip and put three fully loaded magazines into belt pouches behind his left hip. His jacket easily concealed the pistol and magazines. It was unlikely he would need them, but Ed never left anything to chance.

He checked his backpack and confirmed it had everything he needed. He tossed in some granola bars, just in case his body felt hungry later. Today, it would be especially important for Ed's body to be happy. He already had bottles of water in his car.

He walked to the hotel's garage with his backpack and salesman case. At this hour, no one was in the garage. He transferred the rifle to the cloth case, set it on his back seat, and threw a raincoat over it. He put his backpack on the front passenger seat and the salesman case in the trunk.

Now it would be a matter of driving and waiting. Ed did not mind the prospect of waiting. He had waited fifteen years to kill the subject, and a few more hours were immaterial.

Ed was happy.

With any luck at all, he'd be going home today.

* * *

Arthur opened the rear door of the Lincoln and waited for Thornton to sit down. "Where would you like to go, sir?"

"The Near West Side, just west of downtown. There's a neighborhood there called Greektown and a certain restaurant I'd like to try."

They drove down the long driveway, passed through the gate, and turned right onto Route 31. Arthur was glad the police were no longer following them; he'd grown tired of checking his rearview mirror to make sure the officers were still comfortably behind them. Now he could drive normally again and keep his eyes on what was in front of them.

Chapter 48

Thursday, May 21, 1987
11:30 a.m.

Bernie had already been at Area Six for four hours. He'd read the overnight reports and spoken with the patrolmen and detectives who were doing door-to-door interviews. As usual, none of the citizens had seen or heard anything. He didn't like being pessimistic, but interviews were a long shot. They'd have to find physical evidence or turn someone.

He called Marcelle and listened to her complain about having to stay in the hospital; she sounded like her old self again. When she finished kvetching, he told her about Mike's directive to split off from John.

She said, "I thought you'd be ecstatic to be rid of him. How come you sound so glum?"

"He's grown on me. He's a peculiar guy and he can be a royal pain, but he's also got this innocent, naïve side, like part of his brain never got past age eleven."

Fifteen minutes later, John appeared at Bernie's desk. "I haven't seen the South Side, other than the silos."

"You want to go south? We'll go way south. We can start in Pullman and Calumet Heights and take it from there."

They pulled out of the Area Six parking lot, and Bernie steeled himself for a difficult conversation. "We need to talk, John."

"Okay," John said.

"You know there's a lot going on right now, with the Arroyos and all."

"I do."

"The IRS has a long view of these things, but us city cops, we need to show progress and we need to show it fast. The residents, the politicians, the papers—they don't want to hear us say we're building a case against a large organization and it might take a couple years. They want us to catch the offenders, and they want us to do it right now."

"What are you saying?"

"They want me back on the streets, John. This'll be our last tour, at least for a while."

"I understand."

John was hard to read because he never showed much emotion. He gazed out the passenger window, then turned back in Bernie's direction. "Does this mean you won't teach me the secret language?"

"Not at all. We're friends, John. We don't have to work together to spend time together. We can still hang out, right? By the time you leave Chicago, you'll understand the secret language."

"All right."

Neither one spoke for a few minutes, and then John resumed the conversation. "It made me sad to see Marcelle yesterday."

"Me too, John."

"Maybe I could help you catch the people that hurt her."

"Maybe so," Bernie said. "Why don't you think on it, and see if you can come up with an idea for how you could do that."

They drove down the Dan Ryan and on to Pullman. Bernie wondered what he was missing by being in the car with John, and feeling guilty that he wasn't on the streets sharing the burden. John just stared out the passenger window.

They'd been driving around Pullman for ten minutes when John broke the silence.

"The silos," he said.

"What was that?"

"The Damen Silos. I want to go back there."

"What for?"

"I've been thinking about how I can help you find the people who hurt Marcelle. They were probably Thornton's men, right? Maybe the same people who killed the Arroyos at the silos."

"John, we already spent hours there, not to mention a dozen cops who examined the place with a fine-tooth comb. What do you think you'll find?"

"I don't know. I just feel like we must have missed something."

There was no use arguing; John had made up his mind. "You're the boss," Bernie said.

They reached the silos fifteen minutes later. The scene looked much different than it had two days ago. The people and the cars were gone and the crime scene tape had been removed, except for a few stubborn scraps still knotted around the chain link fence and blowing in the breeze. The site had gone back to looking forlorn and solitary, the only sound the chorus of the car engines zooming down the Stevenson a couple of blocks away.

Bernie pulled up near the entrance to the elevator building. "Where do you want to start?"

"The second floor," John said.

They walked up the stairs and into the room. John examined every square inch of the walls, then got on his hands and knees and did the same with the floor, and finally scrutinized every piece of trash. This enterprise went on for thirty minutes, with Bernie sitting and watching the entire time.

"Let's go up to the third floor," John said. "We never went there."

"They already checked it, John. No one had been in it for weeks."

"Maybe they didn't look hard enough."

They went to the third floor and John repeated the process. Bernie was getting antsier by the second, and as he watched John inspect the room, his mind started spinning through the possibilities of what could be happening while he was stuck here.

It occurred to him that Thornton no longer had police protection. Would he still be willing to venture outside his mansion? At some point, the Arroyos might regroup and fight back, or perhaps one of Thornton's many enemies would hit him and save them all a lot of trouble.

But no sooner had Bernie wished it, than he realized there was a worse scenario. If someone made an attempt on Thornton's life, successful or not, how would his men respond? It could turn into a bloodbath.

That did it. He needed to get to his radio.

"John, we've been here nearly an hour. I need to call and check in."

"Then check in."

"My radio's in the car."

"Why didn't you bring it with you?"

"Because it's too damned big and heavy to carry around, okay? Now, are you finding anything or are we just running in circles?"

"I haven't found anything."

"Can we go now?" Bernie asked.

"I suppose," John said.

They walked back down the rickety stairs and on through the building's doorway, John following behind Bernie. "John, when—"

John tackled Bernie and they fell hard to the ground.

Something hit the wall behind them.

The air cracked.

"What the—"

"Behind the engine *now*," John said. He grabbed Bernie's arm, and they dove behind the car's engine compartment.

Bernie was livid. *"What in the hell is going on?"*

"Someone's shooting at us," John said.

"No shit, Sherlock. How'd you—"

"I'll explain later. He's in the warehouse. Right now, we need to keep our heads down and stay behind the engine block."

"We can't just sit here."

"Yes, we can," John said. "Nothing's going to happen for the next few minutes. Right now, he's thinking about what to do next, just as we are."

* * *

The setup was perfect.

Ed was at a second-floor window 150 yards from the building the two men had entered. He had a clear sight line to the building's entrance and an easy exit route. He'd have preferred to be farther back in the room, away from the window, but he didn't have a tripod or anything else tall enough to rest the rifle on and still get the correct angle.

The good news was that the sun was behind him, and the location was ideal in every other way. He knew he wouldn't find another place as good as this one.

Ed put his backpack on the windowsill and removed his rifle from its case. He loaded five rounds into the rifle's magazine, closed the bolt, and confirmed it was off safe. He knelt down, put the rifle's forearm on the backpack, and wrapped himself around the rifle. Satisfied that everything felt correct, he looked through the scope and adjusted his position until the crosshairs were on the building's entrance.

Now, it was just a matter of waiting.

Ten minutes went by, and then another ten, but Ed did not notice the passage of time. His whole world had reduced to this moment. Nothing else existed now except the doorway and the crosshairs.

He told himself not to be surprised when he saw the men come out. He would have only two seconds to press the trigger, and he needed to begin as soon as he saw them.

Another ten minutes went by, then—

Movement.

A foot, a leg, a torso—

The shot broke, but the men dove a millisecond before the crosshairs moved in recoil.

Miss.

He quickly cycled the bolt for a follow-up shot, but it was too late. The men had already scampered behind cover.

* * *

"Patience, my ass," Bernie said. "I'm not just gonna sit here like a damn duck in a shooting gallery."

"What do you suggest?" John asked.

"The last thing he expects—I rush him. I can weave around as I'm running—"

"He's 150 yards away and has the high ground. He'll wait till you're close, when you'll also be tired and slowing down, and then he'll take you with one shot."

"Do you have a better idea?"

"Let me think for a minute," John said.

* * *

Ed kept the rifle trained where the men were hiding. At some point, they'd have to move.

He asked himself what he would do in their situation, and then his blood turned cold.

Do they have—

* * *

"A radio," John said. "Where's your radio?"

"It's in a pouch on the back of the driver's seat." They were on the car's passenger side, and Bernie thought through how he could get to it. "I can crawl to the rear door, open it fast, slide across the back seat, and grab it."

"Bad idea. He'll shoot you dead."

"But the door on the other side—"

"Won't help you. Those bullets will go through that door like it's nothing. The only way we stay safe is to stay behind the engine block. Shooting at us while we're behind the block is almost guaranteed to fail, and he's not going to take a low percentage shot."

Bernie cast him a quizzical look. "How come you're suddenly such an expert?"

"I didn't say I was. It's just logical. He knows that the more he shoots, the better the chance someone hears it. He's going to wait. Right now, we're in stalemate."

* * *

They don't have a radio.

Ed was sure of it now. If they had one, police cars would already be here.

Right now, they were in stalemate.

* * *

"Give me your backup gun," John said.

"My what?"

"Don't play games. Just give it to me."

Bernie pulled the gun out of the holster in his right pants pocket. It was a Smith & Wesson Bodyguard, a small, five-shot, .38 Special snubnosed revolver, designed for close-in defensive work.

John pushed the thumb latch forward and swung the cylinder out. He verified it was loaded, then closed it and rotated it until it locked into place.

Bernie asked, "Do you know how to use that thing?"

"I think so."

"Well, don't waste ammunition. You won't be able to hit anything closer than ten feet with that gun."

"I'll try to remember," John said. "Now here's my assessment: he had one advantage, the element of surprise, but he's lost it. Now we have two advantages over him. It's two armed men against one, plus time is on our side. The sun will set just after eight o'clock, and then it'll be too dark for him to see us."

* * *

Ed was patient, but the men were patient, too. They weren't panicking; they were staying behind cover, and it occurred to him that time was on their side. By eight o'clock it would be too dark for him to see, and they could just slip away.

He had to consider an alternative to waiting.

* * *

Bernie said, "Eight o'clock is over five hours away. If I rush him now, you can fire at him, try to keep him pinned down till I reach the building."

John shook his head. "I can't give you effective covering fire with five rounds from a snubnose at a target 150 yards away."

"They taught you all this in accounting school?"

"No, I just know a bad idea when I hear one. You're brave, but it's a foolish strategy with a low probability of success."

"You still haven't suggested a better strategy."

"All right," John said, "here's my idea. Let's get him out of his comfort zone. As long as we stay together, we make his job easier because he can focus on one place. If we separate, we make his job much harder." John pointed to a weedy embankment of timeworn concrete blocks twenty yards to their right. "I can run down there; they'd give me good cover. If I make it, he'll have to keep track of two different places."

"I don't like it," Bernie said. "You're not qualified for action like this."

"I've passed all the Treasury classes. I'm as qualified as you are."

Bernie stopped and considered it. He wasn't comfortable with John fending for himself, but they needed to get off square one. Separating might break the impasse; it could induce the guy to descend from his vantage point and give them an easier target. The risk was the twenty-yard run to the concrete blocks, but that was less risky than trying to run to the warehouse.

"Okay," Bernie said, "but let me go."

"No. I'm a smaller target and I can run faster."

Bernie couldn't argue with either proposition. "Just make sure you keep your head down while you're running."

"I will."

Bernie pulled his service revolver out of his hip holster, made sure it was loaded, and kept it in his right hand, finger off the trigger. "Once you're down there, we won't be able to communicate, so let's figure out our plan now."

"Okay," John said. "After we separate, one of two things will happen. First is, he may try to wait us out. If that happens, just stay right here until it's dark and then crawl away. Second option is that he comes down from his perch and comes at us. If that happens, stay in a crouch, lay your arms on the hood and shoot."

"We won't be able to see him," Bernie said. "We can't lift our heads above cover, because he might take a head shot. How will we know he's coming?"

"We'll hear him."

"What if we don't?"

"Stop thinking about failing and start thinking about succeeding," John said. "If you stay calm, you'll live."

John turned to the right, took some deep breaths, and started sprinting.

* * *

Movement, right to left.

It surprised Ed, and it took him a second to recover. He shifted the rifle left, traced the man's path with the crosshairs, got the crosshairs in front of him—

The man dove behind the blocks.

Smart. Ed had expected him to be good, and he was. They'd separated, and now Ed had to split his concentration between two different places.

Very, very smart.

Now, time was even more on their side. It was hard enough to maintain focus on one location. How long could he keep it up with two?

Waiting was no longer viable. He had to force the issue, and he couldn't do that from a distance with the men behind cover. He had to assault them on the ground, flank them, and get a clean shot.

He was on a catwalk on the second floor. To get to the ground and start his approach, he'd have to run the length of the catwalk, down two sets of stairs, and on to the door. Would the men try to escape in the meantime?

He assessed it as improbable. So far, except for separating, they'd maintained perfect discipline, staying behind cover. They wouldn't break cover now, especially since they'd improved their tactical position.

Ed pulled the rifle off his backpack, put the rifle on safe, and set it on the catwalk below the window. The rifle was no longer the weapon of choice. The fight would be close-in now. He'd need to acquire a sight picture quickly, and he'd have to make fast follow-up shots. It was pistol work from here on out.

He drew his pistol, pulled back the slide a bit, and verified a round was in the chamber. He turned toward the stairwell, filled his lungs with air, and ran across the catwalk, down both sets of stairs, and reached the open doorway.

Ed put his back to the wall next to the doorway, peeked through it, and saw nothing. He had to believe the men were still there. He rested a moment and caught his breath.

Time to go.

Ed turned, walked through the doorway, and began his approach. He held his pistol in both hands, in the high-ready position. His head was upright, his eyes forward, his view alternating between the two targets.

And because he was looking only at the targets and ignoring the ground, he didn't notice the broken piece of concrete that his left foot was about to hit.

* * *

Bernie heard a scratching sound, not a sound of nature, but the sound of something scraping against concrete. He popped his head up and laid his arms on the hood with his revolver in both hands. He saw a man forty yards in front of him, facing in John's direction, holding a pistol in the high-ready position. Bernie brought his head down to his gun's sights and shifted his arms to get the front sight on the man's body, but before he could pull the trigger, he heard two gunshots so close together they seemed almost as one. Bernie's brain, seeing nothing except a narrow tunnel encompassing him and the man, told him the man must have fired at him, because he and the man were the only things in the universe and his brain could draw no other conclusion.

Then the man faltered, his arms went limp, and his pistol dropped to the ground. He looked down at his chest, confused, bewildered, and then his legs folded beneath him and he sat down hard on the ground. Two seconds later, he fell backward.

"Bernie."

Someone was talking to him. He turned to his right and saw John standing next to him.

John opened the cylinder of the revolver Bernie had given him and laid the gun on the hood of the car. "It's evidence now," John said. "It's got my fingerprints on it. Don't touch it." He started walking toward the body.

Bernie felt the way he did when awakening from a dream, that gradual realization that he'd returned to reality, and the gears in his brain started turning again. He looked at the open cylinder of the revolver on the hood, saw three unfired cartridges and two with firing pin indentations in the primers, and that's when he realized it was John who had fired the shots.

He walked around the car and followed John to the body. He saw two bullet holes in the man's shirt, still oozing blood, one over his heart, and another, two inches away, that must have gone through his lung.

Bernie had seen a lot of dead bodies, more than he could count, but even the sheer volume of those experiences hadn't desensitized him to the sight. Every dead body reminded him of his own mortality, and it always troubled him.

It didn't seem to bother John, though. He just stood there, looking at the body like it was a possum on the road.

Bernie knelt down, felt for a pulse and found none, then looked up at John. "Ever seen this guy before?"

"No."

"Then let's see who we've got." Bernie patted down the man's body and felt a wallet in his right front pants pocket. He wrapped his handkerchief around his hand, removed the wallet, and opened it. "Stepanek, Edward J., Belmont, Massachusetts," Bernie said. You could usually learn a lot about a person from what they had in their wallet, but Stepanek's wasn't very enlightening. No photos, no club memberships, just a library card and a driver's license.

"There should be a rifle in the warehouse," John said. "The shot he took made a sonic crack, so the bullet had to be supersonic. That pistol uses subsonic ammunition."

Bernie set the wallet next to the body, stood up, and did something he had never done before: he spoke to a dead man.

"Fuck you, Stepanek, Edward J."

They walked to the warehouse and John looked around, trying to gauge the location from which the man took the shot. "He fired through one of the windows on the second floor, probably that corner over there."

They walked up the stairs to the second floor. The windows were elevated, the access to them was a catwalk. They climbed the stairs to the catwalk and walked down the length of the wall, Bernie following behind John. The room was dim, and the catwalk was bathed in shadow. "Watch your step," John said. "It's hard to see, and I don't know what condition this walkway's in."

They neared the end of the catwalk, and John stopped and pointed. Bernie saw a rifle lying on the catwalk next to the wall, almost invisible in the shadows, and knelt down to take a look. It had an attractive wood stock and a longer barrel than he was accustomed to seeing.

"Nice rifle," Bernie said.

"It's a thirty-aught-six Winchester Model 70," John said.

Bernie looked at the rifle again. There weren't any markings on the side facing up, so he wrapped his handkerchief around the edges of the trigger guard, pinched the guard between his thumb and index finger, and turned the rifle over. There it was, engraved on the barrel:

WINCHESTER-MODEL-70—30—06 SPFLD—

A hell of a guess for an accountant.

He looked up at John. "Let's go call it in."

They walked back down the catwalk, down both sets of stairs, and back to the car.

"How'd you know he was there?" Bernie asked.

"I saw the sunlight reflect off the glass in his scope, and knew it could only be one thing."

"Good call, John. You saved our lives."

Bernie pulled his radio out of the pouch on the seat, made the call, and then leaned against the car and waited for the cavalry to arrive. Thoughts were bouncing all over his head, like pinballs in an arcade game, but one in particular was bothering him: John had lied about how he knew the man was there.

Like any good sniper, the shooter had picked a location where the sun was behind him, precisely so there wouldn't be reflections off the lens in his scope that might give him away. Somehow, John had known the man was there, and he didn't want Bernie to know how he knew.

Chapter 49

Thursday, May 21, 1987
2:58 p.m.

Within minutes, there were two patrolmen, a sergeant, a detective, and an evidence technician at the silos. The patrolmen secured the site, and the ET took photographs of the overall crime scene: Bernie's car, still in the same spot, shown in relation to the concrete blocks, the silos, the warehouse, and the dead man. They always started with the wide shots, and Bernie knew he'd be in them, just as he often was in the photos of his own crime scenes. He wondered if he'd look different as a witness than he did as an investigator.

The detective watched as the ET photographed and recovered Bernie's backup gun and Stepanek's pistol and wallet. The ET then went inside the warehouse and returned a few minutes later with Stepanek's rifle in a cardboard box. In the meantime, the sergeant chatted with Bernie and John, not a full-fledged interrogation, but enough to get the lay of the land.

"What are the procedures now?" John asked the sergeant.

"You'll both go over to Area Four. We've notified Kozinski, and he'll meet you there. One of the patrolmen will drive you over, and Bernie can follow in his own car."

The sergeant spoke with the ET, who confirmed he was done with Bernie's car and they could move it now. They drove to Area Four, and Mike met them in one of the conference rooms. The room looked familiar to Bernie: it was drab, run-down, and half its chairs were broken, which meant it looked just like the conference rooms at Area Six.

"Here's what's going to happen," Mike said. "Alan Urbaniak will interview you guys separately. He'll take John to another room, interview him first, and then Bernie. It won't be the third degree. Just tell him what happened, whatever details you remember. He may ask you questions—nothing for you to worry about, just tell him what you know. We'll give John a ride back to Area Six so he can get his car. Should be able to have both of you out of here in an hour or so. Anyone have questions?"

Neither of them did, and Mike left when Alan walked in a minute later. Alan shook Bernie's hand and said, "We've got to stop meeting this way." Bernie managed a smile.

"I'll take John down the hall," Alan said. "Bernie, you need anything in the meantime?"

"A cold pop would be wonderful."

"It'll be here in a minute. Just relax awhile."

Forty-five minutes later, Alan returned to question Bernie. As Mike had said, it wasn't the third degree. At the end Alan asked, "Any reason to believe it had to do with your Thornton investigation?"

"No idea. It was like a bolt out of the blue."

"Okay. I don't have any more questions, but you may have some for me."

"What happens to John now?" Bernie said.

"As far as I'm concerned, he's a civilian who acted in self-defense, justifiable all the way. The IRS has its own procedures for agent-involved shootings. I don't know what'll happen with that, though I can't imagine he'll catch any fallout."

"When do I get my gun back?"

"A few days, probably. You want a spare in the meantime?"

"No, but thanks. Are we done?"

"We're done," Alan said.

Bernie walked to his car, stood there, and couldn't figure out what to do next. He wanted to talk to Marcelle, but not right away. He needed to decompress a little.

If he went home, he'd just pace around and relive the incident. If he went to a bar, he'd just drink and relive it. Neither would be helpful. He needed to distract himself, just for a little while, and the best way to do that was to work.

He drove to Area Six. Maybe they'd have the forensics reports for the Monday homicides at the silos.

When he got to the second floor, there were four detectives in the room. They gathered around him and expressed their happiness that the shooter was dead. When word had first reached them, it had been Bernie who'd put two in the shooter, and they were having a hard time adjusting to the idea that the weird twerp had done it. Bernie assured them it was true. The conversation was brief; they knew he was tired of talking about it by now.

There were no forensics reports on his desk.

What now?

Time to go see Marcelle.

He started to leave, but stopped when he noticed a red message slip on Marcelle's desk. Someone named Annie McIntire, with a 317 area code, had called her at 12:40 that afternoon.

Annie McIntire. The name sounded vaguely familiar, but he couldn't place it.

He called Directory Assistance.

"Ma'am, could you tell me where area code 317 is located?"

"Indianapolis and central Indiana."

Now he remembered. Annie was the woman who lived near Fort Harrison, whose mother had thrown dances for the people going through the Army Finance School. It could wait until Marcelle got back.

He put the slip back on her desk, then reconsidered. It was nice of Annie to call, and it could be days before Marcelle was up and running.

He dialed the number.

"Annie McIntire, please?"

"Speaking."

"This is William Bernardelli with the Chicago Police Department. I'm Marcelle DeSantis's partner, and I noticed you left a message for her today."

"Yes, I did."

"Marcelle's out of town on vacation right now and, you know, I didn't want to bother her while she was off having fun, so I thought I'd call and see if I could help you."

"That's very nice of you, sir. Did Marcelle tell you about our visit?"

"Yes, ma'am, she mentioned it."

"Marcelle was trying to find the names of the people who'd gone through the Finance School with this John Shepard fellow, and the folks at the base didn't have the information, so they sent her to me. My mother used to put on these dances—"

Bernie was barely listening. He wanted to get off the phone and get to Marcelle.

"—and then she'd make these yearbooks, as she called them, with photos of the students and their names, and if someone missed the dance, she'd put their name on a separate list of those not pictured—"

"Uh-huh."

"—and we thought if we could find the book Mr. Shepard was in, then she could get the names of his classmates, but unfortunately, I didn't have the books. I was so disappointed— Marcelle is just the *sweetest* young lady."

"Oh, I know."

"But I told her my sister Jessica in Minneapolis might have them. I called Jess a couple days ago when she got back home, and it turns out she's got all the books from all the dances Mom put on."

"That's great."

"I'm afraid it's not all good news. The books don't mention Mr. Shepard anywhere."

"Excuse me?"

"Jess started with the 1969 books because that's when Marcelle thought he was here, but his name wasn't in any of them. So, then— you have to know Jess, she's very thorough—she started with the first book from 1965 and went through every book, all the way to the last one in 1972. She looked at every photo, every name, every list of the people not pictured. He's nowhere."

"But how can that be? Could your mother have made a mistake?"

Annie didn't respond immediately, and when she did, her voice was polite but firm.

"Mr. Bernardelli. During those years, the dances and the books were the most important things in my mother's life outside her family. She got the class rosters directly from the Army, and before each book was printed, she checked it against the roster to make sure every person was in the book. She was an exceptionally careful woman, and she would have been mortified if she'd left someone out."

"But there had to be a mistake somewhere."

"I agree," Annie said. "Is it possible someone was mistaken about Mr. Shepard being here?"

Chapter 50

Thursday, May 21, 1987
8:28 p.m.

Bernie stepped off the hospital's elevator and turned toward Marcelle's room. He didn't recognize the guard at her door, but the guy was already standing and facing him, alert as hell. Bernie put him at six-two, early thirties, and he looked like he'd been carved from granite.

Bernie walked up to him. "Bernardelli, Area Six."

"Don Pankiewicz, two-seven. I know who you are, sir. Everyone knows who you are."

"I don't think I've seen you before," Bernie said. "How long with CPD?"

"One year, sir."

"And before that?"

"Army, Seventy-fifth Ranger Regiment."

"An ex-Ranger, huh?"

"A Ranger for life, sir."

Bernie liked him already. "Is she being a pain in the ass?"

Don's face turned pensive. "I think she'd prefer to leave, sir."

"You're going to go far," Bernie said, and he knocked on the door. "It's me."

"C'mon in."

Marcelle sat down on the bed, and Bernie pulled up a chair. "I hope I didn't wake you when I called," he said.

"No, you didn't wake me. I can use some company; I'm bored as hell."

"You look a lot better. They say you're getting out Monday."

"I'm ready to go now. There's nothing wrong with me that Maybelline Concealer can't fix." She paused and scrutinized him for a second. "I don't mean to sound like your mother, but you don't look so good."

"I had a hell of a day," Bernie said.

He told her the whole story, starting with the drive with John and ending with his conversation with Annie McIntire. He tried to do what he wished witnesses would do when he interviewed them: he included every detail he could remember, no matter how trivial it might seem, because even if something seemed unimportant at the time, you couldn't always predict what might turn out to be relevant later on.

When he finished, Marcelle took a deep breath and gradually exhaled it. "You *did* have a hell of a day. Are you okay?"

"No, not really. I'm probably still in shock and not thinking real clearly, so I thought I'd come here and tell the story to the best thinker I know. Can you make sense out of it?"

Most people didn't get Marcelle. They saw a gorgeous woman, or a gorgeous woman who could kick ass, and stopped there. Bernie, though, knew better. What Marcelle really excelled at was what she was doing right now: crunching a mass of facts, arranging and rearranging them into coherent narratives, and assessing each one's probability. She leaned back against the bed's headboard and stared straight ahead for several minutes, oblivious to Bernie's presence, and then she looked up.

"The car you drove today. Does it have a side-view mirror on the passenger side?"

"Well, yeah, but—"

"That's how John knew you were being followed."

"Slow down," Bernie said, "you are way ahead of me."

Marcelle was sitting up now, cross-legged, and getting more animated by the second. "You're driving along, going on another neighborhood tour. Out of nowhere, John says he wants to go back to the silos. It's a weird thing to say, given the context."

"He must have been thinking about them and thought we'd missed something."

"Unlikely. John couldn't even tell you why he thought that, right? He knew we'd had a forensics team go over it. He'd walked around it himself, as much as he'd wanted to. But today you're driving along and suddenly he wants to veer off to the silos just on some amorphous hunch? John's a concrete, linear, literal person. Not the kind of guy who suddenly changes course because of instinct."

"Good point," Bernie said. "Keep going."

"He changed course because he saw something that got his attention. Could have been in front of you, could have been off to the side, but I'm betting it was behind you and he saw it in the mirror, someone following you."

"He knows we're being followed and doesn't tell me?"

"That part didn't make sense to me, either, until I considered what he said about seeing the flash off the sniper's scope. There wasn't any flash because the sun was behind the shooter. An obvious lie, right? Why lie? Only one reason: he didn't want you to know he already knew the guy was there."

"I'm with you on that one."

"And whatever his motive," she said, "it was the same reason he didn't reveal you were being followed. He makes up a lame excuse about being afraid you missed something at the silos, and an even lamer explanation about how he knew a sniper was there."

"But why, Marcelle? Even if I buy your theory that he knew we were being followed, why did he hide it from me?"

"Because he knew the shooter, and didn't want you to know that."

"Now you're stretching," Bernie said.

"No, I'm not. Let's go back to the point right after John shot the guy. You walked around the car and started walking toward the body, right?"

"Right."

"Now think back to that moment. Other than being relieved you were still alive, what was the first thought in your head?"

"I wanted to know who the son of a bitch was that was shooting at us."

"Exactly. Same question I would've had. Same question anyone in your position would've had. So you do the obvious thing—you check his body and go through his wallet. Who is this guy? Where'd he come from? Why was he shooting at me?"

She stopped for a moment to let it sink in. "But John didn't seem interested, did he?"

"No, he sure didn't," Bernie said. "Didn't even ask to look at the wallet. But maybe he's just not the curious sort. He's an odd guy; maybe he thinks differently than we do. You can't just discount that possibility."

"Yes, I can, because of one other thing. You and he get to the second floor of the warehouse. You see the rifle. It's lying in a shadow, barely enough light to even see it, but he knows exactly what kind of rifle it is."

"Someone who knows rifles can spot a Model 70 by its bolt knob."

"Oh, okay. So now, John the accountant is a rifle expert who knows the difference between the bolt knob on a Winchester and the bolt knob on a Ruger? Or between that and a Savage? A little bolt knob—they're practically identical on all those brands—and he sees it and instantly recognizes it in almost total darkness? When he said it, did he say it tentatively, like he wasn't sure?"

"No," Bernie said, "he said it like he knew it for a fact. Plus, he knew what cartridge the rifle was chambered for. These days, most pros shoot a .308, but this guy had a thirty-aught-six. Couldn't have been a lucky guess."

"The part I can't figure is John's motive," Marcelle said. "Would've saved you a boatload of trouble if he'd told you that someone he knew was following you."

"True," Bernie said, "but if he'd told me, let's look at the consequences. I would have called in and set up a trap to isolate the guy."

"Absolutely."

"Now we've got him trapped. He gets out of the car and we find guns and ammunition. Can we prove he was following us and wanted to kill us? No. 'Gee, officers, I was just driving around with my guns.' We don't even have probable cause for the stop. Just because John knows him and thinks he's up to no good, his hunch isn't enough to get us PC. The most we have is a weapons charge, but it's probably a bad stop to begin with—"

"And he ends up skating on the weapons charge," Marcelle said. "Even a bad defense lawyer wins that one."

"Right. John figures that out right away. Telling me the guy's following us gets him out of our hair temporarily, but he'll be back in the fight before long. John doesn't want to give him another chance. The only way to stop him for sure is to draw him out, make him commit, and then stop him. And John has an advantage he doesn't want to waste."

"Which is?"

"He knows the guy is following us, but the guy doesn't know he knows. That gives John a chance to set the table. Where should we go? What gives me the best odds? And it has to be a place the shooter will like. John reviews what he knows about Chicago and remembers the silos. Big place, abandoned. No civilians to get caught in the crossfire. The shooter would like it. So he asks me to drive over there, and what does he do when he gets there? He kills time for an hour to give the guy a chance to check out the site and get set up. And in the end, it worked out perfectly for us, didn't it? The guy goes for it, John kills him, game over."

"It's pretty outlandish," Marcelle said.

"Yeah, it is. Can you come up with a better explanation that accounts for all the facts we know?"

"Not offhand. Now tell me this: who was he shooting at? You or John?"

"John."

"Why him and not you?"

"Two reasons. First off, the shooter was walking toward John, so John had to be the primary target. And second, if I were the target, it'd be too coincidental. There's no way he'd happen to go after me just as I happened to be in a car with someone who just happened to know him."

"You convinced me," Marcelle said. "So let's see what we've got right now. John knows the guy, sees him following you, figures he's the target, but doesn't tell you. And I agree with your theory that John wanted to draw the shooter to the silos and all that. A hell of a ballsy move, but John's now proved he's got a pair, so I can buy that. But here's where I get stuck: once it's over, the guy's dead as hell, what was stopping John from saying, hey, now that I see him, I know this guy?"

"We won't be able to figure that out tonight," Bernie said, "so let's look at a different aspect. Why would someone want to kill John now?"

"He's put away a lot of high-profile offenders. I'll bet there's a slew of potential suspects."

"Yeah, but why now? Why here? John lives in DC. He's been in Chicago, what, less than two weeks? Would've been easier to hit him at home."

"The obvious answer is Thornton," Marcelle said. "He arrives, John arrives, Thornton knows John's on his tail."

"No way. Assassinating a federal agent, any LEO for that matter, is a huge step to take. Thornton's smart. He knows the whole federal government would come gunning for him. Maybe he'd try it if he were desperate, but right now John's not even within sniffing distance of him."

"I'm not ready to leave the Thornton angle," Marcelle said, "because, like you, I don't believe in coincidences. Of all the times someone could choose to hit John, it's in Chicago, after John came here to investigate Thornton. It could be that John pissed him off years ago, and now that Thornton's back it's time to get even."

"Yeah, but if that were the motive, Thornton could have done it long ago. A guy like him, with the resources he's got, has a long reach. Why now, but not earlier? What's changed? And why would drug king Robert Thornton have a personal gripe with John Shepard?"

Marcelle had no answer to that.

Bernie bowed his head for a minute, thinking it through, and then looked back at Marcelle. "Part of the problem," he said, "is we're accustomed to thinking of John as this nervous little nebbish, so let's put aside our assumptions and just look at what we know to be true. John was in mortal danger, but he stayed cool and devised a perfect plan. And to top it off, he shot the fastest double-tap I've ever seen and nailed the guy twice in the chest at forty yards—with a frigging pocket pistol, no less." He shook his head in awe. "Most cops couldn't have made those shots at half that distance, and John did it under massive stress, knowing if he missed, he'd be dead."

"Obviously, there's more to John than we thought," Marcelle said. "You think that plays into why Thornton would go after him?"

"I don't know. I just don't see anything in John's background that would make Thornton want to kill him."

"Maybe not in the background we thought he had. But we learned something new tonight, didn't we?"

Bernie had almost forgotten.

"Thank goodness for Annie McIntire and her sister Jess," Marcelle said, "without whom we would never have known this. Someone falsified John's service record, at least the bit about going through school at Fort Harrison. We know that's baloney, and that means the rest of his service record probably is too. Why fabricate that part but not the rest? And that's not something John could have done. Monkeying with a federal service record is a big deal; only someone high up with a lot of clout could do it. And for some reason, they did it with John."

She stopped, sipped some water, turned it over again in her mind, and continued. "There is something important in John's background that we're missing."

"I agree," Bernie said, "but you're still stuck on the idea that Thornton's the one going after him, and I'm still not buying it. I said it before: he wouldn't target a federal agent unless he was desperate. Give me a good reason why Thornton would want to kill John."

Marcelle unfolded her legs, stretched, and leaned back against the headboard, considering the possibilities. She wasn't going to give up easily.

"You want a good reason for Thornton to kill John?" she said. "Then tell me this: what's the best reason to kill someone?"

"To stop them from killing you."

"Same thing I was thinking. Remember that Green Beret farmer you visited in Iowa? The one who knew Thornton in Vietnam?"

"Steven Johannsen. What about him?"

"He was surprised when you told him Thornton had returned to the US, didn't think the man was brave enough to come back—"

"Because there's a lot of people here who want to kill him," Bernie said.

They looked at each other.

"Maybe we've been looking at it from the wrong direction," Marcelle said. "It's not Thornton that has a gripe with John, it's John that has a gripe with him. Thornton knows John's coming after him, so he sent the shooter to do John before John could do Thornton."

Bernie thought about it, then shook his head. "Ever since John got here, he's done his best to protect the guy. If he wants Thornton dead, why would he do that?"

Even as he posed the question, they both solved it.

"Maybe John wants first dibs," Marcelle said with a smile.

Chapter 51

Friday, May 22, 1987
6:20 a.m.

Bernie had made it through yesterday mostly on adrenaline, and by the time he got home he was crashing, completely worn out. He fell asleep on his bed, still clothed.

But even as he slept, his brain was still working away. He woke up before his alarm went off, fully alert, and focusing on what he needed to do next.

Marcelle was right—they were missing something important in John's background. He needed to find the missing piece, he needed to find it quickly, and there was only one way he could do both.

But now he faced a hard decision. He'd have to use up the most valuable favor he owned just to get his source to look for the information, and there was no guarantee the guy could get it. Bernie felt sick just thinking about it; he could spend the favor and still end up empty-handed.

Bernie showered and dressed, drank some coffee, and reviewed what he'd learned about John. He had a phony service record; he knew tactics; he was a phenomenal shot with a handgun; he was cool under pressure. What else could he do? If he had another skill, the odds were good that Bernie's source could get the information he wanted.

Bernie rolled a plan around in his mind, but before he did anything else, he had to keep his promise to Mike to work the Arroyo murders today.

He went to Area Six and spoke briefly with Mike. Before departing, he swung by his desk and grabbed a file he thought he might need later that day.

He drove to the locations of the three Tuesday evening murders, the dealers Thornton's men had killed for selling Arroyo dope. He examined the scenes and made some street stops. Unsurprisingly, all were DKAs. After three hours of spinning his wheels, he decided he'd done his duty. It was time to pursue his plan about John.

He rolled the idea around some more. It was either a good idea or the worst idea he'd ever had. He wanted to run it by Marcelle, but he knew what she'd say: *high risk, potentially high return, your call.*

He went to a payphone and called John.

"How are you feeling, John?"

"Fine."

"You killed someone yesterday. It's okay not to feel fine."

"I'm fine."

"Look," Bernie said, "I've put in enough time today, and I was thinking—why don't we go for another ride? You know, just for old times' sake."

"Where do you want to go?"

"Manny Garza's right in the middle of all this business. I think we should visit him again."

"He wouldn't talk to you the last time. I don't think he'll talk to you now."

"You're probably right. But he's got no history with you and you're less intimidating, so maybe he'd talk to you. Can't hurt to try."

"All right," John said.

Bernie drove to John's apartment and picked him up. The drive to Manny's bar was a typical John ride, vast stretches of silence interrupted briefly by conversation.

Bernie said, "Is tonight the night Mary Ellen comes over?"

"Yes."

"Are you excited?"

"Yes."

"Have you bought the flowers yet?"

"I'll do it later."

They arrived at Manny's Place and parked. "He may feel threatened if we question him together," Bernie said. "Let's go inside, you stay at the door, and I'll try him first."

"Fine," John said.

They walked in. The only people inside were Manny and the bartender. John stood by the door while Bernie walked over to Manny and sat down across from him.

Manny eyed him warily. "I'm not talking to you."

"I don't want you to talk to me. I want you to do something for me."

Now Manny looked both wary and curious.

"You see that little guy back there?" Bernie asked.

"He was with you the last time."

"Right. CPD's letting him shadow me for a book he's writing, and he's giving me a huge case of the red ass. He seems to think police work is all nice and rosy, and I thought, you know, maybe he needs to see that sometimes it's hazardous. Might convince him to stop pestering me."

"You're shitting me," Manny said. "You want me to beat him up?"

"I don't want you to hurt him. Just shove him around a little."

"How stupid do you think I am? You'll arrest me on the spot."

"Are you Catholic, Manny?"

"Yeah, I'm Catholic. So what?"

"I am, too." Bernie crossed himself. "In the name of the Father, and of the Son, and of the Holy Spirit, and on my father's grave, I swear to you, I won't arrest you. He attacked you and you defended yourself, and I'll back your story a hundred percent."

Manny looked skeptical.

"C'mon, Manny, how often do you get a chance to have a cop owe you a favor?"

Swearing an oath was one thing, but the word "favor" took it to another level.

Manny thought about it.

"Send him over," he said.

Bernie walked back to the door, where John stood. "He won't talk to me," Bernie said, "but he says he'll talk to you."

"Okay."

"I'll stay here at the door so he doesn't feel like we're double-teaming him," Bernie said.

Manny stood up, and John walked over to him. "Johnshepardpleasedtomeetyou," he said, and he extended his hand.

Manny just looked at it. "Are you a cop?"

"No."

"What are you?"

"I'm an accountant."

"You're a fucking *accountant?*"

"No, I'm just a regular accountant."

Manny reached out with his right hand and grabbed John's shirt collar. "Lemme tell you something, Mr. Accountant—"

"Please remove your hand, Mr. Garza."

"Please remove my hand? How about I—"

John's left hand shot upward. He pressed his thumb hard into the back of Manny's hand, slipped his fingers under Manny's palm, and turned the palm up. Before Manny could react, John brought his other hand into play, both thumbs and all of his fingers now pressing from opposite sides into Manny's hand. John took a step back, twisted Manny's wrist to the left, and Manny's body followed and flipped over. As Manny's back hit the floor, John yanked his arm upward and delivered a toe kick to his temple. Manny sprawled out, unconscious.

The bartender walked around the bar.

Uh-oh. Bernie drew his revolver and pointed it at the bartender. *"Stop right there."*

The bartender stopped.

John turned around and looked at Bernie, and at that moment, Bernie saw exactly what he'd come here to see.

John had gone completely still.

There was no fidgeting, no twitching; he looked like he was barely even breathing. His entire image just went flat, as if he were no longer three-dimensional but simply a picture on a wall. John had become nothing but calm.

He was dead calm.

A second later, recognition swept over John's face, the realization that Bernie had set him up, and his expression morphed into that of a child who'd just been caught with his hand in the cookie jar.

He walked past Bernie and out the door. Bernie caught up with him at the car.

"What did he say?" Bernie asked.

"He wouldn't talk to me."

"You had some nice moves back there."

"Thank you."

"Where'd you learn how to do that?"

"In the Army."

"What'd they call your outfit, the Fightin' Accountants?"

"Are you trying to make a point?"

"Not at all. Just a little surprised, I guess."

"Only because you expect so little of me."

There was no point in pushing it. "Look, maybe we're still a little stressed from yesterday. How about I just take you home?"

"Fine."

They drove back to John's apartment building in silence, and Bernie pulled up in front of it.

"Have fun tonight," Bernie said.

"Thank you."

John got out of the car and walked into his building. Bernie waited until he saw John disappear up the stairs, then turned his car around and headed downtown.

Chapter 52

Friday, May 22, 1987
1:22 p.m.

In Chicago, nothing is more sacrosanct than a favor that's owed. It's at the apex of the pyramid of obligations—above morals, law, and ethics, superior to religion, country, and family. It's the lifeblood of the city, the grease that made Chicago The City That Works. And today, Bernie was finally going to collect the favor that was owed to him by Myron Skolnik.

Bernie and Myron had met in the third grade and soon discovered how well they complemented each other: Bernie was big and Myron was small. Even as a child, Bernie instinctively wanted to help people, and he became Myron's protector, saving him from the neighborhood bullies. Bernie was the reason Myron reached adulthood unscathed.

Myron was a good man, with a good wife, good kids, and a good job with the federal government. Bernie didn't know exactly what Myron did—Myron took his duty of confidentiality seriously—but he'd once let slip that he had the highest security clearance a federal employee could have.

Because Myron was such a good man, he never drank alcohol, unless one counted a sip of Mogen David during Sabbath or

Passover. And it was precisely because Myron did not drink that he ended up owing Bernie a favor.

Six years ago, one of Myron's colleagues retired, and the office threw a going away party at a local tavern. Everyone encouraged Myron to drink, and his protestations only made them try harder. It made him feel self-conscious and puny, just like in the old neighborhood, but Bernie wasn't there to save him.

So Myron ordered a beer and took a sip. It wasn't so bad! So he took another and another and then four more glasses. When he left the tavern, he didn't understand all the fuss about people getting drunk on alcohol. He felt fine! He got in his car and made it two blocks before getting stopped by a CPD motorcycle cop, who informed him he'd been weaving in and out of two lanes and scaring the crap out of every other driver on the street.

Myron then did exactly what he'd done throughout his childhood: he sought Bernie's protection.

He dropped Bernie's name with the cop, who radioed in and asked Bernie to come pick up his friend. Bernie arrived in a few minutes and had a brief conversation with the cop, who let Myron go without writing a ticket.

Bernie and Myron never spoke of it again, but they both knew one thing: Myron owed him.

Over the years, Bernie had been tempted many times to call in this favor, but had always resisted it. This one was a big-time, solid-gold favor, the kind you kept in a special box and fondled every now and again just because it felt so good to know you had it. And like all favors, you could use it only once.

Today, though, he had no choice.

Bernie parked in a garage on Dearborn and walked two blocks to the Kluczynski Federal Building, where Myron worked. It was steel and glass, much different from the old federal building of cut granite and Greek columns that they demolished twenty years ago. The lobby was vacant except for an officer at a desk. Bernie handed his star and ID to the officer.

"I can't let you go up by yourself," the officer said. "I have to call him, and he comes down and gets you."

He made the call and Myron arrived a minute later, looking worried.

"What are you doing here?" Myron said.

"Myron, is that how you greet your childhood pal? I was in the neighborhood and wanted to see your office. Let's go upstairs."

They went up the elevator and into Myron's tiny office. The biggest thing in it was a computer screen.

"What are you doing here?" Myron said again.

"I need to see a guy's file."

"You're a cop. Just go through normal channels."

"For reasons you don't want to know, that's not real feasible."

"Bernie, I could lose my job if—"

Bernie spoke the magic words. "You owe me, Myron."

Myron looked around, as if someone might be hiding in his office, spying on him. "Okay, what's the name?"

"Shepard, S-H-E-P-A-R-D, John Taylor."

"There are probably thousands of Shepard, John Taylors. You got a social security number?"

Anticipating this issue, Bernie had brought along the first part of John's file that Mike had given him last week. He pulled it out of his coat pocket and read off the number.

Myron typed in the information. After a pause, green text—all uppercase—scrolled across the black screen. Bernie recognized it as the same file he already had.

"This guy's an accountant," Myron said.

"I know. Now let's see if he's got a deepfile."

Myron turned so fast Bernie thought his head might fly off. "How do you know about deepfiles?"

"I know lots of things. Now go ahead and pull it up."

Myron shook his head emphatically. "No way, Bernie. If I get caught pulling a file without authorization, I get canned. If I get caught pulling a deepfile without authorization, I go to jail."

"What are the odds he has a deepfile?" Bernie asked.

"This guy? One in a million."

"So you make the search. It comes up dry. Even if they find out you searched, you say you did it by mistake. No harm, no foul."

There was a long pause.

"If I search, will we be square?"

"Yeah, we'll be square."

"Even if it comes up dry?"

"Yes, Myron, even if it comes up dry."

Myron took a deep breath, typed in the codes, and then steadied his finger over the "exit" key, ready to punch it as soon as "NO ENTRY ON FILE" flashed on the screen.

But the message never came. Instead, the screen lit up, and both men stared at it, awestruck, as the lines formed.

"Holy shit," said Myron Skolnik.

Chapter 53

Friday, May 22, 1987
2:37 p.m.

"Let me in, John," Bernie said through the building intercom.

"Mary Ellen's coming over at 5:30. What do you—"

"I'll be gone by then. Let me in."

John buzzed him through. By the time Bernie reached John's apartment, John was standing in the doorway. Bernie walked straight into the living room and sat down.

John said, "What's going on?"

"What's going on is that you've been lying to us. You son of a bitch, you've been lying to us all along."

John said nothing.

"You think I'm bluffing? Then let's try this: you weren't an accountant when you were in the service."

"What was I?"

"You were in a classified unit, you and fifteen others, and you were all trained by Thornton."

Bernie pulled a computer printout out of his coat pocket, unfolded it, and tossed it on the table. John stared at it for a moment, then picked it up and began to read.

TOP SECRET TOP SECRET TOP SECRET

BEGIN DEEPFILE ENTRY 69-283

NAME
SHEPARD, JOHN TAYLOR
SSN
985-11-4024

DOB
25 MAY 1947

POB
GREENCASTLE, IN
USA

CURRENT RESIDENCE
2445 MANOR ST NW
WASHINGTON, DC

CURRENT EMPLOYMENT
INTERNAL REVENUE SERVICE
1111 CONSTITUTION AVE NW
WASHINGTON, DC

SERVICE PROFILE
PLACED ON EXTENDED ACTIVE DUTY, US ARMY RESERVE,
2D LT, 3 JUNE 1969
DISCHARGED, CAPT, 11 JAN 1973
NO DISCIPLINARY ACTIONS

COVER PROFILE
ARMY FINANCE CORPS, FINANCE AND PAYROLL
ACCOUNTING

ASSIGNED TO ARMY FINANCE SCHOOL, FT BENJAMIN HARRISON, LAWRENCE TOWNSHIP, IN

REASSIGNED TO FT A.P. HILL, BOWLING GREEN, VA

DEEP PROFILE
OPERATION ARES, TEAM ONE
REPUBLIC OF VIETNAM
20 AUG 1969-11 JAN 1973

PHYSICAL PROFILE

HT 67 IN
WT 122 LBS

VISION
20/15
EXAMINER'S COMMENT: SUBJECT'S LOW-LIGHT VISUAL ACUITY AND CONTRAST SENSITIVITY ARE EXCEPTIONALLY HIGH. SUBSEQUENT REEXAMINATION CORROBORATED THESE RESULTS.

AUDITORY ACUITY
RESULT: H1
SUBJECT TESTED AT -10 DB IN EACH EAR AT EVERY FREQUENCY
EXAMINER'S COMMENT: SUBJECT'S AUDIOMETRY RESULTS NOTED AND VERIFIED.

HEART RATE
REST PULSE 87 BPM
STRESS PULSE 50 BPM
EXAMINER'S COMMENT: SUBJECT'S HEART RATE ANOMALY NOTED AND VERIFIED.

PSYCHOLOGICAL PROFILE

FULL EVALUATION ON FILE
INTERPRETATION AND CONCLUSIONS FOLLOW

THE SUBJECT IS A 22-YEAR-OLD MAN WHO WAS SELECTED FOR PSYCHOLOGICAL ASSESSMENT IN CONNECTION WITH POTENTIAL DEPLOYMENT IN A CLASSIFIED OPERATION. THE ASSESSMENT WAS COMPLETED IN TWO SESSIONS OVER CONSECUTIVE DAYS AND INCLUDED CLINICAL INTERVIEWING AND STANDARDIZED TEST PROTOCOLS. OVER THE COURSE OF THE EXAMINATION, THE SUBJECT PARTICIPATED IN A COOPERATIVE MANNER. HIS RESPONSES WERE STRAIGHTFORWARD AND THERE WAS NO INDICATION OF ATTEMPTS TO EITHER DECEIVE OR PORTRAY HIMSELF IN A BIASED MANNER. AS A RESULT, THE CONCLUSIONS HEREIN REPRESENT A RELIABLE AND VALID INDICATION OF THIS PERSON'S CURRENT LEVEL OF PSYCHOLOGICAL AND INTELLECTUAL FUNCTIONING.

THE SUBJECT DEMONSTRATES SYMPTOMS CONSISTENT WITH A TRANSIENT TIC DISORDER. HE MANIFESTED EYE BLINKS, ABNORMAL MOUTH MOVEMENTS AND HEAD TWITCHES INTERMITTENTLY THROUGHOUT THE EVALUATION PERIOD. OF NOTE, THESE ABNORMAL MOTOR SYMPTOMS DECREASED IN OCCURRENCE DURING THE PARTS OF THE EVALUATION THAT CONSISTED OF HIGHER INTELLECTUAL DEMANDS AS WHEN CONCENTRATING AND SOLVING SPECIFIC TASK PROBLEMS. CONVERSELY, THEY TENDED TO INCREASE IN FREQUENCY WITH LESS-STRUCTURED TASKS THAT FOCUSED MORE UPON FEELINGS, EMOTIONS, AND INTERPERSONAL INTERACTION. IT IS TYPICAL TO SEE AN INCREASED FREQUENCY OF TIC SYMPTOMS DURING HEIGHTENED PERIODS OF STRESS AND ANXIETY. THE SUBJECT HAS LIKELY EXPERIENCED THESE

SYMPTOMS SINCE EARLY CHILDHOOD, WHICH MAY HAVE CONTRIBUTED TO DIFFICULTIES IN DEVELOPING AGE-APPROPRIATE SOCIAL SKILLS AS HE MATURED.

THE SUBJECT TESTS IN THE VERY SUPERIOR RANGE OF INTELLECTUAL FUNCTIONING AS COMPARED TO PERSONS HIS AGE IN THE GENERAL POPULATION. HIS TEST SCORES PLACE HIM ABOVE THE 99TH PERCENTILE WITHIN HIS NORMATIVE GROUP. VERBAL AND PERCEPTUAL REASONING AND PROBLEM-SOLVING SKILLS ARE VERY ADVANCED AND IT IS CLEAR THAT HE CAN DEMONSTRATE RAPID LEARNING AND SKILL MASTERY. HE HAS EXCELLENT SHORT-TERM MEMORY AND CAN RETAIN A LARGE AMOUNT OF DATA WITH A SINGLE TRIAL PRESENTATION DUE TO A VERY STRONG CAPACITY TO FOCUS HIS ATTENTION. HE HAS VERY ADVANCED INDUCTIVE AND DEDUCTIVE REASONING SKILLS, ENABLING HIM TO SOLVE COMPLEX PROBLEMS EMPLOYING MULTIPLE COGNITIVE STRATEGIES. HE WORKS SIMILARLY WELL UNDER TIME CONSTRAINTS, WHERE HE CAN FOCUS HIS ATTENTION AND COMPLETE UNFAMILIAR TASKS MUCH MORE RAPIDLY THAN IS COMMONLY OBSERVED IN OTHERS. MATHEMATICAL COMPUTATIONAL AND REASONING ABILITIES ARE ALSO WELL ADVANCED. OF INTEREST, HIS OVERALL INTELLIGENCE SCORES WOULD HAVE BEEN EVEN HIGHER EXCEPT FOR WEAKNESSES OBSERVED IN TASKS DEMANDING SOCIAL JUDGMENT AND INTERPRETATION OF MORE ABSTRACT AND NUANCED SITUATIONS. HE TENDS TO THINK IN LITERAL TERMS; IS NOT SKILLED IN COMMON SOCIAL NORMS AND BEHAVIORS; AND HAS A RATHER IMMATURE VIEWPOINT WHEN DEALING WITH SOCIETAL STANDARDS OR ETHICS.

WITH REGARD TO PERSONALITY DYNAMICS AND CHARACTEROLOGICAL FUNCTIONING, THE SUBJECT EXHIBITS SOMEWHAT UNUSUAL BEHAVIOR PATTERNS THAT IMPACT HIS ABILITY TO PERCEIVE, RELATE TO AND THINK ABOUT BOTH HIMSELF AND THE WORLD HE ENCOUNTERS. HE

HISTORICALLY HAS TAKEN PLEASURE IN FEW ACTIVITIES AND DOES NOT TOLERATE OR SEEK OUT CLOSE RELATIONSHIPS WITH OTHERS. HE WILL APPEAR TO OTHERS AS ALOOF, DETACHED AND ALIENATED. DUE TO GENERALLY DIMINISHED SOCIAL JUDGMENT, HE IS APT TO PRESENT HIMSELF IN A BLUNT OR UNFILTERED MANNER WHEN INTERACTING WITH OTHERS, SHOWING LITTLE OR NO AWARENESS OF HOW HE MAY NEGATIVELY IMPACT OTHERS. HE DOES NOT EXHIBIT MUCH CONCERN AS TO HOW HIS BEHAVIOR MAY AFFECT THOSE AROUND HIM AS HE SEEMS TO POSSESS LITTLE EMPATHY. HE IS NOT WELL-VERSED IN DEALING WITH EITHER HIS OWN EMOTIONS OR THOSE OF OTHERS AS HE FINDS MORE COMFORT AND A SENSE OF PERSONAL ACHIEVEMENT DEALING INSTEAD WITH TASKS AND SPECIFIC ACTIONS. HE MAY APPEAR TO HAVE NO REACTION TO CRITICISM OR FEEDBACK AND WILL COME ACROSS WITH A DETACHED OR FLATTENED LEVEL OF AFFECT. IN MOST SITUATIONS, HIS MOOD IS APT TO BE UNCHANGING AND STABLE.

THE SUBJECT IS LIKELY TO BE VIEWED AS ODD OR DIFFERENT BY THOSE AROUND HIM. THIS PERSPECTIVE WILL BE FURTHER ENHANCED BY HIS OWN LACK OF DESIRE TO SEEK OUT CLOSE RELATIONSHIPS AND HIS PREFERENCE TO BE LEFT ALONE. HOWEVER, BECAUSE HE POSSESSES INORDINATELY DEVELOPED REASONING AND PROBLEM-SOLVING SKILLS, THIS INDIVIDUAL HAS THE POTENTIAL TO BECOME A KEEN MILITARY ASSET WHETHER IN SPECIAL OPERATIONS, INTELLIGENCE FUNCTIONS OR STRATEGIC PLANNING.

DIAGNOSTIC CONSIDERATIONS:
307.22 CHRONIC MOTOR TIC DISORDER
301.20 SCHIZOID PERSONALITY DISORDER

OPERATIONAL PROFILE

SPECIALTIES
CLOSE COMBAT, SMALL ARMS, EXPLOSIVES

MISSION HISTORY
1. NAM PHUC TRAN, NVN
17°33'N 106°32'E
18 JUNE 1970-24 JUNE 1970
STATUS: SUCCESSFUL
ENEMY KIA (TEAM): 101
ENEMY KIA (SUBJECT): 18

2. DONG CAO, NVN
17°37'N 106°32'E
3 DEC 1970-9 DEC 1970
STATUS: SUCCESSFUL
ENEMY KIA (TEAM): 117
ENEMY KIA (SUBJECT): 23

3. DON BAI DINH, NVN
17°45'N 106°46'E
12 JULY 1971-18 JULY 1971
STATUS: SUCCESSFUL
ENEMY KIA (TEAM): 114
ENEMY KIA (SUBJECT): 25

4. NAM LANH, NVN
17°53'N 106°28'E
7 JAN 1972-13 JAN 1972
STATUS: SUCCESSFUL
ENEMY KIA (TEAM): 102
ENEMY KIA (SUBJECT): 19

5. NE HE, NVN
17°57'N 106°14'E
8 AUG 1972-14 AUG 1972
STATUS: SUCCESSFUL
ENEMY KIA (TEAM): 137
ENEMY KIA (SUBJECT): 28

6. DUC LAM, NVN
18°16'N 105°53'E
31 OCT 1972-9 NOV 1972
STATUS: UNSUCCESSFUL/OPERATION TERMINATED
ENEMY KIA (TEAM): 67
ENEMY KIA (SUBJECT): 67

DOD DIRECTIVES

1. SURVEIL SUBJECT QUARTERLY. ANY CHANGE IN STATUS OR PSYCHOLOGICAL STABILITY SHOULD BE NOTED IN DEEPFILE AND REPORTED ASAP TO GEN. H. SAMPSON, USA.

2. DO NOT APPROACH SUBJECT WITHOUT PRIOR DOD AUTHORIZATION, PER GEN. H. SAMPSON, USA.

3. MAINTAIN MAXIMUM CAUTION DURING ANY CONTACT WITH SUBJECT. SUBJECT SHOULD BE PRESUMED UNSTABLE, HOSTILE, AND DANGEROUS.

4. PURGE DEEPFILE ON DEATH OF SUBJECT.

END DEEPFILE ENTRY 69-283

TOP SECRET TOP SECRET TOP SECRET

John handed the printout back to Bernie.

"You almost got me killed yesterday," Bernie said. "You owe me the truth."

"I was not an accountant when I was in the service."

"No kidding. What in the hell were you?"

"I was in a special operations unit. There were two teams, eight men each. It was called Operation Ares, after the Greek god of war."

"What was your mission?"

"We assassinated people."

"I hate to tell you this, but 'assassination' is just a fancy word for killing people, and that's something a lot of soldiers do."

"Not the kind we did," John said.

"And what kind was that?"

"We assassinated North Vietnamese Army soldiers inside North Vietnam."

"We didn't have ground troops in North Vietnam."

"People also thought we didn't bomb Cambodia until it came out in the press. The difference is that no one ever found out about us."

* * *

Bernie sat back in his chair. "Start from the beginning."

"I graduated from IU and got my commission," John said. "I was supposed to report to Fort Harrison, but they diverted me to Fort Bragg for psychological assessment."

"Why?"

"At the time, they didn't tell me. Later on, I learned they were screening people for potential assignment in what became Operation Ares."

"Screening you for what kinds of characteristics?"

John didn't respond.

"What's the matter, John?"

"I don't want to talk about it."

"Well, I didn't want to get shot at yesterday, so suck it up and tell me."

John grimaced and clenched his jaw. "They were looking for people who lack the capacity to understand how other people feel."

"All right," Bernie said. "What happened after they evaluated you?"

"They held me there for a few days, probably to give themselves time to write up the assessment and pass the results up the chain. The summary of that assessment is what you saw in my deepfile. At that point, I got orders to report to a facility on the outskirts of Quantico for more testing. There were at least two hundred men there, going through the same process. Some had been there for months, doing nothing, and no one had any idea why they were there."

"What did you do there?"

"Nothing for the first three weeks, and then they started testing me. Three days of tests, physical testing in the morning, psychological testing in the afternoon."

"I thought they'd already given you a psych exam."

"The Army ran the initial tests, but Thornton ran the Quantico tests because he wanted his own man to do the psych evaluation. The psychologist who tested me at Quantico was a guy named Rupert, who'd worked for Thornton for years."

"How were his tests different from the first ones?"

"I'll just say his were more comprehensive," John said.

"Okay, they tested you. Then what?"

"Another month went by, and then they ushered me into a room with fifteen other men. At the front of the room were three people: Thornton and his assistant—a Special Forces sergeant named Johannsen—and an Army major named Sampson, who's now a two-star general. Sampson was the head of the operation."

"What did they tell you?"

"They'd chosen us for a covert operation, something extremely hazardous. They told us to assume we wouldn't survive it, and anyone who wanted out should leave right then. No one did."

"You all had a death wish?"

"No. We stayed because of what Thornton told us. He said we were special, that we had talents we weren't aware of, abilities that he'd bring out in us and develop. It was the first time anyone had ever told me I was special, at least in a positive way, and in time I learned the others were a lot like me. We couldn't turn it down."

John paused for a beat. "We all wanted to be special."

"How did they describe the operation?" Bernie asked.

"There were dozens of North Vietnamese Army camps in North Vietnam just over the DMZ, each with hundreds of soldiers. They'd infiltrate into the South, create havoc, then cross back over the border or up the Ho Chi Minh Trail. We weren't supposed to send ground troops into the North, and at that time we couldn't use air power up there either."

"Instead, they sent in your teams covertly?"

"That's right. The two teams trained together, but went on missions separately. The first part of the training took ten months, and then we went on our first mission. Then more training, another mission, and the process repeated itself."

"That's a lot of training."

"Yes, it was. During the three years we were operational, we spent only six weeks in the field. The rest was all training, every day."

"Who ran the training?"

"Thornton. To him it was the opportunity of a lifetime."

"I'm not following you," Bernie said.

"What Thornton had really wanted to be, more than anything else, was a college professor. Things didn't work out that way, but he never lost his academic curiosity. For years, he'd been developing a system for selecting operators and training them. The only thing he lacked was a large sample of men to apply his process to."

"And in came the US government, which gave him a big sample."

"Thornton's dream come true," John said. "To him, it wasn't just a job—he looked at it as a proof of concept, with the government providing the test bed."

* * *

Bernie kept expecting John to stop talking, but he didn't, so Bernie kept going. "You get through the training and you go on missions. What was your mission protocol?"

"They'd insert us at night by helicopter. A UH-1D would drop us twenty kilometers from the target camp, very quick insertion. We'd spend that night and the next two nights approaching the target, then three nights of recon. On the seventh night, we'd attack. We'd have a seven-man assault team, and the eighth man would stay outside the perimeter, armed with a sniper rifle, to cover the team during withdrawal."

"How would you make the assault?"

"Each man on the assault team was assigned a sector. He'd take out the sentries in his sector, then all seven would breach the camp simultaneously from different points. We had one hour to operate after breach, and then we'd withdraw. The Huey would come back to a predetermined LZ a couple clicks away and extract us."

"You had an hour to do what, exactly?"

"The objective was to kill as many soldiers as possible, as quickly as possible, and as quietly as possible."

* * *

Bernie had tried his best to keep up, but he felt like he was missing something.

"Let's stop for a second. I understand wanting to kill the enemy, and from your file it looks like you guys killed plenty, but it seems like a hell of a lot of effort for what you were trying to accomplish."

"Why do you say that?"

"Think about it, John. Not one, but two sets of psych tests, plus the physical tests. Months and months of training. Why bother? We already had special operations units over there—Green Berets, SEALS, Rangers, Marine Force Recon. Why didn't they use the men they already had?"

"I never thought to ask. They gave us a mission, and we performed it."

Bernie frowned and shook his head. "Let's keep going. From your file, it looks like your first five missions were successful, but the sixth wasn't, and then they closed your operation. What happened there?"

"Our sixth mission was Duc Lam, the furthest north we'd ever gone. That night I was the perimeter man. The assault team dispersed. A minute later, all seven were cut down."

Bernie knew better than to say he was sorry. John never understood what he meant.

"They knew I was out there," John said, "and they sent troops after me. I couldn't wait for the helicopter to arrive. I had to keep moving, and the LZ was too hot for it to land, anyway. For the next three days, I evaded them, killed sixty-seven of their men, and finally got to a place where I could be extracted safely. I radioed in, and they came and got me."

"With all that going on, you actually kept count of the men you killed?"

"Of course. Keeping an accurate count was very important. They taught us to always keep count."

* * *

"Let's go back to something," Bernie said. "Your guys were killed before they even attacked. Did the NVA know you were coming?"

"Yes, they did."

"Did you ever find out how they knew?"

"It wasn't hard to figure out. He never showed up for work again."

"Thornton?"

"That's right."

"So, betraying your team was Thornton's ticket to getting in with General Quan?"

"No doubt about it. At that point, the Paris peace talks were progressing, and it looked like the war would end soon. Thornton needed to find his next job."

"That explains why they continued keeping it secret," Bernie said, "even after the operation ended. During Thornton's CIA days, he was in Burma, setting up the KMT, helping them take over and expand the opium trade. Twenty years later, the government rehired him, but it didn't dawn on them that he was now a mercenary, willing to sell out to the highest bidder. He turned on us, got your men killed, and then helped a North Vietnamese general take over the opium trade from the KMT, probably using knowledge he'd gained when he was on our payroll twenty years earlier. A great big black eye for the government, all the way around."

John looked impressed. "You've been busy."

"Busy chasing your bullshit," Bernie said.

"However you found out, you said it perfectly. There were too many people who would have been embarrassed. CIA people, DOD people, who knows how far up it went? There were too many careers at stake, so they covered it up, and over time, the cover-up took on a life of its own. And if all that wasn't bad enough, they had something else to worry about."

"Which was?"

"The nine of us," John said, "the remaining members of Ares. They think we're mentally disturbed, so they monitor us."

"For what?"

"To see if we're a danger to society."

"They're afraid you're going to snap and start mass-murdering people?"

"That's exactly what they're afraid of."

"Well, while we're on the subject of you murdering people—you came here to kill Thornton and avenge your teammates, didn't you?"

"Yes, I did."

"How long have you been planning this adventure?"

"Fifteen years, ever since the operation ended. I needed access to the government's information on his activities, so I used my accounting degree to get a job at the IRS, and asked to be assigned to the Intelligence Unit."

"Does the IRS know about you and Thornton?"

"No," John said. "The information concerning Ares is tightly compartmentalized within DOD. If IRS knew, they would never have let me come here."

"Then tell me how you swung this assignment."

"I monitored Thornton's activities right from the start in 1973. A few months ago, our intelligence suggested he was coming to the US. I went to my superior and recommended we take the case from the DEA, which was glad to oblige because it's so busy with the cocaine cartels. And when we got the case, I volunteered to head it."

* * *

"Let's fast forward to what happened yesterday," Bernie said. "You saw Stepanek following us, and decided to draw him to the silos and flush him out."

"Correct."

"Did you know him?"

"He was on the other Ares team."

Bernie smiled wryly. "This story just keeps getting better and better, you know that? Why didn't you tell me he was following us?"

"I assumed Thornton had sent him to kill me, and I needed to force his hand."

"No, John, you didn't *need* to. You did it because you *wanted* to. You wanted to kill Stepanek so you could send Thornton a message. 'Here I am, Professor, still as good as I ever was. Come and get me.' And all this bullshit about protecting Thornton—you just wanted to make sure no one else killed him before you did."

John didn't look angry—Bernie wasn't sure the man could even get angry—but he took his time responding.

"All my life," John said, "all I ever wanted was to have a friend, but I never had any. And then I joined Ares, and the men on my team became my friends. They liked me, even respected me because of what I could do, and then Robert Thornton murdered them. So, yes, I wanted to make sure no one else killed him before I did, because no one has a better right to kill him than I do."

"That's where you're wrong, John. If Thornton was pointing a gun at your head, getting ready to pull the trigger, then I'd say you'd have a good reason to kill him. But what you're talking about right now is first-degree murder, and that's a crime in this state."

"Then you may feel free to arrest me when I'm done."

"You won't get the chance. I'm going straight to Mike and we're gonna pull the plug on your little party."

"He won't believe you and you can't prove it."

"I can prove it with this," Bernie said, brandishing the printout.

"That file doesn't prove a thing. All it does is describe what I did in the Army. There's nothing in it that ties me to Thornton."

"Then I'll get his deepfile too."

"They've already purged it," John said. "And besides, I don't think you'd show my deepfile to anyone."

"Why not?"

"Because of how you got it. It's a three-month process, but somehow you got it in less than two weeks."

"I got it expedited."

"No, you didn't. No one gets it expedited. You turned someone and got inside. If you show that file to anyone, they'll trace it back to whoever gave it to you, and that person will go to jail. I don't think you'd do that to your source."

Bernie realized John was right. Practically everything he knew was from sources he couldn't disclose. He needed a chance to process everything, talk to Marcelle, and come up with a plan.

But he had one last question before he could leave. "Why were you even willing to tell me all this?"

"As you said, I owed you the truth, and now it's too late for you to stop me."

Bernie stood up and walked to the door, then turned and faced John again.

"I'm disappointed, John, disappointed about a lot of things. Disappointed you lied to us. Disappointed you played us. But what disappoints me the most is that I thought we were friends. I know I'm not perfect, but I'll tell you this for damn sure: I would never put a friend in the line of fire just to carry out a personal vendetta."

Chapter 54

Friday, May 22, 1987
5:27 p.m.

John took deep breaths and tried to calm himself, but when his buzzer rang, his heart started pounding.

Mary Ellen walked in with a loaf pan covered with plastic wrap. "Your apartment is so nice!"

John pointed at the kitchen table. "I got you flowers."

"Oh my God! They're beautiful!" She set the pan on the table and bent down to smell the bouquet.

"You can take them when you leave," John said.

"You are so sweet." She hugged him, and for reasons he couldn't understand, he relaxed.

Mary Ellen said, "I already made the meat loaf to save some time, but I still need to bake it. While it's baking, I can make the rest of the food."

"I got everything on the list," John said.

"I knew you would. You're dependable, aren't you?"

"Yes, I am."

Mary Ellen turned on the oven to preheat it. "Let's open the wine. Do you have a corkscrew?"

"A corkscrew?"

"You know, one of those curlicue things for pulling out corks."

The apartment had come furnished, and John had spent little time exploring the drawers. He fished around the utensil drawer, found a corkscrew, and handed it to her. Mary Ellen removed the cork and asked where he kept his glasses.

"Last cupboard on the left."

She opened the cupboard. "No wine glasses, but regular glasses work too, don't you think?" She filled each glass partway and handed him one.

"Let's clink glasses." She held hers up, he imitated her movement, and they touched their glasses together.

"Cheers!" She took a long drink of wine while John watched her. "Aren't you going to drink any?"

"Um, yes, of course." He took a small sip. John rarely drank alcohol, but the wine tasted good and made him feel more relaxed, so he took a few more sips.

Mary Ellen put the meat loaf in the oven and turned her attention to the potatoes. As she peeled and cut them, she told John about her week. He made sure he listened well and asked follow-up questions, just as Bernie had told him to do. All he had to do was follow the rules, and he felt himself gaining confidence.

Mary Ellen was an efficient cook. She prepared the green beans and boiled and mashed the potatoes and John set the table while she continued chatting. When the kitchen timer rang, she pulled the meat loaf out of the oven.

"It smells wonderful," John said.

"Wait till you taste it."

They brought the food to the table and sat down. Mary Ellen put two slices of meat loaf on his plate, along with portions of mashed potatoes and green beans.

"Try the meat loaf," she said.

He took a bite. "It's delicious."

Mary Ellen clapped her hands and looked delighted. "I told you it was the best!"

While they ate, Mary Ellen told him more about her life. "—and I was a Brownie and a Girl Scout and I got lots of badges."

"Which ones?" John thought it was a good follow-up question.

"Oh my God, let's see—drawing and painting and needlecraft and bibliophile and cook and conversationalist and homemaker—I got so many I can't even remember them all, because I liked getting them and as soon as I got one, I moved right on to the next one."

She was so joyful and enthusiastic, it made John happy just to listen to her. To Mary Ellen, life was something to take delight in, not something to endure.

When they finished eating, John cleared the table, rinsed the dishes and put them in his dishwasher.

"You're a neat person," Mary Ellen said. "I am, too. We're a lot alike, don't you think? Do you want to sit on the couch?"

"Okay."

Mary Ellen sat down first, and John sat down a foot away. As soon as he got settled, she moved closer to him. They were practically touching, and John wasn't sure what to do next. Bernie hadn't addressed this situation.

"I'm surprised you don't have a girlfriend," Mary Ellen said. "You're so nice and thoughtful. Women should line up for you."

"It's hard for me to form relationships, so I keep to myself."

She looked at him curiously. "Why do you say that? You're a wonderful person."

How could he possibly explain it to her?

"Most people have a place inside them where they feel things," John said. "Love and grief and concern for others. I don't have that place."

"You're wrong," Mary Ellen said. "The fact that you know about it tells me you have that place. You just don't recognize it when you see it."

She cupped her hand over the back of his head, drew him toward her, and kissed him.

It felt *good good good good good.*

She pulled away, then kissed him a second time, and it felt good all over again.

She stood up, took his hand in hers, and led him to his bedroom. He felt like he should be nervous, but he wasn't.

She undressed him, then asked him to undress her.

They made love for a long time. It was even better than kissing.

When they finished, John was lying on his back, Mary Ellen straddling him from above. He had no idea what to do now; Bernie's rules hadn't gotten nearly this far. He wondered if she was uncomfortable.

"Do you want me to move?"

"Not yet," she said. "I want to enjoy the moment."

John lay his head against the pillow and gazed at her. He watched her as she shut her eyes and breathed deeply, her breasts rising and falling in sync with her breaths. He watched her as she arched her back, tilted her head backward, and ran her fingers through her hair. He watched her as her right hand stiffened into a spear point.

She hesitated, just for a split-second, and he caught her wrist just before her fingertips reached his throat. She jerked to a halt, and before she could recover, he thrust his other hand upward. The heel of his hand hit the bottom of her nose, snapping her head backward, and her body rolled off his and onto the bed.

John put two fingers next to her carotid artery and felt for a pulse. She was alive, but unconscious.

He sat on the bed, looking at her and cursing himself for being so stupid. Thornton had created what he knew would be John's ideal woman, someone so perfect that his desire for her would repress any suspicions.

He put it out of his mind. He needed to focus on his next steps.

He'd based his entire plan on light. John knew his low-light vision would be superior to that of Thornton's men, but some of them would have night vision goggles that provided illumination by amplifying the ambient light. He'd planned to assault Thornton's mansion next Tuesday night, the evening of the new moon, when the sky would be darkest and the goggles would have the least amount of light to work with.

But Thornton must have deduced his plan, and that explained the events of the last two days. Stepanek was Thornton's Plan A, and the woman was Plan B. She was probably supposed to check in by a certain time, and when she didn't, Thornton would know she'd failed.

John now knew that Thornton was determined not to let him attack next Tuesday. Between now and then, the moonlight would diminish rapidly, and Thornton wouldn't handicap himself by letting John wait to strike. Thornton would have a contingency plan, some way of accelerating John's timetable.

But how?

The classic move would be to take a hostage, but that wouldn't work here. John had no family, no friends, no one he cared about.

No one except Bernie.

John pulled his phone off the hook, dialed Bernie's number, and let it ring ten times.

No answer.

He ran through the possibilities. Bernie could be home, ignoring the phone or sleeping through it; he could be out somewhere; or they could have already taken him.

Mary Ellen was still out, and there was no way to predict when she'd wake up. Different people reacted differently to traumatic brain injury; she could come back in fifteen seconds or fifteen minutes.

He couldn't afford to wait. The woman was irrelevant now. He had to see to Bernie.

John dressed quickly and pulled two bags out of his closet. The first was bulky but light. The second, much heavier, was his old Army duffel bag. This bag was the real reason he'd driven to

Chicago instead of flying. He would never have gotten it through airport security.

He hoisted the bags onto his shoulders and looked at the woman one last time, replaying the events in his mind. She'd come within a hair's breadth of killing him. He was still alive only because she had hesitated.

He walked out of the bedroom and was almost to the door when another thought hit him: his response to her attack was all wrong. Thornton had taught them early on that when someone threatened their life, it was no time for half-measures; you struck back to kill, because anything less might be inadequate. It was a good rule, and following it had saved his life many times, but on this night, when this woman had threatened him, he had deliberately held back.

Chapter 55

Friday, May 22, 1987
8:51 p.m.

Somewhere in Bernie's dream, a phone was ringing.

When he left John's apartment that afternoon, he considered and rejected the idea of going back to Marcelle and getting her advice. He'd just done that the day before, and this time he wanted to be a big boy, figure out a plan himself, and then run it by her.

He was still exhausted from yesterday's events, so he went to bed early. He soon fell into a deep sleep in which dreams came quickly, and his present dream was going along just swimmingly until the phone started ringing. It didn't make any sense in the dream's context, and it was damned annoying.

So annoying, in fact, that by the eighth ring he woke up enough to realize it wasn't in his dream at all. It was the phone on his bedside table.

He turned over and began to reach for it, but stopped short because two men stood next to his bed, pointing pistols at him.

"Good evening, Mr. Bernardelli. Professor Thornton wishes to see you."

"Tell him I'll be in my office first thing Monday morning."

"He wishes to see you now."

Bernie looked at the muzzles of the pistols. "Well, I'm always happy to accommodate the public. You mind if I put some pants on?"

Chapter 56

Friday, May 22, 1987
9:19 p.m.

John kept checking his rearview mirror as he drove to Bernie's apartment. No one was following him, though that meant nothing. They expected him to go there, so they didn't need to follow him.

He parked a few doors down from Bernie's building. He got out of his car, looked up and down the street, and saw nothing suspicious.

He opened his trunk and pulled out the heavy duffel bag and a large, empty backpack. He walked inside Bernie's building and rang the buzzer, but it went unanswered. The vestibule door was locked.

He unzipped his duffel bag and found the pouch that held his lock pick set. He'd practiced repeatedly during the last two months, and the practice paid off: he got the door open in twenty seconds.

He walked up to the third floor, found Bernie's door, and put his ear next to it. He heard nothing but the refrigerator running.

John pulled a pistol out of his bag, inserted a loaded magazine, and cycled the slide to chamber a round. He quietly turned the doorknob, expecting it to stop, but it was unlocked. He threw the door open, swept the space with his pistol, and quickly cleared the rest of the apartment.

He didn't find Bernie, but he did find a note in a familiar handwriting on Bernie's bed:

At 0300 next, your eighth friend will die by my hand.
Come alone.
RT

Chapter 57

Friday, May 22, 1987
9:23 p.m.

Bernie was in the back seat, one man sitting next to him while the other drove. Neither man said a word, and neither seemed the least bit concerned about Bernie. What was he going to do, open the door and roll onto the expressway at sixty miles an hour?

He knew they took him to draw John in, just as he knew he was as good as dead. No one kidnapped a cop intending to let him go. He considered it briefly, then forced himself to ignore it. As long as he was alive, he had a job to do, and now his job was to help John.

They finally arrived at the gate, the same one he'd gotten stuck at a week ago, but this time the gate opened and they drove through. Bernie was surprised at how long the driveway was. The place looked like a forest, and it was dark as hell.

They wound around, reached the clearing, and pulled up to the mansion's front door. They walked inside and down a long hallway, stopping at a carved wood door.

One of the men knocked, and Bernie heard someone inside say "enter." The man opened the door, and Bernie beheld a room so beautiful that it looked like it had come straight out of a movie—a library of wood and marble, and stuffed to the gills with books.

Inside the room was a man who walked toward them. He wore the most expensive suit Bernie had ever seen, and not a single strand of his white hair was out of place. As befit the room, he looked like a movie star.

He gave Bernie a broad smile.

"Welcome, Mr. Bernardelli," said Robert Thornton. "Would you care for something to drink?"

Chapter 58

Friday, May 22, 1987
9:25 p.m.

John dropped his duffel bag onto Bernie's floor and removed its contents. He changed into the camouflage clothes he'd worn in Vietnam; they weren't ideal for the environment he'd be in, but they were only secondary camouflage. He arranged his knife sheath on the right side of his belt. Inside it was the Gerber Mark II he'd used in the war.

John pulled out his rifle, an unsuppressed, semi-automatic H&K MP5. He loaded one 30-round magazine, inserted it and chambered a round, and made sure it was on safe. He was tempted to load another mag, but didn't want the bulk.

Which pistol? He had a 1911-style .45 and a 9mm Glock 17, one of the first to hit American shores. He didn't like the Glock's springy trigger, but it had a fantastic ratio of ammunition capacity to weight, and it was utterly reliable.

He chose the Glock. With two fully loaded mags and one in the chamber, he'd have thirty-five rounds for the pistol. He slid the holster onto the left side of his belt, as he expected to use the pistol much less than the knife.

Now John turned his attention to his demolition materials. Five years ago, the IRS had lent him to its sister agency, the Bureau of

Alcohol, Tobacco, and Firearms, to help it investigate a company suspected of stealing and selling military explosives. ATF had granted his request to be on the raid team, and he surreptitiously siphoned off some of the stolen items and hid them in an air vent. From there, it was just a matter of infiltrating the building later and retrieving them.

John arranged the materials on the floor, starting with the explosives: ten 1¼-pound blocks of US military M112 demolition charges, also known as C-4. He also had three plastic cap boxes, each containing ten M7 non-electric blasting caps; a fifty-foot coil of M700 time blasting fuse; and a twenty-foot coil of Type 1 Class E detonating cord. He hadn't been able to steal any time-delay fuse igniters, so he'd made his own using digital kitchen timers, nine-volt batteries, stormproof matches, and cheap electronic components he'd bought at a hobby shop. He needed to minimize weight, so he put what was necessary into the backpack and returned the rest to the duffel bag.

John finished packing up his gear, some going in the backpack, some in a waist pack, and the rest in his pants pockets. He made one last check and satisfied himself he was ready. He slung the MP5 over his shoulder, followed by a coat and the two packs. He left the duffel bag on the floor; its contents would be safer here than in his car. He made sure to lock Bernie's door.

He walked out of the building, stopped, and looked right and left. Fifth car on the left across the street, exhaust fumes rising from an idling engine. That would be Thornton's man. He had to lose the man or kill him.

John dropped the packs and rifle onto the rear seat of his car and considered his next move. In all those hours driving around Chicago with Bernie, he'd learned two things. The first was that there was a main road every half-mile. The second was this: if a Chicago driver was stopped at a red light, the instant it turned green he shot forward like a rocket.

John pulled away slowly, and the other car pulled out behind him. A block ahead was the main road, with the traffic light facing him on green. As he neared the intersection, the light turned yellow, and he slowed down as if to stop, but at the last second, he gunned the engine and made it through as it turned red. The tail car skidded to a halt as the cross traffic sure enough started instantly. He had a thirty-second head start.

The traffic ahead of him was backed up, and he needed to get out from under it. Halfway down the block, he saw an alley on his right. He turned into it, then stopped immediately. It wasn't a through alley; it dead-ended into a building with a loading dock. There was a two-story brick building on the left, a three-story brick building on the right, and the dock and its building in front of him. On one side of the dock were stairs that led to the top of the dock and the building it fed. The building's entrance was a metal door with a deadbolt lock. He was boxed in on three sides.

He had twenty seconds.

* * *

Johnson saw Shepard turn right. The light finally turned green, and he sped forward. He was only thirty seconds behind. He made the same turn, saw Shepard's parked car in front of a loading dock, and hit the brakes.

Okay, you bastard, where are you?

The choices: inside the car, under the car, in the trunk. He saw the metal door of the building over the loading dock; that was choice number four.

Johnson exited the car, .45 in hand. He dropped to the ground and looked under Shepard's car. Nobody there.

Johnson crawled forward, belly hugging the ground, crunching against the asphalt and debris, and worked his way to the passenger side of the car. He sprang up and swept the passenger compartment with his pistol.

Nothing. Shepard was in the trunk, or he'd escaped through the building.

He checked the driver's door, found it unlocked, and opened it. His pistol was in his right hand, pointed at the rear of the car, just in case. He reached inside the car with his left hand and popped the trunk.

Moment of truth time.

Johnson hit the ground again and crawled to the rear of the car. He lifted his hand over his head and pushed up the trunk lid, ready to fire. He heard nothing, but he was below the opening and couldn't see inside. He crawled backward while facing the rear of the car, gun in hand, until he was five feet directly behind it, then jumped up with his pistol.

The trunk was empty.

Son of a bitch. Shepard had picked the lock and gone through the door of the building. And while he was crawling around the car, Shepard was running through the building and out the front door. He was probably half a mile away by now.

At least it wasn't all bad news. Even though he'd lost the guy, Shepard was now without a car. He'd have to hot-wire one or carjack one. Either way, he'd be behind schedule, and by the time he got to the mansion, he'd be in hurry-up mode. A minor victory, anyway.

Johnson winced at the thought of calling it in, but knew he had to. He holstered the gun and turned back to his car.

John Shepard was crouching four feet in front of him with a knife in his hand.

John lunged forward, the knife in a reverse grip, and punched his hand near the side of Johnson's neck. The blade, trailing behind his hand, slashed through the front and side of Johnson's throat, and when John's arm reached full extension, he reversed it, dragging the blade back through the slash and expanding it. He finished by thrusting the blade through the gash he'd created, cutting through the aortic arch. The entire procedure took less than two seconds.

John looked down at the body. The man was dead because he'd forgotten about the roofs of the buildings. It didn't take long to climb up and down two stories.

He searched the man and his car, found a pistol, a knife, and a radio, and tossed them into his own car. The man's car was blocking his, so he backed it out, parallel-parked it on the street, and returned to his own car. As he shifted into reverse, he made a mental note, just as they'd trained him to do.

One.

Chapter 59

Friday, May 22, 1987
10:04 p.m.

"Coffee, black," Bernie said.

Ten seconds later, Thornton's man handed Bernie a full cup on a saucer.

"Man, these guys give great service," Bernie told Thornton. "You ever rent them out for parties?"

"I admire your bravado, Mr. Bernardelli." Thornton gestured with his right hand. "Shall we sit?"

They sat down in armchairs across from each other, and Bernie set his cup and saucer on a side table. His hands were shaking, and he didn't want to hold the china.

"I suppose you've gathered why you're here," Thornton said.

"I'm bait for John."

"Succinctly stated, and quite correct. Please don't misunderstand, I bear no ill will toward John. On the contrary, I rather like him. He has an endearing, almost childlike quality. He is, however, quite intent on killing me—for good reason, I suppose— and I must see to self-preservation."

"You didn't have to take me," Bernie said. "John was coming after you no matter what."

"I don't doubt that, but I prefer to battle John on my schedule, not his. I thus decided it was time to bring Mohammed to the mountain."

Thornton looked like he didn't have a care in the world, just one man sitting with another in a beautiful, comfortable room, enjoying an evening's chat over tea and coffee. But he was a blowhard, and sometimes blowhards needed deflating.

Bernie said, "You're afraid of him, aren't you?"

Thornton raised his teacup to his lips, took a polite sip, and smoothly set it back down. "How much do you know about John?"

"I know you put him on one of the Ares teams and trained him."

"All of that is true, but how much do you know about *him*?"

"Not much, I guess."

Thornton's eyes sparkled at the chance to tell the story and he reclined comfortably in his chair. "Every once in a great while, a person is born with a special talent. Consider, for example, a major league baseball pitcher. Millions of boys try baseball in their life, but at any given time there are only around three hundred major league pitchers. Anyone with a normal arm and hand can throw a baseball, but a major league pitcher can do it so much better than the typical person that he's on a completely different plane from the rest of humanity. And why is it he's able to pitch so well? No doubt his training and practice have much to do with it, but those factors don't explain it entirely. Another person could receive the same training and practice just as hard, but could never pitch one-tenth as well.

"To put it simply, a major league pitcher can pitch as he does because he's born with a particular set of physical and psychological characteristics, which, in combination, produce the ability to throw a small sphere extraordinarily well. Your friend John, likewise, was born with a set of characteristics that produced a special talent. He was born with the ability to kill people."

"You sick bastard, if you can't even tell the difference between throwing a baseball and killing someone—"

"Don't be so sanctimonious. Abilities have no moral dimension by themselves; it's how they're used that matters. Fighting skill has been valued since the dawn of man and always will be. Your own department has tactical teams, does it not? And what are the criteria for selecting the men for those teams? That they're good, churchgoing citizens?"

Thornton didn't wait for an answer to his rhetorical question. "They're selected because of their ability—and their willingness—to dispense violence at society's request. The Ares teams were no different. The United States government spent a fortune selecting and training the men for those teams, and my methods produced men that performed beyond the government's wildest dreams."

* * *

John turned onto the expressway and was glad to see the traffic moving smoothly. The last two hours had been so hectic he hadn't been able to think beyond the immediate, but as he settled in for the drive, it hit him that he was nearing the end of his fifteen-year journey.

Besides the waiting, the hardest part had been maintaining his skills. He'd gone to martial arts schools to find sparring partners, but inevitably, the questions would come: *Where did you learn that? Do you compete? Can you teach me?* And when the questions became too uncomfortable, he would go to another school and find new sparring partners. It wasn't the best way to train, and the men he'd be up against had a better training regimen, but it was the best he could do.

For the last ten days, he'd been gathering intelligence and formulating his plan. The materials the county gave him last week told him everything he needed to know about the buildings. That covered the inside, but he still needed to cover the outside, so he'd spent two nights reconnoitering the property to learn its layout and to see how they set up their defenses. He knew, though, that there was an important difference between then and now. On those nights, Thornton had assigned a low probability of attack so he didn't field all his men. Tonight, John would face the full complement.

* * *

Thornton just loved the sound of his own voice, and Bernie realized how he could help John: keep the guy talking and distract him from running his men.

"What methods are you referring to?" Bernie asked.

Thornton looked eager to answer the question. "With the help of a psychologist, and applying many years' worth of my own observations, we devised a system for predicting fighting skill. We isolated and created tests to measure the particular physical and psychological traits that produce the ability to fight well, and then we trained the men to exploit that ability to its fullest. Do you know how many men we tested before we chose the sixteen men for the teams?"

"I sure don't."

"Three hundred, Mr. Bernardelli. The Army gave me three hundred men chosen without regard to any skill sets they might already have had. The testing process alone took six months. As for the sixteen men we selected, none had any prior experience in the fighting arts. Relying only on our testing process, we selected sixteen men who appeared thoroughly unremarkable, and then we made them into superlative man-killers."

"It's hard to accept," Bernie said. "John's so, you know—"

"Small?" Thornton's lips curled in disgust. "Just like a Westerner to confuse size with skill. Asians have known for centuries there's no correlation. John is the perfect combination of the characteristics we search for."

"Like what?"

"It's much too involved to cover in a brief conversation, but I'll give you two examples. The first is that John has a very useful heart rate anomaly."

"Now you've lost me."

"Nearly all people have a lower pulse rate when they're in a non-stressful situation—or at least what you and I would consider non-stressful. Put them under stress, especially a situation that presents danger, and their heart rate and adrenaline escalate rapidly, which, in turn, increases their strength and speed. Those were evolutionary, adaptive responses that helped the species survive. But with modern fighting methods and weapons, those responses are often counterproductive. They impede the exercise of judgment and degrade fine motor skills."

"And John's the opposite?"

"Precisely. No doubt you've noticed his high anxiety level and motor tics in everyday situations. What most people think of as normal life makes John nervous, but put him in a situation where he's called upon to perform, particularly one involving jeopardy, and his pulse declines. He becomes nearly serene, able to function at a high level, without interference from an accelerated heartbeat or adrenaline surge."

"You said you'd give me two examples."

"Very well. I suppose this one will further offend your sensibilities, but among the prime characteristics we look for is a lack of empathy. During my time in China, I came into possession of a film captured from the enemy. It's much too awful to describe, so suffice it to say it depicts soldiers committing horrible atrocities against helpless people. Over the years, we've shown that film to over a thousand men as part of our testing process. Well over eighty percent of them vomited when they saw it, which should give you some notion of its contents. You'll be pleased to know that John had the flattest, most impassive response of anyone we've ever tested."

"I don't believe it," Bernie said.

Thornton gave him a dismissive wave. "Believe what you will. The data do not lie, nor does John's performance."

* * *

John ditched his car at the forest preserve, a mile from Thornton's mansion. He opened his visor mirror and applied his face paint—shades of black, brown, and green—putting the darker colors on the higher areas of his face and the lighter colors on the lower ones. He made sure he painted his neck, ears, and eyelids. He put on a camouflage watch cap, then retrieved his rifle, backpack, and waist pack from the back seat. Finally, he opened the second bag he'd taken from his apartment and pulled out his ghillie suit. He'd made it himself from netting and dyed burlap, and enhanced it with fir needles, leaves, branches, and ground vegetation gathered during his two nights of recon.

Fully geared up, John began the trek to Thornton's property. He walked at a moderate pace, scanning constantly in case Thornton had sentries in the forest preserve, and he ran through his plan one last time.

The property was thirty-three acres, densely forested with firs and hardwoods, the ground covered with vegetation. In the center of the tract was a clearing in which the buildings sat. The clearing was roughly circular, with a diameter he estimated at 150 yards.

Darkness was his ally, light was his enemy, and there would be some of both. The buildings had floodlights at six-foot intervals just below their roofs, but McHenry County had turned down Thornton's request to install lights in the woods, saying it would harm the area's natural ambience.

It meant he could be invisible as long as he was in the woods. The hard part would be the last fifty yards from the edge of the trees to the buildings.

His first priority was eliminating the lights. The primary power supply was a distribution transformer on a pole at the perimeter of the property. The backup power supply was a commercial-size generator, just behind the mansion, fueled by natural gas. During his recon, John hadn't been able to get close enough to see how they'd secured the generator, but Thornton would have fortified it as best he could.

The last backup was the emergency lighting system. Each exterior wall had a battery-operated light that automatically switched on if the power supply went down; likewise, the main stairwells in the mansion and the annex had an emergency light at each floor. Each light had its own battery and its own switch; there was no way to shut them all off simultaneously. Even if he killed the power supplies, there would still be some light outside and in.

As for Thornton's men, they were well-equipped. Each one had a pistol, a suppressed MP5, and body armor. The one sentry he'd seen roving the woods had night vision goggles.

Those were the knowns. Now he had to contemplate the unknowns.

The first unknown was how Thornton would deploy his forces. Twelve men—now eleven—were too few to saturate such a large area. Thornton would have to post them judiciously.

During his recon, John had spotted the one roving sentry in the woods and stationary guards at the electrical pole and the generator, but there was no guarantee Thornton would do the same tonight. He would certainly have a man on the annex roof and another in the room with Thornton and Bernie. That left the perimeter of the buildings and the remaining interior spaces. Thornton would have to choose between concentrating his men where he was located, or spreading them out to maximize their chance of stopping John before he got close.

The biggest unknown was Thornton's location. John knew Thornton's ego wouldn't let him retreat or barricade himself. He would stay put and ensconce himself in the grandest room available. That meant the ballroom in the annex or the dining room or library in the mansion, which, not coincidentally, were the only three rooms with their own emergency lights.

* * *

Bernie could tell Thornton was slowing down. He needed to get the man going again.

"John told me the story this afternoon," he said, "and there's something I can't figure."

"I'd be pleased to enlighten you."

"The military wanted to kill the soldiers at some enemy bases— that much I get. What I don't get is why they went to so much trouble to test so many people and train them for so long. We had hundreds of special ops guys over there who could've done the job. Why didn't they just pick sixteen and call it a day?"

Thornton's eyes tightened, and he sat up. "Is that all John told you?"

"It is."

"Then perhaps he still doesn't know as much as he thinks he does."

A man walked in, leaned down, and whispered something to Thornton. Whatever it was, Thornton looked unhappy. He gave a curt response, and the man left. It had to mean John was still alive.

"Trouble in paradise?" Bernie asked.

"Nothing we haven't planned for."

Bernie sat back, looking as smug as he could. "John's pretty good, isn't he?"

Thornton again declined to rise to the bait. "I gave you examples of John's characteristics. Now I'll give you an example of the ability his characteristics produced. I presume he told you about his last mission?"

"Yeah, and how you double-crossed them."

Thornton ignored him. "The plan called for seven men to infiltrate the compound, with an eighth man to hold on the perimeter to cover the others during withdrawal. The eighth man was supposed to be someone other than John, but that's irrelevant now. The salient point is that we knew a man would be out there, so we planned for it. As soon as we stopped the team's assault, we sent one hundred troops in pursuit of the eighth man, who turned out to be John.

"Now ponder that, Mr. Bernardelli. One hundred men who were prepared for the situation, who knew the terrain intimately, against one man who was surprised and in unfamiliar surroundings. John nevertheless evaded his pursuers and killed two-thirds of the men who were hunting him. It's a shame, really, that the operation was classified. He should have become a legend, and his tactics taught in military academies."

"Even though he beat you, you sound pretty proud of him."

"Indeed, I am," Thornton said. "John is my creation. I found him and trained him and sent him forth."

"Well, you should've gone after him when you had the chance. Now he's on his way and he gets to choose how he's going to do it."

"We did go after him," Thornton said, "twice in the last two days, as a matter of fact. The second attempt failed a short time ago."

"And the first was yesterday when you sent Stepanek, right?"

"Ah, yes, poor Edward. I didn't fancy the idea of waiting for John to attack, so naturally I put certain countermeasures into motion. I did not, however, send Edward directly."

"Then who did?"

"I knew Edward had continued to practice the art I'd taught him—as I'm sure you can appreciate, assassins with his level of skill are well-known in my particular business—but I didn't deem it prudent to engage him directly. Instead, I prevailed upon the government to hire him, which, incidentally, already knew how

Edward earned his living. Unfortunately, Edward was engaged in another project, and it wasn't until late last week I knew for certain he was coming here."

"There are lots of contract killers," Bernie said. "Why him?"

"Edward was the logical choice, not only because he was highly competent but also because he knew John's techniques."

"There's more to it than that," Bernie said. "You wanted to know whether John still had his stuff after all these years, and that's why you picked Stepanek. You knew Stepanek was still in the game, still keeping his skills sharp. What better way to test John than to match him against one of his classmates? If Stepanek won, your problem's solved. And if he failed, at least you wouldn't be sacrificing one of your own guys."

"Very perceptive," Thornton said. "Even my closest advisor didn't deduce that."

"What puzzles me most is your strategy. Here you are, with a dozen highly trained men, and there's John, all alone and unprotected. Why not just send in a team and take him out?"

"There is a maxim in the art of assassination," Thornton said. "It is easy to kill someone; the hard part is getting away with it. Sending in a group like that draws attention and increases the possibility of evidence being left behind. We prefer to kill with minimal commotion, which leaves us with two methods."

"Which are what?"

"To kill from afar and to kill at touching distance. Unfortunately, we tried both, and neither succeeded. Our only alternative now is to face him here, but at a time of our choosing."

"You know he's coming," Bernie said. "Why are you even still here?"

"Leaders lead. They do not run."

"Very inspiring, but you know damn well that's not the only reason."

Thornton's eyes blazed, but he said nothing.

"What would happen," Bernie said, "if John made it all the way to this room and you weren't here? You were safe in Thailand, but now you're in the States, and you know John would keep hunting you." He thought back to what Gene Richards had told him in New York. "It would be one thing to see John in front of you—that'd be frightening enough—but the thought that John might stand over you while you're sleeping and cut your throat is absolutely terrifying."

Thornton's continued silence told Bernie he was right. "You don't want to be running, scared every minute, so you picked the least bad option and stayed in your fortress. And you're conceited enough to think you can talk him out of it."

A trace of a smile played across Thornton's face, as if Bernie had accomplished the nearly impossible task of earning his respect.

"You won't talk him out of it," Bernie said. "He's gonna walk in here and kill you."

"Perhaps he will, but after facing death countless times over the last forty-five years, I've accepted its inevitability. And of all the ways I could die, there are worse ways than to be killed by a master."

"That's how you think of him?"

Thornton had projected invincibility ever since Bernie arrived, but now an air of sadness came over him. "Of all the men I've trained, John is without question the most proficient. Had I been empowered to grant degrees, his would have been *summa cum laude*."

Chapter 60

Friday, May 22, 1987
11:42 p.m.

John reached the fence.

It was only five feet high, intended mainly to keep out the idly curious. He lowered his ghillie suit, rifle, and packs over the side. He backed up several yards, sprinted forward and jumped the fence, landing silently on the soles of his feet.

He donned his ghillie suit and the packs, and slung the rifle over his shoulder. He was at the southeast side of the property and ready to begin the first sequence: eliminate any sentries around the electrical pole at the northeast end and rig the explosives to disable the primary power supply.

Only sprays of moonlight filtered through the trees. The wind was moving in a cycle, blowing awhile, then ebbing, then resuming; it provided some cover. He advanced in a crouch, making sure he avoided a steady rhythm, moving when the wind blew and stopping when it receded. He saw and heard nothing out of the ordinary, and stopped when he was seventy-five yards from the electrical pole.

No guard was there, or at least none he could see. Thornton had either given up on the primary supply, choosing to rely only on the generator, or it was a ploy to draw John in and induce him to let his defenses down.

John stowed his packs near a tree and covered them with vegetation. He listened, heard nothing, and began crawling.

Human beings tend to behave in patterns, consciously or not. Even the best-trained sentries can unintentionally fall into a pattern of movement, favoring certain areas and avoiding others. Twenty yards from the electrical pole, John found what he was looking for: a depression in the vegetation and fallen foliage formed by footsteps extending northeast toward the electrical pole and southwest toward the mansion. He followed it for a spell and came upon an intersecting depression. Two sentries roving in a crossing pattern.

John crawled back toward the pole, following alongside the first path he'd seen. When he found a suitable spot, he went prone, face down, two feet to the side of the path. For the next few minutes, he'd have to rely only on his hearing.

John was now part of the earth, just leaves and branches and fir needles and grass in harmony with the terrain. He filled his nostrils with the dampness and smell of the ground, imagining himself not as being on it but as being part of it. He listened, filtering out the ambient sounds of wind and the occasional car driving down Route 31, and finally heard a sound that shouldn't be there, coming from behind him and getting closer.

The sentry was walking at a deliberate pace, no doubt scanning all around. John waited until he heard the footsteps barely pass him.

He leaped up with his knife in a reverse grip. Cupped his hand over the man's mouth and pulled his head back to expose the neck. One forward slash against the side of his neck and a reverse slash that ripped his throat out. Keeping his hand over the man's mouth, he took a step back, lay him on the ground, and then fell onto his face and neck to muffle the inevitable gurgling that accompanies a cut throat.

Two.

John waited thirty seconds, listened, and heard nothing but the wind. Now he could figure out what type of body armor Thornton's men wore.

There are vests that stop bullets, vests that stop edged weapons, and vests that stop both. He thrust his knife down and, sure enough, it stopped abruptly and deflected.

Was it bulletproof as well? Only one way to find out.

He picked up the man's suppressed MP5, flipped the selector lever to semi-automatic, and fired once.

He removed the vest and examined it. There was a hole in the front, but not in the back. Stab proof and bulletproof. It meant the torso was off limits.

But even though the war gods had taken something away, they'd also given him something. He now had a suppressed, fully automatic MP5.

The sentry wore AN/PVS-5 night vision goggles. John had trained with them once at a Treasury class.

He pulled the goggles off the body, put them on, and remembered why he didn't like them. They were heavy and bulky. They reduced the three-dimensional world to two dimensions, like looking through two tunnels, and diminished his depth perception. They also reduced his field of view from 190 degrees to 40 degrees, which meant he'd constantly need to turn his head to scan for threats.

Worst of all, the image was terrible. The goggles reduced his visual acuity from his normal 20/15 to 20/60, and contrast and resolution were awful.

He took the goggles off and tossed them aside. He could do better without them.

John crawled to the second path he'd seen earlier, lay down next to it, and waited again. Five minutes later, he heard footsteps, but this time they were coming toward him.

He let the footsteps pass, then stood straight up, pivoted around, and launched himself with his knife in hand.

But the sound of the pivot had given him away. Just as John reached him, the man turned and his rifle turned with him, swinging toward John's right.

Before the man could finish his turn, John cocked his body down and left, lashed out with his right leg, and kicked the man's kneecap. The man fell forward with his finger against the trigger, the gun firing on full auto, the only sounds the thumps of the bullets striking the dirt. The man hit the ground and dropped his rifle, but before John could pounce on him, the man rolled sideways and drew a knife from a thigh scabbard.

John dove at him, bending his left arm in front of his chest to block a strike. The man thrust the knife forward and John parried it, the knife scraping across the top of John's left forearm. John plunged his own knife hard into the man's lower abdomen below his vest and slashed it laterally.

The man let go of his knife and lay still. He stared up at John, wordlessly pleading for mercy, his mouth agape, his face a mixture of terror and hope.

The terror was understandable; the hope was not. Thornton had taught every man he'd ever trained: *The only rule of warfare is to make sure the enemy is dead.*

John picked up the man's rifle and put a bullet through his head. *Three.*

* * *

John's left arm felt like someone had poured acid on it.

He looked at the left sleeve of his ghillie suit covering the top of his forearm. The knife had cut through one of the attached branches. John pulled his arm out of the suit and rolled up his shirtsleeve, already drenched in blood. It was too dark to get a good look at the cut and too risky to turn on his flashlight, so he put his eyes directly over the wound and pulled back the skin on both sides, gritting his teeth to avoid crying out. The cut covered the width of his forearm, but didn't appear to be too deep; the branch on his suit had blunted some of the impact.

That was the good news. The bad news was that he was losing blood. He needed to get to the first aid kit in his backpack.

He took four steps toward it and stopped.

His backpack didn't have a first aid kit.

In Vietnam, the kit had stayed permanently in his pack—never removed, so he'd never leave it behind. In time, he'd taken its presence for granted, which was why it hadn't occurred to him when gathering his gear for the trip to Chicago.

He searched the dead man but found nothing useful. He'd have to improvise.

Keeping his left arm elevated, he used his right hand to cut two long strips from the man's pants and wrapped one around the cut. When that strip was saturated, he'd use the other, but he didn't have any adhesive tape or gauze to secure it.

John untied one of the man's bootlaces. He applied pressure to the wound for two minutes, then unwrapped the first strip and wrapped the other. He tied the bootlace around the strip, held one end in his teeth, and knotted it as tightly as he could.

John tested his left hand, clenching and unclenching it. His arm hurt each time, but it was still usable. He had perhaps fifty percent strength in it.

He couldn't spend any more time addressing the wound. He had to get to the power supply.

The question was whether any additional sentries were patrolling the area around the electrical pole. He'd seen no evidence of it, but there wasn't enough time to do a more thorough search.

He retrieved his backpack and made his way to the electrical pole. He would have to climb to the top, rig the explosive on the distribution transformer, and climb back down—a process that would take several minutes, during which he'd be exposed and helpless against an attack.

He opened the backpack, put on a lineman's belt and climbing gaffs, and put his demolition materials in a pouch on the belt. He did a quick scan around the area, then wrapped the safety strap around the pole and climbed up.

When he reached the transformer, he worked quickly but methodically. He'd lost some dexterity in his left hand, so he used his right whenever as he could. He pulled the paper backing off the bottom of a C-4 block and stuck it, adhesive side down, on top of the transformer. It would be loud when it detonated, but it wouldn't give away his position because he'd be nowhere near it.

He primed the block and installed his jury-rigged time-delay fuse igniter. It looked like something a mad scientist would concoct in his basement, but he'd tested several iterations and was confident it would work.

Now he had to set the timer. He thought through his next sequence, estimated how long it would take, and added five minutes. A late explosion would simply delay him, but a premature explosion would critically wound his plan. He worked the buttons on the timer, flipped the switch, and pressed the timer's start button. He looked at his watch and memorized the time; synchronization was key.

He made his way down the pole, took off the climbing gear, and hid it under some bushes.

* * *

Staying well back in the woods, John reconnoitered the perimeter of the buildings. There was one guard on each of the four sides of the connected buildings, plus one on the annex roof. Thornton should have had at least three men per side, so if John killed one, the others could react. But Thornton had wanted a large estate, and what he got was too large to defend appropriately with the number of men he had. That was the price of ego.

The clearing in front of the buildings, on their east side, had a driveway and a few small flower gardens at irregular intervals. The other three sides had lawns and larger gardens of small trees, shrubs, and flowers.

The annex building was on the north side and the connected mansion was on the south side. The generator was behind the mansion on the west side.

Most of the annex roof was a flat rectangle, making it a good patrol platform for the rooftop sentry. The south end of the annex had a tall pitched roof that rose above the top of the flat roof, and the mansion behind it also had pitched roofs. It meant the rooftop sentry would have an unobstructed view of the north, partial views of the east and west, and almost no view of the south.

The guards spoke into their radios intermittently, no doubt checking in, but they didn't seem to do it on a set schedule. That was a smart move; it meant he couldn't predict when the next one would occur. From what he saw, they never strayed outside their respective sectors.

John was twenty yards from the clearing, facing the southwest corner of the mansion, in the rooftop sentry's blind spot. Once he was at the edge of the woods, he'd have to cover fifty yards of open, brightly lit space before he could get to the south guard.

He decided not to use the MP5. The next kills had to be instant and silent, but an instant kill with this subgun at this distance at a moving target was beyond his capability. The gun had a short sight radius and an unknown zero on the sights, not to mention the guards' vests. There was no way he could make a perfect, first-shot head shot.

He'd have to get in close.

He removed some demolition materials and a few other items of gear from his backpack, put them in the waist pack, and fastened it to his body. From here on out, he'd need maximum mobility, and that meant he had to jettison the backpack. The last thing he took out of the backpack was an entrenching tool, a folding shovel with a saw edge on one side and a sharp edge on the other.

John checked his watch. Twenty-six minutes until the transformer exploded. In that interval, he'd have to eliminate two guards and the generator.

He slung the MP5 tight against his back and cinched up his ghillie suit. The only thing in his hands was the e-tool.

He saw the south guard speak into his radio, then the west guard started walking north and the south guard started walking east. Both had their backs to John. He checked his watch: 1:12 a.m. Twenty-four minutes until the transformer exploded.

He ran, dove into the nearest garden, and went prone just as the south guard started turning. The west guard could no longer see him, but John still had to approach the south guard. He watched the south guard complete his pass and turn back around, and when his back faced John again, John sprinted to the next garden. In the next cycle, John made it to the wall.

The wall was lined with shrubs, only two feet high, but tall enough to cover him when he was prone. There was enough space between the wall and the shrubs for him to fit between them. Sometimes it was good to be small.

John reached beneath his ghillie suit and drew his knife.

The guard got to the end of his pass, turned, and began walking toward John, facing John's head. John waited; he wanted to launch a rear attack.

The guard reached the end of the wall and turned again, approaching John from the rear, and the instant he passed, John bolted upright. He gripped the guard's mouth with his left hand and pulled his head back, stabbed the neck three times, and before withdrawing the knife, he pulled it backward, slicing through the right side. He lay the man down and fell on his mouth and neck.

Four.

Sixteen minutes until the transformer exploded.

Time for the west guard.

* * *

Frank was excited and anxious at the same time. After all these months, the night had finally arrived. Thornton had given him the west wall, the one with the generator, which meant the Man had a lot of faith in him. Frank would not let him down.

He heard a noise in the shrubs and spun around, pointing his subgun at the wall.

Nothing.

Okay, son, settle down, it was just a damn squirrel or—

Frank's neck hurt and he felt warm liquid running down it, and in the haze that accompanies death, he wondered how a squirrel could hurt him so badly.

* * *

John wiped his knife on the man's pants.

Five.

Thirteen minutes until the transformer exploded.

John crawled to the generator and looked toward the annex roof. As he'd predicted, the pitched roofs of the annex and the mansion blocked the view between the annex roof and the generator, which meant he could work without fear of being seen by the rooftop sentry.

At last, he could get a good look at the generator. The gas line and the electrical connection to the mansion were underground. The generator's housing looked like steel, probably custom-made. The door in the front was secured with two massive, four-digit combination padlocks. His lock pick set was useless.

He couldn't take a chance on exploding the unit or even just exploding the locks; unless he did it perfectly, he'd ignite the gas line.

It was just as he'd expected: the generator was impregnable. He couldn't get in it, so he'd have to go around it.

John unfolded the entrenching tool and started digging in the space between the generator and the mansion's wall. The gas pipe was steel, and the electrical wires that fed power to the buildings were housed in plastic conduit, required by county code to be buried eighteen inches down.

He soon hit something hard. It was the gas pipe, so the conduit had to be close by.

He dug to the side of the gas pipe, and a few shovelfuls later he felt something soft. He knelt down, dug around with his hand, and saw the PVC pipe.

John turned the e-tool sideways and sawed with its serrated edge, got through the plastic, and saw the wires inside. He drew his knife and cut through them. These wires were the reason he had to disable the generator before the primary supply. If the primary supply went off-line first, the generator would automatically start and send current through these wires, and if he cut through live wires, he'd electrocute himself.

Footsteps, coming from the north. They'd checked in and discovered that two of the perimeter guards were down. Someone was coming for him.

John picked up the e-tool, crouched behind the generator, and waited. He reminded himself to avoid the torso.

He saw a ray of light tracing the ground, a flashlight attached to a rifle. Still crouching, he swung the e-tool in an arc a foot above the ground. The sharp edge hit the guard's shin, his legs buckled, and he fell face down. John lifted the e-tool one-handed and swung its edge hard against the man's skull. The man splayed out, motionless. John dropped the e-tool, drew his knife, and finished with one stab to the back of the neck.

Six.

Seven minutes until the transformer exploded.

John pulled four C-4 blocks out of his waist pack. He primed them using both time blasting fuse and detonating cord, connected everything using a ring main and branch lines, and hooked up the detonator. He looked at his watch and calculated the delay he'd need, set the timer, and started it. He hid the assembly in an inconspicuous spot in the shrubs near the wall. It didn't need to do any damage; it just needed to be loud.

One minute, twelve seconds until the transformer exploded.

* * *

1:36 a.m.

They heard a distant explosion, the lights in the library went out, and five seconds later the emergency light came on.

"That'd be John," Bernie said.

Thornton didn't seem perturbed. "This development is only the first phase of John's assault. He still has to run the rest of the gauntlet."

"So far, so good."

"You should broaden your horizons," Thornton said. "You're thinking purely in terms of physical warfare. There is also such a thing as psychological warfare."

"Oh, I get it. Among your many talents, you can see inside men's minds?"

"Scoff all you wish. John underwent an intensive battery of psychological tests, and I trained him and observed him almost daily for three years. I know the man. I know how he thinks, and I know what he wants."

"Yeah? Tell me what he wants."

"A friend, Mr. Bernardelli. What he wants most in the world is a friend. And if he ever had a friend, he would do everything in his power to avoid disappointing that friend."

* * *

The only outside illumination now was from the emergency lights, one per wall. John positioned himself to the side of the west light, raised the MP5, took careful aim, and fired. The glass disintegrated and the wall went dark. He moved to the south wall and repeated.

There were two more outside lights, one guard on the ground and one on the rooftop. Both guards knew John was at the buildings and that the other guards were down.

Would they depart from their sectors and hunt him?

John waited in a crouch at the southwest corner of the mansion, the darkest spot in the clearing, but saw and heard nothing. The guards were going to stay in their sectors, a smart move. They correctly concluded that he would come for them, and staying within the lighted areas gave them an advantage.

He decided to check the north wall first.

He put his back to the west wall and inched forward, the MP5 in his hands at low-ready. When he reached the point where he could see the annex roof, he stopped and took a step back. He was at the edge of the blind spot, and any further forward movement would put him within view of the rooftop sentry.

He saw a beam of light between the roof and the ground, twenty yards ahead. The rooftop sentry was walking along the wall in John's direction, scanning the ground below with a flashlight.

John backed up another step, further into the blind spot, and went prone. The beam of light disappeared. He waited until he estimated the sentry had rounded the corner for a pass along the south wall.

He belly-crawled along the west wall and stopped at the edge of the north wall, listened, and heard nothing. He made sure his rifle's safety was off, then rolled past the wall, ready to fire.

No one was there. The man he'd killed with the e-tool must have been assigned to the north wall.

He rose to a kneeling position and lifted the gun's muzzle to the north emergency light. One shot later, the north side went dark.

He was at the northwest side of the annex, where the ballroom was located. He took a quick look through the window, saw no one, and took a closer look. The emergency light was on, but the room was vacant. Thornton had to be in the mansion, either in the dining room or in the library.

The annex was larger than the mansion; if Thornton was in the mansion, they'd leave the interior of the annex undefended and focus their forces in the mansion. He needed to eliminate the last two outside guards, then breach the mansion.

John crawled along the north wall toward the east wall, the last lighted, guarded wall. Twice, he saw the rooftop sentry's flashlight beam, stopped, went prone, and waited until it passed.

He got to within ten feet of the east wall. He listened, but all was quiet. He pivoted his head around the corner and saw the east guard walking away from him, almost all the way down at the other end. Before long, the guard would reach the end of his pass and start coming toward him.

And then John noticed two things he'd missed during his recon.

The annex's first floor projected out from the rest of the building, with the top two stories set back from it. The first floor had its own roof, ten feet deep. As long as he stayed against the wall of the first floor, the rooftop sentry wouldn't be able to see him.

The other thing he'd missed was a short tree at the north end of the east wall.

* * *

The east guard was nervous. The other three lights were out, which meant Shepard was coming for him.

The guard reached the south end of the wall, scanned forward and to both sides. He held his MP5 at high-ready, a flashlight attached to the underside of the barrel. Its meager spray of light illuminated perhaps twenty yards; beyond that, the south and west were a black void with a few sprinkles of moonlight.

He turned around and proceeded north again, relieved to be back under the emergency light. As he walked, he scanned forward, right, and backward. He was not going to let this guy—

Something turned from behind the tree, a faceless, non-human mass of vegetation, terrifying in its swiftness and appearance.

The apparition raised a rifle, and that was the last event his brain would process.

* * *

John dragged the body to the side of the wall.

Seven.

He went prone and backed up until he had a line of sight to the roof. He couldn't see a flashlight beam, which meant the rooftop sentry was on another side.

He transitioned to kneeling, brought the rifle to his shoulder and fired. The emergency light shattered and the whole universe went pitch-black.

The rooftop sentry was in *his* world now.

John crawled back under the first-floor roof and removed his ghillie suit, now an unnecessary encumbrance. His left shirtsleeve was heavily bloodstained, but only a little damp. He pressed his right-hand fingers against the improvised bandage. It didn't feel wet underneath; maybe the wound had stopped bleeding.

He climbed up a gutter downspout toward the first-floor roof, propelling himself mostly with his legs and right arm; he couldn't pull much with the left. He reached the roof and was at the second story of the three-story annex.

At the north end was a square tower extending out from the annex at a right angle and forming a corner with it. Halfway up the tower was a narrow ledge. The ledge was just a few feet below the annex roof.

John climbed up a downspout to the ledge and steadied his back against the tower wall. He drew the Glock with his left hand and transferred it to his right, hesitant to trust his left hand. He held his arms down to keep a low profile.

Thirty seconds later, he saw the beam of the rooftop sentry's flashlight, scouring the ground and moving toward him. When the beam was five feet away, John raised his pistol.

The sentry's moment of surprise was all John needed: the bullet entered the sentry's left eye, and he slumped over the roof's edge. John climbed onto the roof and put a second bullet through the man's head.

Eight.

* * *

1:51 a.m.
John checked the sentry's MP5 magazine. It was fully loaded, so he swapped it out for his own.

It was finally time to breach the mansion. John had to start at the top, eliminate any men on the upper floors, and work his way down to Thornton.

The top of the mansion had three openings. Two were chimneys, one at each end of the building, rising above the first-floor fireplaces in the library and the dining room. If the plans he saw were correct, both their flues would be too small for him to fit through.

That left the third opening. Like many stately homes of its era, the Lowell Mansion had been equipped with a manually operated dumbwaiter. The dumbwaiter's mechanism had failed decades ago, and the county had made Thornton remove the car and the other components because they created a hazard.

What that left was an empty shaft that ran from the roof to the basement kitchen, with a door at each floor. If the dimensions in the drawings were accurate, he'd be able to fit inside the shaft.

The now-removed pulley mechanism at the top of the dumbwaiter's shaft had been housed in a rooftop hut. The hut was on a flat area situated inconspicuously among the mansion's gables.

John spent the next ten minutes crossing over from the annex roof to the mansion, ascending and descending slanted roofs, checking his traction before every step to keep from sliding off, and finally made it to the flat area. It was covered with gravel, so as he walked, he lifted his feet straight up and gently set them down to minimize the sound.

He reached the hut. It had a steel door secured by a ten-key pushbutton lock. These people had thought of everything.

John doubted he could shoot it open. Thornton would never make it that easy.

There was no other way into the mansion from the roof. He would have to demolish the lock.

He took off his waist pack and removed his last C-4 block, stuck it onto the lock, and primed it. He didn't need a time-delay. All he had to do was light the fuse.

He knew the explosion would be loud; that they'd know where it came from; and that they'd be ready to deal with him.

He lit the fuse and walked around to the opposite side of the hut to avoid the shrapnel. Thirty seconds later, the explosion blew the lock apart along with part of the door.

John waited one minute, then crawled inside the hut to the side of the shaft. He reached down and slapped his waist pack twice against the shaft's inner wall, imitating the sound of someone rappelling, then jumped out the doorway.

The gunfire from below started instantly, an MP5 emptying its magazine on full auto, the bullets flying up the shaft and pinging off the ceiling of the hut.

When it stopped, John crawled back inside. He lay flat against the floor and shifted his body until his right eye was over the shaft. Part of his head was exposed, a risk he'd have to take. He saw nothing except a dim light at the open, third-floor dumbwaiter door.

John drew his pistol with his left hand, transferred it to his right, and waited.

A head poked through the door, followed by an arm holding a flashlight. John fired three times, hitting the head twice and the neck once.

Nine.

* * *

2:09 a.m.

John took the last pieces of gear out of his waist pack—climbing rope and gloves. He hadn't brought proper rappelling gear, just the rope, because he didn't need to descend far; he could use the rope-only Dülfersitz technique.

There weren't any good anchor points for the rope, so he'd have to improvise. He looped the rope between the hut's door and frame and pulled it down over the door's top hinge. The hinge could cut the rope under the pressure of his weight, but he had no other choice. Fortunately, his right hand, the braking hand, would do most of the work.

John wrapped the rope around himself and rappelled down. He reached the third-floor dumbwaiter door and realized the dead man was still slumped over the sill. He lifted the torso up with his feet and pushed the body onto the floor, then swung his legs through and slid inside.

The dead man's radio came on.

"Come in, Pickett."

Silence.

"Come in, Pickett."

The radio went dead again.

John surmised there was one guard on each of the first and second floors, plus one in the room with Thornton. They now knew the third-floor guard was down. Would they come upstairs for him? Unlikely; it was easier to defend than attack.

He decided to take his chances and move to the second floor. The question was how he'd get there.

He didn't want to try the next floor's dumbwaiter door. It was awkward getting through it, and if the guard was nearby, he'd be defenseless. The main stairway was better, but not ideal. Each floor's emergency light was at that stairway, making it the brightest section of the floor.

That left the servants' stairway, a narrow staircase at the rear of the mansion, used by the servants in days of yore so they could move around the house discreetly.

The servants' stairway had its own door. It squeaked when John opened it, and he told himself to remember that on the next floor.

The stairway was devoid of light. He found the first step and gingerly pressed down on it. These were old stairs, and it creaked accordingly.

He grabbed the railing and shook it, made sure it was solid, and then did something he hadn't done in thirty years—he sat on the rail, slid down to the landing, and repeated down the next flight.

He put his ear next to the second-floor stairway door and heard nothing. The second-floor guard had probably passed this door hundreds of times this evening, and he would remember it was closed.

John opened the door a bit, let it squeak, and left it open. The upper half of the door had a window, and John needed to avoid the sight line through it. He backed to the stairs leading to the floor below and lay his body over them, his head a few feet below the landing and facing it. Now he couldn't see the door's window, which meant someone on its other side couldn't see him. He pressed his feet against a stair to stabilize himself.

John shouldered his rifle, braced his support arm against a stair, and waited.

He heard footsteps, someone moving cautiously next to the wall, where the wood would creak the least.

The footsteps got closer. The man was just a few feet away. A beam of light shone through the door's window. Any moment now, the door would fly open. John placed his finger on the trigger.

The beam disappeared. He heard footsteps again and waited until they receded. He'd need to pursue the man.

John crawled up the stairs and stepped onto the landing. The door was still cracked open, but not enough for him to get through it. He wondered how he could open it a tad more without making it squeak, but as he contemplated that question, he thought of a better one.

Why didn't the man close the door?

He didn't close it because he wanted John to walk through it.

John looked through the door's window. Across the hallway was a bedroom whose door was open. He could see moonlight at the opposite end of the room, not entering through a window but through a glass door.

He thought about the floor plans the county gave him. Each second-floor bedroom had a glass door that opened to a long porch along the mansion's outer wall.

The hallway between him and the bedroom was only five feet wide. He could cover it in under a second. He flipped his rifle's selector switch to full auto.

He slowly pushed the stairway door all the way open. The man in the hallway was probably kneeling with his rifle shouldered and ready to shoot.

John stuck his rifle out the doorway in the direction the footsteps had gone, sprayed the hallway with bullets, and leaped across it. He dove onto the bedroom's floor just as the man answered with a burst of his own.

John emptied the rest of his magazine at the bedroom's glass door, shattering it into a thousand pieces.

* * *

McNally replaced his partially depleted magazine with a fresh one and considered the situation. Shepard either went through to the porch, or he was lying in wait in the bedroom.

Keeping his back to the wall, McNally moved down the hallway toward the bedroom. He took a breath, then swung into the doorway and sprayed the entire space.

The room was empty.

Shepard was on the porch, or he'd jumped to the ground.

McNally walked to the open space where the glass door had been. He knelt down, then swept the right and left sides of the porch.

Nothing.

He walked to the right end of the porch, bent over the railing, and surveyed the ground, using his rifle's attached flashlight for illumination. He saw nothing. He sidestepped down the railing to the left, scanning the ground all the way.

He stopped when he saw a muzzle a foot from his eyes.

There was a flash of light and nothing else.

* * *

John dangled in the air, holding onto the floor of the porch with his right hand. He stuck the Glock back in his holster.

Ten.

He'd been hanging on with one hand for nearly a minute, and couldn't hang on much longer.

Now he had to figure out how to get back up.

Getting down hadn't been difficult—it just required some coordination, and he could let gravity do the rest. But now gravity was working against him, and he needed to do a pull-up with a nearly depleted right arm and disabled left one.

He gripped the floor with both hands, took two deep breaths, and pulled. A bolt of pain shot through his left arm. His brain told him to let go and stop the pain, but he kept pulling, pulling, just a little more—

He got his head above the floor. He pulled down as hard as he could with his right hand and let go of his left, then bent it and laid his forearm on top of the floor. Supporting himself with his forearm, he released his right hand and quickly grabbed a post in the porch railing, then released his left arm and grabbed another post. He pulled himself up, two inches at a time, alternating right and left.

Just four more inches to go and—

His left hand slipped off.

He swayed to the right, holding on with one hand. He swung left and got his left hand back on the post.

Right hand, left hand—

Right hand, left hand—

He got the crook of one arm, and then the other, over the top of the railing. He lifted his legs up, got his feet on the floor, and stepped over the railing.

He collapsed to the floor. Both arms were shaking and felt like dead weight.

He sat up, let his arms dangle, and shook them, trying to get the blood flowing again.

Before long, he felt tingling, then burning, which meant the numbness was dissipating. He flexed his arms and wrists, and that was when he felt moisture on his left hand.

The wound was bleeding again, and the blood was running down his arm.

He unbuttoned his left sleeve and wiped his arm and hand on his shirt. There was nothing more he could do about it, and no point in worrying over it. Within thirty-five minutes, it would all be over, one way or another.

The dead man had two rifle mags in belt pouches, one lighter and the other heavier. John replaced the mag in the man's rifle with the heavier one from the pouch.

* * *

2:29 a.m.

John took the servants' stairs to the first floor. He was at the rear of the house, steps away from the dining room.

He brought his rifle into low-ready and made sure the selector was on full auto. His arms were still shaky, and he didn't trust himself to hit a target with one shot. He put his back to the wall and inched his way to the dining room. The room's emergency light was shining through the doorway, and he stopped at its edge.

No breathing. Nothing. The room was vacant.

John walked inside to the far end of the room and checked his watch. He had twenty-eight minutes until 0300. He felt mortally tired, and now he could rest a moment.

The room was a large, half-empty space that Thornton apparently had not yet had a chance to fully furnish. One side of the room, the side with the fireplace, was empty. The other side had a dining table and sixteen chairs.

John looked at the table. It was classic Thornton: beautiful mahogany with elaborate inlays and waxed to a subdued glow. Nothing but the best for—

"Turn around slowly," said a voice at the door.

John turned and saw an MP5 pointing at him, the handguard pressed against the door frame, the shooter using the wall as a barricade.

"Hands up slowly."

John complied.

From behind the wall stepped a man with a flattop haircut and gleaming, silver-blue eyes.

"I'll be damned," the man said as a smirk creased his mouth. "Little ol' Arthur has brought to bay the great John Shepard." He shook his head in disgust. "Thornton thinks you're the best he's ever seen."

"What do you think?" John asked.

Arthur's eyes narrowed into two slender, shimmering mirrors. "I think you're a myth."

"Maybe so," John said, "but if you shoot me, you'll never know."

Arthur's eyes went down to John's bloodstained sleeve, then came back up again. "I can kill you now or in five minutes, but if you want the five minutes, it'll have to be empty hands."

"Five minutes," John said.

Arthur kicked the door shut. A key stuck out of the keyhole, and Arthur reached backward, turned it, and dropped the key in his pocket.

"Just in case you decide to run," Arthur said. "Now walk over to that window and open it, and if you do anything I don't like, I put you down."

John opened the window lock and pulled the window all the way up.

"The subgun first," Arthur said. "One hand at the muzzle and the other hand at the butt, then rear back and chuck it out there as far as you can."

John unslung the rifle as instructed and threw it out the window.

"The pistol, then the knife, then the magazine on your belt. Thumb and index finger only."

John complied again.

"Empty your pockets."

John removed a small flashlight and his lock pick set and tossed them out.

"Anything else?" Arthur asked.

"Nothing else," John said.

"Go stand in that corner."

John walked to the corner, and Arthur took his place at the window. He disposed of his rifle, pistol, knife, and magazines, then unlatched his vest and dropped it to the ground. He shut the window and locked it.

They took their positions in the empty half of the room at opposite ends. They didn't wave their arms or shadowbox. They didn't want to elevate their pulse or trigger their adrenaline. They fought best when they were calm.

They faced each other, their torsos straight, their muscles relaxed. They moved warily toward each other until they were three steps apart. Now it was a question of who would attack first.

It turned out to be Arthur.

It was a straight punch, propelled explosively and without even the slightest flicker to give it away. But John was fast, too, and before Arthur's fist could reach him, John deflected the punch with a circular motion of his right arm, leaving Arthur's chest exposed. John stepped in, bent his arm at the elbow, and thrust his forearm at Arthur's chest. Arthur stepped back and sunk his body away from the strike, and the blow barely made contact.

Arthur took three steps back, but it wasn't a retreat. Neither one was yet committed to a determined attack. They were assessing each other, each man trying to learn his enemy, how he moved and thought and reacted.

They closed up, and John sensed the man would initiate again. Arthur tilted to his left and his right leg shot forward, aiming a powerful side kick at John's chest. John sidestepped right and dodged it, then stepped forward and hit Arthur's chest with both palms and knocked him down. Arthur rolled backward to put distance between them.

John now grasped his opponent's advantage: time was on his side, so he could draw out the fight and force John to do something risky to meet his deadline. John had to find a way to end it quickly, something that didn't require a fully functional left arm, but he also had to consider what his opponent would do. What would he do if he were in the man's position?

Knowing his opponent had an injured arm, he'd go for it at the slightest opportunity.

A sequence flashed through John's brain. If he could move fast enough, he could deliver a knockout blow, but if the man were faster, he could disable John's arm. It was risky, but John had two potential advantages: the man had not yet seen him initiate an attack, and he was accustomed to people who moved at normal speed.

They converged again and John threw a half-speed, left-hand punch, as if unable to throw a normal punch. Sensing his chance, Arthur struck his hands down toward John's elbow and wrist, a move designed to break the elbow, but John dropped his arm before Arthur could make contact. John then took a step forward and uncoiled his real punch. Turning his waist and shoulders to generate momentum, his right arm rocketed forward, his arm and his fist rotating as they moved, and when he reached full extension, his fist drilled itself into Arthur's chest. The blow knocked him clear off his feet.

The strike had breached Arthur's defense, but it was also a little off. Instead of hitting the solar plexus, John had hit the left side of the chest. The man was hurt, but he wasn't out, and before John could move in, Arthur rolled backward until he hit the fireplace at the opposite wall.

Throughout the battle, Arthur had exuded quiet confidence, but now he had a different expression: the look of a man who'd just realized that for the first time in his life he was outmatched.

He rummaged through the fireplace tools and picked up the fireplace poker.

John looked at the poker, and then he looked at Arthur. "You said empty hands."

"And you're an idiot. Thornton taught us both that the only rule of warfare is to make sure the enemy is dead."

John grabbed one of the mahogany dining chairs and held it out, legs forward.

They walked toward each other, John holding the chair like a lion tamer, and Arthur holding the poker point down and swinging it in an arc forward and backward. John knew what would come next: the man would swing the poker back and around and bring it down at John's head.

Expecting the blow to come from above, John pushed the chair up and forward. But Arthur surprised him—instead of swinging the poker down, he sidearmed it at John's left leg. The poker struck John's thigh, the chair struck Arthur's ribcage, and both of them fell.

Arthur pressed his hand against his ribs. John stood up . . . and promptly fell down. His left leg was numb and couldn't support any weight.

Both men instantly knew the consequences: a man who can't stand is finished.

John stretched out his body and did a sideways roll, rotating his body until he hit the wall behind him. He lay his back against the wall and massaged his thigh, trying to get some feeling back.

Arthur rose to one knee, still rubbing his ribs, but in no hurry to attack. He knew John wasn't going anywhere; he could strike at will. Arthur looked straight at John, his eyes reflecting the emergency light like tiny penlights.

The light.

It was on the wall John was backed against, two feet to his right and seven feet up. With one of his legs useless, John would need his left arm to help support his weight for two seconds. If it couldn't, he was done for, but it was the only move he had left.

He scooted over until he was directly below the emergency light. He lifted himself into a handstand and smashed his right heel through the light. The room went black, his left arm gave way, and he and the shattered glass fell to the floor together.

The only light came from the remnants of moonlight that made it through the window, and both men tried to adjust their eyes to the darkness.

Before long, John could see outlines: the table, the wall, the man at the other end of the room. He couldn't see detail, but he could see enough, and he wondered what Arthur could see.

Arthur stood up, craning his head and scanning left and right and back again. It had to mean Arthur couldn't see him.

Arthur bent down, raised his pants leg, and pulled something out. Even from across the room, John could hear the telltale click of a safety being pressed.

"That's right, Shepard, I kept a gun. Did you really think I'd violate my orders if I didn't have an ace up my sleeve?"

Arthur picked up the fireplace poker, then backed up and pressed his back against the wall to square himself. Even though he couldn't see John, he knew where the light had been. He'd assume John was still there; if John had moved, Arthur would have heard the broken glass scratching the wood floor.

Arthur swung the fireplace poker with his right hand, forming large, looping figure eights. He was practicing, learning how to swing it in a rhythm. His plan was obvious: he'd use the poker to shield himself from any thrust John might make, and if he didn't kill John with the poker, he could use the gun.

John reached around, gently and quietly searching the broken glass until he found what he wanted: a five-inch shard with a jagged edge.

The pistol was in Arthur's left hand, next to his hip, and the poker was in his right hand, still making figure eights. He took two steps forward: one step and the poker went up, another step and the poker went down. He was synchronizing his movements, coordinating his steps with the swinging of the poker.

John pressed the glass shard between his thumb and fingers and waited.

Arthur started walking forward in earnest, his steps and his swinging arm perfectly synched, the poker whistling through the air as it made its figure eights. He was headed straight for John.

Three steps away.

The poker went up.

Two steps away.

The poker went down.

One step away.

The poker went up.

John pushed off the wall with his good leg and slashed the glass down Arthur's inner right thigh from groin to knee, and at the bottom of the stroke he curved upward and reversed, slashing the other thigh from knee to groin, and finally curved once more and slashed from right to left across the stomach. Arthur's finger reflexively worked the trigger, sending two bullets into the wall a foot to John's right. He dropped the pistol and fireplace poker and fell onto John.

Arthur flailed, but all he did was accelerate his blood loss. A few seconds later, the flailing stopped, and he went still.

John pushed the man off and looked at him. He'd cut Arthur's femoral and abdominal arteries, and the man's blood was gushing out of him. John knew he'd be dead within two minutes.

But being dead in two minutes wasn't the same as being dead now.

John dragged himself to the fireplace poker. He picked it up with both hands, turned it point down, and raised it over his head.

"You cheated," he said, and he drove it through Arthur's heart.

Eleven.

* * *

2:53 a.m.

John did a quick status check. He could put some weight on his leg, not much, but enough to limp. His left arm had little strength, but the fingers still worked. His weapons were somewhere on the grounds outside; there wasn't enough time to look for them. The kitchen would have knives, but it was in the basement, a floor below, and he wasn't sure he could make it all the way down the stairs and back up again. The dead man's pistol would have to be his only weapon.

He checked it quickly. It was a .45 ACP Detonics Combat Master, and after the two spent rounds, it had four in the magazine and one in the chamber. Whatever he might need a weapon for, it would have to be something he could do with five or fewer gunshots.

John pulled the key out of the dead man's pocket. He opened the door and walked toward the library, his left foot scraping against the wood floor. So much for being surreptitious.

He put his back against the wall next to the library's doorway, listened, and heard breathing.

He lay down with his head facing the wall, his arms extended in front of him, his hands holding the pistol forward. He made sure it was off safe.

He took two deep breaths and rolled himself to the center of the doorway.

Three men in the room: Thornton sitting in a chair at the far end of the room, directly facing him; Bernie sitting a few feet to Thornton's left; and Thornton's man sitting right behind Bernie, using Bernie as a shield and holding a pistol against Bernie's temple.

"Hello, John," Thornton said. "I expected you a little earlier."

John stood up, keeping his pistol trained on Thornton. He limped forward and was a step past the desk when Thornton spoke again.

"That's far enough."

John glanced at Bernie. "Are you okay?"

"Yeah, I'm great. Your buddy's been talking my ear off."

"You know, John," Thornton said, "I never did get a chance to debrief you after Duc Lam. You realize you disobeyed my orders."

"How's that?"

"You were supposed to be on the assault team."

"So I'd be among the first to die?"

"Of course. Nothing personal, you understand, just trying to manage my risks."

"I switched with Martinez."

"And ruined my plan. Martinez would never have made it out the way you did."

"You have to answer for him, Professor. For him and Krauss and Fuji and Seely and O'Neill and Costa and Skulski. You have to answer for them all."

"I am deeply disappointed," Thornton said. "I taught you never to kill from emotion."

"I've had a long time to calm down."

"Indeed, you have. And true to your word, you appear as calm as ever. It always was one of your most remarkable characteristics."

John ignored the comment. "You have an interesting setup here."

"Thank you. I wanted to give you a clear choice: you can kill me, but your friend dies."

The explosion was loud enough.

The windows rattled and the floor shook. As Bernie dove to the floor, the man behind him instinctively turned to face the sound. John shifted his hands right and pressed the trigger twice. The second shot was unnecessary; the first bullet pierced the man's head and exited, and even before he hit the floor, John arced the gun back to Thornton, the only person in the room who hadn't moved, and who seemed not very surprised at all.

Twelve.

"Well executed, John," Thornton said. "You anticipated the problem and created a diversion."

"I've also eliminated the element of choice."

Thornton shook his head. "No, you haven't. Not by a long shot."

Bernie was just now standing up, finally grasping what had happened. "You did it, John. Let's—"

"Sit down, Bernie."

"John, we can go now."

"I said sit down."

John's voice was perfectly cold, colder than any voice Bernie had ever heard, and it made him recall what Thornton had said: *the flattest, most impassive response of anyone we've ever tested.*

Bernie sat down.

That conversation seemed to amuse Thornton ever so slightly. "It's interesting how things work out," he said. "Edward realized I had taught him a good trade, and he continued to ply it, quite successfully from what I'm told. But not you. No, you turned your back on your considerable skills—and for what? You could have earned a good living in private enterprise, but instead you went to work for the government, doing good for a pittance. What drove you, John? Survivor guilt?"

"I'll address that with a higher authority than you."

"Indeed, you will, but the question remains: how does it feel to be operational again?"

"It all came back to me."

"Until recently I would have agreed, but now I'm not so sure."

"Some flaw in my performance?"

"Hardly."

"Then what is it?"

"You could have killed me without risk at any time in the last two minutes, but you haven't."

"I didn't have any trouble with your men."

"Of course not. You knew they would have killed you, had you not killed them. And the same was true in Vietnam—you were a soldier fighting a war. But now you face a man who poses no threat, and you hesitate."

"You once told me I was born to kill people."

"I remember it well."

"Then why do you doubt it now?"

Thornton paused just long enough to give his words their maximum effect.

"Why didn't you kill the woman?"

John's hands trembled, just an infinitesimal movement, but Thornton didn't miss it because he never missed anything. He locked his eyes on John's and pitched his voice low.

"I know you, John, even better than you know yourself, but there's always been one thing about you I didn't know: do you have it in you to cross that last line?"

Bernie had been watching in rapt fascination, transfixed by the interplay between these men. They were in a different world, operating at a level he couldn't even begin to understand.

But he couldn't just sit there and let John commit murder.

"Listen to me, John," Bernie said. "Just listen. You were born with an ability. You didn't ask for it, you didn't have a choice in that, but you've got a choice now. You can either control the ability or you can let it control you, and if it controls you now, it'll control you forever."

No response.

Bernie swallowed, trying to think of something else he could say.

"Let him go, John. Do it for me. Do it for your friend."

Bernie couldn't tell whether John had even heard him. The two men were completely still, as though they'd been flash-frozen at a pivotal point in time when the slightest motion might destroy them. Bernie looked from one to the other, finally settling on John's hands.

And then gradually, almost imperceptibly, he thought he saw John loosen his grip on the pistol.

A moment later, John's arms dropped to his sides. He pressed the safety up, opened his hand, and let the pistol fall to the floor.

"I was not born to kill people," he said.

Chapter 61

Saturday, May 23, 1987
2:58 a.m.

A motorist driving southbound on Route 31 heard what sounded like an explosion coming from the old Lowell property. At the first opportunity, he stopped at a payphone and dialed the operator, who transferred him to the Diamond Lake Fire Department.

Diamond Lake FD dispatched fire engines and ambulances and called the McHenry County Sheriff's Office. In accordance with a protocol established several weeks earlier in connection with the Quan matter, the Sheriff's Office notified Chicago PD, which called the officer in charge of the Quan investigation, Commander Michael Kozinski.

Mike looked at his clock and cursed.

He sat on the edge of his bed, trying to wake up and figure out what to do next. He telephoned Bernie but got no answer, so he called CPD and asked them to send a car to Bernie's apartment.

They called back just as Mike finished dressing. The two officers dispatched to Detective Bernardelli's apartment received no response when they rang his bell. They proceeded to wake up the building's supervisor, who unlocked the door and let them in, but the apartment was vacant. They also reported finding a duffel bag containing a .45 caliber pistol, a large quantity of ammunition, plastic explosives, and what looked like homemade detonation devices. The bag was olive drab, appeared to be military in origin, and bore a label that read, "SHEPARD, J."

Mike's wife asked, "Is it bad?"

"It's bad," Mike said.

"Do you want some breakfast?"

"Thanks, honey, but I'll pick something up."

Mike had taken plenty of calls like this one, and he knew what he needed to do. He stopped at a diner, got some sandwiches, and filled two Thermos bottles with coffee.

Chapter 62

Saturday, May 23, 1987
3:04 a.m.

Bernie heard sirens in the distance, getting louder by the second. In minutes, this place would be bedlam. For now, though, he was sitting with his head in his hands, savoring the knowledge that he'd escaped his second brush with death in less than forty-eight hours.

When he finally looked up again, the other two men were still in place, still glaring at each other, the pistol still on the floor at John's feet. Neither one had moved a millimeter, and Bernie realized: *They just can't let it go.*

He stood up and cleared his throat. "C'mon, John, let's take this asshole and leave."

That seemed to snap him out of it. John nodded, turned around, and began walking toward the door.

And the instant he turned, Thornton reached inside his coat. He pulled out a .45, clicked the thumb safety down and began bringing the front sight down on John's back.

Before Bernie could draw a breath, John spun around and in the same motion grabbed the blade end of Thornton's letter opener. He locked his wrist, cocked his arm back and released it. The blade slid out of his hand, flipped a half-revolution, and skewered Thornton's throat to the back of his chair.

He didn't have a chance to give his critique. He was too surprised, and then he was too dead.

Bernie just stared, too stunned to say anything.

The other man in the room spoke one word.

"Thirteen," said John Shepard.

Chapter 63

Saturday, May 23, 1987
6:05 a.m.

Bernie sat on the trunk of a CPD cruiser, drinking coffee from one of Mike's Thermos bottles. He couldn't make sense of what was going on, not only because his brain was sluggish but also because the scene itself was surreal.

The fire engines had arrived first, followed closely by ambulances and squad cars. Most of the vehicles were from Diamond Lake and McHenry County, some were CPD, and a few were Illinois State Police. The last car to roll in was an unmarked, black, late-model sedan, from which a man in a suit emerged. By then, the entire area in front of the mansion was full, and they finally closed the gate.

One of the fire department paramedics cleaned out John's wound, bandaged it, and made John promise he'd get a ride to the nearest hospital for stitches and a shot of antibiotic. Meanwhile, Bernie watched the man from the late-model sedan speak with Mike for a few minutes, following which the two of them huddled with the other officers and fire department personnel. When the huddle broke up, they all dispersed in different directions. No one took notes or photographs or diagrammed the locations where bodies were found. They looked like they were in a hurry to find the bodies and clean up the mess, and didn't much care about anything else.

"You sure you're okay?" Mike asked him for the second time.

"Yeah, I'm fine," Bernie said. "I didn't do a thing but sit there. John took care of it all by himself."

Mike spat on the ground. "Hard to believe."

"I wouldn't have believed it either, if I hadn't seen it. Have they checked John's apartment?"

"They checked. The woman was gone."

Bernie drank some more coffee and stretched. "I'm more tired than I've ever been in my life. Can I give you my report on Monday?"

Mike looked away. "You don't need to."

"What do you mean, I don't need to? I've got to—"

"No, you don't," Mike said. "You don't need to do a damn thing. No reports, no conversations, no nothing. I want every piece of paper you have on this case, and then I want you to forget it ever happened."

"What's going on, Mike?"

"It's the feds. They're putting a lid on it, as in hermetically sealed." At that moment, they came across another body—the second roving sentry—and Mike walked off to observe.

Twenty yards to Bernie's left, John stood with the man from the late-model sedan, engaged in what appeared to be a one-sided conversation—the man did most of the talking, and John just nodded politely and spoke sporadically. The longer it went on, the more agitated the man became, and then John said something and the man threw up his hands and stalked away. John looked around and, seeing Bernie, ambled over and sat down next to him.

"Who was that?" Bernie asked.

"FBI."

"He looked mad."

"He was."

"What did he want?"

"He wanted to know what happened."

"What did you tell him?"

"I told him the Department of Defense would answer all of his questions in due course."

"Will it?"

"No," John said. "As a matter of fact, it will not."

Bernie nodded. Hermetically sealed, all right.

"What happens now?" Bernie said.

"Defense has informed Justice that this case concerns a national security matter. Justice will fabricate a cover story and issue instructions to local law enforcement. A few days from now, you won't be able to prove what happened here."

"And that's how it ends?"

"That's how it ends."

They sat there a while longer, silently watching the chaos. At length, Bernie turned and looked down at the man beside him.

"What about you, John? What do you do now?"

John stared straight ahead as he answered.

"I guess I'll be a fucking accountant," he said.

Chapter 64

Sunday, May 24, 1987
8:12 a.m.

By the time John got to Marcelle's hospital room, Bernie was already there, he and Marcelle huddled together and speaking in low voices. When John walked in, they stopped and looked up. Marcelle said, "Hey, John."

"Hello, Marcelle. You don't look as bad as you did the last time I saw you."

"Wow. You really know to flatter a woman."

"Thank you," John said.

She sighed and turned back to Bernie. "I'd like to talk to John for a second."

"So talk."

"Alone," she said.

Bernie walked out and shut the door behind him.

Marcelle got right to the point. "Bernie told me the whole story about you."

"It's dangerous knowledge to have."

"I know that. You don't need to worry."

John said, "I'm sorry I lied to you, Marcelle."

"I understand your reasons, and all is forgiven. But since I've got you in a remorseful mood, I was hoping I could ask you a personal question."

"I'll tell you whatever you want to know."

Marcelle hesitated, unsure how he'd take it, but finally worked up the nerve to ask.

"Before they selected you for that operation," she said, "did you have any idea you had the abilities you have?"

John shook his head. "None of us did. But Thornton told us we had unmanifested abilities buried inside us, that he'd unlock them, teach us how to use them, and make us powerful. I'd always been the small one, you know, the weird one, the one nobody ever wanted on their team, but here was Thornton telling me he wanted to put me on a team and make me powerful. And so, I agreed to join the operation, but I didn't realize it came with a price."

"What do you mean?"

John bowed his head for a moment, then raised it again. "The price I paid was learning I have a skill that most people find repulsive, that would make them fear me and hate me if they found out about it. I told myself I couldn't let that happen, and that's one reason I'm so solitary. If people knew what I did and what I'm capable of, they'd shun me even more than they do already."

"Bernie and I won't shun you," Marcelle said.

"Most people aren't like you and Bernie. Most people would only see a monster."

John looked like he was gearing up to say something else, so Marcelle just waited.

"There's something I want to tell you," he said, "and it's important to me that you believe me."

"I will."

"I never enjoyed it. Not in Vietnam, not this past week, not ever. It never made me feel good."

"How *did* it make you feel?"

John considered it before he responded.

"Like I was doing my job. I guess that's it, really. I just felt like I was doing my job."

* * *

Bernie followed John back to John's apartment, and when they got out of their cars, Bernie handed over John's duffel bag. "The folks at Area Six were very impressed by your stuff, but I think you'll find it's all still there."

"Thank you," John said.

They walked up to John's apartment, and for the next hour, Bernie watched John pack. When Bernie packed for a trip, he stuffed everything in a suitcase and then mashed it down until he could close it. John, though, was the most meticulous packer Bernie had ever seen. He put everything on his bed, arranged by category and stacked in neat piles, and after placing them in his luggage, he still had room to spare.

They carried the bags downstairs. After John put them in his trunk, he faced Bernie.

"I wish I could tell you how sorry I am—"

Bernie put his hand up. "Don't get all maudlin on me. I have a feeling you'll be back."

"I just want to say one thing."

"Okay," Bernie said.

"When I was growing up, I never had any friends, and then I went to Vietnam and I had some friends, and then they were gone and I had no more friends."

John stopped and looked Bernie in the eyes.

"Are you my friend, Bernie?"

Bernie held his hand out, and John clasped it. "I sure am, John. I'll always be your friend."

John got in his car and shut the door, but before he could put his key in the ignition, Bernie bent down and spoke to him through the open window. "There's just one thing I don't understand."

"What's that?" John said.

"It must have occurred to you that Thornton might have a gun, but you didn't pick up your pistol and check him before you turned around."

For the first time since they met each other, Bernie saw John smile.

Acknowledgements

I am deeply grateful to the many people who helped me with this book. Dr. Dennis Lindenbaum, neuropsychologist and shooter *extraordinaire,* gave me invaluable help with the psychology aspects of the story, and did yeoman's service by writing John's psychological evaluation. I hope you clean the Xs, pal.

Susie, Sam, and Gene humored me and listened patiently for years as I blathered on about this book. Don Loft and Alan Perry assured me—with straight faces, no less—that I was on the right track and ought to keep going; I don't know whether they were right, but I do know I wouldn't have gotten this far without their feedback and encouragement. Lt. Mike Casey, Sgt. Brian Forberg, and Sgt. John Foster of the Chicago Police Department generously shared their knowledge and reminiscences with me. My editor, Emily Murdock Baker, handled my manuscript with just the right balance of objectivity and tact. Maj. Gregory Sidwell, USA, Ret., and Capt. Ralph Kuhnert, USA, Ret., kept me straight on many of the Army details. My valiant beta readers—Hans de Kok, Don Loft, Jessica Pardi, Alan Perry, Sam Rabin, Richard Reinhart, Alexia Roney, and Tom Suswal—rolled up their sleeves, put the manuscript under a microscope, and provided tons of good suggestions.

Last but certainly not least: ace prosecutor Dan Piwowarczyk educated me about various procedures described in the story, and, equally importantly, told me about the Damen Silos, which, by the way, are still there as of this writing.

The Dole Mansion in Crystal Lake, Illinois, was the inspiration for the Lowell Mansion in the story. I changed the buildings, grounds, and environs of the property to suit the story I wanted to tell, but the real place is beautiful and well worth your time.

The graffiti Thornton saw on the pavement at the Damen Silos is from the song "Legs" by PJ Harvey. The song was released in 1993, so the graffiti couldn't have been there at the time of the events in the story. In real life, though, that graffiti did appear on the Silos' pavement, so I used a bit of artistic license to move it backward in time.

That admission brings me to a *mea culpa*. This is a fictional story that takes place in the real world, and while I tried to make the story fit the world, sometimes I made the world fit the story. In those instances where I did the latter—or got something wrong—the fault is mine and mine alone.

About the Author

David Rabin was born in Chicago and raised in its Lakeview neighborhood. He later moved to Atlanta, where he worked as a trial lawyer for thirty-three years. Now retired, he writes fiction, runs a competitive shooting program, and competes in rifle sports, including the discipline of Highpower Rifle, in which he holds two High Master classifications. He and his wife, Susie, a former clinical social worker, have two sons, Sam and Gene. *In Danger of Judgment* is his first novel.

Note from the Author

Word-of-mouth is crucial for any author to succeed. If you enjoyed *In Danger of Judgment*, please leave a review online—anywhere you are able. Even if it's just a sentence or two. It would make all the difference and would be very much appreciated.

Thanks!
David Rabin

We hope you enjoyed reading this title from:

BLACK🌹ROSE
writing™

www.blackrosewriting.com

Subscribe to our mailing list – *The Rosevine* – and receive **FREE** books, daily deals, and stay current with news about upcoming releases and our hottest authors.
Scan the QR code below to sign up.

Already a subscriber? Please accept a sincere thank you for being a fan of Black Rose Writing authors.

View other Black Rose Writing titles at www.blackrosewriting.com/books and use promo code **PRINT** to receive a **20% discount** when purchasing.

Made in the USA
Monee, IL
19 February 2024

53790115R00225